W9-BAH-810

M

Matthews, Alex.

Blood's burden

Blood's Burden

THE EIGHTH CASSIDY M^CCABE MYSTERY

ALEX MATTHEWS

INTRIGUE
PRESS

Published by Intrigue Press, an imprint of Big Earth Publishing
923 Williamson St.
Madison, WI 53703

ISBN 1-890768-64-2
LOC 2006921917

Cover design, photos and book design: Peter Streicher

For my husband Allen, who makes all things possible

Acknowledgments

Many thanks to all the people who helped in the birthing of this book: my husband, Allen Matthews, whose fourth career has become book promotion; my editor, Chris Roerden, who would not accept less than my best; my fellow critique group members, Nancy Carleton, Cecelia Comito, Carol Hauswald, and Ginny Skweres, who faithfully refused to let me get away with anything; my publicist, Barbara Young, who applied her vast energy and enthusiasm to book promotion; Oak Park Deputy Chief Robert Scianna, who educated me on police procedure; Mary Welk, who shared her knowledge of emergency room protocols with me; Oak Park Firefighter Lt. Donald Bush, who explained what paramedics do at the scene of an accident; and Linda Schulyer, Director of West Suburban PADS, who told me how overnight shelters work.

Everyone gave freely of their time and expertise.
Whatever errors exist, they are mine.

Blood's Burden

THE EIGHTH CASSIDY M^{C}CABE MYSTERY

ALEX MATTHEWS

Chapter 1

"**Y**OU CAN'T JUST LEAVE!" BRYCE LOOKED AT Kit across the dining room table.

"Sweetie, I hate to tell you, but I can do anything I want." Kit inserted a small bite of lasagna into her darkly outlined mouth. Dinner was turning out to be quite the production.

Cassidy McCabe and her huband Zach sat politely through the argument unfolding between the younger couple. It was obvious to Cassidy that Bryce had made an effort to impress his father: a home-cooked meal; a new, well-appointed townhouse; a pretty—and headstrong—girlfriend.

"Two days ago I checked to make sure your calendar was clear. I mean, after all, the whole idea of this dinner was for you to meet my parents."

Parents, Cassidy thought, a lump rising in her throat. *Never thought I'd hear that word fall from Bryce's lips. At least not in regard to Zach and me.*

"I told you I have a rehearsal tonight," Kit said in a playful tone. "You must've forgotten. Here you are—only a sophomore in college—and your mind's going already."

"No you didn't!" Bryce jabbed his finger at her. "You promised you'd come home early and help me cook. Instead, you waltz in just about the time we're ready to sit down at the table, then five minutes into dinner you spring this rehearsal on me. Which you never mentioned before."

"The lasagna's really good, sweetie." Kit turned toward Cassidy. "Don't you think it's good?"

If you say "yes," it'll look like you condone her bad behavior.

"Everything's delicious," Cassidy replied. "But it's too bad you're going to disappoint Bryce by leaving early."

No, that was wrong too. Sounds like you're trying to rescue him. Like you don't think he can handle Kit on his own.

Cassidy twisted her wineglass on the linen placemat. She didn't mind couples slicing and dicing each other in her therapy office, a place where she had the power to stop them. But she felt uneasy being thrust into the role of spectator while Kit and Bryce went at each other in his townhouse. Cassidy had no authority here at all. She glanced at Zach, who was watching the exchange with a frown on his face. *Well, for once he hasn't withdrawn into his detached-journalist-bystander persona.*

"Goddammit, Kit, if you're going to leave, just do it," Bryce said.

"I've still got five minutes. And besides, it's fun getting to know your parents." Turning to Zach, she said, "One thing I don't understand is why you're not helping Bryce with his college expenses. I hardly speak to my folks and they shell out all the money I want."

Zach said amiably, "I can't think of any reason to discuss this with you, Kit."

Bryce banged his water glass on the table. "Kit! You know I've never wanted to take money from Zach. Why should I? I have a trust fund of my own."

Kit continued as if Bryce hadn't spoken. "I don't think Bryce should have to spend down his trust when he has a family that's perfectly capable of helping him out."

Actually, we're not. Not since we started rehabbing the house.

"What the fuck's the matter with you?" Bryce demanded, a vein starting to pulse along the side of his rough-hewn face. "First you say you told me about the rehearsal when you didn't, and now you're hassling Zach. When you get into one of these moods, I don't even like to be around you."

Kit's lips curved into an icy smile. "Well, sweetie, if being with me is too hard on you, I can always find someone else to shack up with."

A slight shiver ran down Cassidy's arms. *Using threats to keep Bryce in line. To throw him off balance and make him insecure so he always gives in to her.* It reminded Cassidy of what life had been like with her first husband.

"Kit, I believe you said you have a rehearsal to go to," Zach said.

Cassidy felt a tic of annoyance. *You're the one who's supposed to be the expert at people problems. Zach's stealing your thunder.*

"Yeah, just go on—get out of here." Bryce sat tall, his body rigid with anger.

A contrite look suddenly appeared on Kit's finely contoured face. Leaning closer, she laid her hand on Bryce's arm. "I'm sorry—I realize how much this evening meant to you and now I've spoiled it. Sometimes things come out of my mouth and I don't even know why I'm saying them."

"Just go to the damn rehearsal."

Kit stood up, her gaze fixed on Bryce. She was a tall, trim woman with close-cropped hair—dyed black—heavy black makeup, and long black nails. She wore a sheer blouse, only two buttons fastened, and her small, uncontained breasts were visible through the fabric. It looked as if she'd taken a scissors to the bottom hem, cropping it to reveal as much skin as the law would allow.

A vampirish femme fatale who sucks Bryce's blood for the fun of it.

Dragging her feet, Kit went into the entryway and started up the stairs.

The others sat in silence waiting for her to leave. *The evening's not a total bust. After all, this is the first time Bryce has ever wanted to introduce any girlfriends or show off any townhouses. And he's being downright friendly to Zach.*

When Bryce first arrived at their door a couple of years earlier he was a boy, filled with hatred toward the father he'd never met; a hatred instilled by his mother. Later, Bryce came to understand that his mother's stories were untrue, though old habits die hard and his hostility toward his father had never entirely gone away.

Kit came downstairs and stood in the entryway facing the dining room. "I'm sorry I screwed things up for all of you." Blowing a kiss to Bryce, she left.

"Well," Cassidy said, letting out a breath, "that was fun."

"God, I feel stupid." Bryce propped his elbows on the table and pressed the fingers of both hands against the sides of his face.

"I guess we're done." Zach got to his feet and opened the second bottle of wine he'd brought. Refilling their glasses, he said, "Let's go sit in the living room."

Zach's doing good. Getting us away from the scene of the crime.

Cassidy and Bryce followed Zach across the entryway. Zach was just under six foot, broad-shouldered, with a waist that had thickened slightly in the years Cassidy had known him. Bryce was three inches taller, with a lean, flexible build. The only resemblance between the two lay in their bronze-toned skin and straight dark hair.

In the living room a black sofa stood against the far wall, with two black and white plaid chairs facing it at angles. One wall was painted entirely black and hung with several large, primitive masks. The other three walls were a deep red. Cassidy liked the drama but was repelled by the menacing expressions of the masks.

The boy flopped down on the sofa. Cassidy and Zach opted for the chairs.

"Do you and Kit get into fights like this very often?" Cassidy asked, her therapist part coming to the fore.

"Not that much." He paused. "I suppose you think I'm nuts for having anything to do with her."

I think anyone who'd get involved with that drama queen should be required to take hormone suppressants.

"No, of course not."

Zach laced his fingertips together on his wide chest. "I have a little trouble understanding the appeal. Maybe that's because I've never been attracted to women who go around PMSing all the time."

Cassidy threw him a dirty look. *As if once-a-month moodiness was worse than testosterone-driven violence.*

"You don't understand," Bryce said fiercely. "Most of the time she's really sweet. She leaves little love notes around the house. She makes me laugh and cheers me up when I'm down. It's just that she has these anxiety spells. And she can't stand it if she feels like I'm controlling things. I think that's what set her off tonight. She felt like I was forcing her to meet my family."

"A lot of relationships get off to a rocky start," Cassidy said. "Zach and I had a terrible time at the beginning."

Zach shot her a look of surprise.

He always forgets what that first year was like.

"How long have you and Kit been together?" Cassidy asked.

"About three months. When I first met her, she was camping out in her girlfriend's studio apartment. Her family has this humongous house in Winnetka, but she refused to stay there and didn't have any place of her own."

"When you fight," Cassidy said, "does it ever turn physical?"

Bryce raked his fingers through his dark crewcut. "Sometimes she comes flying at me with her fists, but she's never hurt me or anything."

"Have you ever hit her?" Zach's voice was gentle.

A long silence. "Just once. It was late at night and I was tired and she wouldn't let up." He gazed at the floor. "I slapped her. I didn't even see it coming—I just did it."

Yeah, but if a person gets pushed far enough, it's likely that person will lash back. Bryce couldn't possibly have the resources to handle someone like Kit.

Zach said, "You know there was that one time in my life when I got out of control and got physical with your mother." Xandra had been pregnant with Bryce when it happened, although Zach hadn't realized he'd fathered a child until more than seventeen years later. "Ever since then, whenever I start to get too angry, I walk away."

Hate it when he does it to you but you know he's right.

A defiant look came over Bryce's face. "You think I should break up with her, don't you?"

Cassidy jumped in quickly before Zach could endorse the idea. "You're the only one who knows what's best for you. No one else can tell you what to do."

The boy flashed her a grateful smile. "You've only seen her bad side. Most of the time she's really cool. And I love her. I've never loved anyone as much as I love Kit."

†††

Cassidy and Zach climbed into his Subaru and began the long trek from Rogers Park, a neighborhood on the far north side of Chicago, to Oak Park, the near west suburb where they lived. It was the middle of September and the night air was chilly.

"When you made that comment about PMSing, I was wishing I had a table to kick you under," Cassidy said. "In fact, that was so bad, I think I'll kick you anyway the next chance I get."

"Look, I was biting my tongue not to say more. Where are the love police when you need them most? And who would have guessed that Ben Hopewell—the famous family-values minister—would have a daughter who walks around with her boobs showing?"

"Oh, and you were offended at having her flaunt her perky young breasts in front of your face?" said Cassidy, who, at forty, was aware that gravity was beginning to take its toll.

"I thought we agreed I could look as long as I don't swivel my head and drool." Zach turned onto Lake Shore Drive, an eight-lane thoroughfare running between the diamond-bright city on their right and the dark expanse of lake on their left. He said, "You were quick to tell Bryce you didn't think he was nuts—even though I know you do."

Cassidy sighed. "Some of my clients have gotten into horrendous relationships, and I always walk this thin line between pointing out the red flags and making sure I avoid making any criticisms of their beloved."

"I suppose Bryce would stop speaking to us if we told him what we really think."

"Maybe we're being too hard on her. She seemed pretty remorseful at the end." Cassidy had had a few bouts of jealousy with Zach that had driven her to behavior she'd just as soon forget.

Zach gave her an amused look. "You're so incurably sappy. Always trying to find the good in people who don't have any."

"Everybody has some good in them," she said, not quite believing the words as they came out of her mouth.

"They do?" Zach said in the supercilious tone she hated. "What about sociopaths? Or narcissists?"

You should never have educated him about personality disorders. Knowledge is power and you shouldn't give it away.

"Narcissists are often charming and helpful. They seldom abuse anybody outside their immediate families, and, in fact, often go to great lengths to be nice to everyone else."

"I notice you didn't rush to the defense of sociopaths." He put his hand on her knee. "So, I guess there isn't anything we can do to get Bryce unhooked from Kit."

"This is a reversal. When it comes to Bryce, I'm usually the worrier."

"You're not worried?"

"Well, I am a little. Bryce is too much like me. His self-esteem is a tad low—God, how could it not be, given his history? And he's not much of a leaver. So he may just stay on and let Kit torture him. But Kit seems more like you—somebody who jumps ship pretty easily. So I expect she'll release Bryce from his torment before too long and move on to someone else."

"Did you just take a dig at me?"

"Um ... I might have. But it was fueled by envy. I've always wished I could be more cavalier about relationships instead of being so clingy."

Zach laughed and gave her knee a squeeze. "I'm not cavalier about you. In fact, I've fallen into such a disgusting state of adoration, I can't imagine why you'd even say such a thing."

CHAPTER 2

A FEW DAYS LATER CASSIDY WAS STANDING IN their remodeled kitchen with Zach as he, clad in a collarless shirt and jacket, held forth to an assembled group of coworkers and friends. The occasion was a surprise second anniversary party, engineered by Cassidy's grandmother and best friend Maggie.

It was ten PM—two hours into the party—and Zach, leaning against the new mauve countertop, was in a garrulous mood.

"You know how Cass and I met?" His voice was beginning to sound mushy. "I was investigating my brother's—half brother's—death, and she was his therapist."

This is strange. Here Zach's getting drunk right in front of you and you're not even upset.

Zach's drinking had always been an issue between them, although he'd cut back enough of late that it seldom came up anymore. *But this isn't the pounding-down-bourbons kind of drinking you used to get so pissed about. This is more of a laid-back, losing-track-of-beers kind of drinking. Doesn't seem so bad.*

"So Cass was his therapist," Zach repeated, "and I went over to her house one night and pumped her for details, but I couldn't get her to give up any of the confidential information I was after." Opening another Sam Adams, he took a long swig, then set the bottle on the counter behind him. "I made a couple more tries, and then I started to see her as a challenge. I was even willing to take her on a date in hopes of prying something out of her."

He reached for the bottle, fumbled and knocked it to the floor. As he started to lean over, a bald guy from the *Post* quickly retrieved it.

"Hey," the guy said, "you better leave the bending to somebody else. We let you fall on your face, Cass'll make us carry you up to bed."

"I'm out of practice," Zach declared. "Can't hold my liquor like I used to."

Which is a very good thing. If he hadn't given up his old sleazy habits, we wouldn't be having this anniversary.

Catching her eye, Zach smiled a slightly drunken smile. He had smooth dark hair, a high forehead, hawkish nose, and jagged scar across his left cheek.

Cassidy returned the smile but decided she might enjoy the party more if she didn't stick around to witness his further decline. Squeezing through the circle of bodies, she went into the dining room where she spotted the party co-conspirators: her grandmother, a small wiry woman in a red beehive wig, and Cassidy's fellow therapist, Maggie, a woman with a soft face and direct, no-nonsense manner.

Putting an arm around each of them, Cassidy said, "What an incredible surprise. But why'd we rate a party after only two years? Were you afraid we wouldn't make it to number three?"

"We just thought you'd earned it," Gran said.

"Right," Maggie said. "Given the kind of scrapes you two get into, we figured we ought to throw you a party before one or the other of you lands in jail."

"The only person who isn't here is Bryce," Gran said, her mouth puckering in a frown. "I wish he'd made it. I don't get to see nearly enough of him."

"Well," said Cassidy, "his life's kind of complicated right now."

Gran fingered the ruffled neckline of her filmy turquoise blouse. "Complicated—that's one of those code words, isn't it? Sort of a polite way to tell people to mind their own business."

"I have to rescue Susie," Maggie said, referring to her partner. "She doesn't do well in a roomful of strangers." Leaving the huddle, Maggie went around the corner into the living room.

"You should mingle, too." Gran gave Cassidy a push. "I'm gonna go find me some young hunk and hang on his arm."

Cassidy was catching up with some friends from graduate school when she heard the phone trill.

A moment later, her mother tapped her on the shoulder. "I was in the bedroom taking a break from the crowd when the phone rang. It's Bryce. He wants to talk to Zach. I told him there was a party going on, but he wouldn't take no for an answer."

"Thanks, Mom. I'll take care of it." Cassidy headed for the stairs.

His girlfriend's locked him out. Or cut him up with a butcher knife. Or set the townhouse on fire.

Picking up the cordless from Zach's desk, she moved her cat aside and settled into her favorite place on the bed. Starshine, whose girth had increased dramatically over the past few months, threw Cassidy an irate look and stalked out of the room.

"Hello?"

"Cassidy, I have to talk to Zach," Bryce said, his voice shaky.

The good news is he's finally taking his problems to his father. The bad news is his father's in no condition to hear them.

"Zach's pretty busy right now. Maybe you could tell me instead."

"Just go get Zach, will you?"

Maybe you should let him talk to his father. But I can't imagine Bryce would want to hear Zach slur at him over the phone.

"He's packed into the kitchen with half the staff from the *Post.*"

"Zach has to come down to the townhouse right now."

"We can't just walk out in the middle of our anniversary party unless we know what this is about."

"Cass, please … " Bryce was crying. "I need my father."

Her throat constricted. "Okay, we'll be there as soon as we can."

In the kitchen she threaded her way through the crowd and slipped up close to Zach, who reeked of beer. Pulling his head down, she whispered in his ear, "I need you to come upstairs."

"Not now." He gestured to the guests. "I'm talking to my friends."

"There's something I have to tell you. It's important."

"Oh-oh," one of the young guys said, "Zach's in trouble now."

"Just come hear what I have to say." She took his arm and dragged him up to the bedroom.

He rested his hand on the back of his desk chair to steady himself. "If you hauled me up here just to chew my ass for getting a little sloshed, I'm going to be pissed."

"Bryce called. I could hear him crying on the phone. He refused to tell me what was wrong. Just said he needed his father."

"Oh shit." Zach stared at her, his eyes slightly glazed. "Whatever the problem is, I'm in no shape to fix it."

"Yeah, but we have to go."

Running a hand over his face, Zach said, "I don't wanna let him down."

Cassidy's gaze softened. As she looked into Zach's face, she could see the effort he was making to pull himself together.

"You okay to drive?" he asked.

She nodded.

Cassidy located her grandmother in the dining room, chatting up a good-looking man in his fifties. Pulling her aside, Cassidy explained why they were leaving.

"Don't you worry," Gran said. "I'll just tell everybody you thought it would be more romantic to celebrate your anniversary at the Sybaris." Gran winked.

Cassidy grabbed a lightweight jacket to put on over her ankle-length wine-colored dress, then led the way out to the garage. She backed her Toyota into the driveway, and Zach climbed in beside her. "Buckle your seat belt," she said, her voice catching as she realized how much the alcohol had slowed him down.

"This is your fault, really," he complained. "Before you gave me so much shit about my drinking, I could slug down booze all night and nobody knew how ripped I was. I could walk and talk as if I were perfectly okay, even though everything was jumbled in my head."

"Feeling nostalgic about your glory drinking days?" *Which clearly are not entirely in the past.*

"Just mad at myself for getting loaded."

CHAPTER 3

BRYCE'S TOWNHOUSE STOOD IN THE SHADE OF a parkway tree, the property blanketed in darkness except for a row of glowing windows on the second floor. His Miata was the only car in the drive. *Kit broke every dish in the house by throwing them at Bryce, then drove away, leaving no forwarding address. Or her car's in the garage and she's holding Bryce hostage with a blowtorch.*

She looked at Zach. "You ready?"

"Yeah." He pressed his fingers against his left temple.

On the sidewalk, she touched his arm. "How you doing?"

"I'm fuzzy. If I say something stupid, don't hesitate to correct me."

Zach pushed the bell and Bryce opened the door, the hinges squeaking noisily. Even though the entryway was unlit, Cassidy could see his face was shiny and wet from crying. Drawing back from his father, he raised an arm and held it in front of his face. *The cloud of beer fumes must've hit him. So he won't be surprised if Zach's not exactly on top of his game.*

Bryce led them into the dining room and collapsed into a chair at the head of the table. He said to Zach, "Guess you're not going to be the tower of strength I was hoping for."

Speaking slowly and distinctly, Zach asked, "What's going on?"

"See for yourself." Bryce waved toward the living room.

Cassidy turned to stare in the direction Bryce had indicated. She noticed a familiar coppery odor, the smell mingling with the malty aroma exuding from Zach.

This isn't a surprise, is it? You had a hunch about what you were going to find when you got here. As Cassidy and Zach started toward the living room, she grabbed Zach's arm with both hands, momentarily forgetting that she'd have to be the rock tonight.

"You stay here," he said, evidently forgetting also. He crossed the entryway, Cassidy less than a step behind. He stopped near the short wall that separated the entryway from the living room and ran his hand down the wall in search of a switch. The entryway fixture flicked on.

Blood was splattered in a wide arc around the plaid chair that stood closest to the hall, facing the sofa. At first all Cassidy saw was the blood, then she became aware of an arm in a wide floppy sleeve dangling limply over the side of the chair.

Turning away, Cassidy sucked in air. She stepped back and leaned against the front door, her legs so weak she doubted they would hold her. Zach, a veteran crime reporter who'd witnessed a number of murder scenes, turned his back to the body, his shoulders hunched.

His defenses are shot. Beer-soaked brain cells will do it to you every time.

Straightening, Zach said, "Have to see if she's dead." He went into the living room. Cassidy remained against the door, and a moment later Zach returned. He shook his head.

"We should call the police," Cassidy said.

"I need to talk to Bryce first." They walked into the dining room and sat at the table. Zach addressed his son. "Did you do it?"

"What?" Bryce's voice swooped up an octave. "Don't you know me at all?"

The kid wouldn't hurt anybody. How can Zach even think it?

Reaching across the table, Zach laid a hand on Bryce's arm. "Tell me what happened."

Bryce ran his free hand over his face, the same gesture Cassidy had seen Zach use any number of times. "We were upstairs. Studying. I was at the computer, Kit was in the bedroom—I don't know what she was doing. I heard her go downstairs." He gazed down at the table. "Then I heard the shot."

"This must be hard to talk about," Cassidy said.

He looked up from under his brows, his eyes soft and moist. Running his hand over his face again, he continued. "I didn't go down right away. I kinda froze. I knew I should get my ass down there as soon as possible. That Kit might need me. If only I'd gone downstairs ... or called an ambulance ... "

"She died instantly," Zach said. "There's nothing you could've done. If you'd shown up too soon, you might've caught a bullet yourself."

Bryce spoke to his father in a harsh voice. "You wouldn't've been scared, would you? You'd've gone straight down the instant you heard the shot. You might even have stopped the killer from getting away."

Zach never can win. If he screws up, like coming here drunk, Bryce is disappointed. If he does everything right, Bryce feels he can't live up. No wonder Zach's reluctant to throw himself into fathering.

Squinting at Bryce, Zach looked as if he were trying to formulate his thoughts. "I get scared. The only reason I don't freeze is that I've got all these years of experience."

Cassidy asked, "How long did you stay upstairs?"

"Don't know." Bryce shook his head. "I didn't have any sense of time. But I got myself to go down into the living room and look at her." His brown eyes filled with tears. A hot red flush crept up beneath his bronze-colored skin. "When I saw all that blood, I went running into the bathroom to puke. I didn't even check to see if she was alive."

Beating himself up, the way he always does. But it makes sense he'd fall apart. Only a couple years ago he saw his mother's blood splattered around a room.

"You knew she was dead," Zach said softly. "The back of her head's blown off."

Bryce looked away. "I started to cry. I sat on the floor over there," he tilted his chin toward a corner of the dining room, "and just couldn't stop crying. I knew I should call 911, but I kept picturing these cops busting into the townhouse, cuffing me, and hauling me down to the station."

Of course he's scared of cops. He was almost killed by one.

"Isn't it time we made that call?" she asked Zach.

The furrows between Zach's brows deepened. "A few things I need to do first."

"The longer we wait, the harder the cops'll be on Bryce."

"I'll say it was me who made us wait." Zach looked at Bryce. "Were the doors locked?"

"Um ... yeah. We're always pretty careful about that."

"Are you sure? Did you have to unlock the front door to let us in?"

"Yeah, it was dead-bolted."

"Maybe she let the killer in," Cassidy said.

"And then threw the dead-bolt?" Zach asked.

Cassidy glared at her husband.

Bryce said, "She didn't open the door. You know that creaky sound it makes? I always hear it."

"Maybe you were listening to music. Or concentrating so hard you missed it."

"She didn't like my music so I turned it off. I always hear the door. There were times she sorta disappeared on me, so I'm real tuned in to it."

"Then it must've been a break-in," Cassidy said.

"I'm going to see where it happened." Zach headed toward the entryway, with Cassidy right behind him.

They examined the lock on the front door, which showed no sign of having been tampered with. The windows in the living room and the half-bath were open, but the dust and cobwebs on the ledges bore witness to the fact that the screens had not been removed. The closed windows also appeared undisturbed. As Cassidy went from one window to the next, she could feel a growing sense of alarm. The last thing they inspected was the back door. Its lock was securely fastened also.

What does this mean? That Bryce killed her? No—there has to be some other explanation.

As they returned to the table, Cassidy noticed that a remote look had settled on Zach's face, the expression he wore when he wanted to distance himself. Seeing that look alarmed her.

Zach said, "There's no sign of a break-in."

"What?" The boy's shoulders jerked. "Oh shit," he muttered under his breath. Pinpricks of light appeared in his eyes, and a muscle quivered in his cheek. "Maybe I should say the doors weren't locked."

"No lies," Zach said. "You have to tell the exact truth. We all do. Cass and I have to tell them everything. We'll even have to describe that fight we saw between you and Kit."

"Whose side are you on?" Bryce demanded. "I shouldn't have called you. Just go home and let me handle it."

"One of the first things the cops are going to ask is whether you and Kit were fighting today."

Bryce didn't respond.

"Were you?" Zach pressed.

"Not much." Bryce glanced at his father, then away. "Just the usual."

Cassidy laid her hand on Bryce's forearm. "I know it feels like we're grilling you, but we need to ask these questions. What about keys? Did either you or Kit give out extra keys to anybody?"

Bryce took a while to reply. "Maybe Kit did. I mean, I guess she must have. I didn't give anyone else a key."

"Listen," Zach folded his arms on the table, "this is why it's so important to tell the truth. The police will look at the evidence—you and Kit alone in the house, your history of fighting, no forced entry, the fact that you didn't call it in right away—and they'll assume you're guilty. But cops are like walking lie detectors. If every word out of your mouth is the truth, it'll make them less suspicious. It'll encourage them to look elsewhere."

Cassidy kept her gaze on Bryce. The boy had bent forward and was rocking slightly in his chair.

Kid's scared half to death. Zach should just shut up.

Yeah, but he needs to be scared. If he isn't scared enough, he might not tell the truth.

"The good news is," Zach said, "I think they'll let you go in the end. They won't charge you."

"Why the fuck not? After what you said, I'd charge me."

"If they don't have a confession or any forensic evidence, it won't stand up in court. That's why they're going to sleep deprive you, threaten you, use every trick in the book to get you to confess."

Cassidy's brain buzzed with anxiety. "They wouldn't get physical with him, would they?" *No, of course not. Only black guys get tortured by Chicago's finest.*

"Not with a reporter standing by, they won't. But cops really know how to mess with a person's head. The police have the right to hold you up to seventy-two hours, although they can't keep you against your will. You could try to walk out, but if you do, they'll arrest you on the spot, then drop the charges later. And in the long run, you'll get the cops off your back faster by cooperating." Zach paused. "One option would be to say you won't talk without an attorney present, but then they'd make you sit and wait while we tried to run somebody down. And if a suspect lawyers up, they always assume he's guilty."

"Why get an attorney if all I have to do is tell the truth?"

"An attorney might be useful. He could provide moral support. He could also keep the cops from doing anything too outrageous. Plus he could make sure you don't say anything you shouldn't."

If Bryce is supposed to tell the exact truth, how could there be anything he shouldn't say?

"It's Saturday night, and we might not be able to get hold of an attorney till Monday morning."

Bryce said, "What about Victor? My trust attorney? He's always been sort of like an uncle. I bet he'd come right away."

An Uncle Victor we never heard of? I guess Bryce hasn't opened up as much as I thought.

"A trust attorney? Yeah, that'll work. You have any kind of attorney, it'll keep the cops in line." Zach handed Bryce his cell phone. "Go ahead, call him."

Bryce dialed, then explained the situation to Victor. After listening a moment, Bryce held the phone away from his ear and said to Zach, "He's in his car and could be here in a few minutes, but he says we should get a criminal attorney instead."

"Let me talk to him." Zach took the phone. "This is Bryce's father. All we need you to do is stay with Bryce while the police question him."

Zach listened, then said, "God knows how long it'd take to get a criminal attorney to return my call. Please just help us out tonight."

Zach listened again, then snapped the phone shut. "He says he'll do it."

"So *now* we call the cops," Cassidy said.

Rubbing his forehead, Zach looked as if he were still having trouble holding onto his thoughts. He asked Bryce, "Did Kit have her own computer?"

"Hers crashed so she's been using mine."

"You know her password?"

Bryce nodded.

Zach said to Cassidy, "I want to print up her email and track the websites she's been visiting. While we're doing that, why don't you take a quick look around?" He gave her his handkerchief. "Use this so you don't leave any prints and make sure you put everything back where you find it."

"I'll be disturbing the crime scene."

"Okay, then don't do it."

Only chance to look through the townhouse before all the evidence gets carted away. Besides, you've already done so much to irritate the cops, what's one more infraction?

Tucking a notepad into her pocket, she went into the kitchen, surveyed the half-eaten pizza and dirty dishes on the counter, and poked through the garbage under the sink.

Upstairs she wandered into the study where Zach and Bryce were hovering over the computer, then crossed the hall to the bedroom. She stood in the doorway, her eyes skimming the space: a small desk in the corner, black apparel tossed on the desk chair, a skimpy bra and thong underpants on the floor next to the unmade bed. She thought she detected a faint aroma of sex but couldn't tell if the smell was real or just her imagination working overtime. A creeping sense of shame came over her at the thought of invading Bryce's privacy, and she almost turned away.

Zach's told you over and over—you have to develop thicker skin if you want to be an investigator.

Squaring her shoulders, she stepped into the room and rummaged through the papers on the desk, all of which appeared to be schoolwork. Next she went through Bryce's clothes in the tall bureau, and after that, Kit's clothes in the long chest. Pushed back into the far corner of the middle drawer she found a photo. A thin woman clad in a worn-out shirt and jeans, straggly light blond hair framing a youthful face. For an instant Cassidy wondered if the picture might be a pre-vampire version of Kit, but she had difficulty imagining that the combative woman she'd met could ever have looked so vulnerable. *And yet it happens all the time. People turn aggressive to hide their insecurities.*

The doorbell rang and she put the photo back in the drawer. Following Bryce down to the entryway, she stood in the background as the boy ushered a medium-sized man into the house. The attorney glanced at the murder scene, then turned away. Raising a hand to shield his eyes, he took a moment to compose himself. He had a long narrow face with sandy hair that sprang in untidy tufts from his head. Although he was dressed in a style befitting his profession, his polo shirt, khaki pants, and wingtips had seen better days.

You were expecting high-powered and glitzy. Somebody who'd fit into Xandra's upscale crowd. Bryce's mother, a high-class madam, had traveled in some of the same circles as Chicago's biggest power brokers.

Bryce introduced Victor to Cassidy. The two exchanged polite words, then the attorney clapped the boy on the arm. "My God! This is horrible! I hope you'll forgive my saying it, but I'm glad it was your girlfriend who walked in on that thug and not you."

"I almost wish it was me." Lowering his head, Bryce wiped the corners of his eyes. "Zach's upstairs. He wants to talk to you."

As they gathered in the study, Zach rose and introduced himself. "Look," he said to Victor, "I hope this doesn't come across as pushy, but I've been observing cops for a long time and I know what Bryce needs to do to come through this interrogation in one piece." Zach repeated what he'd said earlier to Bryce. "The cops'll be doing all kinds of things to piss Bryce off, and it'll be up to you to make sure he remains cooperative."

"I should be able to handle that," Victor replied. "I know this kid's innocent and I'll do whatever it takes to help him." He threw an arm around Bryce's shoulders.

Wouldn't you love to see Zach do that?

Giving the cell phone back to Bryce, Zach said, "Okay, call it in."

CHAPTER 4

Z ACH LOOKED AT CASSIDY. "DID YOU CHECK the bathroom?"

She frowned, annoyed at her husband's peremptory tone, then decided she might as well finish the job. As she left the study, she heard Bryce explaining to the emergency operator that an ambulance wouldn't be necessary. She stepped into the white-tiled room at the end of the hall. A few cosmetics were strewn across the Formica counter, but other than that, the room was in good order. She peered inside the medicine chest. In addition to the usual items, she found a dial dispenser for birth control pills and two prescription bottles, one quite large.

Cassidy used Zach's handkerchief to check out the dial dispenser, which displayed four weeks of pill slots, each week marked Sunday through Saturday. Only two pills remained, a Friday and Saturday. Cassidy's first thought was that Kit had missed yesterday's pill, but then she noticed that the refill date was August 2. *Stopped more than two weeks ago. Maybe she started a new birth control method.*

Or maybe—God forbid—trying to get pregnant. Whatever she was up to, I hope Bryce knew about it.

After jotting down the information from the birth control dispenser, she took out the large pill bottle and read the label: Thorazine, twenty-five milligrams four times a day, prescribed to a Margaret Polanski.

Thorazine! My God, that's an antipsychotic. What would either Kit or Bryce be doing with Thorazine? And how did this woman's pills get into Bryce's medicine chest?

She copied the information from the Thorazine label onto her notepad, then looked at the smaller bottle. Erythromycin, a common antibiotic, prescribed to Kit, with instructions to take two pills a day for ten days. The date on the bottle was August 11. Ten out of the twenty pills were gone. Cassidy wrote everything down and replaced the bottles.

On her way back to the study, she nearly bumped into Zach, coming through the doorway with a sheaf of printouts in his hands.

"I'm locking these in the trunk," he told her. "You have anything to go with them?"

She gave him her pad.

As Zach was hustling toward the door, Victor came to stand beside her at the top of the stairs. "Don't worry. I won't let the cops eat him for breakfast."

Bryce, standing in the doorway to the study, shot the attorney a grateful look.

Returning a few moments later, Zach said, "There's something I'm forgetting." He rubbed his forehead. "Oh, yeah, the key to the townhouse." He looked at Bryce. "If you give me a key, I can get someone in here to clean up as soon as the seal's lifted."

Digging a bunch of keys out of his pants pocket, Bryce fumbled to remove one.

A knock sounded at the door.

Cassidy opened it to find two beat cops standing on the porch, two more approaching rapidly from the street.

The uniforms were shepherding everyone outside to sit in separate squads when an unmarked car jerked to a stop at the curb. Two detectives, one black, the other white, jumped out.

The white guy, athletic build, bleached blond hair, swaggered up to Zach. "Well, if it isn't the hotdog reporter from the *Post*."

"Good to see you too, Detective Lyons."

† † †

Cassidy sat in a windowless room in a straight-backed chair, a wooden table in front of her, a second chair across from her. The only person she'd seen since the cops put her there was the black detective, an amiable guy who, amazingly, listened to her entire story without making a single snide remark. But regardless of his pleasant demeanor, Cassidy found it embarrassing to admit to so many transgressions. On top of that, she hated having to say she was acting on instructions from Zach. Pointing the finger at her husband made her feel like both a snitch and a mindless follower. But she had to tell the truth.

Letting out a heavy breath, she tapped her fingers on the table. As time wore on, she flipped back and forth between feeling sorry for herself and sorry for Bryce.

When she was feeling sorry for herself, she focused on how edgy and frustrated she felt, how slowly time was moving. But whenever she caught herself wallowing, the critical voice in her head told her that she was being shallow and self-centered to even think about herself when Bryce's situation was so much worse.

Each time she flipped into feeling sorry for Bryce, the fear and sadness she felt for him created a tight band around her chest that made it difficult to breathe.

Zach said the police won't charge him, so at least they'll let him go when they're done.

Assuming Zach's right. Which he isn't always. You just like to believe everything he says because it's easier than thinking for yourself.

A while later Detective Lyons came into the room. Sitting in the chair across from Cassidy, he thumbed through his notepad. She stared at his stylish blond coiffure, wondering if the old-timers sneered at things like manicured nails and bleached hair.

"So, Ms. McCabe, why did you search the premises before calling it in?"

"Zach thought it would be a good idea."

"Because?"

"He didn't say."

Lyons' face creased in annoyance. "Why do you *think* he wanted you to?"

"Zach may decide to investigate."

"I hope you're aware that a civilian investigation could constitute an obstruction of justice."

Cassidy pulled herself up straight. "Zach's a reporter. He has a right to investigate anything he damn well pleases."

† † †

After Lyons let her leave, Cassidy found Zach waiting for her in the area between the detectives' desks and the interview rooms.

He said, "I want to have a word with Victor before we go. One of the dicks just went to get him." Zach wrapped his hand around her upper arm. "How you doing?"

"An hour ago I was sure Lyons would come in and find me certifiably dead of boredom. But I'm okay now."

Victor, his sandy tufts of hair looking even more unkempt than when she'd first seen him, came out of one of the rooms.

"How's Bryce holding up?" Zach asked him.

"He's taking the girl's death pretty hard, but he's been entirely clear and consistent in his statement."

"How much longer are you going to be able to stay?"

"I was just getting ready to leave."

"Here are some numbers where you can reach me." Zach wrote his home and cell numbers on a card and handed it to Victor. The attorney reciprocated.

Zach said, "Tell Bryce to call me when they let him go. I want to make sure he doesn't get dropped off in front of his townhouse."

A beat cop ferried Cassidy and Zach back to the Toyota. Since Zach had sobered up, he offered to drive home. After adjusting the seat and the rearview mirror, he drove south to Chicago Avenue, then headed west toward Oak Park. At two thirty in the morning, the city was wide-awake, the landscape awash in hazy light, pedestrians clustered on sidewalks, music blaring.

Cassidy looked at her husband, who appeared more alert than she felt. "What you said about not wanting him dropped off at the townhouse. Is that because you think he might be suicidal?"

Less than a year earlier, Cassidy had wrested an admission from Bryce that he was thinking of shooting himself. Zach had taken the gun.

"The thought crossed my mind," Zach said.

She pondered for a moment. "He's still in shock, so I doubt that he's suicidal now. But we'll have to watch him. He could go over the line at any moment."

"I'll be counting on you to keep an eye on him."

She nodded. *One of the scariest things about being a therapist.*

They drove in silence for a while. Cassidy felt exhausted by the night's events, yet, at the same time, so wired she didn't know how she'd ever get to sleep.

Zach glanced at her, then said in a gentle voice, "Has it occurred to you that Bryce may be lying?"

"What?" Cassidy's stress level intensified, growing so loud she could actually hear it—a low staticky buzz at the back of her brain. "You can't be saying you think he shot her!"

Zach didn't answer.

She gritted her teeth, angry that he could even conceive of such a thing. *If there was ever a time Bryce needed our support, this is it. Victor doesn't seem to have any doubts. Zach shouldn't either.*

He said, "We know Kit and Bryce had a stormy relationship. They were alone together in the townhouse, the doors were locked, there's no sign of forced entry. Kit gets shot, Bryce doesn't call 911." He paused. "We took an illegal gun off him once before and there's no telling whether or not he replaced it."

Cassidy drew her brows sharply together. "He didn't. He had no reason to. He wasn't planning to kill himself or anybody else."

"I don't like what I'm thinking any better than you do, but we can't ignore the facts."

"Stop it. I don't want to hear this." Biting off the words, she stared out the side window as they drove past a group of bikers standing around a black-fronted tavern named Hog Heaven.

Too late. Seed's already planted. Besides, those same thoughts would have eventually cropped up in your own head.

Turning back toward Zach, she said, "You saw the tears on his face when he opened the door. And there were a couple of times after that when he welled up. He's obviously devastated by Kit's death. And ashamed of himself for falling apart."

"Yeah, I could see that."

"Besides, Bryce just isn't the type to shoot anybody. We've never seen any sign of violence in him, and even though he gets angry a lot, I think that's just a defense. Under the surface he's really pretty soft."

Bryce isn't the type. What a pathetic argument. You just can't stand to have Zach not agree with you. The downside of being so married—harder and harder to hold opposite points of view.

"Look, I'm not trying to convince you," Zach said. "I'm glad you believe in him. But you're more intuitive than I am. You can just run with your feelings. I can't."

There was a long silence, then Zach started up again. "Cass, I've seen people be overwhelmed with grief at the death of someone they just killed. And I can't tell you how many stories I've written about nice guys who got pushed around once too often and snapped."

"I thought you weren't trying to convince me."

"I'm not."

He doesn't like it that we're on opposite sides either.

She said, "I noticed you started looking detached after we didn't find any sign of a break-in."

"I was having a lot of doubts and I didn't want him to see it in my face."

"What he needed to see was that you believed him."

"What the hell do you expect of me, Cass? I was having a hard time. It took all my concentration just to stay focused."

"I expect you to be a father!"

"What does that mean? That I should shut my eyes to the facts?"

Cassidy took in a breath and let it out slowly. *Only reason you're attacking Zach is there's some part of you that has the same doubts he does. A part you'd like to throttle.*

"I'm sorry." She laid her hand on his thigh. "I just have this social-worker fantasy of how I'd like things to be between you and Bryce."

Zach's voice softened. "It's that sappy side of you again." He turned north on Austin Boulevard, the border between a poverty-stricken Chicago neighborhood and their middle-class suburb.

Cassidy thought back over the events at the townhouse. "Were you able to learn anything from looking at the body?"

After a short pause, he said, "I was still so drunk I don't even have a totally clear memory. The entry wound was in her forehead … looked like the shooter was standing straight across from her … I think she was wearing a bathrobe." He shook his head. "There was something about the lack of forced entry, something knocking around in the back of my mind, but I can't get hold of it."

Zach turned left onto Briar, the street that ran alongside their corner house. He stopped to let Cassidy out, then rolled into their detached garage. While waiting beside the driveway for Zach to emerge, Cassidy listened to the wind sweep through the surrounding trees, the lofty elms that canopied the street and the shorter maples that grew under them. Drawing her jacket up tight against the cold night air, she glanced across Briar at a bungalow that used to belong to the neighborhood cat lady but now was inhabited by a young gay couple. The porch light was burning. Beneath it sat a cat.

She walked out into the middle of Briar to get a better look at the feline, hoping it might be Milton, the gimpy old tom Cassidy had come to know when she'd launched a campaign to rescue feral cats. At that time Olivia, the Cat Lady, had collected a large colony of strays. Then Olivia was murdered and Cassidy felt responsible for saving the colony from Animal Control. She found a cat-rescuer who trapped all the strays except Milton and took them to a sanctuary in Wisconsin. The wily old tom evaded the traps, then moved away from the block, with occasional return visits to his home territory. Cassidy assumed he'd found a new cat lady somewhere else.

Staring at the cat on the porch, she could see that one ear was missing. *It is Milton! He's still with us.* It always surprised her that any cat could survive year after year on the street, considering the toll disease, starvation, and Chicago winters took on strays. A Milton-sighting gave her hope. It made her feel that anything was possible.

Milton walked stiffly down the porch steps, trotted out to the sidewalk, sat down on the curb and stared back at her.

"Hey," Zach said from behind her, "what are you doing out in the middle of the street?"

"Greeting an old friend."

CHAPTER 5

A SHRILL SOUND INVADED CASSIDY'S DREAM, TRIGGERING AN
image of Bryce shooting her in the forehead with his cell
phone. Rolling onto her side, she pulled the covers more tightly
around her. Cat whiskers tickled her nose.

The waterbed surged as Zach sat up. She heard him say, "Yeah,"
followed by a pause, then "Shit," another pause, and "Yeah, okay."

Cassidy propped her back against the headboard and watched
Zach put on his blue robe. Starshine danced around his feet, uttering
a series of *mwats* that translated to "Breakfast! I want breakfast!"

Cassidy said, "Victor?"

"Coffee first."

"What did he say?"

Zach's face looked drawn and tense. "Not till I have a mug in my
hand." He started downstairs with Starshine bouncing along beside
him making her chirpy little noises. Unlike Cassidy, who would have
preferred to skip mornings, the calico adored them.

The clock on the bureau said seven thirty. *Less than five hours
of sleep.* Cassidy threw water on her face, combed her hair, dressed,

and hurried downstairs. The first floor was all spruced up, no vestige remaining of last night's party.

In the kitchen Zach was staring out the window above the sink while Starshine gobbled from her bowl on the new mauve counter. The coffeepot gurgled, sending out a rich aroma. Cassidy noticed that Zach had given the calico the high-fat food she loved instead of the diet food Cassidy was trying to foist on her.

"What did Victor say?"

Zach turned to face her. "The cops found a .357 Magnum. In the corner under one of those brick and board bookcases. No prints on the gun." He paused. "I didn't even see the bookcase, did you?"

She pictured Bryce's living room: polished wood floor, sofa, two chairs, a couple of lamps and end tables, a wall full of masks. "I didn't either." Gazing into her husband's face, she could see he was looking ragged. Since he'd sobered up long before going to bed, she doubted it was a hangover.

"Did you get any sleep?"

"Not much. I was up most of the night trying to devise some scenario that didn't result in Bryce popping his girlfriend."

He poured coffee into Cassidy's purple cat mug, added cream and sugar, and handed it to her. "You go pet Starshine while I take a shower and clear my head." He filled his own mug and started for the stairs.

†††

Cassidy watched the calico scrub her small triangular face. "Now that you've gotten what you want, are you willing to put in some lap time?" Starshine had been withholding favors ever since Cassidy started her on the low-fat diet three days earlier.

The cat bestowed a moist green-eyed gaze on her human.

She's buttering you up. Providing positive reinforcement for Zach's feeding behavior in hopes of motivating you to do the same.

After washing her orange ear, then her black ear, Starshine marched out of the kitchen, turning her head in the doorway to make sure her human was following. Cassidy obediently trailed after her. The calico, with her short body and tail, had always looked quite svelte. But the previous spring, she had started to blimp out. She went from a petite cat—so small she appeared only half grown—to a plump little sausage. The vet instructed Cassidy to switch her to a low-cal dry food and restrict her meals to twice a day. Zach, who paid no attention to fat grams or carbs, voted to ignore the vet's advice, but Cassidy had overruled him.

In the bedroom Cassidy seated herself on the unmade bed, pillows behind her back, the burgundy sheet and comforter piled around her. Starshine went to sit on the radiator board beneath the west window, her back to her human. Before climbing onto Cassidy's lap, the cat typically went through an elaborate pretense of indifference.

Starshine picked her way over the cluttered nightstand, stepped across Cassidy's body, went to the far corner of the bed, then returned to settle on Cassidy's stomach.

"So, now that your belly's filled with the fattening stuff, I'm back in your good graces. Unconditional love is definitely not a cat thing."

Purring rambunctiously, Starshine leaned forward to touch her mouth to Cassidy's lips, then extended her chin for scratching.

"Thank God for coffee," Zach said, coming through the doorway in the buff. "Another cup or two and I won't even notice the sleep deficit."

"This revolver they found. You think someone might've planted it to make Bryce look guilty?"

"The killer must've been an amateur. He probably got scared, dropped the gun, and ran out. Or Bryce dropped it." Zach donned his standard garb: a black tee that said I'M HERE FOR THE BEER and a pair of black jeans.

"That doesn't make sense," she said. "There's no reason Bryce would drop the gun and just leave it there." *Unless he wanted to get caught.*

Zach leveled his eyes at her. "Maybe we shouldn't work on this together."

"We always work together."

"Yeah, but I don't want you snapping at me every time I express an opinion you don't like." Zach sat in his desk chair to put on his gym shoes.

Cassidy stared at the window, wondering how she could not snap when Zach's comments made her feel so tense.

"We may get on each other's nerves a little but we can't stop talking."

"I realize I won't be able to keep you from investigating, but I'm going to be damned pissed if you make me fight you at every turn."

She had a history of insisting that Zach do things her way and she knew she needed to stop it. "I'll try not to make any trouble."

He looked at her for a moment, then nodded. "While I was up last night, I went through that pile of paper we brought home from the townhouse. Let's sit at the dining room table and I'll show you what I've got."

Moving Starshine off her lap, Cassidy followed Zach into his computer room across the hall, where he picked up a stack of papers, his spiral notepad on top, the pad she'd used at Bryce's apartment just beneath it. Seeing the pad reminded her that she wanted to look up Thorazine, so she made a side trip into the den to grab her copy of *The Prescription Drug Guide.*

She carried the fat paperback downstairs, refilled her mug, and sat at a right angle from Zach, who also had a fresh mug of coffee in front of him.

"Before we start," she said, "how bad is it that they found a gun? Does it mean they'll charge him?"

"Not unless they can trace the gun to Bryce, and the odds are he didn't go out and buy a legal firearm. So far, the evidence is all circumstantial. And the fact that Kit could have given a key to someone raises reasonable doubt."

The tension in Cassidy's chest eased.

Zach gazed into space for a couple of seconds, then shook his head. "Remember I told you there was something I couldn't get hold of? Something about forced entry? Whatever it is, it keeps flitting around the edges of my mind but I still can't pin it down." He shook his head again. "If I hadn't been so damn wasted, it probably would have jumped right out at me."

"It'll come sometime when you're not thinking about it."

He picked up the pad with Cassidy's notes. "Birth control pills Kit had stopped taking and Thorazine prescribed to a Margaret Polanski. After we're done here, I'll Google the Polanski woman."

"Maybe Bryce can explain about the birth control."

"And maybe the autopsy will show she was pregnant."

What if Bryce wanted her to get an abortion and she refused? What if they had a big fight and he killed her? No, he'd never do that.

Zach continued to stare at the pad. "Isn't Thorazine something they use on schizophrenics?"

"They used to. But the new antipsychotics are so much better, I don't believe they prescribe it much anymore. Since I've never worked with the mentally ill, I don't know a lot about it. But it's not the sort of thing you'd expect to find in a college student's medicine cabinet." Cassidy paused to consider the possibilities. "Bryce said Kit had a problem with anxiety, so maybe she was taking it for that. Although I can't see why she'd be using someone else's Thorazine instead of getting her own prescription for Xanax or Klonopin." Opening the drug guide, Cassidy skimmed the section on Thorazine. "It says here the usual dose is three hundred to eight hundred milligrams, so a hundred milligrams per day would be pretty low."

"Kids are always passing pills around. Maybe Kit or Bryce got it off a friend."

"You don't think Bryce does drugs, do you?"

"I've only seen him high that once, when he was staying with us. But if he did have a drug problem, I doubt he'd tell us about it."

"I can't believe someone just gave them a bottle of Thorazine. I've had a few clients with mild psychotic symptoms, so it's possible Kit did suffer from psychosis but managed to keep it hidden. She might have seen a psychiatrist under an alias." Cassidy paused. "But that still doesn't make sense, because there wouldn't be any reason for a doctor to use such an old drug."

"We'll have to see if Bryce knows anything."

Cassidy stared at the physician's name. "I wish we could get this Dr. Winslow Leonard to tell us who Margaret Polanski is and why he prescribed Thorazine for her, but that's not going to happen."

"Let's move on to the websites Kit's been visiting."

Cassidy read the list Zach put in front of her. "Three of these sound like sites for tracking missing persons. The rest don't mean anything to me."

"I looked them up last night. Most are the kind a college student would use to do research. But these missing person sites are curious. Makes me wonder if she was adopted."

"There certainly are some biological parents who don't want to be found, although it's hard to imagine that having your long-lost daughter show up at your door would be a motive for murder."

Zach gave her a cynical look. "I thought you were supposed to know about people."

"Okay, okay. Show me what else you've got."

Zach handed her the next sheet on the pile, an email from Kit to a person named Angie:

We're reading Shakespearean sonnets in lit. Thought they'd be bo—ring, but some of them are actually kinda cool. Romantic and sexy. Too bad guys dont write poetry to their girlfriends anymore. But you know what? I think I could get Bryce to write me some cool erotic verse. An

ODE TO KIT. IF I GAVE HIM WHAT HE WANTED. WHICH I USUALLY DON'T.

DID I TELL YOU I SAW RAUL? BRYCE IS NICE BUT RAUL IS BIGGER. OF COURSE YOU WOULDN'T KNOW ANYTHING ABOUT THAT, WOULD YOU?

Cassidy's hands clenched. *If Kit weren't dead already, I might kill her myself.*

"I'd bet my next big story that Bryce was reading her email," Zach said. "And if he was, just seeing what she had to say about him could constitute motive." Zach handed his wife another email. "Here's Angie's response."

YOU'RE SO MEAN TO BRYCE. BUT NO MATTER WHAT YOU DO, HE COMES PANTING BACK FOR MORE. MAYBE THE REASON I CAN'T GET A BOYFRIEND IS THAT I'M NOT MEAN ENOUGH. YOU COULD GIVE LESSONS. MEANNESS 101.

"Sounds like Angie and Kit were pretty close."

"They emailed each other at least once a day. Kit had other email buddies, but Angie was the only one she maintained such regular contact with. In that first email, Kit came across as pretty patronizing, but in some of the others she doesn't sound so bad." He laid another email from Kit to Angie on the teak table.

OMIGOD! THAT'S SO UNFAIR! I KNOW HOW HARD YOU STUDIED FOR THAT TEST. WHY DONT I COME OVER TONITE AND WE CAN HAVE A SLEEPOVER, JUST LIKE WHEN WE WERE 12. I'LL PICK UP A DVD AND SOME POPCORN, YOU MAKE THE HOT CHOCOLATE.

"The other side of Kit," Cassidy remarked. "Just like Bryce said. Sometimes she was warm and sweet, other times this poisonous little viper. The worst part for Bryce was never knowing which side he was going to run into next."

"Yeah, I know what that's like," Zach said, grinning so she could tell he wasn't serious. "Most of the time you're this kind empathic person, then you suddenly turn snarly when I disagree with you."

Cassidy grimaced at him. "We should set up a meeting with Angie."

"I emailed her around five AM."

"I suppose the cops will already have interviewed everybody before we get to them."

"They'll be way ahead of us."

Lifting her mug with both hands, Cassidy stared through the wide dining room window at the charcoal bungalow with the concrete porch Milton had occupied in the predawn hours. "The police have so many more resources than we do. How are we going to find anything they haven't gotten to first?"

"The police always have more resources, but that's never stopped us before. This isn't like you. You're usually chomping at the bit when it comes to investigations."

"But this is different. This time it's Bryce." She took in a breath. "And we don't know what we're going to find."

"Cass, I know you don't want to hear what I'm about to say, but I have to ask the question. If we were to find evidence of Bryce's guilt, what would you want to do with it? Turn it over to the police, or look the other way?"

"That isn't going to happen so there's no point talking about it."

"You keep swinging back and forth. Half the time you sound convinced he's innocent, the other half you sound afraid he's guilty."

"Of course that's how I feel."

"You know, the best thing might be for us to just stay out of it."

"What?"

"I may be even more worried about the outcome of this case than you are. Worried that we'll find damaging evidence and you'll pressure me not to turn it in. Or that we will turn it in and you'll never forgive me. I really don't want to be the bad guy on this one. Not with you or Bryce."

Would you pressure Zach to conceal our findings? She couldn't see herself withholding evidence, but she also couldn't see herself doing anything to harm Bryce. *Yes, but wouldn't letting him get away with murder be worse in the long run than sending him to prison?*

"We have to investigate," she declared. "I don't believe either one of us could stand it if we didn't do everything in our power to find out whether or not Bryce is guilty."

"Okay, then we'll continue as is."

CHAPTER 6

Zach laid four more emails in front of her.

From DC@worldcast.net to Kit:
THIS HAS TO STOP. NO MORE PHONE CALLS. NO MORE EMAIL. NOTHING.

From Kit to DC:
ARE YOU TRYING TO TELL ME IT WASN'T GOOD FOR YOU?

From DC to Kit:
I'M TRYING TO TELL YOU THAT WHAT WE'RE DOING IS WRONG. AND BOTH OF US COULD GET INTO A LOT OF TROUBLE IF ANYBODY FINDS OUT.

From Kit to DC:
THEN WE HAVE TO MAKE SURE NOBODY DOES.

Cassidy said, "So Kit was sleeping with somebody who wanted her to back off. Somebody taking a big risk. A married guy, or one of her teachers."

"A family member, or her therapist if she had one. And if she didn't, she certainly should have."

Cassidy reread the "from" line at the top of the page: DC@worldcast.net (ABC). "I thought the sender's name was supposed to go here," she said, pointing to the ABC.

"The sender can substitute anything he wants."

"How do you do that? No, don't tell me, I wouldn't understand it anyway. Isn't there some way we can trace these emails?"

"Not that I know of. Worldcast isn't about to release any customer information without a court order. Now the police won't have any trouble getting DC's name, and they'll give him a good working over, but we're not going to get anywhere with this email. Although it's always possible Angie or Bryce or some other friend of Kit's will be able to point us in DC's direction."

"I hope so. He sounds like somebody Kit might've given a key to."

Zach scratched his jaw. "I doubt it. DC's obviously nervous about the affair, and the last thing he'd want is to be seen going into her home."

"But Kit might've pressed it on him. In fact, I bet it'd be just like her to pull a power play like that. Maybe he couldn't get her to go away. Maybe she threatened to tell his wife or the authorities or whatever. That'd give him motive, and if he had a key he'd also have means."

"Yeah, but why would DC go into the townhouse with Bryce's Miata parked in the driveway?"

Why would anybody go in with Bryce's car there? Shit, the more we talk, the worse it sounds.

"Unfortunately," Zach added, "these emails are more damaging to Bryce than anyone else."

"I suppose the cops will say Bryce read the emails, discovered Kit was cheating, and killed her for it." Cassidy shook her head. *But most people with unfaithful lovers just leave. Or hang around until they're left, like you did with Kevin.* Narrowing her eyes, she asked, "Do you read my email?"

"Sometimes. Don't you ever read mine?"

"Of course not. It never even occurred to me." She scowled. "Why on earth would you want to?"

"No reason." He drummed his fingers on the table. "It just goes with the territory of being a reporter. Whenever the opportunity presents itself, I automatically snoop around."

Anger started to bunch up in her stomach. Then she remembered what he'd said about not wanting to fight with her and she let it go. This was a time when they needed to pull together.

Zach said, "The one thing I didn't get done last night—"

The phone interrupted him. Cassidy lifted the handset from the wall just inside the kitchen doorway.

"This is Angie Meggins." A tremulous voice. "Is Bryce's father there?"

The email Angie. "I'm Bryce's stepmother. Would you mind talking to me instead?" *No reason I can't set up a meeting.*

"Um … … I guess that'd be okay."

"I suppose the police have been in touch with you?" *God, I hope so. I certainly don't want to deliver a death notification over the phone.*

"They got me up at four AM. Kept buzzing and buzzing. The guy said he was a cop but I was afraid to let him in at first. Then I did and he told me and … " Cassidy heard a sniffle, "I just couldn't believe it. I mean, I can believe it, I can see how it could happen, but at the same time I can't. You know what I mean?"

"Yeah, me too." Cassidy wondered if Angie had jumped to the conclusion that Bryce was guilty. And if she had, how they could get her to talk to them. "Did the police say anything about Bryce?"

"They wanted to know everything. How did Bryce and Kit get along? Did they ever fight? All this personal stuff. They kept pushing me, trying to get me to say something against Bryce. But he's a friend of mine. I know what he's like. He wouldn't kill her."

An ally at last! "We feel the same way." *At least half of us do.*
"We want to talk to everyone Kit was close to and find out who
else had a motive."

"But don't you have to be a cop or a private eye or something
to do that?"

"Zach—Bryce's father—is a reporter at the *Post*. He does this
kind of thing all the time. So, will you help us get started?"

Angie said she would and they made arrangements to meet at
three PM at the Café Unicorn, a coffeehouse not far from Northwestern. "I'll be wearing a purple sweater with a big red rose on the
front," Cassidy said, "and Zach will be all in black."

As Cassidy sat down again, Zach said, "The other thing I need
to do is run a search on Kit's father, Ben Hopewell. You've heard of
him, haven't you?"

Prior to 9/11, Cassidy had avoided reading papers or watching
the news on the grounds that way too much of it focused on triviali-
ties such as sex scandals and who wore what at the Oscars. But on
the other side of the attack, she'd been glued to the television like
everybody else, and now found herself reading the *Post* and listening
to NPR on a regular basis.

"Isn't Hopewell one of those right-wing ministers? Another Jerry
Falwell or Pat Robertson?"

"He's smoother than those other two. Probably holds the same
basic beliefs but manages not to offend the hell out of everybody left
of Ashcroft." Zach went into the kitchen and emptied the coffeepot
into his mug. "I'm going to spend some time at the computer. If I
find anything interesting, I'll let you know."

††††

Upstairs in the bedroom, Cassidy sat in her swivel chair, stared
at the phone on her desk, and let out a sigh. She owed explanations
and thank-yous to her mother, Maggie, and Gran. *What's the matter
with you that you don't want to pick up the phone? You know Maggie*

and Gran will be understanding, and even your mother will basically be on your side.

Yeah, but there's no way to avoid telling them about the murder, and saying everything out loud will make it sound like Bryce is guilty—even to your ears.

First she called Maggie, who was supportive and empathic, just as Cassidy had known she would be. Her friend encouraged her to tell the whole story, so Cassidy let it all out. As she disconnected, she felt a sense of relief. *Here you are a therapist, you can't seem to hold onto the idea that talking is just as good for you as it is for everyone else.*

She provided a summarized version for her mother. Cassidy knew her mother still felt critical of Zach for having had a child out of wedlock—even though he hadn't known about the pregnancy—and critical of Bryce for having had a madam for a mother. Helen made an effort to sound sympathetic, then advised Cassidy not to get involved.

Dialing again, she heard a perky "Hiya!" on the other end.

"Hiya? You've never said 'hiya' before."

"It's my new hobby," Gran said. "I'm trying to think of as many different ways to answer the phone as I can. Tomorrow it's gonna be," her voice deepened, "'You've reached the residence of Ms. Mary McCabe.'"

"Well, Ms. Mary McCabe, I'm calling to thank you for the terrific cleanup you and Maggie did. The place has never looked so good. You two must've worked your little buns off."

"Far as I can tell, my buns are on my backside right where they belong. Maggie did most of the cleaning. I just wandered around finishing off the beer and wine people left in their plastic cups. And your mother came tagging after me, preaching about how people my age shouldn't drink."

"I don't think your liver's in any danger. And there's no question that your brain cells are doing fine."

"So," Gran asked, "is Bryce okay?"

As Cassidy searched for words, Starshine planted herself on the radiator board and stared out the window.

"Not that you have to explain anything," Gran said. "If you'd rather not talk about it, it's okay by me." She paused. "Well, not exactly okay, but I could live with it."

"No, I want to tell you." Cassidy went on to recount the whole story.

"That poor kid, his girlfriend murdered and now he's locked up in that old police station. And of course you're right about him not being guilty. Zach'll come to his senses, you'll see. I almost feel sorry for him that he can't just go with his heart the way we do."

"He might not be able to work as a reporter if he did."

"It's a shame Bryce wasn't at the party. It would've made a perfect alibi. Did you find out why he wasn't there?"

"I didn't get a chance to ask, but I'd bet my brand new kitchen that Kit wouldn't let him go. He told us she liked to control things. Well, she certainly wouldn't have wanted to hang out with such uncool people as us, so I think she put her foot down and made him stay home with her."

"I don't get it," Gran said. "There are so many fish in the sea. Why didn't Bryce just throw her overboard and go find somebody who'd let him do what he wants?"

"Don't get me started on that one."

"I suppose you and Zach are already working on tracking down the real killer. Well, don't you forget—I'm a dang good detective myself."

Cassidy pictured her tiny, wrinkled grandmother bouncing on her toes and patting her red beehive wig.

"So," Gran continued, "what can I do to help? Maybe I could smuggle a file in to Bryce. Or tail somebody. I've never done that before and I sure would like to try my hand at it."

Cassidy smiled at the idea of Gran attempting to be inconspicuous in her fire-engine red Chevy. "I'm not even sure yet what we'll be doing. But if I think of anything, I'll let you know."

† † †

Starshine stepped from the radiator board onto the desk. She sat directly in front of her human and turned up the volume on her motor.

"This is just a ploy to get me to feed you again, isn't it?" Even though Cassidy could tell Starshine wasn't in the mood for petting, she still attempted to scratch behind the cat's ear. The calico, behaving as always when on a food quest, backed just out of reach.

"I know it's hard," Cassidy said, trying empathy. "All this time you've been used to eating whatever you want, whenever you want. Now the rules have changed and you don't know why. Since your skin never gets tight the way waistbands do, you probably don't even realize your girlish figure disappeared about five months ago. And my saying it's for your own good carries about as much weight as a letter from me to Bin Laden telling him to turn himself in."

Starshine nipped Cassidy's finger, then jumped down and trotted into the room across the hall where Zach was working. A few seconds later, Zach's footsteps sounded on the oak stairs. Cassidy went out into the hall and called after him, "You're not going to feed her, are you?"

Her words caught him just as he hit the bend in the staircase. "Oh, yeah, I forgot about that starvation diet you've got her on."

"I thought you agreed to go along with me on this. You know the vet warned us about the health risk of letting her carry all those extra pounds." *Not to mention I want her to look adorable and kittenish again.*

The phone rang. As Cassidy headed back toward her desk in the bedroom, she knew that Zach and Starshine would make use of the interruption to fulfill their food-related mission.

† † †

"More bad news," Victor said. "The police called me in for a third interview after the autopsy." Cassidy heard a click: Zach picking up in the kitchen. "It turns out Kit was between three and four weeks pregnant," Victor finished.

At least we were prepared for this one.

Zach asked, "How did Bryce react?"

"Pure shock. I'm sure he didn't have a clue."

"Then it won't hurt his case."

"Won't the cops try to use it as motive?" Victor asked.

Cassidy said, "I think they'd have to prove he knew about it. I assume they'll run a DNA test to see if he was the father."

"They swabbed him right away." Victor paused. "There's more. A neighbor claims he heard shouting between Bryce and Kit a couple of hours before the shooting. Says he recognized Bryce's voice. Bryce denied it." Cassidy could tell from Victor's tone he wasn't buying his client's story.

No one spoke for about three beats.

"He lied to the cops," Zach said flatly.

"That would be my guess."

"Well, that's it, then. He's going to be booked."

"He already is. After this third round of questioning, I said 'Charge him or let him go,' and they started processing him."

Anxiety sluiced through Cassidy's system.

"The bond hearing will probably be sometime Tuesday," Zach told the attorney. "We'll need around fifty thou to bail him out."

"I'll have to sell some of Bryce's stock," Victor said. "It'll take three working days to get my hands on the cash."

"You don't have fifty grand that's liquid?" Zach asked, an edge to his voice.

"Bryce rented a pricey townhouse, furnished it with high-ticket items, and paid his college expenses all in the past few months. He spent down all the loose change."

"That doesn't sound right to me. I thought Xandra left him a bigger pile than that. Enough to accommodate the expenses you mentioned and still have plenty of liquidity."

"The fund isn't as large as you might think."

"Then borrow on margin."

"Margin trading is *verboten*. Xandra had it written into the trust. She tried it once and lost her shirt."

"We have to have the money by Tuesday," Cassidy said. "Otherwise they'll keep Bryce overnight at Cook County." *Along with the roaches, the rats, and the rapists.*

"You could put up your house," Victor suggested.

"That takes time too," Zach said. "We still couldn't spring him till Wednesday."

"Why don't we think about it and get back to you," Cassidy said.

Shortly after she hung up, Zach came into the bedroom, his brows drawn, his bronze skin a shade darker than usual. "After everything I said, Bryce went ahead and lied to the police. Not only did he lie, he did such a lousy job of it that even Victor could tell he was bullshitting." Zach stood for a moment in front of the west window, hands on hips, then turned back toward her. "Did you know that if a case is hanging in the balance, a lie can make the difference between getting arrested and not getting arrested?"

Cassidy pressed her lips together, wanting to defend Bryce but realizing that anything she said would only make Zach angrier.

It would be better to show a little empathy for your husband. Who, after all, is doing everything he can to help.

He looked at her. "Why aren't you arguing with me?"

"Wouldn't do any good."

Sitting in his desk chair, he asked, "So, what do you think we should do?"

"Borrow the money from your Uncle Martin."

"They wouldn't throw Bryce in with the general population, you know. One night in jail wouldn't do him any harm. In fact, it might teach him a lesson."

She gritted her teeth, then said the words she'd been trying to hold back. "You're just pissed because he didn't do what you told him to—even though I doubt that you ever followed anybody's advice in your life. He was probably scared shitless and just reached the point where he couldn't stand to give the cops one more piece of ammunition to use against him. I think Bryce has been through more than enough already, and that we should do whatever it takes to bail him out on Tuesday."

For a moment Zach's face remained stony, then he softened. "You're probably right. I don't know why I'm so hard on him, considering what a fuck-up I was at his age."

"That's *why* you're so hard on him. So—you'll get the money from Martin?"

Zach squeezed the back of his neck. "You know how I feel about borrowing from my family."

"But the money's going to be yours someday anyway. Besides, you haven't hit Martin up that often and I never had the impression he gave you any flack about it."

"It isn't Martin, it's me. I hate doing it."

Rolling her chair closer to Zach's, she laid her hand on his arm. "You're asking for Bryce, not yourself. And you can repay Martin in a day or two."

"Okay, okay." Zach phoned his uncle and made arrangements to pick up a check on Monday night, then swiveled back toward Cassidy.

She said, "How long before they get the DNA results?"

"Eight or nine months. Could be up to a year."

"I thought it only took a couple of weeks."

"If it's a heater case. If it's low profile and an arrest has already been made, it goes to the bottom of the list. The state lab is underfunded and seriously backed up. You should hear the dicks grumble about it."

"Will they tell Bryce when the results do come back?"

"They won't tell him shit."

"So he won't find out if he's the father until it goes to trial?"

"The cops'll have to hand over everything they've got to his attorney, but that's still way off in the future. And if we get lucky, the case'll be dropped before then." Zach folded his hands on his chest. "Now let me tell you what I found—or I should say didn't find—on Margaret Polanski. Google couldn't come up with a single reference to anybody by that name in Illinois. Switchboard listed twenty-seven Polanskis, but none of them was Margaret or even had the initial "M," so I'd have to conclude that the woman is fairly anonymous and doesn't have a phone listed in her name."

"Maybe a college student with a cell? I suppose I could call all the Polanskis and ask if they have a daughter at Northwestern." Cassidy grimaced, realizing how much she didn't want to do that. "I'll put it at the bottom of my list and if nothing else pans out, I can always come back to it."

"After giving up on Margaret, I turned my attention to Ben. Just before Victor called I was checking out the website for Hopewell's church. You want to take a look?"

CHAPTER 7

CASSIDY FOLLOWED ZACH INTO HIS OFFICE ACROSS the hall, where they sat side by side at the long wooden table he'd built to hold his computer equipment. The monitor displayed a photo of The Church of Our Blessed Savior, an ornate gray stone building replete with multiple spires, gargoyles, and heavy stone arches. According to the small print beneath the picture, the building was located in Winnetka, a wealthy lakeshore suburb directly north of Chicago.

Zach clicked on THE MINISTER. A curving block of text with photos on either side filled the screen. Cassidy gazed at a family portrait: Ben and his wife, Adele, seated in the center; a young child, Heidi, in front; two older children, Forest and Katherine, aka Kit, in back. The wholesome-looking eldest child in the portrait bore no resemblance to the darkly made-up young woman Cassidy had met. She guessed that the picture had been taken when Kit was around fourteen.

Adele, a small-boned woman with a somber face, had bequeathed her silvery blond hair to all three children. In contrast, the father had the body of a linebacker, thick dark hair, and a confident smile. *Kit rejected her mother's blondness, adopted her father's dark aspect instead. Suppose most teenaged girls want to be as different from their moms as possible.*

Cassidy, who considered right-wingers to be paternalistic and anti-feminist, focused on the pastor. *An alpha male. Religious zealot who wants to sexually repress everyone in the world—except possibly himself. Nice little family to make him look good, with the exception of rebellious daughter Kit, who refused to toe the line.* Looking at the idyllic family picture, Cassidy could almost understand why Kit had swung to such an opposite extreme.

Skimming the text, Cassidy learned that Hopewell had taken up the ministry of the Winnetka church seven years earlier. He also had penned several books and was in demand as an inspirational speaker. At the bottom he was quoted as saying, "I see it as my calling to reinvigorate family values at a time when the traditional family is under attack."

"A proponent of family values," Cassidy said. "What a surprise."

"We lived together before we were married so I guess we wouldn't qualify."

"I can't think of a single person I know other than Gran who isn't gay or hasn't had an abortion or a divorce or a child out of wedlock."

"There's one guy at the *Post* who's married with a couple of kids, but he's young yet."

Cassidy pictured Kit with her dyed hair, black lipstick, and see-through top. "What do you think?" she asked Zach. "Did Kit show up at Sunday services in her vampire costume?"

"She said her family forked over all the dough she wanted, so maybe they were paying her to stay away."

† † †

It was almost three thirty when a tall, rail-like woman came dashing through the doorway of the Unicorn Café. Spotting Cassidy and Zach, she hurried over to their table. "Are you Bryce's parents?"

"We are." Zach stood and introduced himself and Cassidy, then asked Angie what she would like from the coffee bar.

"Uh, bottled water, I guess."

Doesn't look anything like Kit. But you should have known that from the emails.

Zach left to get the water and Angie sat down.

"Sorry I'm late." Her puffy eyes regarded Cassidy through the lenses of her black-framed glasses. "I never get anywhere on time. I keep trying to improve, really I do, but somehow I'm still always late."

"Well, we're not in any hurry," Cassidy said, concealing her irritation at having to wait so long.

Angie pinched her lower lip. "This is just so creepy. Murder doesn't happen to people you know. Except it really has happened to my best friend. And Bryce—my gosh, this must be so awful for him. Is he with you? How's he holding up?"

Cassidy was explaining Bryce's situation when Zach returned to the table, placed a water bottle in front of Angie, sat down, and took out his pad. The coffeehouse was crowded with people who looked like university types, casually clad folks who were reading, working on laptops, or talking in small groups.

"I called Bryce just yesterday," Angie said. "I was worried about my math exam but he kept telling me everything would be fine. Whenever I get nervous, I talk to Bryce and he makes me feel better. I think that's why Kit wanted to be with him. Deep down inside she really loved him, even though she didn't always act like it."

"Did it bother you that she wasn't always nice to him?" Cassidy asked.

"Well, yeah, it did a little. I'm the one who brought them together, you know." Angie gazed at a large wood-framed mirror on the far wall. "Kit started sleeping on my couch after she walked out on Raul. She should've had her own apartment—she certainly could've afforded it—but she had all these guys buzzing around her and she got in the habit of staying with one for a while, then moving on to somebody else. But Raul gave her a pretty hard time. She told me he hit her and she was sick of it and didn't want anything more to do with him. So after she left him—well, she sort of left him—she stayed with me for a couple of months."

"And that's how Kit and Bryce met?" Cassidy prompted.

"Bryce would drop over sometimes and Kit would be there and she just decided to go after him." Angie pressed her fist against her mouth. "I was happy for Kit," she said, not sounding happy. "I thought Bryce would be good for her. He's always so easygoing and stable. I thought he might help her calm down."

Easygoing and stable? A side of him we haven't seen.

Zach said to Angie, "We just learned that Kit was about four weeks pregnant. Did she say anything to you about it?"

"Pregnant? Oh my gosh! Oh my gosh! That means an innocent baby was killed along with Kit. She didn't let on to me at all. Are you sure she knew?"

"I think she probably did." *Considering she'd missed a period and stopped taking her pills, I'd say she knew.* "We were wondering about paternity. If there was anybody besides Bryce who might have been the father. You said she 'sort of' left Raul. Does that mean she was still sleeping with him?"

"I'm not sure she ever stopped. Raul's a dope dealer. A real piece of slime."

"Kit's dope dealer?" Zach asked.

Angie shook her head. "She hardly ever used drugs. Maybe a little pot now and then, but that's all. She didn't drink much either. Always said she didn't like to be out of control."

"So tell us about Raul."

Angie's mouth flattened with disgust. "Sometimes after she'd been out with him, I'd see bruises. I used to get so mad at her. And then I'd get mad at myself. When Kit was staying with me, there were times she'd bring Raul home and tell me I had to get lost so they could do it in my bed."

Cassidy's gut knotted with anger just hearing about it.

"I know I shouldn't have let her bring Raul over," Angie continued. "It went against everything I believe in as a Christian. But anytime I tried to stop her, she'd make fun of the fact that I've never had a boyfriend. She used to laugh at me because I'm still a virgin." Lowering her head, Angie grabbed a handful of her short curly hair. "What she said—it really hurt. I've talked to a minister here on campus and he's praying for me, but I never did get to the point where I could stand up to her."

Cassidy said, "So you're pretty religious then."

"My parents belong to Pastor Hopewell's church. That's where I met Kit—in the junior high class."

"And you feel a little odd about still being a virgin? There are women a lot older than you who haven't had sex yet." *Had clients in their thirties whose maidenheads were still intact.*

Angie's cheeks flushed. "Well, no, I don't feel odd about it. Not exactly. I mean, if you're a good Christian you have to abstain until after you're married, don't you? But Pastor Hopewell says we shouldn't even date. I love babies and I've always wanted a big family, but the way things are going I don't see how it's ever going to happen."

"I can understand why you'd feel discouraged, but I think you just need to give it a little more time."

Angie turned her head sharply away. "It's so unfair. Here Kit had all these guys chasing after her, and she wasn't the least bit interested in getting married or having a family. But good girls just aren't in demand."

Although Cassidy had never been especially good, she could remember that during her college years she'd felt as if not one member of the entire male population knew she existed. "Having a friend like Kit would be hard for anyone."

The younger woman looked at her watch. "Oh gosh, I'm late again. I was supposed to be at a youth ministry meeting at four o'clock."

Haven't even gotten to the Thorazine yet.

"Before you go," Zach said, "do you have any idea how to reach Kit's dope dealer boyfriend?"

"Got his cell number right here." Angie pulled a notebook out of her backpack and read off a number. "His plate number too. Kit wanted to make sure the cops could find him if she ever went out and didn't come back."

What's this? Our whack-job Kit displaying some frontal lobe activity?

"How 'bout a last name?" Zach asked.

"Estevez."

"There are some other things I'd like to go over with you," Cassidy said. "When could we get together again?"

"The funeral's in the morning." Angie used her index finger to push her glasses farther up her nose. "Call me after it's over and we can set up a time."

"When's the viewing?" Zach asked as she started to leave.

"Ten AM at the church."

CHAPTER 8

Zach called Raul's number. He asked the dope dealer if he'd heard about Kit's murder, then said, "I'm Zach Moran, a reporter for the *Post*. I'm also Bryce's father. I've got my wife here, and the two of us would like to set up a meeting with you."

Clipping his cell phone to his belt, Zach told Cassidy, "The cops were able to roust him out last night, so he knows about Kit. He said to get on over to the campus and wait for him on a bench across from the Rock. If he likes how we look, he'll approach us."

"You told him the truth. I thought for sure you'd make up some story about wanting to buy dope."

"Nah, he'd think I was a narc. I figured my best shot was to say I was a reporter. For some reason, the whole world is in love with the idea of playing Deep Throat."

†††

Cassidy and Zach sat across from the landmark Rock on a wooden bench at the north end of a small plaza. The rock itself was a jagged purple-painted boulder, about four feet high, with white letters announcing a student event scrawled across its face. Several trees rose from the plaza's faux cobblestone surface, their still-green leaves breaking the light into shifting pools of sunshine and shadow.

A constant stream of foot traffic crossed the cobblestoned area, but no one glanced their way. Cassidy began to worry that Raul had given up on them during the half hour they'd spent searching for a parking spot. Then she looked again and he was there, a slender Hispanic guy standing beside the rock staring at them.

"Here he comes," Zach said, as Raul started toward them, walking with a long-legged, hip-rolling stride.

He stood over Zach. "So you're the pussy's old man."

Zach looked through him.

Such a talent for indifference. Exactly the right approach for these big ego types.

A beat passed. Zach got to his feet, with Cassidy following suit. The dope dealer had penetrating eyes, sharply defined features, and a short, stubbly goatee. *Handsome, arrogant, and dangerous looking. Kind of guy women should steer clear of but never do.*

"You going to talk to me?" Zach asked.

"Depends." Thrusting his hands into the pockets of his khaki pants, Raul turned his head to look back over the plaza, then shifted his weight.

Zach gazed past Raul into the middle distance. *Acting as disinterested as Starshine when she doesn't choose to acknowledge your existence.*

After a long silence, Raul looked at Zach. "What do you want?"

"I was told that Kit lived with you before she moved in with Angie."

"Yeah, she stayed at my crib for a while."

"Why did the two of you split up?" Cassidy asked.

"Got tired of her shit and threw her out."

"You ended it, not Kit?"

"That's what I said."

"Evidently Kit had a real need to be in control."

"You got that right."

"But you don't seem like the kind of guy to let any woman push you around."

Raul looked down at Cassidy through slitted eyes, not bothering to answer.

"So why would she move in with someone who wouldn't let her be in control?" *Besides the fact that he's handsome, arrogant, and dangerous looking.*

Raul's face broke into a predatory grin. "Because it pissed off her old man. She even brought me to church one Sunday. We left before the end of the service and stood outside smoking weed while the rest of the congregation came out. I never seen her get such a kick out of anything as she did blowing smoke in the faces of everybody who walked past."

"What did her father do?" Zach asked.

"Acted as if nothing happened." Raul slanted his face away for a moment, then looked at Zach again. "Here's something you might find interesting. She told her dad she wanted to buy me a guitar and the old fool actually gave her the bread to do it. I guess he was too much of a wuss to stand up to her."

"She gave you a guitar?" Zach repeated.

"Top of the line, dude. Top of the line."

Cassidy said, "I understand she continued to see you after she moved in with Angie."

"She was a real hottie, man. Hot enough I didn't mind giving her what she wanted as long as she didn't try to order me around."

"When was the last time you saw her?"

"Look, dude, I don't keep a record in my Palm Pilot of who I fuck when."

Cassidy edged a little closer. "Have you seen her in the past four or five weeks?"

"Not since she moved in with your kid. But she was getting bored with him. Bryce was such a pussy—she wouldn't have stayed much longer."

"How would you know that," Cassidy asked, "if you hadn't seen her?"

"She called a few times. Wanted to get it on with me. But by then, I had me this new bitch so I cut Kit off." The predatory grin. "Couldn't cheat on my new little lovebird, now could I?"

He wouldn't cheat on his new girlfriend like the Republicans wouldn't snuggle under the sheets with big business.

Zach said, "Kit tell you she was pregnant?"

"Didn't say a word about it, man. But I wasn't the one who knocked her up, so why would she?"

"So," Zach said, "you know of anybody who had a beef with her?"

"Shit, she pissed off everybody. But the only person with a reason to kill her was Bryce. I kicked her out after a few weeks. If I'd had to put up with her as long as he did, I woulda popped her myself."

Makes perfect sense. Who wouldn't want to kill her if they had to live with her so long?

Raul's pager went off. He read the message, then told them he had business elsewhere.

After Raul was gone, Zach recorded the dealer's comments in his notepad. Cassidy knew he frequently refrained from taking it out in the presence of a reluctant source.

†††

"You have such an instinct for dealing with these arrogant types," Cassidy said to Zach as they hiked toward the Subaru. "I understand how the game works, but I'm never very good at playing it."

"You didn't grow up with my mother."

Cassidy pictured Mildred, with her regal bearing and aristocratic face. *Arrogance personified. Especially directed at Zach, the kid she didn't want. No wonder he hates to borrow from his family. Mildred will find out and consider it further vindication of her belief that her son is a waste. And even though Zach and his mother never speak, he'll know she knows.*

Pulling away from the curb, Zach started the long diagonal trip across the city from Evanston to Oak Park. Rush hour was in full swing, so Cassidy knew they'd be stuck on the road for at least an hour.

She said, "Raul claims he threw Kit out because of her shit, and Kit told Angie she left because he hit her. Since Angie saw bruises, I think we can assume the hitting part was true."

"Yeah, but there's no way to know whether it was Kit or Raul who decided she should move out."

"Maybe not, but I think we can assume Raul was jealous of Bryce. Why else make such an effort to insult him?"

"Nah, Raul's comments were aimed at me. You know, young Turk challenging old Turk."

"No, I'm sure Raul was jealous. Guys who slap their women around are almost always insecure and possessive."

"Insecure? Raul? This isn't a CEO battering his wife—it's a dealer hitting his girlfriend. Dealers and pimps beat on their women. It's part of the gig."

"Just hear me out," Cassidy said. "I'd bet anything Kit was the one who left. She left and Raul's big fat ego couldn't stand it. He couldn't stand having any woman walk out on him, but especially not a hottie like Kit. For a while, she made herself available to him, and that helped to take the sting out of it. As long as she was at Angie's, it didn't seem so bad. Then she moved in with Bryce, and Raul's jealousy started to spiral. A few months later, something else happened—she laughed at his erection, or she moved DC into his time slot, or she told him to get lost—and that was the last straw. He went out of control and killed her."

"And you think she gave this jealous, hot-tempered guy a key?"

"She gave him a key so they could sleep in Bryce's bed, just like they'd slept in Angie's. Or because she was bored and wanted to stir up a little excitement. Or because she was grandiose and thought she could handle anything."

"Okay, Raul lets himself in and waits in the living room, but he has no way of knowing who'll show up first—Kit or Bryce. He doesn't even know whether either one of them will come downstairs. Maybe they'll both just go to bed."

When you think of it that way, it's hard to imagine that anybody other than Bryce could have done it.

She stared into space, desperately trying to devise a credible scenario. "Raul was stoned or drunk. He didn't think it through. He barged in, planning to kill both of them, but he panicked after shooting Kit and ran out."

"Well, you did it. You found a way to set Raul up as a suspect that I can't instantly shoot down. But give me time, I'm sure I'll think of something."

Couldn't stand that Bryce was the only name on Zach's list, could you?

"What puzzles me," Zach said, "is this thing about Kit's father giving her money to buy Raul a guitar. That, along with what she said earlier about her parents shelling out all the dough she wanted. Hopewell's a powerful guy. I can't see why he'd roll over for his daughter like that—especially since she must've embarrassed the hell out of him."

"What are you thinking?"

Zach stomped on the brake as an SUV cut in front of him. "I'm beginning to wonder about incest. Wouldn't that explain her bizarre behavior?"

"There was a time when therapists jumped to conclusions about incest any time they had a female client who was acting out—especially if she was promiscuous. These therapists made some very bad calls, which led to a lot of pain and suffering for families, so we're careful not to make that assumption any more. Incest is a possibility, but I don't see any evidence pointing in that direction."

"So why wouldn't the pastor have disowned her? Or at least stopped financing her escapades?"

"I guess some fathers are so doting with their daughters they can never say no."

Zach turned south onto the curving boulevard that cut through Humboldt Park, a traditional expanse of grass dotted with statues. A battered car displaying a Puerto Rican flag zipped past them. After several seconds of silence, Zach said, "I was surprised to hear Angie get so emotional about babies. I thought women didn't do that until their biological clocks were about to run out."

Speaking with more intensity than she intended, Cassidy replied, "A women of any age can want a baby."

Zach looked at her in surprise. "What are you saying?"

"Nothing." She turned her head to gaze out the side window.

"Are you telling me that you want a baby?"

What you want is for him to drop it. You put this to rest a long time ago and you don't want him dredging it up.

"Hey, Cass, what's going on? You can't not talk to me about this."

"I used to want a baby, but that was a whole lifetime ago."

"What happened? Kevin say no?"

"Our marriage was rocky. Kevin was hugely self-centered and couldn't hold a job. I just decided it wouldn't be right to bring a child into a situation like that."

Zach put his hand on her knee. "Why haven't you ever talked about this? I thought we were supposed to tell each other everything."

"I stopped thinking about it long before I met you."

Zach drove for several blocks in silence and Cassidy assumed the conversation was over.

"If you could have a baby now, would you still want one?"

"I'm forty."

"Women have babies at forty."

"You don't want a child, do you?"

"A baby." He let out a breath. "I don't seem to be doing such a great job with the kid I've got, so I suppose I shouldn't even think about having another."

CHAPTER 9

WAITING ON THE STOOP FOR ZACH TO unlock the door, Cassidy gazed across the street at the porch where she'd seen Milton the night before. To her surprise, the gimpy old tom was wandering diagonally across the bungalow's front yard toward the street. This was the first time since Milton had moved on that she'd seen him two nights in a row.

You assumed he'd found a new cat lady on some other block. So why would he be hanging around his old feeding station? Because his new feeding station is out of business?

Zach went inside to turn off the security system. Milton crossed the street and disappeared behind their garage, which stood on the far corner of their lot.

Now don't go worrying about Milton. You know cats are inscrutable. Soon as you think you have their behavior figured out, they change it.

Cassidy followed Zach into her client waiting room, a cheerful space with white wicker chairs flanking a large window framed by raspberry sheers. Her therapy practice took up the entire rear section of the house; waiting room in the southeast corner, office in the northeast corner, a bathroom in between. A freestanding oak closet served as a room divider, separating her professional area from the rest of the house.

In the kitchen Starshine sat on the counter complaining to Zach about the contents of her bowl. Cassidy knew most of the calico's sounds: the seductive *mwat* she used when she wanted to be fed, the amiable *mrup* she used when in the mood for conversation, the demanding *mror* she used when confronted with a closed door. But the sound she was making to protest her low-cal diet was a new one: a short, snippy *mrit*. Her ears were back, her whiskers retracted. The tip of her tail twitched. *Mrit! Mrit! Mrit!*

"She isn't going to eat this stuff," Zach said. "We might as well throw it out."

"She's testing us. She thinks that if she holds out long enough, we'll give her what she wants."

"Well, isn't that what's going to happen? How long do you think we can tolerate her hunger strike?"

"She isn't going hungry. Just this morning you gave her the canned food again. As long as she receives intermittent reinforcement, of course she'll refuse to eat the new food." *He doesn't want to put Starshine on a diet because it reminds him that he needs to do the same.*

"This dry food looks about as tasty as gravel. Since I have no urge to force her to eat something she hates, why don't you take over her feeding?"

"But then I'd have to get up first and go downstairs to serve her breakfast. You know what a zombie I am before I've had my coffee."

"Make her wait till you're conscious."

"Make Starshine *wait*? C'mon Zach, parents have to present a united front. You don't want to see her have a heart attack because we were too wimpy to enforce a little discipline, do you?"

"All right, I'll try." Zach wrapped an arm around Cassidy's shoulders. "But I can't promise I won't occasionally succumb to those big green eyes of hers. She's almost as hard to say no to as you are."

Glaring at her humans, the calico jumped down and stalked out of the kitchen.

"Well," Zach said, "now that Starshine's made her decision about dinner, what about ours?"

"I have some hamburger in the freezer," Cassidy ventured. Up until they'd started rehabbing the house, dinners consisted primarily of eat-outs and take-outs. She used to view cooking as tedious and unnecessary, and generally managed to avoid it. But given the large sums going out to contractors, Cassidy decided she needed to increase her contribution by cooking. She'd soon discovered that the biggest difficulty wasn't the cooking itself, but the planning ahead and shopping.

"How 'bout hamburgers and a salad?" she said. "I don't feel up to tackling anything major."

"This has been a rough weekend. Why don't we treat ourselves to dinner out?"

Yes! You deserve a break today! she sang to herself.

Then, sighing, she said, "I set this goal of five meals a week, and if I don't stick to it, I'll never acquire the habit of cooking on a regular basis."

Why is this so hard? Your mother's a great cook and she makes it look easy.

Your mother has nothing else to do.

"Up to you. I could eat hamburgers almost every night of the week."

It's a good thing, since hamburgers seem to be my default setting.

Cassidy took a package of ground beef out of the freezer and Zach went upstairs. She defrosted it in the microwave, tossed a salad, and broiled four patties, leaving the meat to drain on a thick layer of paper towels atop one of the new Dansk plates they'd bought to go with their new kitchen. As she was setting the dining room table, she heard a crash behind her.

Hurrying into the kitchen, she saw Starshine hunkered down amidst a pile of rubble: chunks of hamburger, pieces of broken ceramic, greasy paper towels. The cat was eagerly filling her stomach.

"Oh shit!" Cassidy made a grab for the calico but the cat zipped between her legs and disappeared into the front part of the house.

After Cassidy cleaned up the mess and Zach left for the deli, she plunked down on the top step of their back porch. One of their new dishes was broken, Starshine refused to eat her low-cal food, Cassidy had failed meal-planning 101, and Bryce was facing a murder charge.

She pictured her stepson with a small black cloud over his head. In the two years she'd known him, Bryce had lost the mother he loved, been forced into a relationship with the father he hated, and suffered a depression so severe it had brought him close to suicide. Cassidy wondered if Bryce had the resources it would take to start over one more time.

CHAPTER 10

Z ACH HELD CASSIDY'S HAND AS THEY MOUNTED the wide front steps leading to the entrance of Our Blessed Savior. It was Monday morning, another warm fall day, with pale light emanating from a pearl-colored sky. They crossed the vestibule and entered the sanctuary, an immense room filled with men in suits and women in dresses with cardigan sweaters. Cassidy and Zach had made an effort to dress appropriately, Cassidy in a lavender silk blouse, Zach in a jacket and black jeans. *This time, you really did want to fit in. But once again, you're not quite up to par.*

The closed casket stood in front of the altar, Kit's parents to the right, a receiving line snaking along the right-hand wall. Ben Hopewell looked much less powerful than he had in the picture on the website. As he shook hands with the mourners, his demeanor was grave, his gestures subdued, his large body hunched in on itself. His small, silvery-blonde wife sat beside him, making no effort to speak. On the opposite side of the casket, Forest Hopewell, a slender tow-headed boy in his mid teens, paced back and forth between the casket and the doorway to the vestibule.

Cassidy felt a lump rise in her chest as she gazed at Adele Hopewell. Adele's eyes were downcast, her hands together in her lap. *Violent death of a child. Nothing could be worse.* Cassidy turned toward Zach, not wanting to even think about the pain Kit's mother must be suffering.

"What's the plan?"

"Thought I'd hang out in the crowd for a while, see what people are saying. Then I want to introduce myself to Hopewell."

"Isn't that going to be hard on him? To have to shake hands with the suspect's father?"

"I want to get some sense of how he's likely to react when I call for an interview."

"Okay, I'll wander around and eavesdrop too."

As she headed toward the center of the throng, Cassidy stopped to listen to a woman speaking to another woman. "She used to babysit my twins. They just adored her, and from the way she talked about her brother and sister, I got the impression she mothered them as well. I can't imagine how a girl from such a good family could go so wrong."

Moving on to an elderly couple, Cassidy heard the wife say to her husband, "Ben's a strong person. I know he'll be all right. But I worry about Adele. I don't think she has any friends. And she doesn't seem to have a thing to do other than oversee that house-keeper of theirs."

Someone jostled Cassidy from behind and she started moving again, halting a few moments later to tune in to a conversation between two men. One, in his twenties, appeared earnest and soulful. The other, nearly twice that age, was overweight and a little slovenly. The younger man said, "Last year we had that rash of suicides, but I don't know how long it's been since we had a murder."

"Thank God it didn't happen on campus. But it still means we won't get any work done until the students settle down."

"Excuse me for interrupting," Cassidy said, "but you two sound like you're from Northwestern."

"That's right," the older man said.

"I'm Cassidy McCabe, Bryce Palomar's stepmother." She thrust her hand toward him, hoping his social training would compel him to grasp it and introduce himself.

He resisted for a moment, then shook her hand and said, "Morrie Schweitzer."

"Bryce Palomar," the younger man said. "Wasn't he Kit's boyfriend?"

"Kit was living with him. In fact, they were both in the townhouse when she was killed." Cassidy paused, wishing she could think of a way to make Bryce sound less guilty. "The police have him under suspicion, but his father and I are convinced he didn't do it. We're talking to people who knew Kit, trying to come up with an alternative theory." She turned to the younger man. "Would you mind telling me your name?"

He hesitated.

They think I'm nuts.

"Jeff O'Donnell."

"Did you both have Kit in class?"

The overweight guy squinted at Cassidy. "Um ... you sure you're not with the press?"

"I really am Bryce's stepmom. We had dinner with Bryce and Kit just a couple of weeks ago. Kit had to leave early for a rehearsal."

"*Hedda Gabler*," Schweitzer said. "She had the lead role. I have an understudy, of course, but the production's really going to suffer from Kit's loss."

"What was she like to work with?"

"Good on stage. Fiery. High-spirited. Some days she'd come in and be totally cooperative. Other days she'd fight with everybody, including me."

"I didn't have any problem with her," Jeff O'Donnell said. "She was very bright, always got her papers in on time. There's a girl in class who was having trouble with Shakespeare, and I know Kit helped her more than once." He stared across the room for a moment. "I hope your stepson isn't guilty. But whoever did it, I'd like to see him put away."

Recalling that Kit had liked the sonnets, Cassidy said to O'Donnell, "You must be her lit professor." The man nodded. She turned toward the older guy. "And you're directing the play she was in."

"Yeah, I was both her director and her coach. She'd been taking private lessons with me for over a year."

"This has hit everybody so hard," Cassidy said.

As the lit professor nodded soberly, the director started to edge away.

"Well, thanks for talking to me."

Cassidy leaned against a pew and wrote the men's names in her pad. Shifting her weight, she folded her arms and gazed out over the room. Zach moved slowly through the thickest part of the crowd. A group of college students poured into the church. Ben Hopewell bent down to speak to Adele, who grabbed his hand with both of hers.

Cassidy suddenly realized that the reason she'd had such a mean-spirited reaction when she looked at the family portrait on the website was that she wanted to dehumanize them. *See them as a bunch of religious kooks. Not the same as you and Zach. Turn things around so Bryce can be the victim, not Kit and her family.*

†††

Cassidy noticed a strange-looking woman slip through the doorway to the left of the casket and go to stand against the left-hand wall. Her coat was much too heavy for the seventy-degree weather and there was a general air of unkemptness about her. *Ruffled and ungroomed, like a stray cat.*

The woman stayed where she was for a couple of minutes, her eyes fixed on the area near the casket, then she raised her hand in a small wave and went back out. Thirty seconds later Forest Hopewell followed her through the doorway.

Cassidy hastened across the room, through the vestibule, and out onto the porch. Her eyes darted along the concrete walkway that led to a circular drive. To the left was a parking lot; to the right, a grassy area dotted with trees. A number of people were standing around, but Forest and the scruffy woman were not among them.

Where would you go to conduct a secret meeting? Climb inside a car in the parking lot? Circle around to the back of the church? Behind the church, she decided, and began hiking across the grass.

When she reached the rear of the gray stone building, she moved in close to the corner and peered around it. An oak tree stood at a distance of about fifteen feet, with Forest and the woman in a huddle beneath it. The boy, his back to Cassidy, was gesturing broadly. The woman, facing Cassidy, had her hands clasped together at her throat.

Although Cassidy couldn't hear what they were saying, she was able to get a good look at the woman. Her hair, either light brown or blond, was pulled severely back from her face, and her features were regular. It occurred to Cassidy that the woman may be an outcast member of the Hopewell clan. *A mentally ill aunt. A cousin nobody talks about.*

After Forest and the woman conversed for a short time, he hugged her, then watched as she headed off toward the parking lot. Turning around, he trudged toward the corner where Cassidy was hiding.

Oh shit! You'll never be able to talk your way out of this one.

Just before he stumbled across her, she stepped out into his path.

The boy stopped abruptly. His pale blue eyes blinked in surprise. "Who are you? What're you doing here?"

"I'm Bryce Palomar's stepmother."

"Bryce? That's the prick who killed my sister."

"No, I'm sure he didn't. He loved her. It had to be somebody else."

"So what're you doing here? Spying on me?"

"I saw that woman leave the church, then you went after her. I wanted to see what was going on. I have to find out what happened to Kit."

"You *are* spying on me."

"I just want to learn more about Kit's family." *God, how lame is that?*

"You can't possibly think it was somebody in her family that killed her!"

"I know I shouldn't have spied on you, but I need to learn everything I can about Kit. Please talk to me. Just answer a couple of questions."

"I don't know anything about you. Why should I talk to you?"

"Because the police think Bryce did it and they're wrong. Because I want to see Kit's killer punished as much as you do. Because you might be able to help me figure out who really did it."

Tension lines cut into his face.

I think he does *want to talk to me.*

As he started to brush past her, she grabbed his arm. "I'm a therapist. You've just been through a huge trauma and talking helps." She took out her card and pressed it into his hand. "Hang onto this just in case you change your mind."

Forest tucked her card into the pocket of his gray slacks and hurried toward the church entrance.

At least he took your card. Yeah, but he's too well-mannered to litter so he's probably just carrying it to the nearest garbage can.

Just before he rounded the corner, he turned and asked belligerently, "Are you going to tell my father you saw me talking to that girl?"

"I won't say a word to your father." *Just to Zach, and Forest doesn't need to know about that.*

††††

After Forest was gone, Cassidy waited about a minute so it wouldn't look as if she and the teenager had been together, then went back inside and joined Zach in the receiving line.

When their turn came to speak to the pastor, Cassidy stepped in front of Zach so she could be the one to make the introductions. Even though she would have preferred to leave Hopewell alone on the day of his daughter's funeral, as long as they were standing in front of him, she'd rather be spoken to than ignored.

Watching the pastor's face as she explained who they were, she saw a brief flicker of surprise, followed by a warm smile. *This guy's good.*

"Thank you for coming." Hopewell looked deeply into her eyes, making her feel as if she were the most important person in the room. *Well, what do you expect? He's a charismatic preacher.*

"Sorry for your loss," Cassidy murmured.

"You'll have to excuse my wife." Ben glanced down at Adele, who stared blankly into space. "She hasn't recovered from the shock."

"Of course."

"I met your son." The pastor looked from Cassidy to Zach. "I liked him. I thought he'd be good for Kit."

After Raul, Bryce must have seemed golden.

"The only way I can make sense out of this is to tell myself it was God's will."

Zach said, "I prefer to make sense out of things by finding out why they happened."

The pastor offered a small smile. "I'm sorry for you if you don't have a faith to take comfort in. But I hope you and your son will find solace wherever you can."

† † †

"Didn't you tell me you have a client this afternoon?" Zach asked Cassidy as they buckled their seatbelts.

"Not till three thirty."

"Then you'd have time for a quick stop at Victor's on the way home."

"Sure."

Zach flipped open his cell phone. "Hey, Victor, any chance of getting in to see you about forty-five minutes from now?" A pause. "An hour? Okay, sure, that'll be fine."

"Why are we going to see Victor?"

Zach started the ignition and turned south, heading toward the city. "I want to nail down exactly when he'll get the bond money to us. And also discuss the thirty grand retainer we'll need for a defense attorney."

"Where's his office?"

"One hundred block of South Michigan."

"Michigan Avenue? That sounds more high-end than I would have expected." Cassidy pictured Victor's narrow face, his sparse hair sprouting upward from his scalp. *A man who clearly doesn't indulge in expensive haircuts.* "I didn't get the impression he was all that affluent."

"We're not talking the Magnificent Mile here. Some of the older buildings along Michigan are pretty third-rate. By the way, did you recognize any of the famous faces at the viewing?"

"I never recognize famous faces."

"Henry Hyde was there, along with a couple of state reps. The fact that three politicos showed up on practically no notice confirms my estimation of Hopewell as a well-connected guy." Zach stopped at a light behind a white stretch limo. "You come up with anything?"

She told him about the two professors and the woman Forest had met behind the church building. "There was something about the way he reacted when I tried to get him to talk that makes me think the family has something to hide—something bigger than just a weird relative the pastor chooses not to acknowledge."

Zach looked at her as if she were being naïve again. "Of course the family has something to hide. You know of any family that doesn't? But given that this is a fundamentalist family, the big secret could be that the parents occasionally sneak out to go dancing. Or that the kids are allowed to watch MTV."

CHAPTER 11

CASSIDY AND ZACH PASSED THROUGH A REVOLVING door into a long narrow lobby, the ceiling at least two stories high, the time of construction long before Cassidy was born. *What you'd call vintage. Office space definitely not at a premium.* Due to the miracle of having found street parking a mere three blocks away, they were half an hour early.

In Victor's waiting room, Zach parked himself next to a handsome artificial fig tree. Sitting beside him, Cassidy picked up a *Redbook* and started hunting for quick-and-easy recipes.

Fifteen minutes later a man came out of Victor's office. He looked to be in his fifties, although he walked with a cocky little strut that made him seem younger. He was on the short side, lean and muscular, clad in work pants and a long-sleeved shirt. He wore a ball cap pointing backward and had lively blue eyes, a small bristly mustache, and a relaxed, easygoing smile. He gave Cassidy a broad wink and then was out the door.

Although she knew she ought to be offended, she could not suppress the small glow of pleasure she felt from being winked at. *Suppose a chorus of hardhat wolf whistles would really make your day.*

"Evidently he approves of my choice," Zach said.

Victor invited them into his office.

"So, when's the bond hearing?" Cassidy asked.

"Tomorrow, the afternoon session. I believe it starts at one." He looked at Zach. "You know where to go?"

"Central Bond Court. I'll have the money with me. I assume you'll be able to repay me on Wednesday."

"I'll messenger the check over to you. Now how soon will you need the defense attorney retainer?"

"I've got a call in to John Spredl. I won't know the details until I talk to him, but it's going to be around thirty grand."

"Yeah, Spredl, he's good. I'll start the process right away."

Cassidy pressed her curled fingers beneath her chin. "Have you seen Bryce recently? How's he doing?"

Victor met her eyes, a small frown etching itself into his forehead. "Saw him this morning. He's pretty worn down but he hasn't wavered in his statement, so I'd say he's doing as well as can be expected."

"I'm glad you're getting in to see him so often." She wondered whether Zach, if he'd been in Victor's place, would have done as well.

Visiting isn't Zach's strong point. But he'll be relentless in tracking down the killer. And in the long run, having his name cleared will mean more to Bryce than a warm, avuncular shoulder to lean on.

† † †

The back doorbell rang, signaling that Cassidy's three thirty client had arrived. Cassidy went around the room divider into her waiting area. Jan—early forties, straight dark hair, winsome face—rose from one of the wicker chairs. Her hands twisted a water bottle. Her smile was a shade less confident than usual.

She said, "I'm so glad to be here."

They went into the office, Cassidy sitting in her new chair, Jan perching on the new tropical print sofa.

"What happened?" Cassidy asked.

"I don't know where to start." Jan blinked, gulped water from her bottle, and wrapped her fingers around the base of her throat.

Cassidy glanced at the window behind Jan's head. Wind lashed the small tree in back of her office.

"Is Tony in trouble again?" Cassidy asked, referring to Jan's fifteen-year-old son. When he was doing well, Jan was bright and animated.

"The principal wants to suspend him. They've made up this story about him shoving a teacher into a wall. Nobody's even listening to Tony. But I'm not letting them get away with it. I have an appointment with my attorney tomorrow." Jan unscrewed her water bottle cap, started to take a drink, then screwed it back on.

"What exactly is the school's version?"

"What difference does it make?" Jan asked, an edge to her voice. "He says he didn't do it and I believe him."

Walking a fine line here. Need to get her to see that her son is no angel, but if you sound like you're taking the school's side, you'll be one of "them."

"I'd just like to know the whole story," Cassidy replied.

Jan frowned briefly. "There's this teacher, Miss Barrows. Tony had her for math last year and she seemed to take an instant dislike to him. For talking in class or something. As if everybody didn't do it. Well, yesterday he was headed toward the library, minding his own business—I guess the bell had already rung—and this teacher got in his face and demanded to see his hall pass. He had one, but he couldn't remember which pocket it was in. So this teacher starts verbally abusing him, and I guess he said a few things back. Two or three other kids were in the hall—I don't know why she wasn't harassing them—and naturally they crowded around to see what was going on. One of them bumped into Tony, and he stumbled into the teacher, and she fell back against the wall. Now she's claiming he cussed her out and deliberately shoved her. But she's only saying that because she had it in for him already."

I ask for the school's version and get this?

"Can't one of the other students back Tony up?"

A look of disgust swept over Jan's face. "They're all afraid of being labeled troublemakers. Look what happened to Tony. There was that one little incident at the beginning of his freshman year, and ever since then, the administration sees him as a bad kid."

Cassidy remembered that the one little incident had been a case of Tony beating up a much smaller kid.

"There've been a number of times when Tony said one thing and the school said another. What makes you so sure Tony always tells the truth?"

Jan tossed her bottle from hand to hand. "Because I know him. He's a good kid. He wouldn't do the sort of thing the school accuses him of."

Cassidy forced herself to breathe evenly, not to let out the sigh she felt accumulating in her chest.

"Besides," Jan continued, "I'm his mother. It's my job to stand up for him."

Choosing her words carefully, Cassidy said, "If you keep fighting his battles for him, how will he ever learn to handle problems on his own?"

"He shouldn't have to handle problems like this. He's been unfairly treated since he first started high school. If I let the administration decide he's a punk, sooner or later he'll start believing them."

Since silence was always an option in a therapy session, Cassidy moved her gaze to the window and gave herself time to think. *When people hang onto denial, it's because they're afraid the truth will destroy them. Never a good idea to rip it away. But if she doesn't stop bailing out her bad-ass kid, she'll have a monster on her hands.*

Cassidy said to her client, "I know you believe Tony always tells the truth. And you may be right. Parents have an instinct about their kids."

Jan's mouth relaxed into a smile.

"But what if he couldn't face your disappointment so he fudged a little? What if he was at his breaking point and he did push that teacher? The only way he'll learn to control his behavior is if he's forced to face the consequences."

Jan's face sagged. She moistened her lower lip. "He can't be lying. I'm a good mother. How could I have raised a kid who'd push his teacher? I give him lots of attention, made sure he had a happy childhood. He can't be this thug the school says he is." She drank from her bottle, twisted the cap on, took it off again. "Cass, I need your support. That's why I come here."

"I can understand that this whole thing is very hard on you. But I wouldn't be doing my job if I only told you what you wanted to hear."

When the session was over, Cassidy closed the door behind her client, went into the kitchen, and took out a bag of peanut butter cups. She bit one in two, chewed, and swallowed.

Everybody slips into denial some of the time. And when they do, they're absolutely convinced they're right, regardless of all evidence to the contrary. So how do you know you're not being Jan?

She didn't. There wasn't any way to tell. She decided not to think about it anymore.

† † †

Later that night Martin Lawrence, an elegant white-haired man, ushered Cassidy and Zach into his condo, a unit in a Prairie School building not far from the intersection of Lake Street and Oak Park Avenue. They were there to pick up the uncle's loan of bail money.

"Cassidy," Martin took her hand in both of his, "I'm glad my scapegrace nephew brought you with him this time."

"Scapegrace? He hasn't done anything that would qualify as 'scapegrace' in ages. Aren't you ever going to let him live down that old reputation?"

"Hey, who says I want to live it down? I kind of like being the family fuck-up."

Only way they know how to relate to each other is for Zach to be the acting out kid, Martin the admonishing adult. You need to butt out.

"Well," Martin said, "would you care for some brandy? Or a Jack Daniels, if you prefer."

"We'll take a pass," Zach said, falling into his old habit of speaking for her.

After they were seated, Martin said, "Did I hear that right? Did you just turn down a drink? This wife of yours must be quite the good influence."

"Cassidy keeps me on the straight and narrow."

"He listens to you?" Martin peered at her through the lenses of his wire-rimmed glasses. "Then perhaps you could bring some influence to bear regarding this estrangement between him and his mother."

Cassidy raised both hands, palms out. "I'm not getting into the middle of this one." *Besides, you aren't any fonder of Mildred than Zach is.*

Martin looked directly at his nephew. "It was her sixty-fifth birthday last June. You didn't even call."

"Why would I? Mildred and I practically stopped speaking years ago, and I'm sure she doesn't miss me any more than I miss her."

"She was quite upset when she didn't hear from you."

"No she wasn't. She just used it as an excuse to bitch about me."

"I realize Mildred can be difficult. But you're older now. More settled. I know your mother disapproved of your lifestyle when you were single, but I believe she'd look on your situation more favorably now." Martin smiled at Cassidy.

Fat chance. Especially considering how much she doesn't like me.

Zach rested his forearms on his legs. "Martin, you know as well as I do it wasn't just my lifestyle. It goes clear back to the beginning. Her not wanting a second child. The fact that I look like my black Irish father instead of you blond Waspy Lawrences. If I were to start calling now, she'd just use it as an opportunity to harangue me with all the ways I've disappointed her."

"Perhaps you could make allowances. After all, she is your mother." Martin's thin mouth tightened. "Families ought to stick together."

"Sorry, Martin, it's not going to happen." Then, his voice softening, "You've always been decent to me. Lent me money, bailed me out of trouble. I remember all your lectures back in high school." Zach smiled. "Didn't you used to warn me about the dangers of becoming a dope fiend? Mildred, on the other hand … " He shook his head. "I just don't need the aggravation."

"Well," Martin said, handing Zach an envelope, "even if I can't convince you, I'm glad you came. I hope everything goes well with Bryce." He patted Cassidy on the shoulder. "You know, you don't have to wait for a crisis to come see me."

† † †

Since Martin's condo was only a mile or so from their house, they had taken advantage of the pleasant evening weather and walked to his building. Now, as they approached their back gate, Cassidy wondered if Milton was still around. Seeing no sign of him, she felt a twinge of disappointment. *You've got it all wrong. Should be hoping he's returned to his new cat lady and she's keeping his bowl full. 'Cause if she isn't, you might feel tempted to take on the job yourself.*

Before turning in at their gate, Cassidy glanced back one more time and caught a glimpse of movement in the dark shrubbery beneath the bungalow's front window. *Could be anything. No reason to think it's Milton.*

Inside the house, Starshine plopped down from one of the waiting room chairs, rubbed against Cassidy's ankle, and purred ardently.

Hoping you'll prove more seducible now than you have over the past few days. Zach went straight through the kitchen and out the dining room doorway, making it clear he wanted no part of the contest of wills between Cassidy and Starshine.

Gathering herself to jump onto the counter, Starshine paused to gauge the distance, then propelled herself upward in a leap that wasn't nearly as effortless as it used to be. Cassidy remembered how the calico had flown through the house when she was young and lithesome, racing up and down stairs, springing to the top of the refrigerator, exploring all the high places. "But it's not too late. All you have to do is eat this low-cal food and you can get your old zoomy self back again."

It did not appear that Starshine had eaten any of the brown nuggets Zach had measured into her bowl that morning. Cassidy let out a heavy sigh.

Mwat, Starshine said, begging sweetly. She patted Cassidy's arm and rubbed her head against Cassidy's side. As Cassidy reached out to scratch behind the calico's ear, Starshine nuzzled her hand.

Almost against her will, Cassidy opened the cabinet where the wet food was stored. At the beginning of the diet, there had been only two cans on the shelf, one of which Zach had opened Sunday. Now there were six.

So damn sure Starshine would win, he went out and bought more food. Now you absolutely can't back down.

Cassidy dumped the old brown nuggets in the garbage and refilled the bowl with new ones. "When you get hungry enough, you'll eat."

The cat's large green eyes turned cold and yellow. *Mrit,* she replied.

CHAPTER 12

SINCE IT WAS ONLY NINE PM, CASSIDY went upstairs and called Angie. "How you doing?"

"The meeting was good. Everybody prayed for Kit. They even prayed for me, that I'd get through it." Cassidy heard a sniffle on the other end. "But it's hard. All I can think of is Bryce locked up in some awful little cell at the police station."

"We'll have him out tomorrow. The bail hearing is set for one, but I'd like to see you before then, if I could. I still have some questions."

Angie agreed to meet Cassidy at the student union food court at ten the following morning.

Swiveling away from her desk, Cassidy noticed Zach leaning against the doorframe. "What are you doing there?"

"Procrastinating." He sat at his desk, which stood a few feet from hers. "I've got a call to make but I've been putting it off. Then I heard you set up your meeting with Angie and I realized I better get busy and set up my meeting with Hopewell."

"You're going to call him tonight? On the day of his daughter's funeral?"

"Yeah, I know, I'm being an asshole. But we can't afford to lose any more time." Zach picked up the cordless from his desk. "Feel free to listen in."

Holding her desk phone to her ear, Cassidy heard a woman's voice answer, "The Hopewell residence."

Zach asked to speak to the pastor.

"He's not taking any calls tonight. You can leave a message and he'll get back to you later." The voice was crisp and decisive.

"Look, I realize this is a bad time, but I'd appreciate it if you'd at least tell him who's on the line. The name is Zach Moran. I'm Bryce's father and I'm also a reporter at the *Post*."

Both sound like reasons Hopewell wouldn't want to talk to him.

"He really isn't taking any calls."

"Would you please just deliver the message? If he doesn't want to talk to me, I'll leave my number."

"If you insist."

When Cassidy heard dead air on the other end, she said, "I can't think of a single reason why he'd come to the phone."

"He's a public figure. It's wired in that he wants to maintain a good relationship with the press. Now he obviously doesn't want publicity around Kit's murder, but at the same time, he doesn't want to piss me off."

Several seconds later Hopewell said in a flat voice, "My housekeeper tells me you won't take no for an answer."

"I'm sorry to intrude, but I need to meet with you as soon as possible."

"I'm a little confused," Hopewell said. "Are you calling about your son or a news story?"

"My son. I only mentioned the *Post* so you'd realize I know what I'm doing when I say I'm investigating your daughter's murder. I'm not convinced Bryce is guilty."

Not convinced. Now that's about as lukewarm as you can get.

"Of course you'd want to believe he's innocent, but from what I hear, the police have a pretty solid case."

"Yeah, but look at all the wrong guys who've been sent to death row. If you were in my place, I expect you wouldn't just assume the police were right either."

"So what is it you want from me?"

"A chance to talk to you and your wife."

"We can't help you. Adele and I know next to nothing about Katherine's personal life."

"I need to understand her background. It's how I work. Investigations don't come together for me unless I'm able to see the big picture. And of course anything you say will be off the record."

"Adele is extremely distraught and I can't say that I feel up to an interview either."

"One way or another, I'm going to get at your daughter's history. It would be easier for all concerned if you and your wife would agree to talk to me."

What Zach just said slid by so smoothly you almost didn't notice it was a threat.

After a short silence, Hopewell said, "I can fit you in on Wednesday—let's say four o'clock. Since you insist Adele be present also, it would be best if you come to the house."

Hanging up, Zach turned to Cassidy. "You have any clients then?"

"I already rescheduled my Tuesday clients." *Hate putting clients off. But skipping a session doesn't do any real harm, and you couldn't stand to miss the Hopewell interviews.* "I've got a couple of people scheduled for Wednesday afternoon but I don't think they'll mind missing a week."

† † †

After the phone call, Cassidy headed out to the back stoop, where she settled on the top step to conduct a Milton-watch. A walkway led from the stoop out to the rear alley, and to the left of the walkway, in the far corner of the yard, stood the garage. A lamppost on the opposite side of Briar illuminated her garage doors, and the glow from houses flowed into the center of the street. But the strip along the base of her garage was dense with shadows.

Cassidy heard the whap of Starshine's cat door, located in a basement window around the corner from where she sat. A moment later the calico joined her on the porch, sitting with her back to her human, a signal that she wanted companionship but not petting. Cassidy gazed toward the bungalow where Olivia used to dwell, remembering what it had been like when the feral cats hung out there.

Starshine hissed. Standing on all fours, her back arched, she stared at the band of darkness along the bottom of the garage. Following her gaze, Cassidy saw Milton melt away from the shadows and glide across the yard. He sat down in the middle of the walkway. Starshine, a puffed-up little butterball, took mincing sideways steps in his direction. The tom did not appear to notice.

Cassidy grabbed Starshine and locked her in the house. When she returned, Milton had moved a few steps nearer. Seeing him so close, his gaze fastened on her, Cassidy remembered the experience she'd had the night of Olivia's murder. As she'd stared into the old tom's eyes, she'd gotten the distinct impression he was reading her mind. *A link forged between you. You saved his life by fending off the village animal control and that makes you responsible for him.*

Shaking off the memory, she focused on the fact that Milton had now shown up three nights in a row, which convinced her he wasn't being fed elsewhere and probably hadn't eaten in a while.

Just what you need—two hungry cats. One who's too finicky to eat little brown nuggets and another whose recent cat lady closed up shop.

Cassidy now faced for a second time the dilemma that had presented itself after Olivia's murder: What to do about a needy stray. If she put out food for Milton, she would become a magnet for all the homeless cats in the neighborhood. They would come to eat and stay to reproduce.

Yes, but Milton is only one cat. Olivia must've had fifteen. How do you think she got fifteen?

Cassidy pressed her knuckles into her cheek. If she became the new cat lady, the neighbors would revile her, the male felines would spray her property, and her house would start to smell the way Olivia's had.

Your clients would abandon you and Zach would be entirely within his rights to move back to his condo at Marina City.

Yes, but you can't let Milton starve. She decided she would open one of those extra cans Zach had bought and hope that the cat grapevine had crashed.

By the time she returned with Milton's food, he'd disappeared. She set the bowl she'd prepared for him in the corner between the porch and the house, then went inside to watch through the window in the door. After fifteen minutes, she gave up and went upstairs to make her confession to Zach.

He leaned back in his computer chair, hands behind his head, frown lines creasing his forehead. "This is not a good idea."

"I couldn't let him go hungry."

"Starshine's empty stomach doesn't seem to bother you."

"She's just being finicky. And besides, Milton and I are linked because of our shared experience the night Olivia died." *You shouldn't have said that. That does not help your case.*

"Should I be thinking about taking you in for a psych eval?"

Cassidy didn't believe in the paranormal any more than Zach did, but she couldn't rid herself of the sense that a special bond existed between her and the tom.

"If I turn into a cat lady, will you leave me?"

"No, but I might have to call in a cult deprogrammer to bring you to your senses."

The next morning, when Cassidy checked the bowl she'd left outside, she found it had been licked clean.

CHAPTER 13

CASSIDY SAT IN A BENTWOOD CHAIR AT a table in the student union. A clatter of voices, some from students, others from the TV sets attached to every post, buzzed in her ears. A few students sported strangely colored hair and tattoos, but most looked as if they'd just stepped off a Gap billboard.

Having waited for more than twenty minutes, Cassidy reminded herself that she shouldn't begin the interview by snapping at Angie. *Your fault, really, for arriving on time. You knew she wasn't going to suddenly develop an aptitude for punctuality.*

At ten thirty Angie came rushing in and seated herself across from Cassidy. "Oh gosh, I'm late again."

Surprise.

"I'm just glad you're willing to talk to me," Cassidy said, making an effort to keep the irritation out of her voice.

"Well, of course I am. I want to help Bryce just as much as you do."

We of the blind-faith clan.

"I'd like to start by getting the timeline straight. When did Kit move in with you? And then when did she leave to go live with Bryce?"

"Um ... " Angie pinched her lip. "The beginning of June—sometime that first week—Kit brought this huge pile of boxes over. I don't know how we managed to find places for all her stuff, but somehow we did. And then the time she left—that's easy to remember because it was over the July fourth holiday." Angie smiled broadly. "It was so good to get my space back. The only problem I had was that I was a little worried about Bryce. Back then, I thought I was being silly, but now it turns out I was right." Angie's face creased with tension. "One of those times you really wish you'd been wrong."

"Kit and Bryce had minds of their own and there was nothing any of us could have done to prevent what happened." Cassidy glanced at the list of questions she'd jotted on her notepad. "Do you know if either Kit or Bryce was taking medication?"

"Kit had some kind of pills she carried around with her and it seemed to me like she took way too many of them."

Xanax, most likely.

"I was afraid she'd get addicted. I told her if she'd just come back to Jesus, she wouldn't need so many pills. I used to beg her to get off them, but she insisted they mellowed her out and made her less of a ... well, you know, less of a witch." Angie shoved her black-framed glasses closer to her face.

"It's certainly possible she was overmedicating. But people with anxiety disorder are really miserable inside their own skins. They often need medication just to feel normal and keep functioning. As long as the meds are taken properly, they're not a bad thing."

Angie gave her a skeptical look.

She believes in prayer. You believe in pills. And you're just as unwilling to accept her treatment modality as she is to accept yours.

Looking down at the word "Thorazine" on her pad, Cassidy asked, "Did Kit take anything else?"

"I don't think so."

"What about Bryce?"

"He never mentioned anything."

Cassidy paused, working her way up to a harder question. "Do you know if Bryce is using drugs?"

"Um … why don't you ask him?"

Cassidy felt her stomach sink. "So that means he is."

"We used to argue about it," Angie said, running a fingernail along a crack in the table's wood trim. "I don't believe it's right for people to despoil the temple of their body with any kind of substance, but Bryce always said a little weed now and then didn't hurt anything."

As much as you don't like drugs, he may be right.

"So you don't think he was using a lot of it?"

"I'm sure he wasn't. I hardly ever saw him high."

Cassidy gave an internal sigh of relief. "Well, the next item on my list is keys. Did Kit ever give you a key to the townhouse?"

Angie shook her head vigorously. "I can't imagine Kit handing out keys to anybody."

"Why not?"

"I don't know … I guess because it would mean giving up a certain amount of control."

"I can see your point. But the thing is, there was no forced entry. If Bryce didn't kill her, someone else must've had a way to get inside."

"Then I suppose she must've given a key to someone."

"What about boyfriends? Do you think Kit might have given Raul a key?"

"Maybe. I suppose she might've gotten off on the idea of Raul letting himself in when Bryce wasn't around. Or maybe she even thought it'd be cool if they bumped into each other." Angie scowled. "Gosh, that would be so mean."

Closer to sadistic.

"What about other boyfriends?"

"There were quite a few before Raul but I can't remember any of their names."

"Raul told us he hadn't seen Kit since she moved in with Bryce, but you were under the impression that Kit and Raul never really broke up."

"All I know is what Kit said. When she moved into my place, she told me she was through with Raul, but then she kept going out with him anyway. And even after she moved in with Bryce, there were lots of times she said she'd been with Raul again."

Raul and Kit—one as bad as the other. They had to be soul mates.

"So which one was lying?"

Angie shrugged helplessly. "I suppose Kit might've said she was still seeing Raul just to bug me. She knew how much it upset me to think of her cheating on Bryce. Or maybe she was sleeping with Raul just like she said and he lied to keep people from thinking of him as a suspect."

"Do you know whether or not she gave Raul a key to your apartment when she was staying with you?"

"She didn't."

"How can you be so sure?"

"I came home one time and found him waiting at the door, swearing like crazy because she'd invited him over and then she wasn't there. He certainly didn't have a key with him then."

"After Kit moved in with Bryce, did you ever get the impression Raul was jealous?"

"Kit and Raul both seemed too cool to get jealous." Angie stared at some point beyond Cassidy's left shoulder. "I guess that's what it's like when you have plenty of choices. Me, if I ever had a boyfriend, I'd probably turn into a green-eyed monster. I'd feel like he was my last chance and I'd be scared to death of losing him."

Cassidy touched Angie's arm. "It's natural to get jealous. Most people find they have a few jealous bones if they're in love with someone who isn't fully committed to them." *And who would know better than you?*

"Well, maybe." Angie gave Cassidy a direct look. "But I don't think Kit was ever jealous, and she never said anything about Raul's being jealous, either."

"How did you and Kit ever come to be such good friends?" Cassidy asked. "You don't seem to have a thing in common."

"We did at first. When I met Kit in that Sunday School class, she was kind of loud and sometimes she asked too many questions, but other than that she was really nice. She read the bible, prayed, talked about when she was saved—all the same things I did. And she absolutely adored her father. She was so proud of his work as a pastor."

"When did that change?"

"I'll never forget." Angie pinched her lower lip again. "We were fifteen. It started when she missed a Sunday School class a few weeks before Easter. First class she'd ever missed. I left messages at her house but she didn't return my calls. A couple more classes went by, then she finally showed up again the Sunday after Easter. And boy, was she mad. She called her father a hypocrite, said she hated him, said she didn't even believe in God anymore. I was completely shocked." Angie ran her hands through her short curls.

"Was that when she started acting out?"

"Not right away. She said she didn't want to be my friend anymore and she stopped attending church, so we didn't talk for quite a while. But we went to the same high school, and when I returned in the fall, I started hearing rumors. First she got boy crazy, then she began hanging out with a bad crowd, and the next thing I knew, she was partying every weekend."

"I thought you said she mostly stayed away from drugs and alcohol."

"That was later, after she'd done some experimenting in high school."

"How did you get to be friends again?"

"It was in our senior year: She went through a pretty bad depression and she needed to talk to somebody she knew really cared about her, so she started calling me. For a while I only heard from her when she was down, but after we started college, she wanted to get closer again." Angie paused. "I asked her over and over why she'd turned her back on God, but she refused to talk about it."

"You must've had some guesses."

"Well, Kit's renunciation of her faith seemed like an attack on her father. The fact that she was so mad at him made me suspect he'd disappointed her somehow. She used to think he was so perfect, but nobody really is. I mean, the church teaches us that everyone sins to some degree. So maybe she found out that her father had human failings just like the rest of us, and it turned her world upside down."

"Sounds like she treated you pretty badly. Why'd you stick with her after she started getting so mean?"

"What kind of Christian would I be if I just abandoned her? Especially since I could tell she was hurting. I kept hoping I'd find a way to bring her back to Jesus. And to her parents. Pastor Hopewell and his wife have helped so many people. It must've just killed them to see what Kit was doing to herself."

This girl is far more loyal and unselfish than you could ever be.

✝ ✝ ✝

Cassidy carried two tuna fish sandwiches and a bag of chips to the dining room table, Starshine trotting along beside her, her nose twitching. Knowing that the calico was planning to sit on the table and beg for food, Cassidy snatched her up and shut her in the basement.

"Hey, why'd you do that?" Zach asked, bringing a glass of water for her and a fully leaded Coke for himself to the table. He had arrived home from the *Post* at noon to pick her up for the bond hearing.

"So I don't have to feel guilty about not sharing my tuna."

A mournful lament sounded from the other side of the basement door.

"So instead of feeling guilty about not feeding her, you can feel guilty about exiling her."

But not as guilty as when you have to look into her big, green, reproachful eyes.

Cassidy said, "So how exactly is this bond hearing going to work?"

"Victor will argue that Bryce has ties to the community and isn't a danger or a flight risk. He'll also say that the family has fifty thousand for bail. Then we keep our fingers crossed that the judge is in an agreeable mood and doesn't have any particular vendetta against homicidal white boys from privileged backgrounds."

"Stop it!"

"Sorry."

Cassidy picked up her sandwich, which was oozing tuna around the edges. "What will the prosecutor say?"

"Based on the nature of the crime, he's likely to recommend that Bryce be remanded without bail. But since the kid doesn't pose any danger, the judge'll probably agree to the fifty grand. After the bail is set, we pay up, then wait for Bryce to be processed out."

"But you're not expecting anything to go wrong."

Swallowing the food in his mouth, Zach said, "I'd be really surprised if Bryce isn't released by late this afternoon."

Cassidy had finished her sandwich and was picking up globs of tuna with her fingers when Zach pushed his plate back and folded his arms on the table.

"I have something to tell you but I don't even know where to begin." A three-beat silence. Then, "Remember that conversation we had about babies?"

"What?"

"I know this is nuts, but ever since you asked if I wanted a baby, I haven't been able to get the idea out of my head."

Cassidy's jaw went slack. Taking in a breath, she asked, "Does that mean you *do* want a baby?"

"I don't know what it means. Fatherhood was never part of my plan. Ever since Bryce appeared at our door, I've been trying to adapt to this new role that I don't seem to have any aptitude for. Given all that, it seems pretty ridiculous that I'd even consider taking on this huge task of raising a child." Zach ran a hand over his face. "I shouldn't even be thinking about this. I wouldn't be any good at it."

"What makes you say that?" she asked in a neutral tone.

"Don't play therapist with me."

She shook herself. "I'm sorry. I just … I'm so blown away I went on auto pilot."

"Yeah, I'm kind of blown away myself." He stared out the window. "This is probably a bout of temporary insanity. I only told you because I thought you should know it was on my mind."

"What exactly are you thinking?"

"That if we had a baby together, it'd be completely different from having a teenager drop out of the sky. That a newborn would be easier to love. That I could be a better father with a child we raised from scratch than I'll ever be with Bryce."

"People sometimes feel an urge to repeat an experience they haven't quite succeeded at. They want a second chance to get it right."

"You're doing it again."

Good thing he catches you or you'd end up being his therapist. Which'd be about the worst thing that could happen to this marriage.

Zach wrapped his hand around her wrist. "So, we should just forget about these bizarre ideas I'm having, right?"

CHAPTER 14

BRYCE, HIS HEAD ERECT, HIS CARRIAGE ON the verge of being cocky, came through the double-glass doors on the far side of the room where Cassidy and Zach were waiting. She started toward him, wanting to give him a big hug, but halted abruptly when she saw the dark look on his face. Deciding that Zach's approach of letting Bryce come to him was the better choice, she retreated to where she'd been standing beside her husband.

Bryce stopped in front of them. Up close, Cassidy could see that despite the little strut he'd managed to inject into his walk, he looked pretty haggard. His face was lined with fatigue, his cheeks stubbled, his clothes grimy and rank.

The two men eyed each other but neither spoke.

Oh shit, not this again. Bryce taking his anger out on Zach, Zach withdrawing in return.

"It's really good to see you," Cassidy ventured.

A pause, then, "Good to see you too."

Zach shifted his weight, letting his body go loose. "These past few days must've been pretty miserable."

"I need to get my car," Bryce said, looking between them.

"We'll take you to the Miata, then we can all drive out to Oak Park," Cassidy suggested.

"I wasn't planning to go to Oak Park."

"What?" Cassidy felt a small pang in her chest. "But I thought you'd be staying with us."

He afforded her a disdainful look. "I'm not seventeen any more." That was the age Bryce had been when his mother sent him to live with Zach just before she was murdered. At that time he'd slept in their spare room for a couple of weeks because he had no other place to go.

"You're not going to the townhouse, are you? Not with all those memories attached?"

"Figured I'd hang at Angie's for a while."

"She lives in a studio."

"I'll sleep on the couch."

"You can stay wherever you want," Zach said, "but Cass and I need you to answer some questions before you do anything else."

"Look, man, I gotta get some sleep. Just take me to my car. I'll hook up with you later."

The kid's exhausted. We should let him go. Yeah, but if we do, we might not be able to catch him again any time soon.

"I can understand that the last thing you want is to have to answer any more questions, but we can't afford to wait. The case is getting colder by the minute. We need this information right away."

Bryce directed a hostile stare at his father. "You showed up drunk. The first time I ever needed anything from you, you were so loaded I thought you were going to fall on your face."

Cassidy's head jerked in surprise. *Why would he care about that? Looking for an excuse to be mad?*

"And how was that a problem?" Zach asked.

"I guess it wasn't—for you." Bryce started to turn away, then pivoted back toward his father. "But I have to say, it would've been nice if you could've come through for me for once in your life."

"I thought I did."

"I guess we see it differently."

After three days in lockup, I suppose he's got a right to be surly and unreasonable.

"It's unfortunate you feel that way, but I still need you to come to Oak Park."

"You know, I am an adult. I don't have to do what you say any more."

"Was there some time when you did?"

Bryce drew in a long breath. "Oh hell, considering you just bailed my ass out of the slam, I guess I owe you something."

I'd say he owes a lot more than this—although I guess it's stupid to expect any kind of payback from kids.

† † †

Propping his elbow on the dining room table, Bryce rested his forehead on his hand, then sat straighter and chugged from the beer bottle he had taken out of their refrigerator. "You gonna ask the same questions the cops did? The same thing over and over till I'm absolutely sick of it?"

"The questions will be pretty much the same, but we won't make you answer them more than once."

Cassidy hesitated for a moment, then jumped in. "The first floor was dark when we arrived. Is that how you found it when you came downstairs?"

The boy nodded.

"Why wouldn't Kit turn any lights on? Or do you think the murderer turned them off?"

"I figured she just went down for a book or something and didn't bother with the lights. She kinda liked being in the dark."

"Now that you've had time to think things over, do you have any idea who might have killed her?"

Bryce shrugged. "The only thing that makes sense to me is that she walked in on a burglar."

"Let's assume for a moment that the murderer came to the townhouse with the express purpose of killing Kit. Who might've had a motive?"

"I know she pissed off a lot of people, but I can't believe anybody hated her enough to kill her."

Being pissed off is a motive.

"Don't try to think of an answer. Just let your mind go blank and see what comes up." *Some hunch swimming around in the soup of his subconscious.*

Bryce stared into space. "Her father." He paused. "No, that can't be right. Her father loved her."

"So why would her father pop into your mind like that?"

"Well, she gave him such a hard time. Her parents had us over for dinner once, and she went out of her way to be obnoxious. Her clothes were totally outrageous and every other word out of her mouth was 'fuck' or 'shit.' I could see by her dad's face that he was pretty upset, but he kept his mouth shut."

Kit must've been so disappointed when he didn't take the bait.

"Her father seemed pretty happy to see her, and then, when we were leaving, he reached out to give her a hug, but she pushed him away. Afterward I told her she should give him a break, but she didn't want to hear it." Bryce took a swig of beer. "She used to rant about him being such a hypocrite. Sometimes I thought her whole purpose in life was to get back at him."

"Back at him for what?'

"Being a hypocrite, I guess."

"What did he do that was hypocritical?"

Bryce shrugged. "She didn't say."

Usually takes more than that to generate a vendetta. But Kit was probably a narcissist and they can create vendettas out of nothing at all.

Zach said, "What do you know about Raul?"

"Um … he was her ex-boyfriend."

"You don't expect me to believe you didn't read her email, do you?"

A flush rose on Bryce's stubbly cheeks. "I guess I know she told Angie she'd seen him."

Is there a carnal sense of seeing like the carnal sense of knowing?

"I confronted Kit about the email and she said she made up the part about Raul just to give Angie something to stew about. Because Angie was always lecturing her that she should treat me better. I just wish she'd followed Angie's advice."

"So," Zach looked steadily at Bryce, "did you believe what Kit said?"

Bryce stared through the window, drummed his fist on the table, looked down at his hands. "There were times when she stayed out all night. She always said she'd gone clubbing and crashed with a girlfriend, but I suspected she was with Raul."

"So you thought she was lying about not having sex with him," Cassidy said.

"I didn't know what to think. Sometimes I figured if she really was sleeping with him, she'd throw it in my face when we were fighting just like she threw everything else. Other times I figured she was seeing him on the side but she'd never tell because she got such a thrill out of getting away with it."

"It must've been hard not knowing."

Bryce shrugged again.

Zach started to slide some email printouts down the length of the teak table to Bryce, but Cassidy intercepted them. Reading the top page, she saw that they were the correspondence between Kit and DC: DC telling Kit he couldn't see her anymore, Kit telling him he'd have to find a way. Cassidy handed the pages on to Bryce.

He finished his beer and went to the refrigerator to get a second. After taking a long swallow, he said, "Okay, I know she was sleeping with this one."

"Who was he?" Zach asked.

"No idea."

"What did you do when you saw the email?"

"I got pissed. We had a big fight. I told her to get out of my house. Then she turned warm and sweet like she always does—I mean did—when I tried to break up with her and I backed down." He rubbed his eyes with his fingertips. "I guess I can see why everybody thinks I did it."

"My ex used to cheat on me," Cassidy volunteered. "All the time. But I never could leave either."

Bryce's gaze settled on her face. "It's okay for women to be suckers but guys don't have the luxury."

Are you going to let him get away with that?

After all he's been through, I'll grant him a one-day free pass on egregious stupidity—but if he ever says anything like that again, I'll clobber him.

"When you and Kit were fighting," Zach said, "did you ever threaten her?"

"I said I wanted to break her little neck. I didn't say anything about shooting her. The only time I ever had a gun, you busted me." Scraping his chair against the hardwood floor, Bryce pushed it back and stood up. "Look, I need a break. I can't answer any more questions right now."

Zach rose also. His voice softening, he said, "I'm sorry we have to grill you like this."

"Have to?"

"You want us to find out who shot her, don't you?"

"You mean, you *don't* think I did it?"

Zach looked away. "I intend to learn the truth about what happened that night."

Dammit—why can't Zach just put an arm around the kid's shoulder and say he believes him?

"My old man—the guy with all the answers." Bryce tucked his fingertips into his back pockets. "At this moment in time, I don't give a shit what you intend or don't intend. All I care about is getting out of the house. I've been sitting in a cell for three days, man, and I gotta get outside and move around."

† † †

Bryce left to walk around the block and Zach went upstairs to check his email. Cassidy shuffled through the papers Zach had piled on the table, removing the notes she'd made about the contents of Bryce's medicine chest. She wandered into the kitchen, where she saw a mound of brown nuggets in Starshine's bowl. *Looks like she didn't eat a bite of breakfast.* Hardening herself, Cassidy refused to think about how long the calico had gone without food.

Cassidy grabbed a bag of Reese's out of a cupboard and began munching peanut butter cups, biting each one neatly in two as she stared through her kitchen window into the kitchen of the house next door. Her neighbor gave a friendly wave. Forcing a smile, Cassidy returned the gesture.

Replaying the discussion with Bryce, she puzzled over his reaction to Zach's having shown up drunk on Saturday night. *Maybe he needed something to hold against his father so he wouldn't feel so bad about his own behavior. The best defense, etc.* She wondered how truthful Bryce was being. *Zach caught it right away when Bryce tried to pretend he hadn't read the email about Raul. Does that mean Bryce is such a bad liar he won't be able to pull anything over on us?* She knew it didn't. People got away with small lies all the time, and for all she knew he'd deceived them about several things already. The best she could hope for was that Bryce was basically honest and had no real skill at telling whoppers.

When the three of them reassembled around the dining room table, she was relieved to see that Bryce had not fetched another beer. *After three days with no sleep, any more alcohol and he'd probably pass out. Then he'd have to find something other than drinking to be pissed at Zach about.*

"Anyone else Kit might've been sleeping with?" Zach asked.

"The only reason I suspected her of messing around were the emails about Raul and those other emails between Kit and DC."

"Okay, then let's move on to—"

"Hey," Cassidy laid her hand on Zach's arm, "my turn." Looking down at her notepad, she said to Bryce, "What do you know about the Thorazine I found in your medicine cabinet?"

"It showed up a couple months ago. Kit told me a friend gave it to her for the nights she couldn't sleep. She used to have a big problem with insomnia but the Thorazine knocked her out." He creased his brow. "But I'm not sure I believe her story about getting it from a friend. That name on the bottle? I never heard Kit mention her."

"So you don't know much about the Thorazine?"

"I looked it up on the web and found out it was an antipsychotic. That sort of weirded me out—I thought it might be screwing up her system. I almost called you to ask about the risks, but I figured Kit wouldn't listen to me anyway, so I was probably better off not knowing."

"It's possible she could have had some psychotic symptoms. Did she ever mention hearing voices? Did her thinking seem delusional or paranoid?"

"Some of the things she said sounded a little strange, but doesn't everybody get a little strange now and then?"

"So you don't think she could've been psychotic?"

"Nah."

"Angie told me Kit carried some other medication around with her. Was it Xanax?"

"Yeah. I used to get down on her for taking so many pills, but then I did some reading on anxiety and I could see why she needed them."

"Well," Cassidy took a breath, "let's talk about the pregnancy."

"When that cop told me, I was like, man, that can't be true. At first I thought he was making it up. I mean, no matter how freaked she was, she always took her pill at exactly the same time every day."

Zach said, "You don't think she could've gotten pregnant on purpose?"

"Not a chance. I remember her saying once that it would ruin her life if she got pregnant. I told her it was no big deal—she could always get an abortion. Then she said this thing that seemed to come out of nowhere. That she'd burn in hell if she ever got an abortion. I suppose it must've been some leftover idea from her childhood, because I don't think she even believed in God anymore.

"Anyway, after I thought about it, she could have thrown up the pill. That's possible, right? If she took her pill and got sick?" He frowned. "But the thing is, I don't remember her puking. And she had a pretty strong stomach. Of course, if she was out with her friends and hurled after drinking too much, I wouldn't have known about it."

"Angie said Kit wasn't much of a drinker."

"Yeah. But she was so unpredictable, you never really knew what she might do. Whatever the reason, she must've puked because how else would she have gotten pregnant?"

Is throwing up the only way? Something began to rattle around at the back of Cassidy's mind. She studied the notes she'd taken from the birth control dispenser, then moved on to the information she'd copied from the erythromycin bottle. The antibiotic prescription had been filled over a month earlier. *Around the time of conception.* Suddenly a memory from a long-ago therapy session burst into Cassidy's consciousness.

"It was the antibiotic. Antibiotics can cancel out birth control. I had this client once who came into a session so angry she could spit. Her doctor had prescribed an antibiotic without telling her about the possible drug interaction, and this poor woman was stuck with an unwanted pregnancy."

"Kit got pregnant because she took antibiotics?" Anger flashed across Bryce's face. "Man, that fucking doctor! What a prick! I remember her getting the prescription but I don't remember when."

"She took the pills for five days, starting on August 11. So I'd guess conception occurred between the eleventh and the fifteenth."

"But she didn't know she was pregnant, did she? I mean, if she'd known she would have told me."

Cassidy debated about telling him the truth, then decided he'd find out eventually anyway. "She stopped taking her pills about three weeks after she took the erythromycin. I think she must've missed a period and taken a home test."

A look of pain washed over Bryce's face. "Why didn't she tell me?"

"I don't know," Cassidy said. "But before we jump to conclusions, let me call a pharmacist and make sure the erythromycin could've interacted with the birth control."

Cassidy picked up the phone on the kitchen wall a few feet behind her chair. The pharmacist verified Cassidy's hunch. She returned to the dining room.

Bryce said, "She had a cough that wouldn't go away so I insisted on her seeing a doc. We stopped on the way home to pick up the drugs. That whole week she kept her distance from me. Even though she bounced right back, she kept saying she didn't want to pass on her germs. We didn't have sex for quite a while. I remember being pissed about it."

"So you couldn't have been the father," Cassidy said softly.

Bryce's body gave an involuntary little jerk. His teeth clenched and the cords stood out on his neck. "There's no reason I should even care whether the baby was mine or not. I mean, I already knew she was fucking around. And so what if she was? It's not like we were married or anything. It's just too damn bad I wasn't smart enough to do the same. And since the baby's dead—since there isn't going to be a baby—what the fuck difference does it make who the father was?"

"It's still got to be something of a shock."

"No, it's not. I don't give a shit about Kit *or* the baby." He ran the back of his arm across his forehead. "Look, I don't think I can do this any more. Just take me to my car, will you?"

"I know this is grueling," Zach said, "but I've got one more question." He waited, giving Bryce time to compose himself. "A couple of hours before Kit was killed, a neighbor heard you yelling. What was that about?"

Bryce looked Zach in the eye, calmness settling over his features. "The guy was wrong. We weren't fighting. It must've been the TV he heard."

Well, now you know. Bryce can lie with the best of them.

CHAPTER 15

"I STILL HAVE YOUR HOUSE KEY," ZACH SAID, pulling it out of his jeans pocket and handing it to Bryce. The three of them were standing on the sidewalk in front of Bryce's townhouse, his Miata in the drive to their left.

"I had a copy made," Zach went on, "because I knew I'd need to search the townhouse again. In fact, we better do it now, before Kit's parents pack up her things. At least I assume they haven't been here since nobody's asked for the key."

The boy glared at his father. "You don't have any right to go through my house without my permission. Or to have keys made either. And I'll box Kit's things up for the Hopewells."

"I need to conduct a real search," Zach said. "I had almost no time the night of the murder."

"The cops've probably already carted everything away. And besides, I don't want you pawing through my things. Or Kit's."

Zach stood with his feet planted wide, his hands on his belt. "Do you also not want us to investigate?"

"Well, I see you're finally starting to get it. What I want is for you to stay the hell out of my business."

Anxiety roiled in Cassidy's stomach. "But why wouldn't you want us to try to clear you of suspicion?"

"I just don't, that's all."

"You don't get to make that decision," Zach said. "I have a key and Cass and I are going inside to search the place."

"Oh hell—who cares?" Bryce turned on his heel, climbed into his Miata, and drove away.

"The only reason I can think of that he wouldn't want us to investigate is that he's guilty," Cassidy said.

Zach drew his arm around her shoulders. "More likely he's just pissed at me. Here he's been feeling powerless for days, then I come along and start ordering him around. If I were Bryce, I'd probably push back, too."

"Then maybe you shouldn't have come on so strong."

"I've got a job to do. I don't have time to wait around until he's in the mood to cooperate."

"You sure you're not just reacting to Bryce's hostility?"

"I probably am. I'm not very good at being sensitive to people who come at me the way he does."

Can't blame Zach for not liking to be snarled at.

He headed down the walkway, unlocked the door, and went into the townhouse. Cassidy hesitated when she reached the porch, bracing herself before following him inside. A cleaning company had scoured the room and a strong antiseptic smell hung in the air.

They stopped in the foyer to survey the crime scene. Drapes were drawn across the window, rendering the evening light murky and subdued. The hardwood floor showed no sign of stains. The black sofa remained in place against the dark red wall. The brick-and-board bookcase, which Cassidy had failed to notice the night of the dinner, stood opposite the sofa. The two plaid chairs, which had stood at angles facing the sofa, were now lined up against the black wall beneath the display of masks. *Kit's taste, obviously. Just like her personality—oppressive and overblown.*

"Where should we start?" Cassidy asked.

"Upstairs. I want to go over every piece of paper I can find."

The two desks in the study had been swept clean of everything except Bryce's printer. A bulletin board had also been stripped. A pile of books sat on the floor, and three tall file cabinets were lined up against the wall to their right.

"You really think the cops missed anything?"

"It's always possible." Zach opened the top drawer of the nearest cabinet, which was crammed with files. "Well, here's something they didn't take. In fact, I doubt they even went through this stuff. Despite what you see on TV, the forensic guys don't catch everything. They especially don't when the dicks on the case think they've already got the murder sewn up."

Zach carried a stack of folders to Bryce's desk. "This is going to be pretty boring, so whenever you get sick of it, feel free to go do something else."

† † †

Cassidy grabbed a handful of folders from the third cabinet and sat down at Kit's desk to go through them. They were mostly papers Bryce had written for various classes.

By the time she finished the bottom drawer, her concentration was flagging. She went to stand in the doorway and tried to imagine what had been going on in this room just before the murder. Bryce was staring at his monitor, completely absorbed in his task. She started to picture Kit at her desk, then remembered that Bryce had told them she was in the bedroom.

Crossing the hall, Cassidy wondered what Kit might have been doing just before she was killed. *Working at that small desk in the corner, reading, whatever. Then she decides she wants something from the living room.*

Cassidy went downstairs and moved the two easy chairs back where they belonged, then returned to the bedroom and sat at the corner desk. *Okay, now I want something from down below.* She jumped up, trotted downstairs, and whipped around the corner into the living room. Angling toward the small table at the far end of the sofa, she positioned herself in front of the chair Kit had fallen into and visualized a figure at the opposite end of the sofa with a gun in his hand.

She realized she was picturing a male, although she had no reason to assume the killer had a Y-chromosome. *Just easier than imagining an androgynous figure.* In her mind's eye, she watched the figure extend the gun, pull the trigger, then jerk backward as the gun recoiled. While he was off balance, the firearm slipped out of his fingers and skittered across the floor to disappear under the bookcase. The killer searched frantically for the gun, then turned and fled through the doorway at the far end of the room.

Cassidy followed the figure into a short hall that led to a half bath, the back door, and the kitchen. She remembered from the inspection she and Zach had conducted Saturday night that the back door had a button lock, which meant it would latch if the killer closed it behind him. She visualized the figure running into the hall and out the back door. Her picture didn't work. In her scenario, the figure had gone racing out and left the door open.

She returned to the living room and played an edited version of the tape. This time the killer planted the gun to frame Bryce, checked the door to make sure the lock was set, then went out and deliberately closed the door behind him.

There were two options, each of which had a slight glitch. One featured a killer who panicked and fled the scene, yet stopped to close the door behind him. The other featured a killer whose intent was to shoot Kit and frame Bryce, but who set his trap in the living room without any certainty that Kit would come downstairs.

There is another possibility, whispered a voice Cassidy had been trying to silence.

No there isn't. Bryce didn't do it. End of story.

You can't afford to be closed-minded. You have to try a scenario with Bryce in it.

She assumed that if Bryce had done it, it would have started with a fight upstairs, the fight the neighbor had heard and Bryce had lied about. Returning to the bedroom, she visualized Bryce and Kit yelling at each other. Before long, Bryce announced that he just wanted to get away from her and stomped down to the living room. Kit, screaming that he had to stay and finish the fight, went storming after him. Bryce told her to leave him alone, warned her that he would hurt her if she didn't. When she wouldn't stop yelling, he picked up a gun from the table and shot her. The instant he saw her fall, he dropped the gun and ran into the bathroom to throw up. Then he crawled into the corner of the dining room, broke down, and sobbed.

In this scenario, the only glitch was the presence of the gun on the end table. The table was not a likely place to leave a firearm. Other than that—*and the tiny fact that you don't want it to be Bryce*—the tape had played out smoothly.

It doesn't mean a thing. When you finally get to the truth, it'll be completely different from anything you ever could have imagined. Pushing the pictures out of her head, she went upstairs to join Zach in the study.

He looked up from the folder he was sorting and gave her a grin. "I found a bonanza. Well, maybe not a bonanza, but enough to justify strong-arming Bryce into letting us search the place."

He didn't let you. He just couldn't stop you.

"Her cell phone bills," Zach said, holding up a handful of paper. "Six months' worth."

Cassidy skimmed one of them. It listed the numbers Kit had called, along with the time, date, and duration of each call. Cassidy estimated there were at least fifty numbers on the bill, although many were repeat calls to the same person.

"You were right. The ETs didn't take everything."

"The cops on *Law and Order* may follow up on every little detail, but in real life, they have more than one case at a time, and once they satisfy the ADA that they've got enough for a conviction, they can't keep screwing around. That's where we have the advantage. We don't have the time pressure."

"Except that I'm starting to get hungry," Cassidy said. "Where did you leave off?"

"I just finished the top drawer of the middle cabinet."

Cassidy spent another half hour sorting, then stopped for a bathroom break. As she was returning to the study, she remembered the snapshot she'd found in the back of Kit's drawer.

It was right where she'd seen it before. An attractive young woman with shoulder-length blond hair. Cassidy studied the face, trying to determine whether it was the same person Forest had met behind the church.

She showed it to Zach. "This could be that scruffy woman who showed up at the wake. Look how blond she is. Same hair color as Adele and the kids."

"Yeah, she's probably a relative. This must've been taken before she went nuts or homeless or something."

"So I guess we should take this picture with us," Cassidy said, feeling squeamish about removing anything as personal as a photograph.

"What do you want to do?"

He's not going to let me foist the responsibility onto him.

"Yeah, we should take it."

††††

Cassidy put a pound of ground beef into the microwave to defrost, then removed a package of Hamburger Helper from the pantry. *No real cook would be caught dead using this imitation food.*

By no real cook, you mean your mother. The real reason you avoided cooking for so long is that you didn't want to compete in a field where your mother rules.

"What I can do to help?" Zach asked, coming into the kitchen.

"Why don't you toss the salad?"

While the meat was frying, Cassidy turned away from the stove and watched Zach break chunks of lettuce into a bowl. Starshine landed on the counter next to him and tried to grab a piece of lettuce out of his hands, but when he set it down in front of her, she gave it a brief lick, then knocked it to the floor. Casting a disdainful look at the untouched food in her bowl, she began pushing it toward the edge of the counter as well.

Zach snagged the bowl and emptied it into the garbage. "We can't let her go without eating indefinitely."

"I know." Cassidy stirred the hamburger, reminding herself that she had to watch it closely so Starshine didn't get the opportunity to forage for herself again. "I'll call the vet tomorrow and see what she says."

Announcing that dinner was ready, Cassidy carried the food to the table while Zach poured wine. She sat on the long side, with Zach at a right angle from her. Starshine jumped onto the chair at the opposite end from Zach, then climbed laboriously onto the table, where she sat tall, her ears pricked forward, her gaze fixed on each forkful of food Zach lifted to his mouth.

Cassidy tried to ignore the cat's hungry stare. *You should put her in the basement like you did last time. Yes, but I hate feeling so mean.*

Taking a swallow of wine, Cassidy let out a sigh.

"What's that about?"

"Oh, I guess I'm disappointed at Bryce's reaction to us. I never expected him to be so angry. Here we left our party and went running to his rescue, then you borrowed money to bail him out. I guess I was hoping for a few crumbs of appreciation, which just goes to show how little I know about motherhood. From what I hear, appreciation is not something you ever get from kids." *So why would you want to have one?*

"But you're not his mother, so you don't get to blame yourself for his faults."

Blame—the other thing that goes with motherhood.

As they busied themselves eating, the calico hunkered down and began inching toward their plates.

Finishing his dinner, Zach said, "One of us needs to tackle those cell phone bills."

"I'll do it. You've got a job to go to and I usually have some extra time during the day."

Moving a little closer, Starshine leaned forward and snatched a bite of Hamburger Helper off Cassidy's plate.

"Okay, I give." Cassidy pushed her plate toward the calico, who quickly scarfed down the remainder of the food, polishing the blue Dansk design until it shone.

CHAPTER 16

THEY CLEANED UP THE KITCHEN, THEN ZACH went into the computer room and Cassidy settled at her desk to look through the cell phone bills. Before she'd gotten very far, Zach came into the room, sat in his chair, and swiveled to face her. "I just read an email from my editor. He tried to reach me on my cell but it must not be working. Anyway, this is not good news. Jerry—he came to our party—you remember him?"

She shook her head. She'd been introduced to at least ten people from the *Post* that night.

"Jerry started having chest pains at the office today, and when they got him into the hospital the doctor confirmed it was a heart attack."

"Oh—that's too bad."

"Yeah, the guy's only in his fifties. But the part that affects us is Jerry's investigation. He's been looking into a hospital where a large-scale Medicare scam is going on. This was his story but I've been helping around the edges so now the whole thing's going to fall into my lap."

"How did Jerry find out about it?"

"A whistleblower started calling him. A woman who works in billing. She's convinced there's a ring of doctors ripping off Medicare by transferring nursing home patients into the hospital when there's nothing wrong with them. And then, of course, these same doctors order a bunch of unnecessary tests. The problem is, the billing records alone don't constitute proof. Most of the whistleblower's information came from her cousin who's a nurse there, and Jerry thinks the nurse is about ready to talk to a reporter. If he's right, I could get a break in the story fairly soon."

"Does this mean you won't have time for our investigation?"

"Pretty much. Even if the nurse talks tomorrow, I'll still need corroboration. I will make time for the Hopewell interview—I wouldn't miss that for anything—but everything else'll have to go on hold."

"Well, but I can keep working on Kit's murder."

"I don't like the idea of you just going off on your own. I'd rather have you wait till we can do it together."

"I won't be going off on my own. We can confer as often as you like by phone. Besides, you told Bryce just this afternoon that we couldn't afford to wait."

"Yes, but … " Frown lines appearing on his forehead, he turned his face toward the window.

"But what?"

"I don't have any reasons. I just don't like it."

"You're afraid something will happen to me."

"Something always happens to you."

"It happens whether you're there to protect me or not."

Zach was silent for several seconds. "I'm racking my brain trying to come up with a logical reason to say no but I can't think of any."

"Say *no*?"

"You know what I mean. After all, who's the one who always gives in around here?"

Cassidy knew that she won most of their arguments, primarily because she was more stubborn than her husband. "So you won't give me a hard time if I continue without you?"

"*Me* give *you* a hard time?"

Standing, she dropped a kiss on his forehead. "I promise I won't run amuck. And I'll keep you posted on everything."

As Zach returned to the computer room, she pondered what it would be like to work without him.

You'll miss him. You always like doing things together.

Yes, but you've been getting too dependent. It'll be good for you to do something on your own for a change.

A moment later she followed him into the computer room. "Since I'm going to be doing the legwork, I should have Bryce's key."

"I don't see why you'd need to go back to the townhouse."

Doesn't want to give up control.

"Maybe I won't, but I'd still like to have it."

He gave her the key.

†††

She sat at her desk staring at Kit's cell phone bills. *So many numbers and so many repetitions. You can't just start calling at random.* She decided that the numbers needed to be organized by frequency. The trouble was, she couldn't face the task of doing it. She'd had a long day, it was almost ten o'clock, and her mind had shut down. The sensible thing would be to wait until morning, but the following day she had three clients before noon and the Hopewell interview at four, which didn't leave much time for organizing and calling.

Gran! She can organize the numbers. She's probably better at that sort of thing than you are, and nothing makes her happier than to get her fingers into an investigative pie.

Cassidy picked up the phone.

"You found something for me to do?" Gran said. "Oh goody! I'll get those numbers whipped into shape in no time. In fact, if you want me to, I could get the addresses from reverse directory and go pay all those people a visit."

"What would you say?"

"I'd tell 'em I was Kit's granny and I had a terminal illness and had to find out who killed her before I died. People have a weakness for old folks, you know."

"I think it'd be better if I just called. The majority are probably cell phone numbers, so reverse directory won't have many of the addresses."

"Why don't you fax the bills over now? I can get them organized and have the info back to you before you're up tomorrow."

"You're not going to stay up and work all night, are you?" Cassidy said, feeling a pang of guilt that her grandmother was willing to keep going so much later than she was.

"Oh, it won't take that long. I'll probably be done in an hour or so."

Cassidy felt another pang for having made her little molehill of a project into a mountain. "I'll get them over to you in a few minutes. Just don't work too hard, okay?"

"I'm at a point in my life where a little work is just what I need."

†††

"I'm going into the office early." Zach set Cassidy's mug on her nightstand and leaned over to kiss her good-bye.

"It's only seven," she protested.

"I should've been out the door before this. I have to get up to speed on Jerry's story and then I'm planning to take time off this afternoon for the Hopewell interview."

As soon as the caffeine began to percolate in Cassidy's brain, she went into the computer room to pick up the fax from Gran: a sheet of paper divided into four columns, the first a list of phone numbers ranked according to frequency, the second a list of dates on which the calls had been placed, the third a list of destination points, and the fourth a half dozen or so names and addresses for the landline phones. There were thirty-two numbers that had been called more than once. Cassidy doubted she could ever be as organized as Gran.

Isn't going to be easy. First you have to devise an opening line that distinguishes you from telephone solicitors, then you have to lure people into answering questions they'd rather avoid. She decided to wait until after she'd seen her clients to tackle the first call.

She showered and dressed, then phoned the vet.

"If she won't eat the food we gave you," the vet said, "we'll have to try her on something else. I have another dry food here that a lot of cats like. It's a little higher in calories but it'll do the job."

"I'm not sure she'll eat any dry food."

"Eventually she'll have to if you don't give her anything else."

That's what I've been telling Zach, but I'm beginning to have my doubts.

"Okay, I'll run over and pick up the new food right now."

When Cassidy returned, Starshine met her at the door, then jumped onto the counter to sit next to the bowl Zach had filled earlier that morning. The calico's eyes deepened; coaxing sounds came from her mouth.

"Well, here's hoping."

Cassidy dumped the old food, opened the bag of new food, and poured it into the calico's bowl.

Mrit!

Maybe you need to find a new vet.

†††

After her sessions were over, Cassidy grabbed a bag of peanut butter cups, took out her notepad, and sat at her desk to study the sheet Gran had faxed her. She looked for Bryce's cell number, which was right where it was supposed to be, at the top of the list. Next she looked for Angie's and Raul's numbers, which she had recorded in her notepad. Angie's was just below Bryce's, and Raul's was a third of the way down. She examined the dates beside Raul's number. *Lot of calls during the three months before Kit moved in with Bryce, not so many afterward. But still a call every week or so. Except for August. No calls from the eighth to the thirtieth—which includes the dates she could've gotten pregnant. So why was this hot woman not talking to her lover during the hottest month of the year?*

Unwrapping a peanut butter cup, Cassidy tried to think of any other information that might be gleaned from the list itself. When nothing came to mind, she ate the Reese's, took a deep breath, and dialed the third number down. Since there was no name or address attached, she assumed it was a cell.

A male voice said, "Yeah."

"I'm investigating Kit Hopewell's murder and I see by her phone records that she talked to you on a regular basis."

"Who'd you say you were?"

"Cassidy McCabe. I'm working for the defense."

"You mean you're looking for some way to get that dickhead who killed her off the hook."

"Um … have you heard of the concept 'innocent until proven guilty?'"

"Look, man, I ain't no lawyer. I don't have to go along with that shit."

"I can understand that you're angry about the murder and you want to see the guilty party put away."

"You got that right."

"All I'm trying to do is make sure the right person gets convicted. Now I gather that you and Kit were fairly close because she called you so often."

"We were both drama majors and we both had Morrie as our coach. He'd assign a scene for us to practice together and then we'd go hang out afterward."

"Did you know her live-in boyfriend?"

"I met him."

"Did Kit say anything that might lead you to think he had a motive?"

"She hinted around that she had some other guys on the side. So I figure he found out about the competition and popped her."

"A lot of other guys?"

"I don't think she was into one-night stands or anything. Maybe just a couple dudes she got together with on occasion."

"Were you one of those dudes?"

"I would've jumped at the chance, but she said she had too many balls in the air already and I'd have to wait in line."

"I've been told her relationships were pretty volatile. Did you and Kit ever get into fights?"

"Oh sure. She reamed me out a new asshole plenty of times. But what do you expect, man? She was an actor."

"Is there anything else you can tell me?"

"Yeah—the police have the right guy."

"Would you mind giving me your name?"

"Why should I? Because I have this great urge to help the defense?" Cassidy heard a click on the other end.

So Kit only had a couple of other lovers, not all the males in the drama department. That is, if you can believe this no-name drama dude. Which you have no reason to do, considering he's not likely to admit to having slept with Kit now that she's been murdered. So what do you expect to get out of making these phone calls, anyway?

Maybe nothing, but you still have to do it. That's what investigative work is—planting your butt and being thorough, even when the odds of a payoff are practically nil.

The next eighteen calls yielded no useful information. Then she dialed number twenty-one, a landline with an address. A male voice said "Hello."

She informed the voice that she was investigating Kit's murder. "I see by her phone records that she placed a number of calls to you."

"Not me. We got five people living here. It must be Iris you're looking for. She's been blubbering all week about somebody dying. Hold on—I'll go get her." He plunked the receiver down and yelled Iris's name. Music blared in the background.

A short time later the music was turned down and a woman came on the line.

Cassidy repeated her introductory statement.

"I thought they'd arrested Kit's boyfriend," Iris said, a quaver in her voice.

"The evidence is all circumstantial. I doubt they'll get a conviction."

"Oh, but I'm sure the boyfriend did it. The police obviously think he's guilty." A brief pause. "I'm sorry, what was it you called about?"

"Could you tell me something about your relationship with Kit?"

"Let's see … we met in a play last year. I was just a freshman. I didn't know anything and she sort of took me under her wing. Showed me around, introduced me to people, explained how things worked." Another pause. "Tried to keep me out of trouble."

"What kind of trouble?"

"Oh nothing. I don't even know why I said that. I've just been so upset ever since I heard about her murder. She did so much for me. I should've done more for her."

More of what?

"Do you know of anyone besides Kit's boyfriend who might've had a reason to kill her?"

"No, of course not. I'm sorry but I don't have anything to tell you." Iris hung up.

Why would she think she should have done more for Kit? Because she suspected Kit was at risk?

Cassidy studied the dates of the calls to Iris. The highest concentration occurred before Kit moved in with Angie. After that they continued on a less frequent basis and finally tapered off to almost nothing.

CHAPTER 17

"How's Jerry?" Cassidy asked her husband as they cruised north on the Edens Expressway. To save Zach the time it would take to drive to Oak Park and pick her up, she had ridden the el into the city and met him at his office.

"His cardiologist is optimistic. I stopped at the hospital today to assure him his investigation is at the top of my list."

"I guess I won't be seeing much of you until you get this Medicare thing wrapped up."

"Probably not. You know, I really appreciate that you never give me any grief over the hours I put in. Some of the guys at work ended up in divorce court because their wives claimed they were never home."

"Those guys probably *weren't* ever home. But you're pretty good about not going out after work. Most nights I find you at the computer after I finish seeing clients." She stopped to reflect on a thought that had popped into her mind. "If we were to have a baby, I don't think your hours would be a problem. Considering that I only see about twenty clients a week, between the two of us we'd have more time for parenting than most working couples."

"So then you'd be the warm nurturing mom and I'd be the distant workaholic dad."

"Why would you even say that?"

"Because I don't know what kind of dad I'd be." He looked at her, his face displaying a degree of uncertainty she seldom saw there. "When I think about having a baby, I see myself as this great father who pours time and attention into his kid. But in real life, I like to come home, plop in front of the computer, watch television, and read. One reason our marriage works is that you never hassle me about it. If we had a baby, I'd have to play with it, change its diapers, put it to bed. This kid would have to become the center of our lives, and I'm not sure I'm unselfish enough to move me out and put a baby there."

"You were able to put me there."

"That's because I get so much back from you. I'm not sure I'd feel the same about a baby."

"That's where bonding comes in. Bonding makes parents feel like they're getting a tremendous amount back. They hold this infant in their arms, look into its eyes, and before long keeping that baby safe and happy is the most important thing in the world."

Glancing behind him, Zach switched into the right lane to pass the rusted-out station wagon that was slowing him down. "Not all parents are able to bond."

He's thinking of his parents. Afraid if they couldn't do it with him, he wouldn't be able to do it with his child.

"So are you saying you don't want a baby?"

"I'm just saying I'm scared. Scared I won't be the kind of dad I'd like to be. But it's up to you. If you want a baby, let's go for it."

One part of her wanted to say, "Yes! Let's start working on it tonight!" But she knew that having a baby was too big a decision to simply foist onto Zach.

"This has to be something we both want."

† † †

He parked in front of a capacious frame house set a good distance back from the road on a beautifully landscaped double lot. Climbing out of the car, they headed down a curving walkway toward a colonnaded verandah. Above the second story, a triangular dormer decorated with fish-scale shingles faced the street.

Zach pressed the bell and a tall, robust woman opened the door.

Zach gave their names.

"Mr. and Mrs. Hopewell are expecting you." It was the same crisp voice Cassidy had heard over the phone. The housekeeper had a sculpted face that might have been almost beautiful if her features hadn't been set in such a stern expression. *An intimidating presence. Just what you want in a gatekeeper.*

After ushering them into the living room, the woman assured them that the Hopewells would be out shortly, then disappeared around a grand staircase to their right. Cassidy's gaze moved up the staircase to a balcony that overhung the living room, with a row of closed doors behind the balcony's railing.

"Well, Zach and Cassidy," Ben Hopewell said as he came into the room, his small wife clinging to his arm, the housekeeper following after them. "I'm sorry I can't say I'm happy to see you, but you must understand this isn't personal. I don't bear any ill will toward you or your son. Everything has a purpose, even the worst tragedy, and I'm sure that Adele's and my suffering won't be in vain. I hold you both in my prayers," he looked from Cassidy to Zach, "and I'm praying for your son's redemption as well."

Cassidy felt herself bristle. *How patronizing. Deciding that Bryce is guilty and in need of redemption. Imposing his prayers where they haven't been asked for.*

"Please make yourselves comfortable," Adele said wearily. She gestured toward two cream-colored chairs standing in front of the window. A velvet loveseat faced the chairs, with a polished wood coffee table in between.

After both couples were seated, she turned to the housekeeper. "Bring out some refreshments, would you, Peg?"

The woman nodded and left the room.

"I'd like to keep this brief," Ben said. "Talking about Kit and her problems is bound to be hard on Adele."

Cassidy's heart went out to the pale woman who looked as if she could barely hold herself upright.

"You mentioned Kit's problems," Zach began. "What exactly would you say they were?"

"She was rebelling against her religion. As her father and pastor, she was particularly rebelling against me. Keeping one's children on the path of righteousness is difficult in a society where temptations abound."

This guy talks in sermons.

Peg carried in a silver tray holding tea and cookies and set it on the table, but nobody made a move to take anything.

When Peg was gone, Cassidy said to the Hopewells, "It must've been hard to see Kit flouting everything you believed in."

"She was extremely close to Forest and Heidi," Adele said. "I was always afraid they'd follow in her footsteps."

Ben reached for his wife's hand. "If Kit had only lived long enough, God would have reclaimed her." He looked at Zach. "You may scoff at our beliefs, but we've witnessed the power of prayer many times over. The whole congregation was praying for Kit. In His own good time, God would have brought her back to us."

So what took Him so long? If prayers are such a sure thing, why didn't He get around to it before Kit was killed?

Zach said, "The one time we met Kit, she told us you gave her all the money she wanted."

Movement from above caught Cassidy's eye. Glancing up, she saw Forest creeping along the balcony. She quickly lowered her gaze, not wanting to betray his presence. Since the boy was walking soundlessly and his parents had their backs to the balcony, she was fairly certain they didn't know he was there.

"Kit said we were giving her money?" Ben shook his head. "We paid for her college expenses but that was all. Unfortunately, her maternal grandparents were never able to say no to their first-born grandchild. I wanted them to stop indulging her, but they kept handing out money behind my back."

Shifting in her chair, Cassidy took another quick look at the balcony. One of the doors stood ajar. *So Forest is listening in. Well, what teenager wouldn't?*

"We were told," Zach said, "that Kit brought her drug-dealer boyfriend to one of your services, and that the two of them left early so they could smoke pot in front of your parishioners as they came out."

A brief frown appeared on Ben's face, then his features smoothed out into his usual expression of benevolence. "That's true."

"Did you do anything about it?"

"When she first started acting out, I tried to stop her. But every time I attempted to exert control, she'd stage a huge temper tantrum, then go out and do something worse. It didn't take long to realize that anything I did or said simply fed into her rebelliousness. So Adele and I had to learn to bite our tongues." He expelled a long breath. "One of the toughest things I've ever had to do."

Cassidy felt a grudging respect for the minister. *Accepting the things you can't change.* She knew from personal experience how difficult that was.

"You told us you paid her college expenses," Cassidy said. "Does that mean you approved of her choice of schools?"

"Not at all. We wanted her to attend a religious college, but she made it clear it had to be Northwestern or nothing. Since we were certain she'd eventually outgrow the terrible stage she was in, we didn't want to deprive her of an education."

Cassidy continued. "We talked to Bryce yesterday. He said Kit called you a hypocrite. He had the impression it was Kit's mission in life to get back at you because you'd disappointed her in some way."

Hopewell stared at the window behind them, then looked at Zach. "My patience is wearing thin. I've already answered a number of questions that were none of your business."

"You have," Zach agreed.

"Now you're accusing me of being a hypocrite."

"That's not what I said," Cassidy replied. *And he knows it. Just trying to set up a diversion.*

A short silence. Then Ben said, "If I don't address this subject, I suppose you'll go hounding my parishioners for information they don't have." A look of dislike crossed his face. "Since I don't want you bothering anybody else, I suppose I better tell you myself."

"We'd appreciate it," Cassidy said.

"When Kit was fifteen, she came barging into my church office and found me with my arms around a woman from the congregation. This woman—who was highly distraught—had come to me for counseling and I was trying to comfort her. I explained to Kit, then the woman explained, but Kit refused to believe either one of us. She accused me of being unfaithful, insisted I'd betrayed my calling. Adele and I tried to calm her down, but she just got more and more hysterical, then she went running out of the house and didn't come home until the next morning. Before that incident, Kit and I were exceptionally close. I never had to worry about her or discipline her. She was everything a father could want in a daughter. And then, she jumped to this one wrong conclusion and suddenly nothing I did was right."

"That must've been a terrible loss."

Ben managed a weak smile. "God never gives anyone more than they can bear."

We better get out of here, because if I have to listen to one more religious platitude, I'm going to gag.

† † †

Once they were back on the road, Zach said, "Hopewell's story about Kit's going nuts over finding him with a parishioner doesn't ring true to me. If Kit idealized her father the way Angie said, why wouldn't she take him at his word? The only reason I can think of is that Kit saw more than Hopewell's admitting to."

"That's certainly possible. The fundamentalist minister taking advantage of his dewy-eyed parishioners is as much of a cliché as the politician with his interns." Cassidy mulled it over. "But—as much as I hate to give the pastor the benefit of the doubt—I can imagine one scenario that would lead to Kit's blaming her father unfairly. When Kit was fifteen, she undoubtedly was high-spirited, curious about the world, and totally repressed. As long as she had her father on a pedestal, she couldn't go against his wishes without incurring a ton of guilt. But if she could knock her father down—if she could convince herself he was a hypocrite instead of a saint—she could act out all over the place without having to feel guilty. But in order to hold the guilt at bay, she'd have to keep reminding herself of her father's failings, which would explain why she was so obsessed with his hypocrisy."

"So you think Hopewell's story might be true?"

"I don't know what to think. I just have this need to come up with theories about everything."

CHAPTER 18

ZACH HAD TO RETURN TO WORK AND Cassidy wanted to borrow the Subaru so she could pay a visit to Iris. When they arrived at the *Post*, Zach kissed her good-bye and she slid behind the wheel to head back toward Evanston. Before they got to the *Post*, they'd squabbled briefly over who would ride the el home that night. Cassidy contended that since she was borrowing Zach's car, she should leave it at the *Post* and take public transportation. But Zach was adamant that he didn't want her riding the el across the west side of Chicago at night, so she gave in to him.

Iris's address belonged to a slatternly looking Victorian located a couple of miles west of the campus. As Cassidy mounted the porch steps, she smiled at a soft-sculpture black and white cow seated on an old-fashioned wooden swing, a flowery wide-brimmed hat on the bovine's head, a cigarette dangling from her mouth.

Just think—if you have a baby, someday you might be visiting your own kid at a great whimsical place like this.

You'd be almost sixty before your child even started college.

Doesn't matter. The boomers, who get their way about everything, are going to pass a law against aging.

The door was opened by a youthful male with piercings attached to most of his visible skin. *Probably his invisible skin as well,* Cassidy thought, an X-rated image flashing through her mind.

"Is Iris here?" Cassidy asked.

"Dunno," Metal Boy answered in a tone of utter indifference.

"Would you mind checking?"

He hesitated, his mouth dipping into surliness. "Oh, all right."

He was gone so long Cassidy began to suspect he had forgotten his mission, but then a slight woman with dark shaggy hair entered the foyer. Stopping about two feet back from the threshold, she asked, "What do you want?"

"I'm Cassidy McCabe. We spoke on the phone earlier."

Iris grasped the open door. "I don't have anything to say to you."

"You were a friend of Kit's. You probably find it painful to talk about her."

The woman nodded. Cassidy detected a hint of anxiety in her large brown eyes. Iris had milky skin, straight eyebrows, deep hollows beneath her cheekbones, and a couple reddish zits on her pointed chin. She wore an oversized white shirt over baggy black pants.

Cassidy said, "I can understand that you wouldn't want to talk to me, considering you've never met me before and you don't know whether or not you can trust me."

She nodded again.

"But even given all the reasons you'd rather not talk to me, I can't imagine that you'd want an innocent person to go to jail. So I'm going to ask you to at least let me explain why I'm working on Bryce's defense. If you hear me out and still don't want to talk to me, I'll leave you alone."

After a long pause, Iris said, "I guess I could do that."

"Is there some place inside where we could talk?"

"Just my room. It isn't very comfortable."

"Then let's sit in my car."

Twisting her head to look past Cassidy, the woman gazed out toward the curb. She nodded, then followed Cassidy to the Subaru and settled into the passenger seat. Cassidy began telling her about Bryce, the loss of his mother, his love for Kit, his difficulty finding a place for himself in the world. *He'd hate it if he knew I was saying these things, but I need to make him into a real person for Iris.*

"The police have a lot of evidence against him," Cassidy acknowledged, "but they don't have fingerprints or DNA or a confession. Bryce is the kind of person who's quick to feel guilty, who blames himself even when it isn't his fault. If he'd killed Kit, he would have confessed instantly. He'd never have refused to accept responsibility if he'd really done it."

"He sounds a lot like me." Iris stared at the motorcycle parked in front of them for several seconds. "Okay, what do you want to know?"

"To begin with, there are a couple people I'd like to find out about. The first is a guy who was sleeping with Kit and uses DC as his email name. Did Kit ever mention that she was having sex with someone besides Bryce and Raul? Or do you know of anyone with the initials DC?"

"I never heard of him. I had no idea she was sleeping with anyone else."

"The second person is Margaret Polanski. This woman might've been a friend of Kit's."

"I don't know anything about her either."

"Well ... " Cassidy paused, not quite sure where to go next. Deciding she should start with something easy, she asked, "Where are you from?"

"Iowa. That's part of my problem. I grew up in a small town with overprotective parents, which left me totally unprepared for a place like this. Kit recognized how green I was and took it upon herself to show me around."

"What did she show you?"

"Parties." Iris looked down at her hands. "Well, that's not the only thing but it was the parties that got me in trouble. I don't want you to think she was out to corrupt me, because she wasn't. The only reason she took me to parties was that I didn't have any friends and she thought I could meet people there. She gave me a long talking-to beforehand. Made me promise to stay sober and not go home with any guys. Said she'd keep her eye out for people who weren't stoners and make sure I got to meet them."

Cassidy remembered the dates of Kit's early phone calls to Iris. "That was during the time she was living with Raul, wasn't it?"

"Yes."

"What can you tell me about their relationship?"

"They were crazy about each other. Kit knew all about him before she moved in. She knew he was a dealer and that he got physical with women, but she thought she could handle him. She told me she was always able to control the guys she was with, and she assumed she'd have Raul eating out of her hand before very long. She loved the challenge, the excitement. You could almost see the sparks flying between those two."

"But she moved out after about a month, didn't she?"

"I guess she thought she could stare Raul down and he wouldn't hit her, but he didn't fall into line like her other boyfriends had. Once the honeymoon was over, he started beating on her just like he had with everyone else, so she went to stay with Angie. But the sparks were still flying. As soon as she moved out, Raul went chasing after her, and she didn't always say no."

"How did he react when she moved in with Bryce?"

"Well … " Iris moistened her bottom lip. "By the time Kit moved out of Raul's apartment, I was attending parties on my own. And I wasn't sticking to the rules. During the early days when I wasn't using anything, I was so shy I could barely hold a conversation. But then I started drinking and suddenly I became this funny confident person I'd always wanted to be. Then Raul and Kit split up—at least I thought they did—and he started coming on to me and giving me free samples of coke. I just felt this tremendous sense of chemistry. I knew all the reasons I should stay away from him, but I wasn't able to do it any more than I was able to stay away from the booze and the drugs." She sighed again. "I hate to admit it, but I think one of the reasons I was so attracted to Raul is that Kit was the most dazzling woman I'd ever met and he was her ex."

"Did Kit find out about you and Raul?"

"Are you kidding? Nobody could ever keep anything from Kit. She hunted me down and read me the riot act. Not because I was sleeping with her boyfriend, but because I was doing coke and hanging out with a guy who beat on his women. She said she was strong enough to deal with him but I wasn't. And God, was she ever right!"

"She wasn't mad that you were having sex with him?"

"I think she knew he was just using me to get back at her."

"So did you go on seeing him after that?"

"Oh God, this is so hard to talk about." Iris pressed her fist against the base of her throat. "Raul and I would go to his place and get high, then we'd have sex, and afterward he'd start talking trash about Kit—what a bitch she was, how she should never have left him, that sort of thing. But at that point he was just grumbling—not hugely pissed—because she was still at Angie's and they were still seeing each other fairly often."

"Did it get worse after she moved in with Bryce?"

"The day she did, Raul hit me for the first time. Even though she was still having sex with him, he started getting a lot more violent."

"Did Kit ever say why she kept seeing this slimeball who beat on her?"

"She told me she loved Bryce and really wanted it to work out with him, but that she craved the rush she got from Raul. It was only by seeing him now and then that she could be satisfied with Bryce."

Terrible for Bryce, but not so great for Kit either. Think how awful it would be to be hooked on a wildman like Raul. Since Cassidy had failed to leave her ex even though he cheated on her, she could understand women getting addicted to bad boys.

"You said Raul got more violent after Kit moved in with Bryce."

"He started hitting me and making threats. And both kept getting worse." Iris pulled out the seatbelt and began twisting it with both hands.

"Tell me about the threats."

"He went on and on about the things he wanted to do to Kit and Bryce—well, mostly Bryce. Things like castrating him, feeding his balls to the dogs, shoving a cattle prod up his rear end."

"What about Kit?"

"Um … let's see … cutting her face, getting his friends together and gang-raping her. He didn't make nearly so many threats against Kit as he did against Bryce."

"How did you react to hearing him say these things?"

"They were so outlandish I didn't take him seriously. At least, I didn't at first."

"What do you mean, 'at first?'"

"I didn't take him seriously until after he'd done something terrible to me." A sheen of perspiration appeared on Iris's brow. She wiped it away with an unsteady hand.

"That's all right," Cassidy said softly. "Just take your time."

Several beats passed. Then, "One night I was at Raul's and he started telling me everything that was wrong with me. I was too shy, too skinny, too boring. A terrible friend because I was sleeping with my best friend's boyfriend. I started to cry and he ordered me to stop but I couldn't. So he put duct tape over my mouth and tied my wrists together with one end of a long rope." Iris began breathing rapidly through her mouth.

"You must've been terrified!"

The younger woman smiled a gruesome smile. "There was a steel hook in his ceiling. I'd asked about it before but he wouldn't tell me anything. Well, that night I learned why it was there. He threw the loose end of the rope over the hook and yanked on it until he'd lifted me about a foot off the floor. Then he tied the rope to the bed. I felt as if my whole body was coming apart. I'd never hurt like that before in my life."

"Oh my God! He tortured you!"

"The next thing I knew he had a razor in his hand and was cutting my clothes off. After he got me naked, he started punching me in the head. Thank God I passed out fairly soon." Iris rubbed one of the blemishes on her chin. "When I came to, it was almost dawn, and I was lying in bed with Raul asleep beside me. I was too scared to move for a long time. Then I gathered my courage and got up. Raul's cell was on the bureau, so I took it into the bathroom and called Kit."

"You actually got through to her at that hour?" *Thank God kids never turn their cells off like you do.*

"I told her what had happened and asked her to bring me some clothes. Half an hour later she was pounding on the door. I let her in, and she shook Raul awake and started screaming at him. It was as if one of the ancient Greek Furies had been let loose in the room. Raul just stared at her with this dazed look on his face. She told him if he ever came near me again, she'd press charges for all the times he'd battered her. Later on I realized she couldn't really do that, but she sounded so sure of herself at the time, I think he believed her."

Cassidy pictured a small naked Raul cowering in the corner, an oversized Kit coming at him with a chair and whip.

"So Kit rescued you?" Cassidy asked.

"She took me to the nearest ER, and after they said I was okay we went to Bryce's townhouse. She got me settled on the couch, and told me she wouldn't let me leave until I promised to attend at least one AA meeting a day for the next week. I was so scared and ashamed of myself, I would have agreed to anything."

"Did you keep your promise? Have you stopped using?"

"I've been clean and sober ever since that night. Raul called a couple of times but I hung up on him, and I haven't had any urge to go to parties. I guess I've retreated into my shell, but at least it feels safe here."

"Did you and Kit continue your friendship?"

"She used to check up on me from time to time but I kind of avoided her. It was really hard to face her after what I'd done."

"What about Kit and Raul? Did she continue to have sex with him?"

"We never talked about Raul after that. But if I had to guess, I'd say she did."

Cassidy tried to think if there was anything else she should ask.

Looking directly into her eyes, Iris said, "I think I should tell you that I *want* Bryce to be guilty. No matter how good a guy he may be, no matter how much you care about him, I want Bryce to be the one who killed her."

Cassidy's head jerked slightly in surprise. "Why? What have you got against him?"

"This isn't about Bryce, it's about Raul. I want Raul not to have killed her. Because if he did, I'd be partly to blame. I heard him make all those threats and I never warned her."

"Not even after you stopped seeing Raul?"

"I was too ashamed. So I convinced myself that he didn't mean what he said, that he was harmless. Even though I knew he wasn't."

"What Raul did to you—that was really horrible. Nobody could go through an ordeal like that without suffering some repercussions." *Post Traumatic Stress for sure.* "I wonder if you've ever thought of seeing a therapist?"

"No," Iris said in a tone that let Cassidy know her sales pitch would be in vain.

But she made it anyway. "Even if you just went for a few sessions, it could help put this behind you. Here, take my card." Cassidy fumbled in her purse, then held a card out to Iris, who apparently was too polite not to take it. "If you change your mind, I could give you a referral."

"I have to go now." Iris bolted from the car.

Pulling away from the curb, Cassidy felt certain Iris wouldn't take her advice.

You shouldn't even have mentioned therapy. People always resent it if they think you think there's something wrong with them.

The sky had turned a dusky blue and the daylight was almost gone. *Seven o'clock Wednesday night. Hard to believe it's only been four days since the murder.*

CHAPTER 19

STARSHINE TWINED HERSELF BETWEEN CASSIDY'S LEGS, THEN squatted on the floor, her eyes fastened on the countertop in preparation for lift-off. A small leap like this, effortless when she was thin, now required a degree of concentration. After a couple of seconds the cat launched herself onto the counter, making a less-than-perfect landing.

Just think how mortified she'll be if the day ever comes when she misses. As bad for her as it is for you when you have that dream where you greet clients in your underwear.

Scratching at the Formica, the calico ritualistically buried her bowl of dry food, then fastened a liquid green-eyed gaze on her human. Cassidy could feel herself weaken.

You have to get her to eat.

Wasn't it just last night she helped herself to your Hamburger Helper? And the night before that she captured a platter of meat patties?

Yes, but she hasn't had a full meal since breakfast on Sunday—and that was more than seventy-two hours ago.

As Cassidy reached out to scratch behind Starshine's ears, the cat uttered a beseeching *mwat*. Cassidy opened the cabinet and stared at the three remaining cans, the other three having gone to feed Milton.

Okay, you can give her a spoonful of canned food. Just this once. Because you've witnessed so much sadness today and seeing your cat go hungry is just too much to bear.

She divided the can between Starshine's bowl and Milton's. Carrying the tom's dish outside, she watched him eat, then returned to the kitchen where Starshine was washing her face.

Upstairs the calico climbed onto Cassidy's lap, kneaded her chest, brushed her mouth against Cassidy's lips, and purred rapturously. *This is the real reason you fed her, isn't it? You didn't want to miss out on the cuddly brand of comfort only Starshine can provide.*

When Zach came home at ten, Cassidy was at the computer doing research on the psychiatrist who'd prescribed Margaret Polanski's Thorazine. Cassidy logged off and followed her husband into the bedroom.

"I'm on page one out of four," she said, sitting on the bed while Zach parked himself in his desk chair. "So far the only thing that stands out is that this Dr. Leonard's practice is in St. Louis, not Chicago."

"So—let's see—how did Kit get her hands on Margaret's Thorazine? Margaret's a Northwestern student who lives in St. Louis. So one day Kit's visiting Margaret and she steals the Thorazine out of her medicine cabinet. Or Margaret stops taking her meds and gives them to Kit."

"Or Leonard's one of those sleazy docs who prescribes over the Net. Maybe Kit ordered Thorazine because she wanted a heavy duty sedative for her insomnia. And she used an alias so that—if Leonard ever got caught—the authorities wouldn't come knocking at her door."

"No way to tell." Zach folded his hands across his chest. "I finally got a call back from the defense attorney. He agreed to take

Bryce's case, so now I have to pry thirty grand out of Victor. The next step is for Bryce to make an appointment. I left messages on both Bryce's and Victor's cells."

Zach went on to tell her that the nurse in the Medicare investigation had not yet agreed to talk to him, then Cassidy recounted what she'd learned from Iris.

"So your initial take on Raul was right. The guy has both a history of violence and a clear cut motive to whack Kit." Zach got to his feet. "I'm going to fix a drink. You want anything?"

"Bring me a glass of wine."

He headed downstairs, returning shortly with their drinks. Handing Cassidy a glass of Merlot, he went into the den next to the computer room, sat in one of the two side-by-side chairs, and clicked on the TV.

"I guess you're done talking," Cassidy said, standing in the doorway.

"You have something else on your mind?"

"Not really."

He turned off the television. "Don't be ridiculous. You wouldn't have said that if you didn't."

"Yeah, but you've had a long day."

"What's this? My wife with something she's not just spitting out? Why aren't you twisting my arm?"

Sitting in the chair next to his, she took a long swallow of wine. "I don't even know what I want to say. It's just that I had a real reaction to seeing Adele Hopewell today. I kept wondering what it would be like to put your heart and soul into raising a child, only to have that child turn against you. And I don't mean just stop speaking to you. I mean repudiate everything you ever believed in."

"Yeah, but that wouldn't happen to us."

"Why not? When I was young and naïve, I used to think that any child with two good parents would automatically grow up to be a decent human being. But I've seen too much evidence to the contrary to believe that anymore. The old simplistic notion that all it takes is love just isn't true."

"When it comes to Kit, we're not talking about a kid who mysteriously went bad even though she was raised in a warm, fuzzy family. Old Ben was probably an overbearing tyrant, plus she had all these religious strictures hemming her in. What kid with any spunk wouldn't rebel?"

"Okay, I agree that Kit's problems were probably the result of her upbringing. But a lot of kids have perfectly fine parents and still get in trouble. I've had two clients—each a mother who came into therapy over the loss of her child. One had a daughter who overdosed, the other a son who'd been sent to prison for twenty years. Both kids had intact families and parents that loved them." Propping her elbow on the leather arm of the chair, Cassidy rested her forehead in the palm of her hand. "Having a baby is such a huge undertaking. There's always the chance that we'd screw it up. Or that the kid would go bad even if we didn't screw it up."

Zach took her hand out from under her forehead and held it. "If that happened, we'd just have to get through it. The way we've gotten through everything else."

But is it worth the risk?

Cassidy smiled and pulled her hand away. "I guess I just needed to vent. I'm ready to go read my book now and let you flip channels."

When the phone rang nearly an hour later, Cassidy was in the bathroom brushing her teeth. She rinsed out her mouth and dashed into the bedroom to answer it.

"This is Forest Hopewell." His voice was just above a whisper. "I hope it isn't too late to call."

"It's fine."

"I heard you talking to my parents today."

"You did?" *As if you didn't know.*

"I think it's important that you find out who killed my sister. I mean, if her boyfriend did it, that's fine. But if he didn't, I wouldn't want the real murderer to get away. And I guess you'd have a better chance of figuring it out if you had all the facts."

"Absolutely."

"So ... um ... there's something I think I should tell you."

"I'd really like to hear it."

"Could you meet me at the Old Orchard Mall at five tomorrow? By that fountain just outside Marshall Field's?"

Although Cassidy had never been to the north suburban mall, she instantly agreed. As she hung up the phone, she could feel some part of her perform a gleeful little dance. *Forest kept your business card and now he's going to rat out his parents. And then you'll know what's been going on behind those closed Hopewell doors.*

† † †

As soon as she was dressed the next morning, Cassidy went to the website for the Old Orchard Mall to look up the address. It was in Skokie, a suburb west of Evanston, not far from Northwestern. *A few clients in the morning, nobody else the rest of the day. Long as you're headed north, maybe you can visit Bryce.*

The boy's failure to contact them was a source of mounting anxiety. She felt a great need to see him in person, to get a sense of how he was faring, to find out what he was doing with his time. *Only eight thirty. Will he yell at you if you wake him up? Doesn't matter. Your need to check on him trumps his need to sleep.*

She tried Bryce's phone, then Angie's, but both numbers routed her to machines where she left messages. *Wonder if he's screening his calls. Refusing to talk to you or Zach.*

Since it appeared that Bryce might be avoiding her, she thought the best use of her time would be to find someone in the vicinity of the campus to interview. Flipping through her notepad, she came across the names of the two professors she'd met at Kit's wake. She left a message on each of their machines.

When her last session ended at one, she went upstairs to find the light on her answering machine blinking twice. She pushed the button, hoping to hear Bryce's voice, but the first message was from Jeff O'Donnell, the English teacher. "I'm booked solid except for a ten-minute slot at two-fifteen. If you can be at my office then, I'll squeeze you in." He gave directions to his office.

The second message was from Morrie Schweitzer, the heavy-set drama teacher. "Tell you what. You show up at my office around three, you can walk across campus with me."

† † †

She sat in a small room in front of an oak desk piled high with paper. Behind the desk, O'Donnell waited for her to begin. He was athletic and supple, with curly brown hair above a narrow face. His dark chocolate eyes were sincere. He had high cheekbones, a sensual mouth, and a firm chin. He gave off an air of quietude that made him easy to be with.

"What was Kit like in class?" Cassidy asked.

"Insightful. She saw things the others missed, and her enthusiasm for literature drew everyone else in. The only problem I had with her was that she always needed to be the center of attention."

"What do you know about her personal life?"

"Not much." Picking up a letter opener, he tapped it against the back of his left hand.

"But you do know something."

"I heard she had more than one boyfriend."

"You mean she slept around?"

"More like she had a couple of different relationships going at the same time. Although how anybody would have the energy for that is beyond me."

"Me too."

He gave Cassidy a shy smile.

"I've been told she was pretty flirtatious and I'll bet you were one of the men she flirted with."

"That seems to be a universal problem with college women. They all want to flirt with their teachers. My first year was kind of hard but I've learned not to offer any encouragement so they usually give up after a while. Prospective teachers should take classes on how to fend off moonstruck students."

"Kit was pretty determined. Did she give up the way the others did?"

He hesitated. "Eventually."

† † †

A knock on the door signaled that Cassidy's time was up. After thanking O'Donnell, she left the Liberal Arts building and found her way to the Dramatic Arts building. Sitting on a bench in the thin fall sunlight, she breathed in the restful campus atmosphere, with its stately stone buildings and gnarly old trees. Patches of yellow were beginning to show in the surrounding greenery.

She fished out her cell phone and tried Bryce's number again. This time he answered.

"I was afraid you'd stopped speaking to us," she said.

"I wasn't speaking to anybody," he replied in a flat tone, "but now I am. So, why'd you call?"

Because I needed to hear your voice. Because I'm worried sick about you. Because I want to smother you with unwanted attention and love.

"To see how you're doing."

"I'm fine."

"There's not a single thing in your life that's fine."

"All right, then, I'm shitty."

"Did you get Zach's message about the attorney?"

"Yeah, and no, I haven't called him yet."

"Why not?"

"Well, you see, I've been so busy with classes and homework and all these parties."

"Considering your girlfriend's dead and you're facing a murder charge, do you think you might acknowledge that you could be a little depressed?"

"Nah, I'm enjoying the hell out of life."

"Antidepressants really can help people get through difficult times."

"I'd rather medicate myself with liquor like Zach does."

Why is it that people who are happy to ingest all kinds of non-prescription mood-altering substances consider it a character defect to take meds?

Cassidy elicited a few more non-answers from Bryce, then gave up and said good-bye.

CHAPTER 20

SHE KNOCKED ON MORRIE SCHWEITZER'S DOOR AT a few minutes before three. He yelled "Come in," and she opened it to discover a student sitting in front of Morrie's desk.

"Give me a few more minutes," the professor said.

While Cassidy was waiting, a young woman wearing a tattered sweatshirt, a long knit skirt, and hiking boots approached her. "You have an appointment with Morrie?"

"Sort of." *The privilege of walking across campus with him.*

"Could I have a word with him before you go in? He's my drama coach, see, and I need to ask him a quick question about my assignment."

"Sure."

After the woman left, Morrie donned a ratty cardigan and pulled the straps of his backpack over his shoulders. "You ready?" he asked, running stubby fingers through his hair.

"Anytime you are."

"So, how you doing with the save-the-stepson campaign?"

Wish to hell I knew. "We're making progress, I think."

They trotted down a marble staircase and headed toward a glass double door.

"On one hand," Morrie said, "I admire your dedication. But on the other, I get truly pissed at families who move heaven and earth to protect their little darlings from the consequences of their own stupid behavior. That's why we have a whole generation of students who see themselves as the center of the universe."

"I'm a therapist and some of my clients have that same exaggerated sense of entitlement you're talking about. Sometimes I'd like to tell them to just get over themselves." *But you can't because they need your help as much or more than anybody.* "However, Bryce isn't like that. His expectations are pretty low. And I'm not on any mission to get him off if he's guilty. I genuinely believe he's innocent."

Morrie turned to look at her. "I wonder if you know Bryce as well as you think you do."

"What makes you say that?"

"I saw him in action once—at least I assume it was Bryce—and I got the impression he was as self-centered as they come. In fact, it struck me as odd that two people as narcissistic as Kit and Bryce could get along together."

"Did Kit tell you it was Bryce? What makes you think it was him?"

"I can't remember if she named any names, but he was her boyfriend, wasn't he?"

"She lived with Bryce but she was also seeing a dope dealer on the side."

"Oh, then it must've been the dealer she brought to rehearsal. They were sitting in the middle of the theater staging a porno love scene for all the world to see. After I kicked him out, he hung around the door and tried to pick up some new customers. Let me tell you, I was really pissed at Kit. Told her I'd yank her out of the production if she ever pulled anything like that again."

"What did he look like?"

Morrie rubbed his chin. "Thin, Hispanic, a small goatee."

"Do you recall when this happened?"

"About three weeks ago."

Just what you were looking for! Proof Raul was lying when he said he hadn't seen Kit since she moved in with Bryce.

"How did she react when you threatened to pull her out of the play?"

"Just laughed and said it'd be a flop without her."

"You know, I talked to Jeff O'Donnell and he didn't think she was so bad."

"She was playing nice girl in his class because he's so pretty."

"It seems like she came on to a lot of different men."

"That's pretty common with these prima donna types. Their egos need constant feeding."

"What about you? Were you one of the men she came on to?"

"Me? When she had O'Donnell in her sights?" He clapped his hands on his belly. "I don't think I quite fit the profile. It's the McDonald's french fries. My wife says I'm addicted." He halted in front of a staff parking lot. "Well, this is it."

"You were her coach and her director. I can't believe she didn't get seductive with you."

"Oh, she did—when I was handing out parts. But once she got what she wanted, the cooing stopped."

† † †

Six o'clock. The time Cassidy had decided she would officially give up on Forest, although emotionally she'd given up much earlier. At a quarter to five she sat down in front of the fountain, her mind bouncing from one thing to another as she tried to imagine what the boy had to tell her. At five o'clock she began pacing, her eyes scanning everyone within viewing range. At five fifteen she sat back down, reassuring herself that Forest was simply running late. *Another nonpunctual person like Angie.*

At five thirty she started compiling a mental list of all the possible reasons for Forest's failure to appear. *You went to the wrong fountain. Or he changed his mind. Or his parents caught him. Or he was simply playing with you in the first place.* When she ran out of reasons, she started berating herself for not having exchanged cell phone numbers with the boy.

At five forty-five she sat hunched forward, her elbows on her knees. She still glanced at each approaching shopper, but without any real hope. *You can't leave yet. It's still possible he's stuck in a mammoth traffic jam.*

At 6:01 she rewarded herself with a call to Zach, whom she had not contacted all day because she knew how busy he was.

"You waited a whole hour?" he said.

"I just knew he'd show up the minute I was gone. In fact, I still feel that way."

"Look, it's simple. Last night he was stoked. This morning it didn't seem like such a hot idea. Snitches stand me up all the time. Considering how much you hate to wait, you deserve a medal for being so patient."

Dropping the cell phone back in her purse, Cassidy reflected on the implications of Forest's call. *Said he has info that might help identify the killer. Must be something that points to a family member. You have to get Forest to talk.*

† † †

Disappointment weighing heavily upon her, Cassidy drove home, went upstairs to the bedroom, and found that she had one message on her answering machine.

"This is Angie. You've got to call me right away." The voice was gasping and breathless. "Bryce just left to go to the townhouse and he's so down on himself I'm afraid for him to be alone."

Her chest tightening, Cassidy sat at her desk and dialed the younger woman's number.

"Oh thank God. Bryce went off and forgot his cell phone and I left messages for everyone on his speed dial, but you're the only one who's called back. I've just been going crazy."

"Why did he leave?"

"We shouldn't waste time talking. You should just get over there right away."

One part of Cassidy wanted to jump in the car and start driving, but another part knew she'd be better prepared to work with Bryce if she understood what had brought on his sudden retreat to the townhouse.

"I need to know what happened."

"Gosh, this is so hard. Well, to begin with, he insisted on going to classes and it was just awful. Nobody would talk to him. They all looked the other way and pretended he wasn't there. When I came home this afternoon, he was watching TV and drinking beer. I fixed something for him to eat but he wouldn't touch it. Then I got him to turn off the television and talk to me. I thought it would help but it just made things worse. He kept going over everything he thought he'd done wrong. He told me they'd had this big fight before Kit was killed. He even seemed to think he could have saved her if only he'd called 911 or gone downstairs right away." She paused. "Maybe I shouldn't tell you this, but he said Zach was a jerk with women and he was just as bad." Another pause. "From the way he was talking, I thought he might be … you know."

Oh shit! Making himself feel worthless. Maybe even justifying that he doesn't deserve to live.

"I should have called the cops, shouldn't I?" Angie said. "The only reason I didn't is I knew how mad he'd be."

"I think it's better you didn't. Having the cops bang on his door would be just one more humiliation. Now tell me, how long ago did he leave?"

"It's been almost two hours."

"Have you tried calling him?"

"I know I should have … but I was afraid he wouldn't want to talk to me."

"Did he say anything about hurting himself?"

"If he'd done that, I *would've* called the cops."

"Then he's probably fine." *You know the really serious ones don't give warnings.* "Okay, I need to hang up now and try calling Bryce."

† † †

He answered on the ninth ring. "Go 'way. Don't wanna talk to anybody." The phone clicked down.

Cassidy let out a breath. *Due for a hangover in the morning but at least he's alive.* Despite what she'd told Angie, Cassidy would have called the police if Bryce hadn't answered.

She wondered whether or not she should go to the townhouse, considering how clearly Bryce had stated his wish to be left alone. *Have to check up on him. People've been known to aspirate in their own vomit.*

After giving Angie a quick call back, she drove to Bryce's block. Her stomach lurched. The Miata, which had been parked in the drive every other time she'd visited, wasn't there.

Out cruising with all that alcohol in his system? Maybe looking for an embankment to plow into?

Stop it! He probably just put his car in the garage.

Cassidy parked and got out of the car. A pale light filtered through the living room drapes; a bright light shone from the uncovered windows in the dining room. The second story was dark. She pressed the doorbell twice, then reached into her purse for the key. *Good thing you made Zach give it to you, even though you didn't think you'd need it at the time.*

In the living room she found mussed sofa cushions, empty beer bottles, and a garbage bag filled with Bryce's belongings. Hoping he was in bed, she sprinted to the top of the stairs, where she could see that the doors to the study, the bathroom, and the bedroom were all open. She turned on the hall light and slipped quietly into the bedroom. He wasn't there. She tried to think if there was anything more she could do before she had to report in to Angie that Bryce was missing.

You didn't look in the garage.

No reason for him to be there.

Oh yes there is.

She rushed into the kitchen and opened the door that led to the garage. The Miata sat in front of her, its top up, its engine running, an indistinct figure behind the wheel. Taking a deep breath and holding it, she dropped her purse, turned on the garage light and hurried down the short flight of stairs to the concrete floor. *No—wait! Open the garage door first.* Scrambling back up the stairs, she searched for the pad and pressed it. The door slid upward. She went to the driver's side window, reached through it, and touched Bryce's arm.

Warm!

'Course it's warm—he was alive less than an hour ago. Doesn't mean he's alive now. Knowing that carbon monoxide could kill in a matter of minutes, she didn't take time to search for a pulse.

Turn off the engine.

No—leave it on and roll the car out of the garage.

Wedging her head and shoulders into the tight space between Bryce and the steering wheel, she shifted into neutral and pushed the car backward. It moved slowly until the rear wheels reached the downward slope of the driveway, then picked up speed. Trotting along beside it, Cassidy felt as though the Miata was about to get away from her. She scurried through the garage-door opening, her right hip bumping up hard against the wooden frame.

When the front wheels hit the incline, the speed increased again and she suddenly realized that the car was on a crash course with a vehicle parked on the opposite side of the street. Thrusting her head inside the window a second time, she shoved the gearshift into drive, causing the car to slow down. Then she yanked the key out of the ignition and the Miata came to a shuddering halt crosswise in the middle of the street, its rear end only inches from the car behind it.

Cassidy let out her breath in a whoosh. Her mind went momentarily blank, then it hit her that she had to get the paramedics as soon as possible. Going back through the garage, she grabbed her purse from the kitchen floor and dialed 911. Since she didn't know Bryce's address, she had to go out the front door and read the house number posted above the entrance.

"I don't know if he's alive," she told the dispatcher, after explaining what had happened. Clicking off, she sank down on the top step and tried to pull herself together. As soon as her legs would hold her, she returned to the Miata. Bryce's body had been disturbed by Cassidy's thrusting herself in and out of the window. His head had fallen forward and his torso was tilted sideways. She straightened his body and raised his head, then opened the door. His skin was pale. His eyes were closed. She couldn't detect the rise and fall of breathing.

Because he's unconscious. People don't breathe as hard when they're unconscious, do they? She grasped his wrist and searched for a pulse, moving her thumb from one spot to another, not quite sure where to find it. Then she felt something. A faint movement. *He's alive! Oh God, he's alive!*

When the fire truck and ambulance pulled up, she was pacing beside the Miata, hugging herself against the shivery feeling inside her. Two paramedics, a man and a woman, jumped out of the ambulance, removed a stretcher from the back, and hurried to the Miata, while several firemen climbed down from the truck. Neighbors were starting to cluster around the vehicles.

"What's his name?" the male paramedic asked.

"Bryce Palomar."

The man shook Bryce's shoulder and called his name but the boy didn't respond. Then the woman leaned over him, blocking Cassidy's view.

As Cassidy tried to move closer, a fireman grasped her arm and pulled her away from the car. "You have to stand back."

"No! I need to see what they're doing." She tried to jerk her arm away but he wouldn't let go.

Don't be stupid. Of course you have to get out of the way.

She stepped back and the fireman moved off to the side. As the medics worked over Bryce, she caught glimpses of what was happening. They folded down the Miata's top, then attached an oxygen mask to his face. After that, they lifted him out of the car and laid him on a stretcher. While the man was strapping Bryce down, the woman approached Cassidy.

"Does he take any medication?"

"I don't think so."

"Allergic to anything?"

"I don't know."

"We're taking him to St. Francis."

The woman headed back toward the stretcher, with Cassidy dogging her steps. "He's going to be all right, isn't he?"

"You'll have to talk to somebody at the hospital."

The medics carried the stretcher into the back of the ambulance.

"Can I ride with you?"

The woman jumped down. "You a relative?"

"His stepmother."

"Okay, you can come along." She slammed the ambulance doors shut.

"No, wait! I want to ride in back."

"Gotta sit in front and buckle yourself in. It's regulations."

CHAPTER 21

"A SUICIDE ATTEMPT!" ZACH SAID. CASSIDY HAD REACHED him on cell phone as the ambulance arrived at the hospital.

"Yes, and he meant it too. Some attempts really are a cry for help, but what Bryce did was as lethal as you can get. He clearly intended to die."

"I'll be there as soon as I can."

"This may take awhile and there's no reason for you to waste time sitting around an ER."

"You just said that because you want to impress me with how independent you are, right? You really know there's no way you could stop me from coming to the hospital."

"I was pretty much counting on it."

"I assume somebody put the Miata back in the garage."

"The paramedic said the firemen would take care of it."

Finishing with Zach, Cassidy called Angie, who became hysterical when she learned of the suicide attempt. The young woman went on and on, blaming herself for Bryce's despondency, while Cassidy tried to soothe her and talk her down.

When Angie sounded calmer, Cassidy said, "I have to get off the phone now. I'll let you know as soon as I hear anything."

"You won't need to call me. I'm cabbing it over to the hospital."

Oh no! I'm just not up to being her personal therapist tonight.

"I'm afraid that wouldn't be a good idea," Cassidy replied, thinking fast. "You saw Bryce at his worst today and I'm pretty sure he won't be ready to face you yet."

There was a silence filled with resistance. Angie put up a few arguments but in the end Cassidy convinced her to stay home.

Stuffing her phone in her purse, Cassidy vowed to cease communication with everyone other than Bryce and Zach. *You had to work harder in that five-minute conversation with Angie than you do in most hour-long sessions with clients.*

† † †

After a two-hour wait, Cassidy and Zach got to their feet as a stocky, gray-haired nurse approached them.

"You can see Bryce now. He's been awake for some time but he kept saying he wasn't ready for you to come in yet. I explained that he couldn't get out of here till he made arrangements with you folks to take him home, and he suddenly decided he was ready after all." She patted Cassidy's arm. "These kids! They'll drive you crazy."

"You're right about that."

The nurse led them into a small room where they found Bryce sitting up on a cart.

"Sorry I didn't let you in right away," he said. "I just wanted some time to myself to see if I could remember anything. I knew you'd have questions."

"You don't remember?" Cassidy asked.

"I remember going into the townhouse, drinking some beer, talking to you on the telephone, then falling asleep on the couch. Next thing I know, I'm in the hospital."

Cassidy's eyes narrowed. *Could be he blacked out. Or could be he doesn't want to admit he just tried to kill himself. Maybe using the drinking as an excuse.*

"You're telling me you don't remember going out to the garage or getting in the car?"

"Not any of it." He stared at some point beyond Cassidy's head. "Last year you took that gun away from me. Back then there were times when I thought about offing myself. Sometimes I'd take the gun out of my drawer and fantasize about sticking it down my throat. But this time I wasn't even thinking about hurting myself." He looked at Cassidy. "You said I was depressed and it's true. This is the worst it's been since my mother was killed. But I feel like I can handle it now. Even if they send me to the joint, I'll survive."

So maybe he is telling the truth. Maybe he didn't intend to kill himself. She caught her lip between her teeth. *Or maybe somebody else put him behind the wheel of his car. No, that's crazy. You have to get hold of yourself.*

Bryce fastened his eyes on Zach. "I suppose you don't believe me."

"I think there's a strong possibility you blacked out and don't remember what you did."

"But you're not sure."

"I don't know that I can ever be sure of anything I don't personally observe."

"My word isn't good enough?"

"Look, I wouldn't blame you if you embellished your story a little. People prevaricate all the time. I try to make a habit of not lying to you or Cass, but if I have a good enough reason, I'll lie to pretty much everybody else."

Cassidy glared at her husband. *So why doesn't he fib a little and tell Bryce he believes him?*

The boy turned his head away. "So what happens next?"

"We take you to our house." She braced herself for an argument.

"Yeah, I figured."

She wondered if she should wait until the next day to tell him the rest. *No, do it now. That way he'll have a chance to get used to the idea.* "And tomorrow I get you in to see a psychiatrist who will undoubtedly prescribe medication. And then I make sure you take it."

"I'm too tired to fight you. Why don't you wait in the other room while I get dressed."

Not just tired. Humiliated, beaten-up, and defeated.

In the waiting room, Cassidy addressed Zach. "I don't get it. You just told us you lie to practically everybody, so why not tell a little white lie to make Bryce think you trust him?"

"I suppose that's what I should've done. I don't know why, but when it comes to Bryce I can't seem to do anything right."

"You do a lot of things right." *Just not lately.*

"This business of not lying to you or Bryce. It started when I first realized how important you were to me. Since I have such an aptitude for deception, whenever I'm in a sticky situation, I'm tempted to improvise my way out of it. I was afraid that if I ever started lying to you, I'd just keep doing it, and eventually you'd dump me. So I forced myself not to lie to you at all, and it seems to have carried over to Bryce."

"When you explain it that way, I have to agree. Honesty *is* the best policy where Bryce and I are concerned."

A few minutes later the nurse told them to get their car and wait for Bryce at the emergency room entrance. As Zach drew up to the curb, Cassidy called Angie and told her that Bryce was on his way to their house. Looking through the hospital window, Cassidy could see Bryce seated in a wheelchair in the waiting room, a volunteer standing beside him. Cassidy went inside, and together they walked out to the car, where Bryce climbed into the Subaru's back seat.

Zach said, "We have to go by the townhouse so Cass can pick up her Toyota."

"That's good 'cause I left a bag of stuff in the living room."

Parking near Bryce's door, Zach said to Cassidy, "Give me the key and I'll go get Bryce's things."

She grimaced. "You don't need it. I went flying out of there and never thought to lock up."

"That's all right," Bryce said. "I forgive you."

Zach went into the house and Cassidy stayed in the car. Although she was certain it would be safe to leave Bryce alone, she couldn't bring herself to get out of the Subaru until Zach returned. A short time later he switched off the house lights and exited through the front door.

He handed the bag to Bryce. "There's a pane missing in the garage window. That may have bought you a little more time."

"So there's an upside to letting things go."

"The upside is in having a stepmother who's determined to keep you alive. And don't you forget it when you feel like giving her a hard time over the psychiatrist."

After a short silence, Bryce said, "I'm glad you found me, Cass. I really don't want to die."

"Otherwise," Zach added, "everything was locked except the front door and there's no sign of forced entry."

"Did you think there might be?"

"Not really."

So I'm not the only one who thought somebody might have helped Bryce into his car.

†††

Friday morning Cassidy got up well ahead of the alarm to await a return call from Phillip Helfer, the psychiatrist she referred clients to for medication. She'd left a message on his machine the night before explaining Bryce's situation and asking the doctor to please find some way to squeeze her stepson in. When Helfer called to tell her he had a ten o'clock cancellation, she breathed a sigh of relief. She was aware that new patients frequently had to wait weeks for an appointment.

Getting Bryce to the psychiatrist's office by ten meant that she had to reschedule her own nine o'clock client. She dialed his number and said, "I'm sorry to do this at the last minute, but I'm going to have to switch our appointment. Since I'm the one canceling, I won't charge you for our next session."

"This has been kind of a rough week. Any chance you could fit me in later today?"

You could make time for him, couldn't you?

Bryce nearly killed himself. You have to be as available to him as you can.

"I'm sorry." Not allowing herself to make excuses, she said in a voice dripping with apology, "You'll have to wait till your regular time next week."

She tiptoed downstairs to make sure Bryce was where he belonged. Dressed in sweats, he was zonked out on the sofa, which was several inches shorter than his six foot plus frame. One of his legs was bent at the knee; the other dangled over the sofa's edge. His bag of clothes sat on the floor beside him. Satisfied that he was okay, she went back upstairs, feeling creaky and sore from the bruise she'd acquired when her hip smacked the side of the garage.

It was nearly nine when Bryce, clad in wrinkled khakis and a dark green sweatshirt, came in and sat in Zach's chair. "So now what?" he asked.

"You have a doctor's appointment at ten. Since the office is here in Oak Park, we won't need to leave till a quarter to."

Starshine moseyed in and jumped into his lap. "Hey, it's my favorite kitty," he said, cradling her on his chest. The calico purred loudly and rubbed her face against his. A bond had been formed between Bryce and the cat when he'd stayed at their house before.

"So you're not going to give me any trouble about seeing the psychiatrist?" Cassidy asked.

"Yeah, I am." He made mooshy noises at Starshine for a minute or so, then gently put her down. "I got a good night's sleep. I feel fine. I don't need to see any shrink. What happened last night was just a fluke. A drinking thing. I'll lay off the beer, I promise."

Sure he feels better. Because someone is finally going to step in and get him the help he needs.

"Dr. Helfer will do an assessment. He'll evaluate you for depression, anxiety, suicidality, substance abuse, and a host of other things. If he concludes that you're significantly depressed, he'll put you on medication."

"But isn't it normal to feel depressed when someone dies?"

"It's a matter of degree. When people make suicide attempts—even if they don't do it consciously—it usually means they've fallen into a black hole and need help getting out of it."

"All he's going to do is talk to me?"

"Yes, but I'm going to sit in on your appointment so I can provide an alternative point of view if I think you're fudging."

"What?" Dismay showed on his face. "You can't do that! What happened to doctor-patient confidentiality? This has gotta be a breach of somebody's ethics."

† † †

The appointment held no surprises. Dr. Helfer asked Bryce a number of questions and, as far as Cassidy could tell, the boy answered honestly. Next the psychiatrist explained the link between depression and brain chemistry, then he provided information about the antidepressant he intended to prescribe. He finished by laying out all the reasons Bryce would be better off if he followed through and took his medication. On the way home, Cassidy stopped to get the prescription filled.

As they came in the back door, she said, "I have three things I need to talk to you about."

"I let you drag me to the psychiatrist—isn't that enough?"

"Would you like something to drink? There's pop in the refrigerator or I could make coffee if you want."

"I thought you had a client."

Cassidy filled a glass of water for herself. "Let's go sit in the living room." Piling the blanket and sheet Bryce had used on one end of the sofa, she sat on the other. He lowered his lanky body onto the facing loveseat.

"Do you have any idea what it was like for me finding you in your car?" Cassidy asked. "I thought you might be dead. I thought I might never get the chance to see you graduate, or hear you tell me about your first real job, or sit in the front row at your wedding. That I might never be able to cook Sunday dinner for you, or tell you all the things I haven't told you yet."

Leaning forward, Bryce dropped his head and squeezed the back of his neck.

"I've never even told you that I love you. God, I don't know what's wrong with me that I went all this time without saying it."

"You don't need to say it," Bryce mumbled. "I know already."

"Do you also know that I couldn't stand it if you killed yourself? I just couldn't stand it. I'd blame myself for the rest of my life. I'd never get over it."

"I kinda do."

"Unless you convince me that you'll take your medication and start seeing a therapist, I'll be constantly worried about you. I'll wake up in the middle of the night and wonder if you're still alive. I'll call you ten times a day. I'll break out in a cold sweat every time you don't answer the phone."

"What do I have to do to convince you?"

"Tell me in a way that sounds like you mean it."

Gazing downward, he said, "Okay, I'll do those things you want."

"Would you look at me and say it again?"

He continued to stare at the floor for a moment longer, then raised his head. His dark eyes shone with emotion. "I will, Cass. I'll take the drugs and see a therapist." He paused. "I guess you knew I was planning to toss the pills."

"I had a hunch." *Given all the clients you've had who prefer misery to medication, it's not a huge leap.*

Bryce glanced at his watch. "Didn't you tell me you had a twelve o'clock session?"

"You don't want to tackle the other two items on my list?"

"I'm kinda wrung out. Why don't we wait until after your client?"

"You'll still be here?"

"I might go get something to eat but I'll be back."

"You want to borrow my car?"

"Nah, I'll walk or hop an el."

Cassidy went into her waiting room and turned on the oldies station she used as white noise to cover the sound of voices from her office. Moving on into the office itself, she plumped the cushions on her sofa and picked the dead leaves off her coleus.

Although everything she'd said to Bryce was true, she knew she'd deliberately set out to manipulate him and she didn't feel especially good about it. But she didn't see that she had any other choice. *He wouldn't have taken his meds for himself, but he might take them for you.*

Or he might not. He could just dump them in the trash and throw himself off a bridge. And even if he does take them, they won't kick in for a few weeks. Medication is never a silver bullet.

CHAPTER 22

AFTER HER CLIENT LEFT, SHE FOUND A note from Bryce on the table informing her that he'd gone to get his car. She went upstairs and started paging through her spiral notepad. As she read about the Thorazine, she remembered that she'd completed only one out of the four pages of links in her search on Dr. Winslow Leonard. She was in the process of booting up when the phone rang.

"This is Victor. I was in the neighborhood and I have the check for the defense attorney with me so I thought I'd drop it off."

Why is he driving around with the check instead of messengering it to Zach? Maybe he's disorganized and that's why he isn't as prosperous as he should be. She told him she'd be available until three, then went downstairs and removed all evidence from the living room that Bryce had spent the night.

The front doorbell rang less than five minutes later. Victor came inside the entryway, his narrow face harried.

"I appreciate your bringing the check by," Cassidy said.

"I know I'm a little late but things have been somewhat hectic." He removed an envelope from his portfolio and handed it to her. "By the way, I hear Bryce is staying with you. Is he around now?"

Surprised by the question, she paused briefly before replying. "Not at the moment. How did you find out he was here?"

"That girl—Angie—she told me. I've been leaving messages on his cell ever since he got out of Cook County, but he never gets back to me. So this morning I called Angie and she said he was with you."

"We've been having the same problem," Cassidy said. "There was one time I got lucky and he answered but he wouldn't tell me anything."

"The best I got was a message on my machine giving me Angie's number. But now that you have him under your roof you'll be able to keep tabs on him." Victor gave her a probing look. "Angie was a little evasive about his reason for leaving her apartment."

"Who can get kids that age to tell you anything?" Cassidy said, becoming evasive herself.

"So how's he doing? Is he going to classes? Has he made an appointment to see the defense attorney?"

"I think it would be better if you talked to Bryce directly."

"I *can't* talk to him if he won't return my calls." Lines of frustration appeared on Victor's face. "It's driving me crazy not having any idea what he's up to."

Cassidy experienced a surge of sympathy. *Same way you felt. After all Victor's done for the kid, he deserves to know what's going on.*

Yes, but Bryce's story belongs to Bryce and you can't go spreading it around. "The next time I see him I'll get on his case for not calling you."

†††

Cassidy returned to the computer and typed "Winslow Leonard, M.D." into the Google search box. Continuing from where she'd left off, she read the next two pages of links, which told her of conferences where he'd been a presenter, papers he'd written, boards he was a member of. *Certainly sounds reputable enough. But then so did Enron's CEO.*

In the middle of page four, she came across a first-person essay he'd written for The Coalition to Promote Healthy Families. *What an innocuous name. Sort of like Pro-Life. Nobody could be against it. Except I bet if I knew more about this coalition, I would be.*

In the article Leonard compared his life to the life of his boyhood friend, Roger. During their early years, both boys had been happy, cheerful kids who played sports and received good grades. Then Roger's parents divorced, his stay-at-home mother went to work, and Roger became a latchkey kid. Not long after that, Roger was caught painting graffiti on the school walls, his grades fell, and he began throwing rocks at the neighbor's dog.

Hate this kind of drivel. Intact families are good, divorced families are bad. If you love your children, you'll stick by your spouse no matter what kind of sociopath he may be.

The final paragraph read:

ROGER AND I STARTED OFF WITH FAMILIES THAT HAD MUCH IN COMMON, AND NOW THERE ARE NO SIMILARITIES BETWEEN THE ADULT CHILDREN IN ROGER'S FAMILY AND THE ADULT CHILDREN IN MINE. ROGER'S BROTHER HAS BEEN ARRESTED THREE TIMES, ROGER HIMSELF IS UNEMPLOYED, AND THEY'VE HAD FIVE DIVORCES BETWEEN THEM. IN CONTRAST, I'M THE DIRECTOR OF A MENTAL HEALTH CENTER, MY SISTER EILEEN IS THE MOTHER OF THREE BEAUTIFUL CHILDREN AS WELL AS THE FLUTIST IN THE CHICAGO SYMPHONY ORCHESTRA, AND MY BROTHER OWEN IS THE ESTEEMED SENATOR FROM ILLINOIS.

Owen Leonard is his brother? Our kill-the-abortionists downstate senator?

She sat back and thought about it. Hopewell was a right-wing minister with enough clout to draw a renowned congressman like Henry Hyde to his daughter's wake. Hopewell and Senator Leonard were undoubtedly political buddies, so there was a good chance the minister knew the senator's brother as well.

But what does this mean? A connection between Hopewell and the psychiatrist must have some bearing on Kit's getting the Thorazine, but I have no idea what it is.

Hoping that Zach would be able to make sense of it, she emailed a copy of the essay to his computer at work.

† † †

When she went into the kitchen to get peanut butter cups after her three o'clock session, she noticed a half empty can of cat food enclosed in a ziplock bag next to Starshine's bowl. Having heard the back door open and close while she was in her office, she knew who the cat-feeder was. The brown nuggets that had been in the calico's bowl since breakfast were in the trash. *So Starshine's enlisted another ally in the food wars.*

Upstairs she found Bryce in Zach's chair in the den, the television on, Starshine ensconced in his lap. "See, I told you I'd come back," he said.

"I was beginning to think you'd blown me off," Cassidy replied, settling into her own chair.

"Would I do that to you? Well, I might, but not today. I went to get my car and then I remembered I'd left my cell at Angie's and had to go pick it up."

"Now that you're back, we can take up the next item on my agenda."

"And here I was just starting to relax." Bryce extended two fingers and scratched beneath the calico's chin, the cat stretching her throat and purring in response. "Right before you came up I was thinking that Starshine's the only female who never gives me any grief and that I should stay away from women and get a cat instead."

"What a perfect lead-in for what I wanted to talk to you about. Angie."

His face went tense. "I don't want to discuss her."

"You told Angie that Zach was a jerk with women and you thought you were just as bad."

"I don't remember what I said."

"I think you said that because you had sex with Angie and then felt like a jerk afterward."

"Cass, please, this is none of your business."

"I suppose you don't want to think about it. You'd prefer to push it out of your mind and pretend it never happened."

Bryce avoided her eyes.

"At least tell me this. Did you use a condom?"

"Yeah, of course. I always do."

"You have to talk about this. If you don't, you're going to continue to feel like a jerk, and this is not a time when you can afford to have one more thing to hold against yourself."

"Oh, and you're gonna tell me it was perfectly okay to fuck somebody who's crazy about me even though I have no interest in her?"

"No, it wasn't. But it also wasn't more than a two or three on the scale of bad things people do. Right now I'm sure Angie's feeling hurt and rejected, and I can see that you're mentally kicking yourself all the way around the block, but in the long run it will be fine."

"You know, I think I understand why Zach complains about being married to a shrink. You have this amazing ability to twist things around so black is white and visa versa."

"Angie will get through this."

"Yeah, but that doesn't excuse my behavior. I knew she considers sex a sin. I just wanted comfort and was only thinking about myself. I let her assume I was interested when I'm not."

"And you don't think that happens all the time?"

What are you saying? That bad behavior can be justified on the grounds that other people do it?

I'm just saying that Bryce needs to put this in perspective and stop beating himself up.

Bryce ran a hand over the top of his head. "If I'd done it with anybody else it wouldn't be so bad. But Angie's already afraid that no guy will ever like her and now I've made it worse."

"You've rejected her as a romantic interest. But you've also made it possible for her to have her first sexual experience with someone who's sweet and gentle and cares about her as a friend. What you did was selfish, but we all do selfish things on occasion and I think you're making this into a much bigger deal than it needs to be."

"You honestly don't think it was that bad?"

"I'm sure Angie's feeling some pain over the fact that she had sex with you, but she also has a lot of resources. She has prayer, her minister, a loving God she can turn to for forgiveness. I can't imagine this is going to do her any long-term damage and I really believe it might do some good."

"So I'm not as big a jerk as Zach?"

"Not even close."

"All right, I'll take your word for it. So—now that we've had our little chat—can I go back to the townhouse?"

"What?"

"Look, I know you want to keep me here but it's not going to work. I've got three eight o'clock classes and there's no way I'm going to drive from Oak Park to Northwestern during rush hour."

"You still plan to attend classes? I thought you had a pretty rough day yesterday."

"I have to keep busy. It's the most important thing. The only way I know to do that is to keep going to classes and bury myself in homework."

"Angie said your friends wouldn't even look at you."

"I'm better off in a class where everybody ignores me than in an apartment staring at the wall."

Wouldn't you do the same? You would if you had the courage.

"Isn't it hard to be at the townhouse with all its reminders?"

"Sure it is. But that's where I live. All my stuff is there. I just have to get used to being in the townhouse without her."

He's being more adult about this than you are.

"Okay, I won't try to stop you. But I do want to drive down to the townhouse and fix you dinner."

"I thought you didn't cook."

"I've been learning. I was planning to invite you over and surprise you. I haven't tackled anything very complicated yet but I can put a simple meal on the table."

"Sure, you can come. As long as we can order pizza if the dinner flops."

"I only have two more things I want you to do," Cassidy said.

"More? I thought we were finished with your list."

"The first is to make an appointment with the defense attorney."

"I did already. I'm going to see him Monday. So what else do you want?"

"Call Victor. He's concerned … " *Don't lecture!* "Just call him, okay?"

Promising he would, Bryce agreed to meet her later at the townhouse and took off.

† † †

Cassidy decided that, as long as they had pizza as a backup, she could take the risk of attempting chicken breasts again. She'd tried them once before and they'd come out tough, but she thought that was because she'd overcooked them. She also picked up a package of prepared rice, vegetables for a salad, and six more cans of food for Milton.

Considering that you're probably going to be stuck feeding him for the rest of his life, you might as well buy a case.

Yes, but I don't want to admit to myself what I've done.

Then she added milk, fruit, cereal, bread, and peanut butter to her basket. *So Bryce won't have to live on fast food.*

When they were seated with their dinners in front of them, she asked, "What can you tell me about Forest Hopewell?"

"Kit and Forest were pretty tight. She seemed to feel like she had to watch over him or something. Sort of like a second mother. I always figured brothers and sisters were supposed to fight, but what would I know?"

Swallowing a bite of chicken, Cassidy congratulated herself that it didn't remind her of used chewing gum. "I'd like to talk to Forest but I don't want to call his house. Do you think Angie could help me out with this?"

"She probably could."

"Did you see her when you picked up your phone?"

"No."

"Are you avoiding her?"

He took his time filling his fork and raising it to his mouth.

"You can't do that."

"Just watch me."

"No, listen, if you just disappear on her, it'll turn this whole thing into a big emotional trauma. She'll feel abandoned. She'll feel like you hate her. You could hurt her so deeply she'd never trust men again. But if you go back to being friends, it won't seem like this huge rejection and you'll both be able to put it behind you and be okay."

"I don't know what to say."

"Tell her the truth."

"I could say I'm not ready yet, that it's too soon after Kit's death."

"Then she'd get her hopes up. She'd start fantasizing that once you're over Kit, you'd fall in love with her. It would be kinder to say you just don't feel any chemistry."

"Oh God, Cass, that's awful. I'd hate it if anybody said that to me."

"Would you like it better if they simply disappeared? Or threw you little crumbs of hope?"

"Yeah, definitely. I'd take the disappearing act, any day."

After they finished eating, Bryce banished her from the kitchen, declaring that the cleanup was all his. With nothing more to do, she called Angie.

Chapter 23

"Is he going to be staying with you?" Angie asked as Cassidy came through the doorway.

"He convinced me he'd be better off at the townhouse." She parked herself on one end of a sagging sofa, the only place to sit other than a desk chair and an unmade bed.

Angie plunked down on the opposite end. "You didn't leave him alone, did you? How do you know he won't try again?"

"He's in a much better state of mind. My gut says he'll be okay."

"But what if—"

Cassidy reached over and took hold of Angie's hand. "There isn't anything more to be done. We just have to trust him. Now, tell me how you're doing."

Lowering her head, Angie yanked at a handful of short curly hair. "If only I'd done things differently. If only I hadn't let things get out of control or let certain things happen."

"I know you and Bryce had sex." Cassidy deliberately put it in a blunt way to make it seem ordinary and insignificant.

Her cheeks flushing, the college student stared at Cassidy. "He told you?"

"I guessed. I don't think Bryce would ever volunteer that kind of information."

"I just wanted to comfort him. I knew it was wrong. I knew I shouldn't be doing it. And—the absolute worst—I told him I loved him. No wonder he went running out of here. Now I'm afraid he'll never speak to me again." Angie took off her glasses and wiped the folds of skin beneath her eyes.

"I understand that this is difficult, but I really believe both of you will get through it and be okay. And there's no reason you can't continue the friendship you had before." *Unless he runs out on her, in which case I'll kill him.*

"Now I need to talk to you about Forest," Cassidy said, changing the subject. She told Angie that the boy had set up a meeting for yesterday, then failed to appear.

"That's weird. He doesn't seem like the type to just leave somebody hanging like that."

"I want to hear what he has to say about not showing up, then try to arrange another meeting. But I'm afraid his parents will get suspicious if I call."

"You want me to do it? They wouldn't think twice if I asked to speak to him."

"That's exactly what I was hoping for."

"You don't think Kit's parents had anything to do with the murder, do you? They're such godly people. There's just no way they'd ever hurt anyone."

Evangelical parents killing their daughter because she embarrassed them? It does sound pretty absurd.

"All I know is, Forest had something to tell me." *And he called late at night and whispered over the phone.*

Angie dialed the Hopewell number and asked for Forest. Moments later she put the phone down and looked at Cassidy. "The housekeeper says his grandmother's ill and he went to spend a few days with her. But that doesn't make sense. They wouldn't take him out of school unless she was practically dying, and then the whole family would go."

"I guess his parents found out he was planning to talk to me and sent him away."

Angie shook her head. "Pastor Hopewell wouldn't do that."

† † †

A silvery crescent moon hung in the sky by the time Cassidy walked in the back door. Starshine jumped down from the waiting room chair and uttered a series of scolding *mwats* as she attempted to lead her human toward the bowl on the counter.

"I suppose you're annoyed because I was gone so long and wasn't here to feed you. But since I keep giving you food you hate, I can't see why you'd even want me around. Unless you're hoping I'll cook Hamburger Helper again."

Cassidy went into the kitchen, where she discovered that the can Bryce had left in a ziplock bag was now upside down on the floor. Starshine lumbered over to it and prodded it with her nose.

"Oh what a disappointment. If it had only landed right side up, you could have torn through the plastic with your fangs."

Starshine said *mwat* again, this time in her begging voice. As Cassidy retrieved the can, the calico jumped onto the counter, where Cassidy scrutinized the cat's body for signs of weight loss. *She must be down a little. Look at all the meals she's missed. If you take in fewer calories you have to shed pounds, don't you?*

Starshine did not appear any smaller than she had at the beginning of the diet. *But that's because she's sitting. Cats sit fat and walk lean. And the fur. The fur makes them look puffy.*

You're grasping at straws, looking for any possible excuse to give her the wet food.

Promising herself she would shop for a more appealing brand of diet food when she had time, Cassidy emptied the can Bryce had opened into Starshine's bowl, then filled another bowl for Milton and took it outside.

She was just coming into the bedroom when the phone rang.

"Sorry I didn't call earlier," Zach said. "The time got away from me. So, how's Bryce doing?"

She told her husband that Bryce had returned to the townhouse and appeared to be doing well, but she didn't mention his sexual encounter with Angie.

"I'm glad to hear it. He's been on my mind all day."

"You could have called him and told him that." *Zach would much rather go through me than talk to his son directly. No wonder the kid's pissed so much of the time.*

"I honestly didn't think of it."

"The Hopewells have spirited Forest away," Cassidy said, going on to fill in the details. "This is driving me nuts. I can't stand it that there's this big family secret and no way to break the code."

"You'll think of something. You always do."

"When are you coming home? I feel like I haven't seen you in days."

"Not till after midnight. Of course, I could wake you when I get in," Zach said in a suggestive tone.

Once you zonk out, sex has no appeal.

"No, that's all right. I miss you, but not enough to lose sleep over."

He laughed. "Somehow that doesn't surprise me."

† † †

When she finished talking to Zach, she logged on to the computer and ran a search on the pastor's name, turning up six pages of hits. *Looks like Zach may beat you to bed after all.* Clicking through the entries, she read about boards Hopewell had served on, assemblages he'd spoken at, activities his church had sponsored. She passed up a couple of treatises he'd written, then skimmed a recent interview in which he mentioned the ages of his children. She learned that Kit was twenty when she died, Forest was fifteen, and Heidi seven.

Shortly after midnight Zach came into the computer room, his eyes displaying the dull look of someone who'd spent too many hours staring at a monitor. "Any luck?"

She shook her head. "I didn't really expect to uncover any dirty little secrets on the Net, but I didn't know what else to do."

"You planning to come to bed? I'm too tired to have anything other than sleep on my mind, but it would be nice to spoon for a while."

"I'd really like to finish all these pages before I turn in."

"That's fine." He massaged her shoulders, then leaned over to kiss her cheek. "See you in the morning," he said, heading into the bedroom.

After reading the last hit on page six, Cassidy returned to an earlier entry: an announcement in a Peoria newsletter of a going-away party for Pastor Hopewell, who'd received a call to serve a church in Winnetka. According to the announcement, he'd spent ten years as minister of the Peoria church. From the date on the newsletter, Cassidy ascertained that the move had taken place seven years earlier. *Interesting coincidence. Heidi born around the same time the family relocated.*

Cassidy considered paying a visit to the Peoria church, but she didn't know whether she'd be able to find any former parishioners with gossip to pass on, and if she did, whether they'd be willing to pass it on to a stranger.

Seven years since he left. Not much chance of finding anybody privy to his secrets back then. Besides, you have clients scheduled every day next week.

But not tomorrow. Peoria's only five hours away. You could just jump in the car and go. Even if the church is locked and empty, a trip to Peoria beats a day spent fretting about the case. The thought of tracking down former parishioners and tricking them into dishing the dirt on Hopewell got her juices going. She wanted to do it.

Deciding she would masquerade as a journalist, Cassidy slipped into the bedroom and rooted through Zach's desk drawers until she found the tape recorder he used for interviews. Then she set the alarm for five AM, left a note in the bathroom, and went to bed.

Five AM! That's insane! You should turn off the alarm and forget all about Peoria.

Chapter 24

U SING MAPS SHE'D MADE ON THE COMPUTER before the sun
came up, Cassidy located Hopewell's former church, a pic-
turesque white clapboard building with a bell tower rising from the
roof. She parked behind a green sedan, its exhaust pipe tied up off
the ground with a rope, a sticker on its bumper that said: A FRIEND
OF BILL W. Since Bill W. was the founder of AA, she assumed that
the owner of the car was a member. *A good omen. Twelve steppers
tend to be more enlightened than people who've never been exposed to
the program.*

She pressed the bell next to the church door. *Here's hoping someone answers and that this someone hasn't heard about Kit's murder.*

A thin, ropy woman in her sixties, her face harshly lined, her
hair a brassy shade of orange, opened the door and said in a gruff
voice, "Can I help you?"

"I'm writing an article about Ben Hopewell and I'm trying to
find someone who knew him when he was the pastor here. Were you
in his congregation? Could you talk to me about his ministry?"

The woman frowned. "What kind of story are you writing?"

Acting so normal—she must not know about the murder.

"An in-depth feature. I'm looking for information about the causes he's sponsored, the people he's inspired, what he's like at home. I'm a freelance journalist and I've admired the pastor for a long time, so I convinced the editor at *Christian Family Magazine* to let me do the story. I can give you my card." She pulled out her wallet and searched through its pockets. "Oh dear, I don't seem to have any with me."

"That's all right. I believe you. But if you want information about Pastor Hopewell, why don't you drive up to Winnetka and ask him?"

"I did. In fact, I live in the Chicago area and I spent several hours interviewing him last week. But he's too modest to boast about himself, and since I was driving to St. Louis anyway, I got the idea to stop at Redemption Baptist and see if I could find anybody who'd give me some quotes. It'd be great to include a few comments from people who were inspired by him."

The woman's face softened. "Well, you sure came to the right place for that."

"Then you'll talk to me?"

"Long as you're not out to make him look bad."

Cassidy tried for an expression of innocence. "Has anyone else tried to do that? I can't imagine they'd find anything."

"Not really. But you can never be too careful."

The woman stood back so Cassidy could come inside. "We'll get ourselves a cup of coffee, then I'll just talk your ears off about all the good works the pastor did while he was here. Oh, and my name's Dorothy, by the way."

Cassidy introduced herself, then followed the older woman along a maze of hallways to a large room in the rear. "I'm the church secretary and this is my office," Dorothy said. "I don't usually work on Saturdays but I guess it was meant to be that you'd find me here."

Hope it's also meant to be that I get the goods on the pastor.

Dorothy filled two mugs from a large metal coffeepot. The room held three desks, an assortment of mismatched chairs, and a long table with stacks of church bulletins on it. Although the furniture was scarred, everything was neat and spotless. In the center of the table stood a porcelain vase filled with freshly cut yellow mums.

Once the two women were seated at the table, Cassidy took out the tape recorder and set it in front of Dorothy. "Is this okay?"

"Sure."

"I'd like to start with your own story. Was there a time when Pastor Hopewell particularly inspired you?"

"He saved my life," Dorothy said, her gray eyes misting over. "You see, I used to be a drunk. Me and my old man, we'd go to the tavern every night and get sloshed, and then we'd come home and fight. I don't mean just argue. I mean we'd knock each other around. It wasn't his fault any more than it was mine. I was just as ugly a drunk as he was. Man, I tell you, I was in bad shape. I lost my job, I'd started drinking in the morning, I was sick all the time. I reached a point where I didn't want to go on. Then one day my sister brought Pastor Hopewell to my house. He said God loved me and all I had to do was invite Jesus into my life and I could be saved. The pastor cared about me so much he actually started to weep. When I saw those tears on his face, I could feel the Lord Jesus Christ come into my heart. The pastor took me to an AA meeting that day and I haven't had a drink since."

"Was your husband saved as well?"

Dorothy shook her head. "He was really pissed at the pastor for getting me to stop drinking 'cause there wasn't any point to our marriage after I was sober. I made him move out of the house but I keep praying that someday he'll let Jesus into his heart, too."

"This is wonderful," Cassidy enthused. "It'll inspire everyone who reads the article."

Her crusty voice turning shy, Dorothy said, "Maybe you'd like to see my scrapbook."

"I'd love to."

Shouldn't have said that. You came here looking for the lowdown on Hopewell and this woman is not about to have it in her scrapbook.

Dorothy took a thick book, its cover adorned with lace and ribbons, out of the bottom drawer of her desk and brought it to the table. She opened it to the first page and ran her fingertips over a flowery card. "During the early months, when I was still a tad shaky, the pastor used to send me these encouraging little notes."

"When did you start as church secretary?"

Dorothy turned the page, revealing photos of Hopewell at what appeared to be a church picnic. "A couple of years after I was saved. At first he made up a part-time job for me 'cause I was so broke. Then the secretary quit and I was able to move up." Pressed flowers were affixed to the next page.

Cassidy hoped Dorothy would not feel compelled to explain every item.

They were in the middle of the scrapbook when a family-photo Christmas card appeared. Dorothy said, "Mrs. H. sent these out the Christmas before they left."

Cassidy's eyes widened as she stared at the three children standing in front of Adele and Ben. Forest was on the left, Kit in the middle, and a slightly taller girl on the right. Cassidy thought the unknown girl resembled the blonde in the picture she'd found in Kit's drawer.

"This is the first time I've seen his children."

"I thought you belonged to his church."

"I've been to services there a couple of times but I live too far away for it to be my home church."

"Oh, well, this is Forest." Dorothy pointed to the boy. "This is Kit," she moved her finger along, "and this is Charity. Now Forest, he was the smartest little dickens. He used to make up stories about the characters in the bible. And Kit was so sweet. Sometimes she'd come to my office after school and do little chores to help me out." Dorothy did not go on to say anything about the remaining child.

"What about Charity? She must be the oldest."

"Let's see … Charity was three years older than Kit so she'd be sixteen in this picture." Dorothy wrapped a strand of orange hair around her finger. "She was a good kid when she was little but then she got to be a teenager."

"That's a difficult age."

"The pastor did have his hands full with the two oldest females in his house."

Meek, mousy Adele was a handful?

"You mean Charity and his wife?"

Deep furrows appeared on Dorothy's forehead. "I shouldn't have said that. You won't put it in your article, will you?"

"Oh no. I just want my readers to know about all the good the pastor's done." She waited, hoping Dorothy would continue. When she didn't, Cassidy said, "So I guess Mrs. H. was a little hard to handle."

Moving her head closer to Cassidy's, Dorothy dropped her voice. "Well, Mrs. H. didn't mean to cause any trouble, but she kind of liked to party."

So there is some lowdown to be had here after all.

"I don't mean she used drugs or anything, but she'd come to church events in these short skirts and high heels and sometimes she was a little tipsy when she arrived. Then she'd flirt and tell off-color stories. There wasn't anything really wrong with what she did, but a lot of the parishioners got their noses out of joint. The problem was, the pastor and his wife got married right out of high school and I don't think he knew what he was getting into. He never said anything, but I had the impression he was worried about what the new congregation would think of her."

Cassidy could not imagine the pale woman she'd seen at Hopewell's side living it up in short skirts and high heels. *That was seven years ago. She could be completely different now.*

"That must have been difficult for the pastor," Cassidy said. "Especially since the church frowns on divorce."

"I'm sure he didn't want to divorce her. He just wanted her to behave the way a minister's wife is supposed to."

Minister's wife—that definitely would make it onto the list of top ten jobs you'd never accept.

"Didn't you say that Charity gave the minister trouble as well?"

"Did she ever! She wasn't even sixteen yet when she started running around with this high school dropout—this moron—Bobby Stoddard. He was way too old for her, plus he was a real punk. He used to steal cars and I believe he even got caught breaking into somebody's house once. The pastor couldn't stand the sight of him, but he couldn't keep Charity away from him either."

"What about after the pastor moved? I'd certainly hope that getting Charity away from here would be enough to break them up."

But considering that she disappeared, it probably wasn't.

"I can't say for sure. Once the pastor left town, I never did hear anything more about his family. I get a Christmas card every year, but Mrs. H. never sends any of those nice newsy letters that catch you up on everybody. I wish she would. I'd sure like to know how everyone's doing."

"What about Bobby Stoddard? Is he still around?"

"I think he moved away too."

So they both left town. My, what a coincidence.

"Did Bobby's family belong to the congregation?"

"Oh no. All he had was his mother and I seem to recall there was bad blood between them. She was trailer trash. Well, she didn't really live in a trailer, but you know what I mean."

Cassidy wanted to ask the mother's name but figured that Dorothy was too smart not to get suspicious if she went that far afield. She endured looking at the rest of the scrapbook, then took her leave.

†††

In the car she called the Peoria Public Library and asked for directions on how to find the place. Once there, she sat down with the telephone book and looked up the name Stoddard, which had fifteen listings. *Bobby's mother could have a different last name. But even if she does, one of these Stoddards is probably related to Bobby.* She wrote the names and numbers in her notepad, then returned to the Toyota and began making calls.

The first two were answered by machines. She didn't leave messages.

The third was picked up by a man.

Cassidy said, "I'm looking for Bobby Stoddard. He's the beneficiary of an inheritance and I represent a law firm that's trying to locate him."

"You don't expect me to fall for that old chestnut of a story, do you?"

"No, really, I'm an investigator for a law firm."

"Yeah, right. An investigator who's looking to hound some poor schlub who can't pay his bills. There's no way I'm gonna help you do your dirty work." He slammed the phone down.

Now there's a man who's had his share of experience with collection agencies.

The fourth call was picked up by an elderly woman. "Why, yes, I know Bobby Stoddard. He grew up right here on my block."

"Then perhaps you could help me locate him."

"Well, I always like to be helpful. I've been making afghans for my church circle, you know. We give them to poor families at Christmas. Do you crochet, dear?"

Not going in the direction I'd hoped.

"Maybe you could give me Bobby's mother's name."

"Whose name was that you wanted?"

When Cassidy got to her eleventh call, a man responded to her legacy pretext by saying, "Bobby didn't have any rich relatives."

"It's a small inheritance. A great uncle who didn't have any other heirs."

"This probably isn't legit, but I'm going to pass you on to Lila and let her handle it."

"Lila's his mother?"

"Right." The man gave Cassidy a number. "I haven't talked to her in ages so I'm not sure it's still good."

After thanking him, Cassidy called reverse directory, which informed her that the number belonged to Lila Boon. The name was followed by an address.

CHAPTER 25

CASSIDY PARKED ACROSS THE STREET FROM A powder blue bungalow with peeling paint on the window frames and a wrought iron railing that had fallen off the porch and was lying on the ground. Having been unable to keep up her own house during her poverty-stricken, post-divorce years, Cassidy was sympathetic. She lingered in the car a moment, devising a new story for Bobby's mom.

The woman who answered the door had blond hair dyed an unfortunate shade of yellow, an open, smiling face, and a shapely figure. She wore a stained sweatshirt and tight jeans. At first Cassidy thought she was too young to be Bobby's mother, but on closer inspection, she noticed the fine lines beneath Lila's eyes and the puckers on her chin. *She has way more than a decade on Britney.*

"Are you Lila Boon?"

"That's right."

"I'm Cassidy McCabe. The reason I'm here is that my mother sent me on a mission to find Charity Hopewell. Mom's dying of cancer and Charity's her granddaughter and nobody's heard from her in the past seven years."

"Oh how sad," Lila said. "My grandchildren are the center of my life and the thought of one going missing like that just gives me the willies." She ushered Cassidy into her house. "I can't say exactly where Charity is but I'll be happy to tell you what I know."

The room was messy in a homey kind of way, with toys and crumbs of food strewn across the thin area rug. Across from the door, a happy looking baby bounced in a swing not far from a sofa, which stood against the rear wall.

Her mouth curving into a soft smile, Cassidy sat on the sofa and extended her forefinger so the baby could wrap its chubby hand around it.

"What a beautiful child!"

Lila sat in an easy chair at a right angle to the sofa. "She's the youngest. When my daughter leaves all of them here it's almost too much for me. But Tory's easy. One of those kids who hardly ever cries."

Cassidy couldn't take her eyes off the baby.

"Would you like to hold her?"

Dangerous! Too much exposure to a sweet-smelling baby is likely to send your maternal hormones raging again. Cassidy held out her arms and Lila put Tory into them. The baby nestled against Cassidy's shoulder as she stroked the fawnlike cheek and curled tendrils of silky hair around her fingers. After a while, she reluctantly handed Tory back to her grandmother.

"I could do that all day," Cassidy said, "but I better not."

"Do you have kids?"

"Not yet." *But maybe soon.* Cassidy forced herself to remove her rapturous gaze from the baby and focus on Lila. "I have the impression that Charity and your son left Peoria about the same time the Hopewells moved up north."

"That's right. They went to LA. Bobby and I had reached the point where we weren't speaking to each other, but after he decided to move to LA, he came over and filled me in on what'd been going on. Then I didn't hear from him again until he was arrested—must've been three years later. That's when he called to tell me he needed five grand for bail. Can't imagine why he even bothered to ask. He knows I don't have that kind of money. And to tell you the truth, I wouldn't of given it to him if I did. Too much risk he'd take the money and run."

"Was Charity with him? Did they get married?"

"Far as I know, they never made it legal. They were living together when he got arrested, and then she visited him at the jail for a while, but after that she just drifted off. He's out now, but he's still got a few months to go on his parole. I've stayed in touch ever since he called about the bail. Still hoping for a miracle, I guess."

"It could happen. People do turn their lives around." *Couldn't be a therapist if you didn't believe that.* "Did he say anything about Charity?"

"She was pretty messed up. Into drugs, couldn't hold a job. Bobby probably knows more about her than I do. I'll give you his number and you can call him."

Tory made a long gurgling noise, stood on her toes, and held out both arms toward Lila. Picking up a red stuffed rabbit, Lila handed it to the child. Tory grabbed the creature by one long ear and began dangling it in front of her.

A sense of longing filled Cassidy's chest. *If you and Zach have a baby, will she be sweet and adorable and hardly ever cry? Given the mix of your personalities, it doesn't seem likely.*

Dragging her attention back to Lila, Cassidy said, "Sounds like Charity's had a pretty hard life."

"You know, I feel really sorry for her. She made a lot of the same mistakes I did. We both fell in love at an early age with guys who had a mean streak. My home life wasn't great, but at least I didn't have a holier-than-thou father telling me I was going to burn in hell because I was diddling my boyfriend."

"So you and Charity both picked less than perfect guys." *And so did you the first time out, but thank goodness you weren't sixteen.*

"Yeah, and then we both got pregnant about the same age."

"Charity was pregnant?"

"You didn't know? Well, I shouldn't be surprised. Ben Hopewell was a master at covering things up. He told everyone he'd sent Charity to a private school to get her away from my badass son when he'd really sent her off to have a baby. A few months later, she came home looking nice and thin, minus the newborn. I don't think she said a word to anybody except Bobby. The only reason I know is that he told me about the baby when he came to say good-bye."

"Did they go to California to get away from Hopewell?"

"It was the other way around. Charity came home just before her father moved to that hoity-toity church up near Chicago, and he absolutely didn't want her embarrassing him in front of his new congregation. So he brought Bobby and Charity into his office, gave them a big wad of cash, and ordered them to move some place far away from Illinois. He told Charity he wanted her out of his life and threatened to press statutory rape charges against my son if either of them came near his new church."

"He actually disowned her?"

"That's what I'd call it."

"That poor girl." Cassidy shook her head. "I really appreciate your telling me. At least now I know why she didn't show up in Winnetka with the rest of the family."

"The more I think about it, the more I can see that Charity's life was way worse than mine. I was a teen mom and had to work two jobs to survive, and the reason Bobby's so screwed up is probably 'cause I wasn't around to keep an eye on him. But at least I had a family who pitched in now and then." Lila picked up the discarded rabbit and tickled Tory's face with its ears. "Let me go get Bobby's LA number. He ought to have some information about Charity's whereabouts."

As Lila left the room, Cassidy knelt in front of Tory's swing and continued the rabbit game. When the other woman returned, Cassidy stood, took the slip of paper Lila handed her, and made her farewells.

† † †

The shadows were lengthening as Cassidy drove north. The fall colors were not as vivid as they'd been that morning, but she still found it breathtaking to come across stands of trees that were a mix of green, gold, and burgundy. Except for small wooded areas and an occasional house, the flat farmland stretched in all directions, with no towns to be seen anywhere.

She felt quite pleased with her success at cracking secrets, but after the first hour on the road, her excitement drained away and images of Tory crowded into her mind. Being exposed to a baby had clicked on a switch inside her that triggered her old craving to have a child of her own. When she was in her twenties, she'd felt such intense maternal yearnings that the sight of a child on the street could set off a physical ache inside her. But there were so many reasons not to have a baby that she'd given up on the idea and eventually the switch had turned itself off.

Now the craving was back and it scared her. There was too big a chance she still wouldn't get what she wanted.

Zach said you could make the decision.

Yeah, but this is too big a thing to railroad him into.

She wanted to rush home and tell Zach all about her experience with Tory but realized that even talking about it would be a form of pressure. *You have to do this right. Keep your mouth zipped and let him work it out for himself.* Given how much he loved her, she thought it likely he would decide on his own that he wanted the two of them to make a baby together.

And if he did, they would then have to face the question of whether her ovaries still produced viable eggs. When she'd first protested that she might be too old to get pregnant, Zach had brushed the issue aside. *What he always does. Denies the possibility that things won't be the way he wants. And then you fall right in with him because you don't like to think about negative outcomes either.*

As long as she hadn't been certain she wanted a baby, it was easy to avoid the fertility question. Now she was afraid she'd be disappointed again.

You may still feel young, but your ovaries could be past their freshness date. You've had clients in their thirties who couldn't conceive.

Her thoughts were interrupted by the sound of her cell phone.

"How long you think it'll be before you get home?" Zach asked.

"You sound grumpy."

"It isn't you. It's just that nothing's going right on this damn story. I'm ready for a relaxing dinner out, a bottle of wine, and thou. So, how long are thou going to keep me waiting?"

She estimated that she'd be home by seven.

†††

A waitress filled their wineglasses with Pinot Noir. Cassidy and Zach were seated at a table in Philanders, an upscale Oak Park restaurant featuring early nineteenth century photos of the village taken by Philander Barclay. Two walls displayed sepia-toned blow-ups of a bygone era, and an amplitude of dark wood created a sense of formality. Pink flowers in tiny glass vases graced the linen-covered tables.

"You won't believe what I found out," Cassidy announced, proceeding to fill him in about Charity and her baby. "I'm convinced Ben and Adele took their granddaughter to raise as their own. But they didn't name her. 'Heidi' isn't a name Ben ever would have chosen. We should've known something was wrong when we first heard their youngest was a 'Heidi.'"

"So Heidi is Charity's child."

"That has to be what happened. Neither Dorothy nor Lila said a word about Adele's being pregnant when she was in Peoria, and then she turns up in Winnetka with a baby."

Cassidy ate half her piece of bread, then sipped from her water glass. "The only thing that bothers me is that it's hard to imagine how Hopewell could have pulled off such a major scam. How did he keep the Winnetka people from noticing that Adele wasn't pregnant before she moved? How did he keep the Peoria people from noticing that the Hopewells acquired a new baby right after they left town? And how did he cover up Charity's disappearance?"

"He obviously planned this in advance. The Winnetka search committee would have invited him and his family to visit their church and he would have told them his wife was pregnant. Then he could have brought her along in a nice loose smock or said she was too sick to travel. So the Winnetka church would have expected Adele to arrive with a newborn. And as for the Peoria congregation, he would've had to cut off his ties the instant he was gone. Even if some of his Peoria friends came to visit, he could have kept Heidi under wraps."

"What about Charity's disappearance?"

"Given that everything changed when the family moved, it's possible nobody noticed. And if anybody did, he could have told the truth—she ran off with her boyfriend."

"I wonder how Adele felt about Ben's disowning their daughter. Dorothy said she was a party girl when they lived in Peoria, but we haven't heard a hint about any short skirts or off-color remarks at the Winnetka church. Maybe having her oldest daughter sent away and being given an infant to raise was too much for her and she slipped into depression. What a shame. I think I would have liked her the way she used to be."

"So you think Charity is both the woman in that photo you found in Kit's drawer and the woman Forest met behind the church."

"Yeah, I think she made her way to Chicago after giving up on her boyfriend. Probably because she'd kept in touch with Forest and knew she had at least one person here she could turn to for help."

A busboy added a splash of water to Cassidy's glass, which was about a quarter of an inch down from the rim.

"Remember those missing person websites Kit was visiting? She could've been looking for her sister. So why would Charity stay in touch with Forest and not Kit?"

"I have no idea. We have to find Charity and get her to tell us."

"Here's hoping Bobby Stoddard knows where she is. Otherwise she's going to be almost impossible to locate." Zach looked at Cassidy. "So this must be what Forest was going to tell you."

"He must've thought that if his father was willing to disown one daughter, he might be willing to murder the other. And here's something else. I've been racking my brain trying to figure out who might've had a key to the townhouse. Well, Hopewell probably would've been able to steal one when Kit and Bryce came for dinner."

"Okay—playing devil's advocate—why wouldn't he simply send Kit off the way he did Charity?"

Cassidy stared into space for a moment. "Kit wouldn't go. She must've realized she was better off staying here and milking him for money. Kit was more like her father—a stronger person than Charity. She could stand up to him and Charity couldn't."

"I like it," Zach said. "Bringing down self-important assholes is always a pleasure. But proving any of this is going to be a bitch. Even if we locate Charity and she verifies all our suspicions, we still won't have a shred of evidence to link Hopewell to the murder."

CHAPTER 26

As Cassidy and Zach were walking from the garage to the house, Milton came trotting from the back porch to the gate, scrunched beneath it, and sat waiting for them. But unlike Starshine, the tom never permitted any hands-on contact. When they were a couple yards away, he zoomed past them toward the garage and disappeared into the shadows.

Standing on the porch while Zach unlocked the door, Cassidy said, "I'm going to sit out here for a few minutes."

"Huh?"

"Milton comes and stares at me when I do that." *Sometimes. If he's in the mood.*

"And the reason you'd want him to do that would be?"

"We communicate telepathically."

"So, what does old Milton have to say these days?"

"I can't tell you. It's privileged."

Zach laid his arm across her shoulder. "There are a few rare moments when I think I should have married someone sane."

After he went inside, Cassidy sat on the top step and waited for Milton to show himself. In the week since the murder, the temperature had taken a downward turn. She fastened the top button of her coat and hugged herself. Before long, Milton came and sat on the walkway a few feet from the porch. She looked into his dark eyes but he did not communicate with her or read her mind. *Nothing like that's happened since the night the cat lady died and you know that was just your imagination going into overdrive.*

Her reason for wanting to commune with Milton had nothing to do with mystical experiences, which she didn't believe in anyway. She just wanted to establish a connection with him, even if he wouldn't sit on her lap and purr. A minute later she went inside, filled his bowl, and brought it out to him.

You are such a well-trained cat valet.

† † †

Reminding herself that college students slept in when they didn't have classes, Cassidy waited until noon on Sunday before calling Bryce.

"Yeah."

"I called to see how you're doing."

"This is about the meds, isn't it? You called to see if I'm taking them."

"That's not why I called." She paused. "So are you?"

"I'm doing everything you want. Taking the pills. Going to class. Not drinking. I even set up a session with a shrink. You don't have to hover."

"You said you have an appointment with your attorney tomorrow and I'd like to go with you."

"I'm perfectly capable of handling this on my own."

"It isn't that I don't trust you. I just want to be there."

"This is gonna be a pain in the ass. I have to drive into the Loop, find a place to park. The guy'll probably make me set up camp in his waiting room. Why would you want to put yourself through all that?"

"Because I can't stop worrying. The only thing that helps is to gather up every crumb of information I can get. So if I hear what your attorney has to say, it will ease my mind." *Or not, if he fails to provide the reassurances you're hoping for.*

"Why don't you just let me tell you what he said?"

Because guys never remember word for word. They give you the skimpy, summarized, one-sentence version. "I really want to hear it for myself."

"Well, alright. I guess having you around isn't that bad."

"What time is the appointment?"

"One thirty. We can meet at the attorney's office."

"I'd rather come to the townhouse early and take you to lunch. That way you can drive and I won't have to deal with the traffic and parking hassles."

"You're doing this to check up on me. To see if my kitchen's full of pizza boxes or if there are empty beer bottles on the floor."

"Maybe a little. But mostly I just want to spend time with you."

† † †

After hanging up, she got out the number for Charity's old boyfriend, put her hand on the phone, then halted. Persuading Bobby Stoddard might prove more difficult than persuading Bryce. She would have to tell Bobby the same story she'd told his mother, because Lila had probably called him the minute Cassidy left her house. Using the same story would be good in that it would save her the trouble of inventing a new one, but it also might be bad in that there was nothing in it for Bobby.

Maybe he'll tell you where Charity is out of the goodness of his heart. Except Lila didn't make him out to be a goodness-of-the-heart kind of guy.

Cassidy dialed and a male voice answered. After confirming that the voice belonged to Bobby, she told him her tale of a dying woman who longed to find her missing granddaughter. "Your mother tells me that Charity's in Chicago and you might know where she is."

"I might," he conceded.

"So will you help me find her? It would mean the world to my mother. And to Charity. Those two were so close. Charity'd be devastated if she didn't have a chance to say good-bye."

"I gotta tell you, I got a problem with this. I still love her and I want her back. Been out six months, got me a place to stay, a line on a job. She'd be a lot better off with me than on the streets. I could take care of her, keep her off drugs."

"Um ... is that what Charity wants?"

"'Course she wants to be with me. She's just a little nervous about coming back 'cause she knows I'd make her lay off the dope."

Yeah, right, ex-con Bobby's going to be her drug counselor.

"So what is it you'd like me to do?" Cassidy asked.

"Put her on a bus to California after the old lady kicks. But you wouldn't do that, would you? You'd glom onto her, try to bring her back into the family fold. You get your hands on her, I might never see her again."

You could promise you'd try to convince Charity to go back to him, but he'd know you were lying. The only other option is to beg.

"Oh please, you've got to help me. This is so important. Just think how Charity would feel if she found out you'd deprived her of her last chance to see her grandmother."

A brief silence. "There gonna be an inheritance?"

"I haven't seen the will, but Mom does have some money. And Charity *is* her favorite grandchild."

"If I help you out with this, will you make sure she at least gives me a call?"

"I'll definitely talk to her about it."

"Last time I heard from her, she was sleeping at a homeless shelter. Somebody's Place. Now what was it? Susan's Place, that's what she called it."

"How long ago was that?"

"Oh, I'd say six weeks or so."

Wonder what makes him think he has any chance of getting his hands on her inheritance considering she hardly ever calls? I'd say Bobby spends too much time in his own little fantasy world.

† † †

Cassidy parked next to a brown-brick, two-story, block-long industrial building in the Wicker Park neighborhood of Chicago. There were no signs but she knew it was Susan's Place because the shelter's website provided the address. Cassidy had also learned this was a woman's-only overnight shelter that opened its doors at six at night and locked them again at eight in the morning.

The building itself was old and grimy, its windows composed of glass blocks, but it was spared from ugliness by a string of playful murals across the front. Each mural represented a window, blue sky in the background, the faces of women and animals looking out upon the world.

Cassidy checked her watch. Five thirty. She had come early in hopes of spotting Charity before she went inside. At this point two women sat on the sidewalk with their backs against the building and three others huddled close together on the porch steps.

As more women arrived, Cassidy began to wonder if she'd even recognize Charity. Some of the women wore hats or scarves that obscured their faces and others kept their eyes glued to the ground. A few younger women stared curiously at Cassidy but none of them resembled the eldest Hopewell child.

The door opened and the women filed in. Cassidy waited another half hour to check out the stragglers, then went inside the entryway, where a woman with braided hair stopped her.

"What you be doin' here, girl?"

"I'm a social worker. I need to talk to the person in charge."

"That be Vonda." The braided-haired woman nodded toward a wide doorway leading into the main room. "She be the one in the turban."

In the larger room cots took up about three-quarters of the floor space, with a kitchen area at the far end, long tables, and a counter where women were picking up their meals. Voices clattered and the smell of unwashed bodies hung in the air.

A tall woman wearing a red and gold turban stood near the counter, shelter clients clustered three-deep around her. Crossing the room, Cassidy positioned herself a little apart from the crowd and took the photo she'd found in Kit's drawer out of her purse.

After Vonda had taken care of the shelter clients, she turned her strong-boned, regal face toward Cassidy. "Now what can I do for you?"

"I'm a social worker and I'm looking for my niece, Charity Hopewell. Her grandmother's dying and I'd like to find her before it's too late." Cassidy held out the photo but could see no sign of recognition on the other woman's face.

"If you're a social worker, honey, you know all about confidentiality."

Exactly what you thought she'd say.

"Can't you at least tell me if she's been here?" *You know she can't.*

Vonda gave her a disapproving look. Reaching into the pocket of her voluminous skirt, she handed Cassidy a pad of paper and an envelope. "You can write her a note. If I see her, I'll pass it along."

Cassidy sat at one of the tables and penned a message, then sealed the envelope and returned it.

"You have quite a few people come in here looking for someone?"

"I take in a lot more envelopes than I give out," Vonda replied, her dark eyes filled with compassion.

Cassidy thanked her, then started toward the door. She had taken only a few steps when someone tugged at her arm. She turned to look into a burnished copper face with wicked eyes and a wide grin.

"You be lookin' for Charity, ain't you?"

"You know her?"

"Sure I do. She be here for a while, then she stop comin'."

"Can you tell me how to find her?"

"You can't find her but I could. If you make it worth my while."

Cassidy's eyes narrowed. "Why should I believe you?"

"Up to you, lady." The woman straightened her slender shoulders and walked jauntily away.

"Wait." *Don't do it. You know she's going to rip you off.* "How would you go about finding her?"

"Frieda, she be Chare's best friend. She show up every day on the same bench. Frieda'd know where Chare be stayin'."

"So then you'd find Charity and tell her to call me?"

"If you make it worth my while."

"How much?"

"Fifty for me and twenty for Frieda."

"Twenty for you and twenty for Frieda." *And I'll bet Frieda never sees a dime.*

The woman started to leave again, then paused and returned. "Okay, I do you a favor."

Cassidy wrote a note on a business card: "Please call me. It's urgent that I talk to you. A friend of Forest's."

She gave the card and two twenties to the younger woman. "What's your name? Will you let me know when you've made contact with Charity?"

"They call me Jazz 'cause I'm so hip and cool." She performed a slick little dance step. "And no, I won't be callin'. I be givin' the card to Chare and she decide whether she call or not. You don't hear from her, you just have to wonder if I be cheatin' you."

"I'm really counting on you," Cassidy said, hoping to stir some sense of obligation in a woman she feared might be lacking that sense altogether.

"There ain't no dyin' grandmother, is there?" Jazz turned and flounced off toward the food counter.

The odds that Charity will ever see that card are about as great as the odds of Rush Limbaugh and Hillary Clinton exchanging valentines.

† † †

The bedroom windows had been black for a couple of hours by the time Zach got home that night. Cassidy swiveled in his direction as he came in and plunked down in his desk chair.

"How's it going?"

"Not well." He bent over and started removing his black gym shoes. "Do you remember my telling you about the nurse who's a cousin to the whistleblower? And that this nurse knows about the Medicare scam and it looked like she was ready to talk?"

"What happened? She get cold feet?"

"Yeah, and I can't blame her. She agreed to meet me this afternoon and bring documentation, but last night she got an anonymous call from somebody who threatened to hurt her kid if she went near any reporters. So she did the sensible thing—the sort of thing I wish you'd do when people threaten you. She quit her job and asked me not to contact her again."

"So what are you going to do now?"

"I'll keep doing what I've been doing. Interviewing patients and staff at the nursing homes where these bottom-feeder docs work."

"I suppose they pick on the Alzheimer's patients."

"You have no idea how many people I've tried to talk to who don't know what planet they live on." He shook his head. "But enough about that. I've got something else to tell you. Remember you emailed me that piece where the psychiatrist mentioned his brother the senator? I talked to the *Post's* political guru today and he said that ten years ago, when Owen Leonard made his first bid for the senate, he was up against a popular incumbent and initially was lagging in the polls. Then Hopewell threw in with him and got out the evangelical vote, which—according to my source—carried Leonard into office. So that means the senator would have owed Hopewell big time, and it's possible the guy's brother might have helped him pay down the debt. However, I have no idea how that might translate into the psychiatrist's writing a script for Margaret Polanski."

"This is so baffling." Cassidy shook her head. "It probably has nothing to do with the murder, but it's driving me nuts that I can't figure it out."

CHAPTER 27

"You go to any classes this morning?" Cassidy asked Bryce, seated across from her at a Formica table with dried ketchup glued to its surface. She'd been hoping for a lady's luncheon kind of place, but since she'd let Bryce choose, she shouldn't have been surprised that he'd picked an Italian beef joint instead.

"I overslept." He bit into a huge beef sandwich, juice dribbling down his chin and hands.

"Just trying to make conversation."

"How's the investigation going?"

She hesitated, her therapist part initially stopping her from telling him what she knew about Kit's family. *Charity is not a client. Confidentiality doesn't apply here.*

"Did you know Kit had an older sister?"

"She did? What happened to her?"

"She had a baby and was disowned and now she's homeless." Cassidy felt a delicious little thrill. This was almost like gossiping, a guilty pleasure she seldom indulged.

"Does this mean you're making progress?"

"I can't tell if this is going to take us anywhere or if I'm just going off on a long tangent." Cassidy opened a plastic packet of dressing and dribbled it over her salad, a pile of iceberg lettuce with some shreds of carrot and purple cabbage mixed in. "That first day when you'd just gotten out of jail you said you didn't want us to investigate. You still feel that way?"

"I don't know." He stared toward the window. "Back then I felt like I deserved to go to prison, but now I'd rather die than be locked up again."

"So then you want us to find the killer?"

"I guess." He took several gulps from his super sized cola. "I suppose I should be grateful to Zach."

"But you aren't? Or you don't want to be?"

He looked at her salad. "You hardly ate anything. Maybe we should pick up a bag of peanut butter cups so you don't go hungry."

Well, I guess it's pretty obvious he doesn't want to talk about Zach.

Bryce's phone beeped. He squinted at the screen, then put it back in his pocket. "Victor."

"It's okay if you talk to him. I don't mind."

"I'll call him later."

"Why don't you take his calls?"

"He's got this thing about money. Every time I need a little extra—you know, like renting the townhouse or buying furniture—he gives me these lectures. Here I've got half a mil in my trust fund and he gets bent out of shape when I spend a few thousand bucks. Probably jealous 'cause he doesn't have anything to throw around himself."

"I wonder why he doesn't."

"It's his kid. He was born with some kind of horrible disability. His wife couldn't take it. She walked out before the kid was a year old. Victor had to put him into some kind of home, and then there are always these extra medical expenses coming up."

"I was surprised when I first met Victor. Your mother was always so … " *What? Classy? I suppose there's nothing wrong with calling a madam classy.*

"Yeah, my mother was always so," Bryce repeated, making a joke of it. "You can't understand why Mom picked Victor instead of some glitzy, high-powered guy."

Cassidy nodded.

"Victor and Xandra went to school together in the old neighborhood. Back when she was poor, before she discovered how much her body was worth. The only people she ever really trusted were the friends she had before she moved up in the world. Or down, however you choose to think of it. And besides, she felt sorry for him because of his kid."

"I'm surprised to hear there's a problem between you and Victor. When you first mentioned him, you said he was like an uncle."

"That's how it used to be. When I was little, he always brought me presents when he came to visit. But after Mom died, he seemed to think he needed to steer me in the right direction. I didn't want to listen to all his advice, so I just stopped having much to do with him except when I needed money."

This should be a lesson to you. You need to keep your advice to yourself.

Except it's so damn hard to bite your tongue when there are things you know he needs to hear.

† † †

After walking back to the townhouse, Bryce climbed in on the driver's side of the Miata and Cassidy took her place next to him. He turned the key in the ignition and they heard a metallic click.

"Maybe the battery's dead," Cassidy ventured.

"It's not that old."

"We're running a little late. Let's just take the Toyota and worry it later."

"There shouldn't be anything wrong. This car is like my baby. I'm never even late for an oil change."

"Yeah, but things happen." She dug in her purse for her keys. "Let's get going. I don't want to be late for the appointment."

"Why not? Attorneys always make you wait anyway." He unlocked the hood, causing it to bounce upward, then got out of the car.

"We don't have time for this," Cassidy protested, climbing out on her side. "Besides, you won't be able to tell what's wrong just by looking at the engine."

What's the connection between testosterone and the need to pretend to understand the big lump of metal that makes the car go?

"I might be able to figure it out. I'm really good with cars." He went to the front of the Miata and lifted the hood.

"Omigod!" He took a quick step backward, his olive-toned face turning white.

"What's wrong?" Cramming herself in front of him, Cassidy looked down. Wires that shouldn't have been there ran from the battery to a cylindrical container taped to the firewall in front of the driver's seat. "Oh shit! It's a bomb!"

Bryce clasped her upper arms and started moving her away from the car.

Her knees nearly buckled. "I need to sit down."

They settled on the porch steps.

"Just think if it had gone off," Bryce said.

She pictured the Miata bursting into flames.

He took his cell phone out of his pocket. "This time I'm going to do it right." He dialed 911 and reported the bomb.

After a short silence, Cassidy said, "I left my purse in the car. I have to get it."

"You shouldn't go near the car!"

"I need my purse. If the car didn't explode when you turned the key, it's not going to now, and I can't take the chance that the cops will put it into evidence or anything." She went to the passenger side door, opened it with trembling hands, and retrieved her purse.

The two cops who arrived first stared at the bomb, then hustled Cassidy and Bryce farther away from the Miata. As more uniforms poured onto the scene, one of the cops informed Cassidy and Bryce that they would have to sit in separate squads.

Before they could be led away, Cassidy said to her stepson, "Make sure you call the attorney and reschedule."

Turning his back on her, he didn't answer.

Gotta stop treating him like a child.

They were deposited in the back of two beat cars and driven in opposite directions to a half block's distance from the Miata.

Cassidy's driver twisted around to look at her. "You understand you have to stay here till someone can take you to the station."

"You wouldn't believe how experienced I am at sitting in the back of squad cars."

He gave her a quizzical look, then got out and gazed toward the townhouse.

Now that I think about it, he probably doesn't have the authority to keep me here. But—even though my statement won't enlighten anybody—the don't-make-waves approach is always best when dealing with the police.

She reported in to Zach. Then, turning around and kneeling on the seat, she watched what was going on in the vicinity of the Miata. The first cops to arrive had been uniforms, but now a number of suits had joined the crowd. Cassidy assumed they represented detectives and other higher-ups in the departmental food chain.

Before long, the cops had emptied out the neighboring houses and cordoned off a large perimeter around the car. After that, nothing happened for a while. Cassidy thought they were probably waiting for the bomb squad. She also thought that the detectives who'd been assigned to the case could, if they wanted to, take Bryce and her in for questioning, but that the detectives were far too interested in watching the bomb squad at work to be bothered with the intended victims. *You weren't an intended victim. You would have been collateral damage. It's Bryce who was the target.*

A couple of hours passed, then a detective took her into the station and ran her through a long list of questions, the answers to most of which were "I don't know." Releasing her, he said that as soon as the other detective was finished with Bryce, a cop would return them to the townhouse.

† † †

Bryce unlocked the front door, then turned to Cassidy, who stood on the steps behind him. "I'll be all right. You don't need to hang around and watch over me or anything."

Cassidy remained silent and followed him into the living room. Sitting across from him in one of the plaid chairs, she suddenly realized she was shivering. "I'm the one who can't handle it. I'm so jittery, there's no way I'd be able to drive home. I always need to process things before I move on."

He rested his forearms on his legs and clasped his hands between his knees. "'Process.' I hear that word all the time. What does it mean, anyway?"

"I think it just means to talk it out."

"I don't know what to say. It happened. It's over. I feel a little tense but I'll be okay."

Cassidy pressed her hand against her chest, drew in air, and heaved a large sigh. "I can't seem to breathe right. When I first saw the bomb, I couldn't take it in. Later it hit me that we both could've been killed. And then later still, it hit me that somebody's trying to kill *you*."

"I still don't believe it. I mean, it just doesn't make sense. Why would anyone want to kill me?"

"Can you think of anybody who might want to get rid of both you and Kit?"

"One of her old boyfriends. One of her current boyfriends. Somebody who wanted to be her boyfriend but didn't make the grade. I'm sure she had plenty of guys lusting after her but I don't know who any of them are."

"What about somebody who had a grievance against you?"

Bryce grinned. "Well, there's Larry. He had a paper due on AIDS in Rwanda and his computer crashed so he asked me to get something off the Net for him. So I found this report that seemed perfect but it turns out his teacher had already seen it so he flunked the assignment."

"No, seriously."

"Of course there's always Angie. Of all the people I know, she's got the best reason to be pissed. I can just see her taping that bomb onto my firewall, can't you?"

"Have you talked to her?"

"Not yet."

No lectures! If you don't stop telling him what to do, he'll avoid you just like he does Victor.

"Can you think of anyone else?"

His expression grew solemn. "Believe me, I wouldn't hold out on you with something like this."

"So, are you really going to be all right?"

"I have to, 'cause if I'm not, you and Zach will either drag me to Oak Park or camp out in my living room."

She smiled. "Well, I'm calm enough to drive now."

"You sure?" His forehead creased with concern. "I don't want you taking any chances."

Same song his father sings.

Chapter 28

I T WAS AFTER SIX WHEN SHE GOT home. Parking her Toyota in the garage, she was surprised to see that the Subaru had made it home ahead of her. As she mounted the stairs to the second floor, Zach emerged from the computer room. Gathering her into his arms, he said in a husky voice, "If our mad bomber had been more competent, you wouldn't be here now." He pressed his mouth against hers, gently parting her lips and delivering a deep, warm kiss.

"Sometimes we lose track of our priorities," he said, leading her into the bedroom. Candles glowed from every flat surface, a glass of wine stood on each of their nightstands, and Bruce Springsteen played on the stereo.

They made love until every vestige of light was gone from the sky. Afterward, Zach rose on one elbow and looked down at her. "You hungry?"

"Can't tell yet."

"Every time we have sex, as soon as you're ready to move, you turn ravenous. The temperature's pretty mild so I thought we could sit on the front porch and eat deli food. I picked up a couple of different kinds of meat and cheese."

"Did you get fruit?"

"I knew you'd complain if I didn't, so I even got fruit."

Putting on robes, they went down to the kitchen and prepared a platter of snack food. As they sliced cheddar and salami, Starshine crouched on the counter, obviously hoping for an unguarded moment with the food.

After Cassidy finished arranging the platter, Zach grabbed their glasses and the half empty wine bottle and led the way out to the wide enclosed porch. Cassidy deposited the platter on a coffee table and they settled on the threadbare wicker couch behind it.

As Cassidy was filling her plate, Starshine leapt onto the table, snatched a slice of cheese out of her hand, and darted off to eat it.

"This isn't going to work," Cassidy said. "We'll have to shut her in the house."

"Why not give her a plate of her own? Let her enjoy a whole meal for once."

"Well, maybe she can clean off our plates when we're done, but she has to go in the house for now."

Cassidy chased the calico down, grabbed her by the scruff, wrapped both arms around her squirmy body and shut her in the basement, far enough away so they wouldn't have to listen to her yowl.

Returning to the porch, Cassidy laid a slice of brie on a cracker. "Now that Bryce was almost blown to smithereens, you still think he killed Kit?"

"Okay, I'm convinced he didn't do it."

"The person who planted the bomb has to be the same person who shot Kit. It just doesn't make sense to think there'd be two different people out to kill Kit and Bryce."

"Right."

"And I can't think of a single reason why Ben Hopewell would want Bryce dead. Here I've spent all this time focusing on the minister's family secrets and I was going off in the wrong direction."

"It's possible Hopewell was afraid Kit indulged in too much pillow talk, but that's kind of a stretch. Especially considering what a good candidate we have in Raul."

"Raul—the guy who tortured Iris and made threats against both Kit and Bryce. Kit must have given him a key."

Zach's head jerked up. "No, wait! I've got it. Remember I told you there was something rattling around in the back of my mind? Well, it finally came to me. The locks were probably picked. That would explain why there was no forced entry."

"How can we find out?"

"Bryce's attorney can send the locks to a private lab. If they were picked, there'll be marks on them."

"Why did the cops miss it?"

"They forgot, just like I did. It's a common mistake. So many people have security systems nowadays you don't see that much lock picking anymore."

"So Raul picked the lock and went inside planning to kill both Kit and Bryce. Then what? He shoots Kit, drops his gun, and panics? He seems too cool for that. Why wouldn't he simply turn on the light, find his gun, and finish the job?"

"Maybe he isn't as cool as he seems. Or maybe he figured Bryce had already called the cops."

"Okay, so he panics and runs but he can't give up on killing Bryce because Bryce was his primary target in the first place. So he picks the lock again, finds Bryce passed out on the couch, and sets up a fake suicide."

"That won't work. There's no way Raul could have known Bryce was back at the townhouse. Or that he was trashed."

Cassidy scrunched her forehead. "I have such a feeling the suicide was a setup."

"Yeah, me too. But there's no logical way to explain it."

"Okay, I'll let it go for now. What I really want to know is will the cops drop the charges against Bryce now that it's obvious the killer is out to get him too?"

"I doubt it."

"Damn!" She drummed her fist against the couch's wicker armrest. "Why wouldn't they?"

"They'll probably think Bryce rigged the bomb himself in an attempt to get the case reopened. Which isn't about to happen unless we produce forensic evidence or a confession."

"You mean even if we went to the police with a witness who heard Raul making threats and proof that one of the locks was picked, they still wouldn't drop the charges?"

"Cops and prosecutors are extremely reluctant to do that because it means they screwed up in the first place. If we can prove a lock was picked, it'll weaken their case, but given the emotional nature of the crime—a young pregnant woman, daughter of a prominent minister, shot in her own home—they still might get a conviction."

Cassidy's stomach sank. "How can you be so calm about it?"

"I'm not calm. I just hide my feelings better than you."

"The worst of it is, if Raul's set on killing Bryce, he'll just keep at it till he succeeds. We have to do something to stop him. I have to convince Raul we've got enough evidence to send the police to his door if anything happens to Bryce."

"I don't want you convincing Raul of anything. This guy is violent and unstable and I don't want you going anywhere near him."

"We have to make him understand that if Bryce dies, he'll be next in line for a first degree murder charge."

"Okay, I agree. We do need to get him to back off from Bryce. But before we talk to Raul, I think we should explain everything to Emily." Emily was a Chicago police detective and a friend of theirs. "Raul is likely to take us more seriously if he knows the cops have their eye on him."

"I'll set up a time to meet with Raul, then I'll call Emily."

"I'm the one who needs to talk to Raul, not you."

"No, I need to do it. Remember how challenging he was with you? Anything you say, he'll want to do the opposite. Since I'm a woman, I won't be so threatening. I'll ask him to meet me at the student union. With all those people around, I'll be perfectly safe."

Zach frowned. "I don't like it. I want you to stay away from him."

She put her hand on his leg. "I know you hate it when I do things like this. It makes you feel helpless and vulnerable. But I'll be in a public place. There won't be any danger."

"You just make sure you have plenty of people around you from the time you arrive at the union till you're back in your car with the doors locked. And don't forget to look in the backseat before you get in."

"I'll be very careful." *Amazing! Zach hardly put up any fight at all. Guess he's given up on trying to keep me out of trouble.*

They sat in silence for a while, looking out through the glassed-in porch at a couple of teens standing on the corner. Zach refilled his wineglass, then held the bottle out to Cassidy, who shook her head no.

"I've been asking myself 'Why now?'" she said. "Why kill Kit three months after she moved in with Bryce? Why kill Kit at all, considering Bryce was the one Raul really hated?"

"Maybe she told him to take a hike."

"I don't think so. From what Iris said, I got the impression Kit was practically addicted to him. I think the reason he killed her now is because of the baby. Kit must've figured out that Raul was the father and told him she wasn't going to have an abortion. He couldn't stand the idea of Kit getting one-up on him like that, so he decided to eliminate the problem—which meant getting rid of Kit, and as long as he was getting rid of people, he decided to kill Bryce as well."

Swallowing the last of her wine, Cassidy stood up. "I'm going to call Raul now and try to arrange a meeting." She went upstairs and dialed his number on her desk phone.

"Yeah."

"This is Cassidy McCabe, Bryce's stepmother. Zach and I talked to you a few days ago on campus and now I'd like to meet with you again."

"Why? You lookin' for some good ganja?"

Ganja? What's ganja?

"I have some information for you."

"Why would I wanna hear anything you got to say?"

"I'm sure you'll find this worth your while. I'd like to set up a time when we could meet at the student union."

"I'll be on campus tomorrow. If you're at the union at eleven, I'll talk to you. Otherwise, forget it."

"I'll see you then."

When she returned to the porch, Starshine stood on the table scarfing down food from Zach's plate, which he'd heaped with leftovers.

"At least I didn't let her eat off the platter," he said.

† † †

After her morning shower, Cassidy selected a pair of crisp wine-colored slacks and a brightly patterned sweater to wear to her meeting with Raul. *Definitely a guy who judges women on the basis of designer labels and hot-looking clothes.* Since neither of these things existed in her wardrobe, she doubted that she would rank as high as a three on the dope dealer's scale.

Why on earth would you care?

Because I hate being looked down on by anybody, even slimy Raul.

She slipped her feet into the pointy-toed pumps she wore while doing therapy, then remembered the half-mile hike between the on-street parking and the student union. *Are you really willing to suffer foot pain just to keep Raul from sneering?* She returned her therapy shoes to her closet and put on her not-entirely-clean Reeboks instead.

Once the laces were tied, she followed Starshine down to the kitchen where the calico lobbied intensely to get her human to open a small flat can. The bowl on the counter was empty, Zach having decided it was pointless to keep filling it with brown nuggets the cat refused to eat.

Launching herself onto the counter, Starshine begged for food.

"Why can't you understand that this is for your own good? I'm trying to save you from a heart attack. You put on four pounds in the last six months, and if I let you keep going, you'll reach the point where you won't be able to wash certain portions of your anatomy."

The cat twisted her ears backward and made angry sounds.

"Considering how many fat grams you consumed last night, you can't make me feel guilty."

Cassidy went outside to retrieve Milton's dish. Trotting down the back steps, she turned into the corner behind the porch and came to a sudden stop. Her mouth went dry. The food she'd put out the night before appeared untouched. She'd never known a healthy stray to miss a meal. Or to turn up its nose at whatever food was offered.

† † †

Before leaving the house, she called Bryce. "Did you set up another appointment with your attorney?"

"He squeezed me in at 7:30 this morning."

"Why didn't you tell me?"

"You're never up that early."

Telling you every way he can that he doesn't want to be mothered. Needs to prove his independence.

An internal sigh passed through her. She asked, "So what did he say?"

"Not much. He just asked the same questions everybody else asked. Except he didn't ask if I killed her. Guess he doesn't want to know."

"He must've said something."

"All he told me is it's gonna take at least a year to come to trial. Wouldn't say shit about my chances."

Heaviness settled on her shoulders. *You were so desperate to have the attorney say the odds were in his favor.*

CHAPTER 29

CASSIDY STOOD NEXT TO A POST PLANKED with a light wood veneer. The student union was so crowded she was afraid Raul wouldn't be able to see her if she sat down. Six young women had crammed themselves around a table in front of her, all wearing preppy clothes and talking at once. It reminded her of why she'd declined to make a bid for popularity when she was in college. *Ditz though you sometimes may be, meaningless babble has never appealed to you.*

Before long she spotted Raul heading in her direction with his aggressive, hip-rolling stride. He did not stop until he'd moved in a little too close, stepping just inside her personal space, his tall muscular body looming over her. Catching her lip between her teeth, she forced herself not to step backward.

"Where's your old man?" Raul demanded. "He send you to do his dirty work? Guess he doesn't want to hear any more of my opinions about his sonny boy."

"You know we've been investigating Kit's murder," Cassidy said.

Raul raised a hand to wave at someone across the room. "Whas'up, dude?"

Not seeing anyone wave back, Cassidy wondered if Raul had merely pretended to notice someone he knew as a means of demonstrating his indifference to her.

"All the evidence we've come across points to you as Kit's murderer," Cassidy said, pressing on even though he didn't appear to be listening. "We also believe you planted a bomb in Bryce's car. When you went into the townhouse the night of the murder, you intended to kill both of them, but you failed to get Bryce, so now you're trying to finish the job."

Raul looked directly at her for the first time, his brown eyes sparkling with laughter. "Somebody tried to blow the pussy up? Too bad he didn't succeed. Far as I'm concerned, the little wuss doesn't deserve to take up space on the planet."

"I'll be sure to quote you on that to the cop who's investigating the car bomb."

"So tell me about your so-called evidence."

"We know you have a history of violence, that you lied about not having seen Kit since she moved in with Bryce, that you made threats against both of them, and that you exhibited extreme jealousy when she moved into Bryce's townhouse."

"You think I popped Kit because I was jealous of the pussy?" His thin-lipped mouth broadened into a wolfish grin. "Bryce was irrelevant. Why should I care if he was paying her rent as long as she spread for me?"

"I think you killed her because you were the father of her child. Were you angry that she wouldn't have an abortion?"

He threw his head back and laughed. "What have you and your old man been smoking? She never said a word to me about any pregnancy. Besides, she slept with a lotta guys, so how would she know who the father was?"

"She got pregnant while she was on antibiotics, and she only took them for five days. I think she knew who she slept with during that time. And since it wasn't Bryce, it must've been you."

"Oh yeah? What five days was that?"

"August eleventh to the fifteenth."

He laughed again. "You and Zach are kinda the Keystone Cops of investigators, aren't you? If you'd done your homework, you woulda known I was in Mexico almost the whole month of August. Bein' the good son, goin' home to visit the family."

He's lying, isn't he? But remember that period in August when there weren't any calls from Kit to Raul?

"Regardless of whether you fathered her child or not, you obviously hate Bryce and you're the only one with a clear-cut motive to plant a bomb in his car."

He looked down at her out of slitted eyes, the humor gone from his face. "Why should I give a shit what you think? You had any proof, I'd be talking to a cop, not you." He glanced at his watch. "I gotta be somewhere in five minutes. You got anything more to say, you can walk along with me."

You shouldn't go anywhere with him.

But you haven't told him the most important part.

Raul turned abruptly and headed toward the nearest door, Cassidy hurrying to catch up. Once they were outside, he set off in a direction that led away from the center of campus and toward Lake Michigan. Cassidy's throat constricted. *Zach'd be really pissed if he knew what you were doing.*

"Wait a minute, will you? I have one more thing to say."

Raul didn't slow down. "Go ahead, spit it out."

There were a few people in the vicinity, but they were all moving purposefully along in their own directions.

Cassidy started to jog so she could come abreast of him. "We have a friend on the police force. A detective. If anything happens to either Bryce or us, she'll have you in the lockup before you can even think of jumping a plane to Mexico."

"She will, huh?"

He suddenly slowed down. When Cassidy was a step ahead of him, he grabbed her left arm and yanked it behind her back.

"Omigod!" she gasped, a sharp pain stabbing her in the shoulder.

Lifting her arm higher, he made her walk toward a concrete block building, her breath coming so fast she couldn't speak. When they were a couple of feet from the building, he changed directions, forcing her to walk around behind it. She stumbled as he pushed her forward, triggering such intense pain she almost lost consciousness. He gave her a moment to right herself, then walked her behind a dumpster and shoved her up against the rough surface of the building.

"That man of yours, he don't care nuthin' about you or he wouldn't have sent you to talk to me alone."

Now that she had stopped moving, she was able to gather enough air in her lungs to scream. "Help! Help! I'm being kidnapped! Somebody help me!"

Grabbing a handful of hair, he jerked her head backward. "Go ahead, yell some more. Nobody can see you back here and nobody's gonna come running to the rescue."

Blackness formed around the periphery of her vision.

"Who'd you think you were dealing with, anyway? Some spineless faggot like your stepson? You think some chick can talk to me about *evidence* and then just walk away? Or some bitch cop is gonna make me all scared?"

He turned her around to face him. "You got the message?"

She nodded.

Smiling lewdly, he ran the tip of his tongue over his upper lip. "So now you learned your lesson, you come by my crib, I'll show you what a real man can do."

He strutted away.

She sank to the ground, propped her elbows on her knees, and held her head in her hands. After a while the shaking subsided. Getting to her feet, she started the long trek back to her car.

† † †

"I totally misjudged him," Cassidy said, sitting behind the wheel of her Toyota and talking to Zach on her cell phone. "I thought he'd be less threatened by a woman, but I was wrong."

"I just wish I could get you to listen to me."

"Go ahead, say 'I told you so.' I deserve it."

"It's no fun if you give me permission. So, you believe what he said about being in Mexico?"

"As soon as he said it, I remembered there were a few weeks in August when his number didn't appear on Kit's phone bill and that they included the days when she could have conceived. Raul was probably in some remote area that didn't have cell phone service."

"That doesn't rule him out. He's still the only person we know of who had a motive to kill both Kit and Bryce."

"Yeah, but I think we ought to take a hard look at the guy who impregnated her. Whoever it was, Kit was in a position to milk him for money for the next eighteen years."

"Probably the guy who emailed her—what was his screen name?—DC. At least he's the only other guy we know about who was banging her."

"The drama dude said she didn't have a lot of guys on the side, just a couple."

"The drama dude?"

"You remember Gran ranked the numbers on Kit's phone bill? Well, this guy I called was near the top of the list. He told me he and Kit were taking private drama lessons and they practiced together, but he wouldn't give me his name."

"So if this guy was right and Kit did have only two other sex partners besides Bryce, DC would have to be the father."

"I'd really like to know who DC is, but all I have is an email address and I don't have a clue how to get from there to a name."

"The police don't have that problem. I'm sure they've already talked to him at length."

"Which doesn't mean a thing. Since the cops are assuming Bryce was the only one who could've been in the townhouse with Kit, they're not likely to look at any other suspects." Cassidy tapped her fingers against the hub of the steering wheel. "Have you done anything about getting the locks examined?"

"Bryce's attorney said he'd take care of it."

††† †

She clicked off with Zach, then dialed the Area Three Detective Unit to see if Emily was in. Cassidy thought Bryce had shown uncommon good sense in renting a townhouse in the same area where Emily worked. *Not that she can do anything. But still, it makes me feel better to know there's a friendly cop at hand.*

Emily picked up and Cassidy told her what Raul had done.

"Are there any marks on your body? Any evidence he assaulted you?"

"Unfortunately, he didn't leave a single bruise."

"You know how this works. Without evidence all we've got is a he said/she said thing. But if he does business in Chicago, I could get a tac guy to slap a drug charge on him."

"Yes! Lock him up. The sooner the better."

"The problem is, he'd be back on the street the next day and if he's as psycho as you say, he'd probably have an even bigger hard-on for Bryce. Or for you."

Cassidy gritted her teeth. "So I should just forget about revenge?"

"Oh no, revenge is good. We just need to let a little time go by. When Raul gets nailed in a month or so, he won't see any connection between the bust and you."

"There's one other thing. I have to talk to a detective on the car bomb case and tell him about the threats Raul made against Bryce."

"Which dicks caught the case?"

"Hensley and O'Brian."

"Hensley's at his desk across the room looking like he didn't make it home last night. He's not going to take your statement over the phone so you might as well get your butt over here."

"I feel like such a flake. Yesterday I said I didn't know anything about the car bomb, and today I'm going to say I know somebody who'd make a great suspect. Could you put in a word for me and tell him I'm not as ditzy as I seem?" *Except there's a good chance Emily thinks you are.*

"You were in shock yesterday. He won't think anything of it."

† † †

After talking to Hensley, Cassidy went home and sat at her desk to study the two emails DC had sent Kit. The first said: THIS HAS TO STOP. NO MORE PHONE CALLS, NO MORE EMAIL, NOTHING. The second said: I'M TRYING TO TELL YOU THAT WHAT WE'RE DOING IS WRONG. AND BOTH OF US COULD GET INTO A LOT OF TROUBLE IF ANYBODY FINDS OUT.

Someone who's breaking the rules. Her father? No, if Hopewell was having sex with his daughter, he'd get in trouble but she wouldn't. Someone who's reluctant. Kit seduced him and now he wants out. Someone who'd have an excellent motive for murder if she threatened to expose him or sue for child support. A motive to murder Kit but not Bryce. Not unless he thinks Bryce knows about the affair.

Cassidy took a deep breath and closed her eyes. An image popped into her mind of the young woman who'd spoken to her while she was waiting outside Morrie Schweitzer's office. "Could I have a word with him before you go in? He's my drama coach."

Drama coach! Is that what DC stands for? Morrie's a married man and her professor. A guy who'd be in deep shit if anybody found out he was sleeping with a student.

Yes, but DC could stand for anything. There's no way you could confront Morrie unless you had something that looked like proof.

She wondered if she could email DC and get a response. The address he'd used to correspond with Kit was DC@worldcast.net. If DC was a professor, he'd be on the university network, which meant he'd opened a second account with Worldcast for his personal mail. *For sending notes to students he sleeps with.* If that were the case, he'd have no reason to reply to an unknown person on his private server.

But he might reply to a student. Someone he coaches, like the drama dude. The drama dude had told her he'd met Bryce, so Bryce might be able to supply the missing name. But even if she knew his name, she didn't have access to his university address.

You should know better than to even think about this techie stuff. You never get anywhere and it gives you a headache.

You may not know a JPEG from an HTML, but Zach does, and so does Gran.

Cassidy decided to call Gran because Zach was busy and because she wanted her husband to think she was smarter than she was.

CHAPTER 30

"It's me," Cassidy said to her grandmother. "I need advice."

"Well, you came to the right person. Giving advice is one of my favorite things. Right up there with gossiping."

"It's always fun to tell other people what to do, but since I'm a therapist, I try to restrain myself."

"I thought therapists had a corner on the market."

"Giving advice isn't good therapy but sometimes I can't resist."

"I don't see the harm in it. I shove advice down people's throats every chance I get."

"There's no harm in *your* doing it. You're a wise old woman. You're supposed to give advice."

"Hah! Everybody who's young thinks getting old makes you wise. They want to believe there's some compensation for turning into a wrinkly old prune. Well, take my word for it, getting old makes you creaky, forgetful, and puts liver spots on your skin, but it doesn't make you wise."

Cassidy pictured her small, wiry grandmother, who'd been known to bounce around like a two-year-old when excited. "You're not creaky or forgetful. And you're definitely wise."

"Hah again! You're just one of those young people who wants to believe there's something good about getting old." She let out a boisterous cackle. "Well, here I am rambling on like the forgetful old fart that I am. I didn't even ask what you called about."

Cassidy explained her problem.

"You want to send an email and make it look like it came from the drama dude even though you can't use his university domain name."

"That's it."

"You can send it on AOL. It'll look like the drama dude has a second IP just like the professor does."

"Oh. Of course. I'll bet a lot of university people have accounts outside the network. But the real problem is the screen name. I'm MsCassM, Zach's Acereporter, you're Singlewhitfem. I can't think of anyone who has an address a male college student would use."

"Create a new screen name. Call yourself Dramadude."

"Oh, how simple. Why didn't I think of that?" *Because you've never created a name for yourself and you don't know how.*

"I could do it for you if you like."

"Tempting, but I need to learn how to do it myself."

"Have you thought about what you'll say in the email?"

"Something Morrie will feel a need to reply to." She squinted in thought. "I know—I'll say drama dude had an accident. I'll send it just before I go to bed so Morrie won't get it till he's home for the night and—if I'm lucky—he'll reply first thing the next morning before he has a chance to bump into drama dude on campus."

"That should do the trick."

Next Cassidy called Bryce. She told him about the drama student and asked if Bryce could provide his name.

"I know who you're talking about. Trouble is, I only saw him a couple of times. What was that guy's name? Brad something." A pause. "I think it was Westover. Yeah, that's it, Brad Westover."

Cassidy went to the computer and, after considerable trial and error, succeeded in setting up a new screen name.

† † †

As she logged off, she realized she barely had time to prepare for her two afternoon clients. She'd donned her best outfit that morning, but after being shoved against a wall and sitting on the ground, her clothing showed signs of wear. Little bits of dirt clung to her sweater and dark stains showed on the seat of her trousers. Grabbing an out-of-date pair of black stretch pants and a fuchsia blouse, she dressed rapidly, then ran downstairs and ate yogurt out of a carton while standing at the sink. One of the things she appreciated most about yogurt was that it didn't go bad the second it passed its freshness date. She was scraping the bottom of the carton for the last spoonful when her back doorbell rang.

Showing her second client out at four, she went upstairs to check her answering machine. One message. A soft female voice identified itself as Charity Hopewell and provided a number. *You were so sure that fast-talking woman at the shelter would stiff you. But as it turns out, sometimes your instincts are wrong.*

Even though Cassidy had now convinced herself that the minister wasn't the killer, she was still eager to hear what his eldest daughter had to say. *Just like Gran. You can't resist a juicy story. Which means you are definitely in the right line of work.*

Cassidy called the woman back and introduced herself, then said, "I really appreciate your getting in touch with me."

"Um ... Forest said he was planning to talk to you, and then he couldn't, so I thought I should."

Cassidy glanced at her calendar. *Client at eight. Should be able to get to wherever Charity is and back by then.* "I know this is spur of the moment, but would it be possible for us to get together now?"

"Couldn't we talk over the phone?"

"I'd rather do it face to face." *Harder for people to escape when you're looking them in the eye.*

"Do you have a pencil and paper? I'll give you my address."

Address? Thought we'd be meeting on a park bench.

† † †

Cassidy drew up in front of a well-kept two-story house with a row of dormer windows above the roofline. She rang the bell labeled with the name Charity had given her and a few moments later the door opened. Cassidy gaped in surprise. Charity was a slender young woman with golden hair cut in a sleek, ear-length bob and a pretty face made even prettier by the artful application of makeup. She wore powder blue trousers and a striped tee, both of which looked new. Except for the fresh red scratch marks on the back of her left hand, Cassidy would have taken her for a confident professional woman.

"I'm sorry," Cassidy said, realizing she'd been staring. "I thought I knew what you looked like. I mean, I thought I saw you at the wake but obviously I was mistaken."

"Forest told me about you spying on us behind the church. But that was before I had a bathtub and a cosmetician and a hair stylist. Come on, let's go upstairs. LeToya's at work so we have the place to ourselves."

They climbed two flights, and Charity opened the door of an attic apartment, letting out a cloud of smoke. Blinking rapidly, Cassidy entered a cozy space with cushy white furniture piled with pink and green pillows. Moving one aside, Cassidy sat on the sofa and Charity sank into an easy chair next to a table holding a pack of Camels and a well-filled ashtray. Tapping out a cigarette, she said, "I hope you don't mind if I smoke."

"Not at all." *Much as I hate second-hand smoke, this girl has been through so much, she's definitely entitled to a few residual vices.*

As Charity lifted the cigarette to her mouth, Cassidy could see that her hand was shaking. The younger woman inhaled deeply, then blew out smoke through her nostrils.

"You look like you're a little nervous about talking to me."

"I hate talking about myself. But Forest thought you might be able to help, so it seemed like I should see you."

"What kind of help is he looking for?"

"He didn't say. All I know is, he was scared Dad would find out he called you, then Dad did find out, and now Forest's been shipped off to our grandparents in Houston."

"Have you and Forest stayed in touch all this time?"

"You mean, since I got thrown out of the house?"

"Yeah."

"We've always been able to email each other. When Bobby and I first got to California, we had all this money Dad gave us, so we got a nice apartment and some furniture and a computer. I opened a free account and started emailing Forest. Then Bobby and I got evicted, but I was able to use the computer at the library to keep our email going."

"Would you mind telling me how you got evicted?"

Turning her head sharply away, Charity began digging at the back of her left hand.

"It's okay if you don't want to."

"Oh, hell, I might as well tell the whole story." She took another long drag. "Did you know I had a baby?"

"I heard your father sent you away after you got pregnant. It's my guess Heidi's your child."

"He took her away from me." Charity's eyes misted over and she raised a hand to cover her mouth.

"Your father, you mean."

"He gave Bobby this big envelope full of money—he didn't even give it to me—and told us to get out of his life."

"How did you feel about that?"

"I hated being home when Dad was around. He'd been calling me a slut and a whore since I first started seeing Bobby. Sometimes I think if Dad had just left me alone, I would've figured out for myself what a jerk Bobby was. But I also hated it that my dad was throwing me away. I mean, he was my father, how could he do that? And I was scared to death. I didn't know how we'd ever survive on our own. And the worst of it was, Mom let him do it."

"You thought your mom could have stopped him?" *Like a Volkswagen stopping a train.*

"Mom and I used to be so close. Kit was Dad's favorite and I was hers. Mom always stood up for me. Whenever Dad would start ragging on me, she'd tell him to shut up and he usually did. All Dad cared about was looking good so this snooty church in Winnetka would call him to be their pastor, but Mom kept saying the family was more important. Even after I got pregnant, she didn't give up on me, so I thought for sure she wouldn't let him send me away. I insisted on staying in town a few days after Dad gave Bobby the money 'cause I kept thinking Mom would come and get me. But she never did, so we finally caught a plane to LA."

"Maybe your mother got depressed over the trouble in the family and she didn't have the energy to keep fighting your dad."

"She was always so—I don't know—upbeat and happy, it's hard to imagine her being depressed, but I suppose it could've happened. If I made her depressed, then it's one more thing I did wrong."

"You think you did a lot of things wrong?" *'Course she does. You shouldn't even have to ask.*

"Are you kidding?" Charity flicked a glance at Cassidy, then ground out her cigarette and lit a new one. "I did everything wrong. The only thing I did right in my whole life was to get into treatment and stay clean afterward, but even then it took me three tries to do it."

"I think you're blaming yourself too much," Cassidy countered. "If your father hadn't made you leave home at such an early age, your life would've been completely different."

"I have to take responsibility," Charity said fiercely. "I spent too many years thinking everything was Dad's fault."

Good to take responsibility, but not good to beat yourself up over things that are done and can't be undone.

"So then you went to LA and got this nice apartment but you weren't able to keep it."

Charity moistened her upper lip. "Bobby started dealing and I started using. He'd always smoked a little weed but he was smart enough to stay away from the hard stuff. I wasn't. I used everything he brought into the house. Crack, meth, X—you name it, I used it."

Cassidy remembered what Bobby had said about getting Charity to quit using drugs. "Did Bobby try to stop you?"

"I think he liked it that I was stoned all the time."

"Why?"

"He wanted me to be dependent and needy so I wouldn't leave him. And it worked. I'd still be with him if he hadn't gone to jail."

"He told me he's trying to get you back."

"When I was on the street—before LeToya took me in—there were times when I'd start feeling weak. Life was just so fucking hard. I'd get to thinking I'd be better off with Bobby, so I'd tell him I was gonna come back. But then I'd remember how bad things were in LA, and that always kept me from going."

"Did he abuse you?"

"Not really. But he always had to be right and I always had to be wrong. I know if I went back to him I'd start using again."

"What brought you to Chicago?"

"Forest kept after me to move here so I'd be closer to him. Even though he's eight years younger, sometimes I think he's more of a grown-up than I am. When I first arrived, he paid for a month's rent at the Y. But then I came in stoned and they kicked me out."

"When did you get clean?"

"Almost a year ago. There was an outreach worker who got me into a treatment program. I'd tried before but always relapsed. This time I was so sick of myself I thought I had to either quit drugs or jump off a bridge."

"But you were still homeless when I saw you at the wake, weren't you?"

"Yeah. LeToya was my roomie at the treatment place. She's a hair stylist at this classy salon and when we finished the program, she gave me her card and said I should call. Of course I didn't because I was living on the street, but I made sure to hang onto that card. Then I went to the library just over a week ago and read this email from Forest telling me Kit had been murdered and the wake was the next morning. Well, I just fell apart. All those years I refused to have anything to do with Kit because she took Dad's side against me, and now she was dead." Covering her mouth again, Charity was silent for a moment.

"I knew she'd been searching for me. That she wanted to make things right between us. But I was just so pissed. I'd been carrying this grudge around for years and I wouldn't give it up." Charity turned her head away, let out a sigh, then resumed her story. "If I'd been thinking clearly, I probably could've figured out a way to get to the church on public transportation. But I didn't. I called LeToya and asked her to give me a ride. Then on the way home she invited me to move into her spare bedroom."

"What a great friend."

"You're not kidding. All the stuff she's done for me—it just blows me away. She styled my hair, fixed my makeup, bought me a couple of outfits, even got me hired on at her salon as a shampoo girl." Worry lines appeared on Charity's forehead. "I just hope I don't let her down."

"You think you might?"

"I've never been able to keep a job. But this time I'm gonna try really hard. I'm gonna get up every morning whether I feel like it or not and I'm not gonna miss any days of work."

"You sound really motivated. I bet you do fine."

"I hope." Charity took another drag on her cigarette, then added the butt to the pile in the ashtray.

Cassidy searched through the questions in her mind, wondering if she'd missed anything. *The Thorazine. But Charity didn't have any contact with Kit, so she wouldn't know about it. Still, it never hurts to ask.*

"Have you ever met anybody named Margaret Polanski?"

"Um ... sounds familiar. I think she was a member of the Peoria congregation."

"Was Margaret a friend of Kit's?"

"She was kinda old. We didn't have anything to do with her. She was just there."

You should stop asking about the Thorazine, because everything you hear only makes you more confused.

"All these things you've told me about your family," Cassidy said, "do you think that's what Forest wanted me to know?"

Charity shook her head. "He thought you could help him, remember? There's something he wants from you and I don't know what it is. But I can leave a message on his cell and have him call you. When I was on the street, I didn't have the money to call very often, but since I've been living here we talk all the time."

So why didn't Forest simply call me and tell me what he wants?

"I'm surprised your father didn't take away Forest's cell," Cassidy said.

"Oh, he did. But Forest's friend lent him his."

Charity went into the red and white kitchen, sat at a small polished wood desk, and picked up the phone. Cassidy leaned against the wall to listen.

"Hi, this is me. I just told my life story to Cassidy. She's that social worker you wanted to talk to. Since I don't have any idea why you wanted to meet with her, you'll have to tell her yourself." Charity handed the receiver to Cassidy. "This is on voicemail. Just give him your number."

She did as she was told.

Charity said, "He keeps the phone off because he doesn't want to talk to anybody in front of our grandparents. They're Dad's folks, and if they knew he was talking to me, they'd take his phone away. So I just leave messages and he calls me back when he's alone."

"I hope he follows up," Cassidy said. "I'm curious to find out what he wants from me."

"I'll get on his case if he doesn't."

CHAPTER 31

LATER THAT NIGHT, ZACH CAME INTO THE bedroom where Cassidy was sitting on the bed reading. She immediately noted the tension in his face.

"What?"

"There's something I have to talk to you about."

"This isn't good, is it?"

"It's about having a baby."

He's going to say no. Heaviness settled on her shoulders.

"I'm getting a drink," he said. "You want one?"

"Am I going to need it?"

"Yeah."

"Okay, bring me a bourbon and soda."

She rearranged the pillows behind her back, then sat up straight, folding her arms beneath her breasts.

You were so sure he'd agree. He's always done what you wanted in the past.

Yes, but you never wanted anything as big as a baby before.

His footsteps sounded on the stairs. He came into the room, handed her a glass, then sat in his desk chair, swiveling it around to face her. "There's this reporter, Melissa. She's in her twenties and she and her husband have an eight-month-old baby. I took her out to lunch today to find out what life was like on the other side of childbirth."

"So you're going to tell me Melissa's having a hard time."

"All it took was one question to open the floodgates. She talked nonstop for at least twenty minutes and all of it was bad news. The baby cries constantly. He sleeps during the day and stays up at night. At the beginning, she and her husband took turns walking him, but now her husband's sick of it and he's refusing to do his share. In fact, he's started blaming her because she's the one who wanted the baby in the first place."

"I don't think I like this guy."

"Melissa's exhausted. She hasn't had more than a few hours' sleep a night since the baby arrived and she's feeling so brain-dead she's worried about her job. She says they used to have a good marriage but now all they do is fight. The last time they had sex was before the baby was born." Pausing, Zach gazed steadily at Cassidy, his face full of regret. "She started off really wanting this kid and now she'd give anything to have her old life back."

Cassidy could feel herself puffing up with indignation. "What you're describing is a worst case scenario. Most babies are much easier than that, and if Melissa's marriage really was as good as she says, her husband wouldn't have turned against her. We'd never treat each other that way."

"Maybe we wouldn't, but I don't want any of those things to happen to us. I don't want a baby to come between us. I don't want our marriage to change. I don't want either one of us to turn into a sleep-deprived zombie. Melissa's in her twenties and she's completely worn out. Think what it would be like for you."

"I could handle it," Cassidy snapped. "Most babies sleep through the night after the first couple of months."

Zach raised his glass, rattled the ice cubes, and swallowed a portion of his drink. "What about our marriage? You can't tell me it wouldn't change."

She stared toward the window. "Marriages don't always change for the worse." *Yeah, but remember all those couples you've seen whose marriages started to fall apart after the birth of a child?*

"Okay, tell me about the marriages that change for the better."

Her mind went blank. After a couple of beats, she said, "Well, some couples find that a baby brings them closer." *What a total cliché.* "I mean, it gives them more in common, more they can share. They get all excited about things like the baby's first word or the baby's first step." Zach's expression was so skeptical she gave it up.

"We already have plenty in common. Do you honestly think we could go eight months with a baby who cries all night and *not* turn on each other?"

"It all depends on the maturity of the couple. You and I've been through some pretty rough times and we've always been able to keep it together."

Frowning, Zach lowered his chin. "You seem to be remembering things differently from the way I do."

Okay, so we had a few fights … a few massive fights … but we always patched it up afterward.

Swigging down more bourbon, he continued, "Before Melissa had the baby, I would've said she was damned mature, but over these past few months I've seen her crumble. You may be a highly evolved human being, but I'm not so sure about me."

"We wouldn't *have* Melissa's baby!" Cassidy pounded her fist on her leg. "Some babies are difficult. But a lot are happy and sweet-tempered and hardly ever cry. And the majority fall somewhere in the middle."

"But there's no guarantee our baby wouldn't be difficult. Maybe if I were younger, I'd be willing to take the risk, but at this point in my life I don't want to stay up half the night with a squawling infant. And—selfish as it sounds—I don't want to be relegated to second place with you."

She drew in a long breath. "Dammit, Zach, how could you do this to me? If you hadn't started talking about a baby, I never would've thought of it. But you got my hopes up and now you're stomping all over them."

Rolling his chair up close to where she sat, he leaned forward, his arms resting on his legs, his smoky eyes going a shade deeper. "You're right—I should've kept my mouth shut until I knew for sure what I wanted. Look, this isn't a final no. Let me think about it some more. Maybe I'm just overreacting to what Melissa's going through."

"I'd say you damn well are." Setting her drink on the night-stand, she stood and pressed her hand against her stomach. "I don't think I want to talk to you any more tonight." She headed toward the doorway.

"Where are you going?"

"To sit on the porch and commune with Milton." *Except Milton didn't eat his food last night.*

She put on her jacket, went outside, and settled on the top step.

Zach is so wrong about this. A baby would be good for both of you. It'd bring out his soft side, turn him into a better person. You just have to make him see things your way.

Don't you ever learn? A few months ago your marriage was teetering on the brink because of all the things you made him do.

Forcing herself to stop thinking about the baby, she scanned her yard for Milton, then went out to the sidewalk and scanned the yards on the other side of Briar. Next she walked the length of the alley, and after that, inspected the shadowy area along the base of her garage. Milton was nowhere to be found.

She sat down on the porch, feeling worse than when she'd first come out. She thought of Zach backing out of the baby deal—*wasn't a real deal, you just thought it was going to be*—and got angry all over again.

Eventually the voice of reason asserted itself. *If you choose to stay mad, you'll be the one tossing and turning, not him. Whenever you get pissy and self-righteous, you only hurt yourself.*

She trudged upstairs and into the den, where Zach was watching television. He clicked it off and waited for her to speak.

"I'm sorry I jumped on you. Even though I have trouble holding onto this thought, I realize we shouldn't have a baby unless we both agree."

He stood and reached out for her. Settling into his arms, she laid her head on his chest.

† † †

It was close to midnight when she wrote her email to DC.

MORRIE,

I HAD AN ACCIDENT AND THE DOC ORDERED ME TO STAY IN BED A FEW DAYS, SO I WON'T MAKE OUR NEXT MEETING.

BRAD WESTOVER

She wondered if the word *meeting* was right—if it might be better to say rehearsal or class or lesson—and if Brad would sign both names or just his first. Since there was no way to know, she pushed *send* and went to bed.

† † †

Cassidy was at the computer before the morning coffee finished brewing. When she opened her mailbox, a message from DC awaited her. It consisted of one line: HOW DID YOU GET MY PRIVATE ADDRESS?

Not absolute proof, but close enough.

She left a message on Morrie's machine. "I have two emails from DC to Kit. We need to talk."

The phone rang an hour later. "Something told me I shouldn't reply to that Dramadude email. So, what do you want?"

"To sit down and talk."

"And if I refuse?"

"I may have to take these emails elsewhere." *But you don't want to even think about that.*

He hesitated, then said, "Meet me at The Bull Dog Inn at four."

"Where is it?"

"A clever woman like you shouldn't have any trouble finding it."

She didn't. Switchboard.com gave her an address in Uptown, a Chicago neighborhood that had historically housed many of the city's outcasts, but was now on its way to gentrification. Then she called Zach and told him what she was planning to do.

The Bull Dog Inn was a tavern, the bottom half of its window painted black, a haphazard assortment of neon beer signs studding the glass. Stepping inside, Cassidy waited for her eyes to adjust to the subdued interior light. The room was long and narrow, with a pool table in front, a horseshoe bar in the center, and a scattering of tables in back. A handful of tattooed young people were playing pool, and a few solitary drinkers perched on stools at the bar. Cassidy identified Morrie as the man who sat with shoulders hunched, back to the door.

She slid in beside him and suggested that they move farther out of earshot. Picking up his drink, he followed her to a rickety Formica table in the rear.

"This doesn't look like your kind of place," Cassidy said.

He ran a hand through his thinning, unstyled hair. "You mean, because I'm so debonair?" Laughing humorlessly, he added, "I picked it because there's no chance anyone I know will walk through that door."

Cassidy took a manila envelope out of her purse, removed four emails, and laid them on the table. "It's obvious that you and Kit were having an affair."

"Affair is too strong a word. It was more like a two-night stand."

"I suppose you're going to say she seduced you." *She probably did. Yeah, but what's wrong with all these male authority types that they never say no?*

"Look, I know what a cop-out that is." He sat up straight and squinted across the table at Cassidy. "I know I was the teacher and it was my job to keep anything like that from happening."

"So why did it?"

"She caught me at a weak moment. She'd been after me since her freshman year when she first discovered I was in charge of a lot of the theatrical productions. I don't understand why she thought she needed to bribe me with sex. She was already getting most of the roles she wanted on the basis of her talent."

"Maybe that wasn't the only reason she wanted to seduce you."

"Well, it sure as hell wasn't my matinee-idol looks."

"You were her teacher, her coach, her director. You were in a position of power. I suspect that was an aphrodisiac for her." *Getting power over the people who had power over her. Like she did with her father.*

"I suppose you think I'm the kind of sleazeball who uses his position to get sweet young things into bed. Well, I'm not. I've had college girls throwing themselves at me for years and the only time I ever strayed was with Kit."

"What made Kit more irresistible than the others?"

"She wasn't." He moved his glass in slow small circles. "She was too ballsy, too outrageous for my taste. I like women who have some softness to them, and Kit was all hard edges."

"So how did she manage to have her way with you?"

"It was the timing. My wife and I were having problems. Lorraine took the kids and went to stay with her family. Like I said before, Kit caught me at a weak moment."

"I'd like to hear about it."

"You've got my nuts in a vise, don't you? I suppose if I refuse to divulge every humiliating detail, you'll take these emails to the head of my department. Or maybe the president of Northwestern."

Cassidy had assumed he would talk just because she possessed the emails. She hadn't put much thought into what she would do if he didn't. Her gut turned queasy. *Threats are just another version of blackmail.*

"At this point I'm not planning to show the emails to anybody. I just want to find out everything I can about Kit."

"You think I killed her."

"The fact that you slept with her certainly makes you a suspect. That is, unless you have an alibi."

"I was home the night she was murdered. My wife was there but she turned in early." He chugged down the rest of his drink.

"Tell me what happened. If it sounds believable, I'll go away and leave you alone." *And even if it doesn't, you'll still have to leave him alone, because the cops aren't interested in anything you have to say.*

Morrie gazed into his empty glass. "You want to know how we ended up in bed."

"Yes."

"A bunch of us stayed after a rehearsal to clean up. I mentioned to a colleague that my wife was out of town. I didn't think Kit could hear me, but evidently she did, because she showed up at my door later that night. I don't even know how she got my address. I was lonely, I'd had a few drinks, and I let her in. She was playing the part of an ingénue—you know, all sweet and solicitous. And I was … I was pissed at my wife."

"So you had sex with her twice while your wife was out of town. Sometime between August eleventh and the fifteenth."

"How'd you know when it happened?"

"Then your wife came back and you emailed Kit that the affair had to end."

"I emailed Kit before my wife came back. I just … I came to my senses, that's all."

"Were you able to convince Kit to stay away?"

"I cancelled our coaching sessions, wouldn't give her any office time, just basically cut off all access."

"But she did find some way to get you alone, didn't she? Some way to tell you she was pregnant with your child." *Can't be sure she told him but my instinct says she did.*

He stared at Cassidy, the color draining from his face. "You couldn't possibly know that. The police didn't even know."

"I came to the conclusion that you were the father by ruling out the other two guys she was sleeping with. And Kit would've been proactive about discovering how and when she got pregnant. And she wouldn't have kept it to herself. She would've been mad that you were refusing to see her and she would've used the pregnancy against you."

You'd like to be angry at him for sleeping with a student but you can't help feeling he was more of a victim than Kit.

"I was backstage looking for a script and Kit suddenly appeared. I think she followed me to the theater. When she first told me I was the father, I didn't believe it. I mean, Christ, we only slept together twice and she was living with your stepson. But then she explained about the antibiotics and it didn't sound like something she could've made up. My first thought was abortion, but she cut me off mid-sentence. She had this odd smile on her face and she talked in a cold voice I'd never heard from her before. She said she was going to have my baby, there was no way I could get out of it, and that we'd be connected for the rest of our lives because of the child."

"So what did she want from you?"

He raised his glass, looked into it, set it down again. "She didn't say. If she'd made some kind of threat—if she said she was going to tell my wife or the head of the department—it would've been easier. I knew she had a hold over me, but I didn't know when or how she was going to use it." He swirled the half melted ice. "I went home that night and told my wife. There was hell to pay, but at least I'd taken back a little control."

Cassidy slid the emails back into their envelope. "You must've been relieved to hear she was dead."

A shuttered look came over his face. "I'd rather not comment on that."

CHAPTER 32

CASSIDY MEASURED WATER INTO A SAUCEPAN FOR the couscous mix, put a skillet on the stove for the salmon, and reread the recipe for sautéing spinach. *Three things to get done at once. Wow, this is going to be tough.* Thinking about the holiday dinners her mother prepared, Cassidy felt a twinge of shame that she'd never given Helen proper credit for her ability to make ten different dishes appear on the table simultaneously. *You never wanted to give her credit. You preferred to marginalize her so you didn't have to compete.*

She glanced at the clock. Six thirty. Zach would be home by seven. She sat down and made a list of all the steps it would take to get the meal on the table.

A furry body rubbed against her leg; sharp teeth nipped her ankle.

"Stop that." She pushed Starshine away with her foot.

The cat jumped on the counter and glared, not even bothering to beg any more.

Cassidy had added the couscous mix to the water and was heating oil in the skillet when Zach came into the kitchen, a plastic bag dangling from his hand.

"I stopped at one of those pet super stores and picked up five varieties of diet food," he said, stacking the cans on the counter.

The oil hissed as Cassidy put the filets in the pan. "The vet never mentioned low-cal *wet* food. Probably because she doesn't sell it at her clinic."

Zach opened a can and spooned food into Starshine's bowl. The cat took a tentative sniff.

"What can I do to help?" he asked.

"Um ... " *You're so disorganized you can't even delegate.* "See that recipe over there?" She thrust her chin toward a newspaper clipping on the counter. "You can mix up a sauce for the spinach."

When everything was done, they filled their plates in the kitchen, then sat at right angles from each other at the dining room table. Cassidy looked morosely at the contents of her dish. The salmon was overcooked, the couscous was cold, and the spinach had shriveled into an unappetizing little clump.

Zach took a bite. "Hey, this is great!"

"Don't patronize me."

"Huh?"

"Nothing came out the way I wanted it to."

"Tastes fine to me."

"Well, it's not."

"Since when are you unable to take a compliment?"

"Since I started doing something I have no aptitude for."

"Cooking doesn't require aptitude. All you have to do is follow instructions. I used to cook all the time when I lived at Marina City."

"You have no idea how much that last comment fails to endear you to me."

"Let's start over," Zach said. "You tell me about your meeting with DC and I'll tell you about this new idea I have for investigating Kit's murder."

Cassidy summarized her interview with the drama teacher.

"He certainly had an excellent motive to kill Kit," Zach said.

"But not Bryce."

"The problem we keep bumping into. So what does your gut have to say about the professor? You still like him as a suspect?"

"Yeah, I do. After the way Kit treated him, I could almost sympathize if he did turn murderous."

Cassidy finished her spinach and couscous, then pushed her plate with its half-eaten salmon toward the center of the table. As if on cue, Starshine jumped onto the teak surface and began gobbling the remainder of the fish.

"We shouldn't let her eat that," Zach said. "If she fills herself up, it'll be harder to tell whether or not she likes the canned food I bought." But neither of them made a move to stop her.

Turning toward Zach, Cassidy propped her elbow on the table. "So what's this new idea you've got?"

"Follow the money. The first rule of investigating. I don't know why I didn't think of it earlier."

"What money? Oh, you mean Bryce's trust fund." She gave her husband a skeptical look. "Why would anybody think they could get their hands on Bryce's money by killing Kit?"

"Maybe Kit wasn't the intended victim. Maybe the killer went in planning to pop Bryce and then Kit surprised him in the living room and he popped her instead."

"I suppose it's a possibility."

They carried their dishes into the kitchen and set them on the counter next to Starshine's bowl, which still contained about a tablespoon of food.

"I'd say this first can isn't a winner," Zach commented.

"One down, four to go."

† † †

After cleaning the kitchen, they went upstairs to call Bryce. Zach sat in his chair and picked up the cordless while Cassidy listened in on her desk phone.

Zach said, "It just occurred to me that the person who planted the car bomb might be after your trust fund."

"What are you talking about? People can't just steal trust funds."

"Beneficiaries can inherit them."

"That's crap."

"You're probably right," Zach said pleasantly, "but I'd still like to know who inherits."

"You think my beneficiary killed Kit? Now there's an interesting piece of logic."

"You don't like the beneficiary theory, give me somebody else to look at."

"You're the investigator, not me."

"Since you can't come up with any other option, how 'bout just telling me who the goddamn beneficiary is."

"Don't know," Bryce muttered.

"You don't know who inherits?"

Bryce is already embarrassed, Zach has to rub it in.

"Doesn't matter," Zach said. "I should read the whole trust anyway. I'll need you to sign a consent form and fax it over."

"I don't have a fax machine or a consent form and I wouldn't sign it if I did."

"Oh? And why is that?"

"My trust is none of your fucking business."

"You want to make everything as difficult as possible, don't you? Well, I'm going to get a signed consent form out of you even if I have to chase you down to do it."

No question Zach'll get what he wants. Whenever they go toe-to-toe, Bryce loses.

She said, "This is me. I'm on the line too."

"Oh, hi Cass."

"I think you're probably right. The trust fund is probably irrelevant. But we're running out of leads and I'd feel better if you'd let Zach read it."

"Look, my trust is private. I don't want Zach knowing everything that's in it."

"If we weren't up against the wall, I wouldn't even ask. But somebody tried to kill you and we have to do everything we can to stop them from trying again."

"Shit! So Zach plays bad cop, you play good cop, and I cave?"

"I guess we are ganging up on you."

"Oh hell, what difference does it make? I'll sign the fucking form."

"Let's meet for lunch," Cassidy said. "Only this time we won't go back to your place and find a bomb in your car."

"I don't suppose you want to revisit my fave Italian beef joint."

"This time I get to choose."

As she put down the receiver, Zach swiveled in her direction. He took one look at her face and said, "Don't start."

"Oh yes, I am going to start."

"How can I be nice to him when he's always pissed at me?"

"How can he not be pissed when you're never nice?"

"He was pissed the moment he heard my voice. I didn't even have a chance not to be nice."

"He was pissed because you bullied him into coming to Oak Park right after he got out of Cook County. And now you've bullied him again today."

"So what do you expect me to do? You've been busting your butt to prove him innocent and he keeps refusing to cooperate. I suppose you'd like me to use therapist-speak on him, except I'm not a therapist and I don't know how to talk like one."

"Oh yes you do. I've heard you use empathy to get sources to open up. In fact you use it on me all the time."

"You don't snarl at me the way he does."

"Zach—this is important. You have to think about Bryce and what he needs. He's already built up all this anger at you and every time you talk to him you make it worse. I've had clients who never got past being angry at their parents."

"Well, I hope he finds himself a good therapist."

"Dammit, Zach! He's the kid, you're the parent. You have to take some responsibility here."

A remote look settled on Zach's face.

Withdrawing. What he always does when he doesn't want to deal with things. Cassidy realized she'd lost him but couldn't stop herself from saying one more thing. "Just don't react when he gets hostile on you."

Zach stood. "I'm going to fix myself a drink and then I'm going to flip channels." He left the room.

What's wrong with him? Can't he see how much harm he's doing his son?

Maybe he doesn't care.

Or maybe he's already doing the best he can.

She remembered seeing Zach and his mother snipe at each other in ways that resembled the sniping between Zach and Bryce. Zach's mother was critical and rejecting, and his response was to attack back. It was a side of him Cassidy seldom saw because he wasn't defensive with her or the world in general. *But the world doesn't come at him the way Bryce and his mother do. So when Bryce takes a dig, Zach goes on auto pilot and simply does what he's always done. He probably can't even imagine doing anything different.*

† † †

The phone shrilled. Cassidy burrowed deeper under the covers. She heard Zach's voice, thick with sleep. "Yeah. What was that again? Okay, hold on a minute, will you?" Coming around to her side of the bed, he gently shook her. "Go throw some water on your face. It's Forest Hopewell."

The clock on the bureau said two thirty. She donned her flannel nightshirt and stumbled into the bathroom. When she returned, Zach was standing next to his desk. He handed her the cordless. "You want me in on this?"

"No, that's all right. You go back to bed." Crossing the hall to the den, she sat in her chair. Starshine followed and plopped in her lap.

"Sorry to get you up," Forest said in a soft voice. "I just wanted to make sure my grandparents were sound asleep. That they wouldn't, you know, look in on me or anything. I don't want to get caught like I did before."

"Did your dad overhear you that first time?"

"He had a recorder hooked up to the landline. Only reason I used it was my cell batteries were dead. Now I keep them charged all the time."

"I understand there's something you'd like my help with."

"Well, yeah, sort of."

"Why didn't you call me sooner?"

"I don't know. Guess I was scared. Sometimes it seems like Dad knows everything. But then after Charity called, I thought I should try again."

"So what can I do for you?"

"Well, you see, there's this thing. I mean, it's about Mom." He stopped. "How do I know you won't tell anybody?"

"If you disclose something to me in confidence, I can't repeat it. It would be a breach of ethics if I did." *He's not a client. Doesn't matter. If you promise, you have to keep your word.*

"Ethics don't mean shit. My dad has everybody under his thumb."

My God, this kid is terrorized. "What can I do to get you to trust me?"

Forest let out a long sigh. "Ever since Kit's murder, I hardly get any sleep. Soon as I turn off the light, these thoughts start going 'round in my head and I can't make them go away."

"Can you tell me what the thoughts are?"

"Maybe I should explain about my family first. So you won't think I'm nuts when I tell you about my thoughts. Or maybe I am nuts. I can't even tell anymore."

Starshine nuzzled the hand that was holding the phone and Cassidy obediently scratched the top of the cat's head with her other hand.

Forest said, "You already know about Chare getting thrown out, don't you?"

"She told me."

"Mom didn't know he was going to do it, then after she found out she had a total fit about it. Kit said Mom even threatened to leave him. Kit thought Dad was perfect—that his work as a pastor was so important nobody should be allowed to interfere, not even his wife or daughter. But I thought he was wrong to send Chare away with that dickhead boyfriend of hers. I was sure Mom wouldn't let Dad go through with it. She'd always been able to stop him before. But this time she got sick a couple of days after Chare left. At least I thought she was sick. She stayed in bed a lot, she was really weak, her mind got all jumbled. I told Dad he should take her to the doctor, but Dad and Kit both agreed there was nothing to worry about so I shut up."

"Did your mom get better?"

"No, but it was a long time before I understood why. A few weeks after Chare left, we moved to Winnetka, and then right after that, Peg came to live with us so she could take care of Mom."

"Peg?"

"Our housekeeper. She used to be in the Peoria congregation. Kit didn't want her here. She begged Dad to get rid of her but he insisted we had to have someone to watch over Mom."

Peg has to be Margaret Polanksi!

"Pretty soon after we got to Winnetka, Dad told me he'd taken Mom in for tests and the doctor said she had some condition I'd never heard of and she was just stuck with it. Dad made me swear not to tell anybody."

"That must've been horrible. Almost as if you'd lost her."

"I *did* lose her. Well, it seemed like I did. My real mom was smart and funny and wanted to hear all about everything. Then, after she changed, sometimes she'd ask about school but she couldn't keep track of what I said. With Mom in bed so much, Kit and I started hanging out together. But then, whenever Dad came into the room, she'd forget about me and revolve around him like a little planet. Then she found out about Dad and Peg and she just went berserk."

"How'd she find out?"

"She walked in on them. After that, Kit started doing everything he hated just to spite him. That was when she finally told me the truth." He paused. "Promise you won't tell anybody?"

Cassidy was fairly certain she knew what was coming next. "Not unless you give me permission."

The boy's voice went harsh with anger. "Dad and Peg are feeding Mom drugs. She isn't sick at all—just drugged up. Dad took her life away. So he could get this rich church in Winnetka. So he could have politicians eating out of his hand."

"Your dad got a friendly psychiatrist to prescribe Thorazine for Peg, didn't he? And then they used it to sedate your mother."

"How'd you know that?"

Cassidy told him about finding the Thorazine in Kit's medicine cabinet.

"Kit said she took it just to give Dad a hard time."

"Did she know about the Thorazine from the beginning?"

"I think so. She went along with it because she thought Dad was doing so much good in the world it didn't matter what he did at home. But then—when she found out about him and Peg—she totally changed her mind."

Kit wanted to take her mother's place. Be her father's confidante and companion. Felt betrayed when she found out he'd picked Peg over her.

Cassidy said, "Charity doesn't know about your mother being drugged, does she?"

"I couldn't tell her. It would've been one more thing for her to feel guilty about."

"So—getting back to your sleep problem—what are the thoughts that keep you awake at night?"

"I keep picturing Dad with a gun in his hand shooting Kit. Then I feel like I must be crazy to even imagine such a thing. Then I think about what he did to Charity and Mom and it doesn't seem so crazy."

"Did he have a reason to kill Kit?"

"Well, there are a couple of things. Dad gave Kit money all the time because he was afraid if he didn't, she'd tell the church elders what he was up to. So maybe he got tired of giving her everything she wanted. Or maybe he was afraid she'd tell Bryce. I mean, she was more serious with him than she'd been with anyone else, so maybe Dad thought her being with him was too big a risk."

Could the minister be trying to kill Bryce because he's afraid Bryce knows too much? That'd be pretty paranoid. But then there's no reason to assume Hopewell isn't.

Cassidy said to the boy, "Are you ever afraid your dad might hurt you?"

"I didn't used to be. I just stayed out of his way and he hardly noticed I was there."

"But now he knows you tried to set up a meeting with me."

"Yeah."

No wonder this kid can't sleep at night.

"So is this why you wanted to talk to me? To tell me you think your dad might've murdered Kit?"

"Well, it's part of it. But the main thing is, I thought that with you being a social worker and all, you might know of some way to help Mom."

Yikes! You can report child abuse and elder abuse but I don't know one thing you can do about spousal abuse.

"I'm going to have to think about this. I bet you've been feeling pretty awful, knowing your dad was drugging your mother and not being able to do anything about it."

"I made an anonymous call to the police once but they said they couldn't even go to the house unless somebody official like a doctor reported it. I considered talking to my school counselor, but I didn't think she'd believe me. And even if she did try to do something, I figured Dad would make her sorry she ever got involved."

Sees his father as invincible. But there's gotta be some way to bring this egomaniac down. A glimmer of an idea began to form in Cassidy's mind.

"You know, I think there might be a way we could rescue your mom but we'd need Charity's help. You'd have to give me permission to tell her."

"What're we gonna do?"

"I'd rather not say until I've worked out some of the kinks." *Of which there are many.* "Just let me know whether or not I can tell Charity."

"I guess it'd be okay."

"You'd have to play a part in this too, and it could be fairly difficult. Do you have a credit card?"

"Yeah, sure."

"Is there any way you could fly to Chicago without your grandparents knowing you were gone? I mean, you'd have to keep them from finding out for six or seven hours, maybe even longer. You know, tell them you were going someplace with a friend. Or staying overnight. Or something." *Tie them up. Lock them in a trunk. No, don't even think of things like that. This is harder than you realized. You may be asking the impossible.*

"I can't see how I could get away without them knowing about it."

"Well, maybe we could do it without you." *No you can't. You'll have to wait until his father lets him come home.* "Don't worry about it. If you think of something, give me a call."

CHAPTER 33

CASSIDY SET THE CORDLESS ON THE TABLE next to her chair, her movements unsettling the calico napping on her chest. The cat jumped down, walked into the hallway, then looked over her shoulder to see if Cassidy was following, a sign that she wanted her human to accompany her downstairs and feed her.

"This isn't breakfast time," Cassidy objected. "Look at the window—it's still dark. Just because I'm out of bed doesn't mean you get to eat."

The cat continued to the head of the stairs, then looked back at Cassidy again.

"I want you to come to bed with me. I need you to curl up between our heads and purr me to sleep. Especially now, when I'm upset about Forest and his mother."

Starshine ambled down to the landing in the middle of the stairs, then waited for Cassidy. Keeping her eyes averted, pretending she just happened to be going in the same direction, Cassidy went after her. When she thought she was close enough, she made a grab for the cat, who easily eluded her and scampered down to the living room.

Cassidy returned to the bedroom, where Zach was sitting in his chair reading a magazine.

He looked up. "So what did Forest have to say?"

"He made me promise to keep it confidential."

"Whatever it was, you don't look happy."

"He's got this huge problem and he wants me to help him, but I can't see how I'm going to do it."

Zach's forehead creased in concern. "If there's any way I can help, just let me know."

What she wanted from her husband was to pick his brain, to bounce ideas back and forth, to do joint problem solving the way they always did when they worked together. *Dammit, Forest, why couldn't you have given me a little wiggle room? Confidentiality except with my bed-partner and crime-consultant.*

"We might as well catch a few hours' sleep before the alarm goes off."

Within minutes Zach began to snore softly, but Cassidy remained wide awake. *Someone should invent a purring machine for people whose cats refuse to obey. Which is not to say there any cats who do obey.*

Cassidy went downstairs on a mission to retrieve Starshine. She found the calico on a credenza beneath the dining room window gazing out at the street. *How can these creatures spend so much time staring at nothing? Well, they obviously have a richer fantasy life than you do. For all you know, she's envisioning you as a tiny rodent she's about to have for dinner.*

Starshine left her window and trotted into the kitchen to sit beside her bowl, which still contained a spoonful of the new food Zach had bought. Cassidy knew if she carried Starshine up to the bedroom without filling her stomach, the cat would sit by the door and howl. *Only way you can get her to purr is by giving her the food she wants.*

Cassidy filled the cat's dish, then put on a coat and went outside to look for Milton, whom she had not seen for the past two nights. When she discovered that the food she'd put out earlier that evening was gone, she felt a small bubble of hope. But then she thought of the possums, squirrels, rabbits, and other critters that occasionally strolled through her yard and her bubble burst.

Lowering herself onto the top step, she folded her arms across her chest and reflected on some of the reasons a homeless cat might go missing. There was the heavy traffic on Austin Boulevard a block to the east. The dogs that sometimes got out of their yards and ran loose. The diseases that caused strays to crawl into the bushes and die.

Shivering, she went inside. She didn't exactly feel better, but at least she'd transferred her worries from Adele to Milton. Starshine's bowl was polished, and the cat didn't complain when Cassidy picked her up. Settling into the waterbed, she drifted off to the sound of a lulling purr.

†††

The phone rang while Cassidy was in the basement trying to finish the laundry before she had to leave for her lunch with Bryce. Dashing upstairs, she lifted the handset off the kitchen wall. "This is Cassidy McCabe," she said, panting slightly.

"I figured it out!" Forest announced. "There is a way I can fly to Chicago without my grandparents knowing about it. But it has to be this Friday while they're attending an all-day seminar. They'll be leaving the house around seven and won't be back until after six. Thursday night I'll rig up pillows to make it look like I'm in bed, then sneak off after they go to sleep. That way I can catch the earliest flight into Chicago."

"That's a brilliant idea!"

"I guess I didn't tell you my grandparents run a catalogue business out of their house, which means one or the other is always around to keep an eye on me. But I've been so good—so careful not to make trouble—they finally trust me enough to leave me alone for a day. Heh heh heh," he chortled, "little do they know."

Oh God, you came up with this half-baked plan and now you have to do it.

Cassidy asked, "How were you able to call me if someone's always watching you?"

"There's this library not far from the house that I can go to whenever I want. I guess they think reading is next to Godliness or something. So, what's the plan?"

She took a deep breath. "You and Charity and I are going to kidnap your mother."

"What?"

"We'll wait until your father leaves the house," *Lord, I hope he leaves the house,* "go inside, face down Peg, and take your mother away with us."

"Omigod!"

You're asking a lot of a fifteen-year-old. Yeah, but you can't do it without him. If you and Charity go in alone, it's home invasion.

"This isn't gonna work," the boy said flatly. "Peg'll never let us leave with Mom."

"How could she stop us?"

"She's the enforcer. She tells Heidi and me what to do and we do it. Kit was the only one who could ever stand up to her."

"What makes it so hard to stand up to her?"

"I don't know. I just never felt like I could."

"Sometimes we have to ignore our feelings and simply do what needs to be done. If you believed this was the only possible way to rescue your mother and you had Charity and me standing right beside you, do you think you could do it?"

"I guess," he said in a small voice. "I mean, getting Mom away from Dad is all that really counts, isn't it?"

"Good. Now, do you think your father will be out of the house on Friday?"

"Shouldn't be a problem. He hardly ever stays home."

"The other thing is, we have to get your mother to come with us. Will she understand what we're doing? Do you think she'll come willingly?"

Forest hesitated. "She has good days and bad days. Getting her out might be difficult. She never likes to leave the house and she's pretty scared of Peg."

This does not sound good. All three of us may end up in the joint.

"Well," Cassidy said, "we'll just have to find a way to get her to come. So, do you think you can manage to book yourself a ticket? Or do you want me to handle it from my end?"

"No problemo. That's the easy part."

† † †

Cassidy described the kind of restaurant she had in mind, and Bryce took her to a café in Evanston. The waitress, clad in a simple black dress, had silver hair and a refined face. Savory smells emanated from the kitchen, and Sarah Vaughan's bell-toned voice sang in the background.

Glaring at her from across the table, Bryce said, "Okay, give me the damn form." He signed it with a flourish and handed it back to her.

Cassidy thanked him, then didn't know what to say next. After an awkward pause, she asked about his classes.

Bryce gave a short reply, turned his face toward the window, huffed a little, then slipped into his usual bantering tone.

She was happy to see their food arrive. It gave her an excuse to break off their conversation and consider her approach to the main item on her agenda.

No easy way. You just have to put it out there, then do your best to keep him from shutting down on you.

He just started his hamburger. Let him eat in peace.

Bryce can talk and chew at the same time. The longer you wait, the harder it's going to be.

She took another bite of chicken salad, sipped some iced tea, then cleared her throat and said, "For the past couple of years you and Zach seemed to be getting along pretty well. But now you're mad at him all the time, just like at the beginning."

"You know something? Ever since you pulled me out of my car, you've been treating me like one of your clients."

She grimaced, recognizing that he'd nailed her. "I have?"

"Yeah."

"But you're not angry at me the way you are at Zach."

Bryce gave her a long look. "I suppose you want me to tell you why I'm pissed so you can go home and repeat everything I say to Zach."

She had consistently refused to keep secrets from his father on the grounds that parents needed to maintain a united front.

"Does that mean if I promise to keep it to myself you'll talk?"

"I might."

Cassidy regarded him with surprise.

He's willing to communicate because he wants to improve his relationship with Zach?

More likely because he wants to get you on his side against his father.

"All right," Cassidy said, "I won't tell Zach unless you give me permission."

Sitting straighter, Bryce exhaled a short irritated breath. "You already know why I'm pissed. He keeps pushing me around. He expects me to jump every time he snaps his little finger. I try to tell him to leave me alone but he just leans on me harder until I give in and do what he wants."

"You must hate it when he steamrolls over you like that."

"And the other thing ... well, I don't suppose I have any business being pissed about that."

"You can be pissed about anything you want."

"It kinda bothers me that he didn't believe I was innocent until the car bomb showed up. But I know how bad it looked and I guess I shouldn't've just expected him to take me at my word."

"He's your father and you wanted him to believe you."

Folding his arms on the table, Bryce leaned forward, his dark eyes turning moist. "Yeah, but if I were in his place, I'm not sure I would've believed me either."

"Doesn't matter. It's still okay to be hurt and angry that he didn't." Cassidy took another bite, giving herself time to think about what she wanted to say next. "When you first got out of Cook County, you said you were mad because Zach showed up drunk the night of the murder."

A flush rose on Bryce's angular cheeks. "Well, I guess I can't be pissed about that anymore, considering I got drunker than he did, passed out, and tried to off myself."

"You were angry the night of the murder."

Bryce shrugged. "I guess. But he did okay so there wasn't any reason for me to get so pissed."

"You needed his help and he wasn't as clear-headed as you wanted him to be."

"I don't know. It seems like he always lets me down. But he doesn't really, so I don't know why I feel that way."

"Is there something you want from him you're not getting?"

"Yeah, I'd like him to be a father."

"How would he be different if he were a father?"

"I've never had a father so how would I know? Look, I'm tired of you messing with my head. This conversation is officially over."

Clasping her hands, Cassidy held them against her chest. "Bryce, please, don't cut me off. Your relationship with your father is important."

"No, it's not. Nothing's going to change."

"You need to tell Zach what you told me."

"Oh no you don't! You're not getting me to tell Zach anything."

Leaning in closer, she laid her hand on Bryce's arm. "You've established this pattern with Zach of never getting what you need, and if you don't fix it, you'll just keep repeating the same pattern in other relationships."

Bryce stared out the window for several beats, then allowed his gaze to settle on Cassidy's face. "You mean, like I didn't get what I needed from Kit?"

"Zach can be a good listener. If you don't start taking potshots, he'll be able to hear what you have to say." *At least I hope he will.* "I'll tell him you want to talk, then I can sit in with the two of you to make sure things stay on track."

You're on dangerous ground here. If Bryce says his piece and Zach doesn't change, the kid'll feel even more hopeless than he does already.

"That'll never work."

"Why not?"

"We can't talk to each other."

"Have you ever tried?"

Bryce didn't answer.

"What have you got to lose?"

"Things could get even worse."

"Or they could get better."

"You really want me to say all this stuff to him?"

"I really do."

After a long silence, Bryce asked, "When?"

My God, he's actually going to do it!

"When would you like?"

"Maybe tomorrow night. But you have to come to my place. I'm not going to Oak Park."

"We'll be there." *I'll arrive with Zach in tow, even if I have to threaten divorce to do it.*

CHAPTER 34

"**D**AD'S GIVING MOM THORAZINE? SHE'S BEEN TAKING it ever since I left? I've *seen* people on Thorazine—you know, psychos just out of the hospital. Man, they're all a bunch of zombies." Charity's skin darkened and her jaw clenched. "My father is so fucking full of himself. Thinks he's this great spiritual leader but he's really the scum of the earth. I thought I hated him before but now I want to kill him. I know people ... you know what I mean? I could find somebody to take him out."

"You can't have your father killed!" Cassidy tried to make eye contact but the younger woman refused to look at her. "You'd never get over it. It would haunt you forever."

"No it wouldn't. Look what he's done to the family. He deserves to die."

You and Charity operate out of distinctly different moral codes.

Cassidy said, "Half the people who try to hire a hitman end up soliciting an undercover cop instead."

A sullen look came over Charity's face.

Shouldn't have questioned her competence at arranging murders.

"The important thing is to get your mother into a safe place. Forest is flying in early Friday morning, then the three of us will take your mom out of the house and put her in a residential treatment program. You probably know that these programs are confidential. Once we get her inside the door, there won't be any way your dad can find her."

"We're going into my dad's house? Just the three of us? And we're going to try and get Mom away from Margaret Polanski—I mean Peg?" Charity took several rapid puffs on her cigarette, the smoke drifting into Cassidy's face.

"Are you nervous about confronting Peg?" *Must be one hell of an enforcer if she's able to intimidate somebody who never even lived with her.*

"I'm not afraid of her! But I do remember her yelling at the kids at church. Seemed like she kinda had it in for me."

"You were a teenager then. Now that you're an adult, she won't seem so scary."

"What if Dad's there?"

"We won't go inside unless we're sure he's gone."

"But won't he have us arrested?"

It's true. We could all end up in the slam on kidnapping charges.

Cassidy forced herself to speak calmly. "If he did that, the press would get hold of it." *Zach'd have a TV reporter camped on the minister's front lawn.* "I don't think your dad would risk such bad publicity."

Scratching the back of her hand, Charity said, "It seems impossible. Nobody ever goes up against my dad and wins."

"Your mother's had seven years of her life taken away. Somebody has to get her out of that house, and we're the only ones who can do it."

Charity exhaled on a long sigh. "Okay, I'm in."

†††

Cassidy reached for her Rolodex. Since she wasn't an addictions counselor, she'd never had occasion to place a client in rehab, but she did have contacts. Assembling a list of treatment centers would be easy, but persuading the person in charge to accept a patient who was not in fact addicted would take some fast-talking on her part. *Adele doesn't meet any of the usual criteria, which means her healthcare provider won't pay unless her doctor comes up with a creative diagnosis.*

Cassidy compiled a list of nineteen treatment facilities. The first sixteen administrators responded with a flat no.

The seventeenth facility was located in Lake Bluff, a suburb twenty miles north of the city. She dialed, sat on hold for five minutes, then was greeted by a pleasant-sounding woman who identified herself as the admissions coordinator.

After explaining that she was a therapist, Cassidy said, "I have an adult client whose mother—a perfectly healthy woman with no history of mental illness—is being forced to take Thorazine by her husband. My client has convinced her mother to leave this abusive man, but we both believe the mother needs to go into a treatment facility to recover from the psychological effects of being drugged over a long period of time."

"That poor woman!" the coordinator replied, sounding more human than any of her predecessors.

Cassidy continued to build her case, and in the end, the coordinator said, "This is pretty irregular, but we have to get that woman away from her husband. I have some favors I can call in. You get her here, we'll have a bed available."

†††

Feeling a sense of relief, Cassidy turned her attention to dinner. Between outgoing calls, Zach had gotten through to tell her he would be home around eight thirty.

She went down to the kitchen, racking her brain to think of a meal she could throw together in less than an hour. Opening the pantry door, she spotted a box of macaroni and cheese. Since she considered it to be a shortcut to heart-attack city, something she would never buy herself, she knew Zach had to have been the culprit who brought the box into the house. *Probably has more fat grams than a Big Mac. 'Course you could add a salad. And it wouldn't take any time at all to cook, and even you couldn't screw it up.*

While she was waiting for the water to boil, Starshine landed on the counter and gave her an intense stare.

"You've already nixed three out of the five cans Zach brought home. Do you have any idea how disappointing it is when you get all twitchy, then walk away?"

What do you expect? She's a cat.

Cassidy dished up food from the fourth can. The calico went on high alert and instantly scarfed it down.

"You ate it! You actually ate an entire serving of diet food! Does this mean the war is finally over?"

Cassidy offered seconds and the food disappeared before she could turn around. As she was fitting the plastic lid onto the half-empty can, the calico bit her thumb.

"What was that about?"

Starshine's eyes went cold and yellow.

"Oh, I get it. You like this stuff so much you want the whole can. Which would completely defeat the purpose of putting you on a diet."

Starshine jumped down and stalked out of the room.

So much for a peace settlement.

† † †

"You did what?" Zach demanded.

"I arranged for you and Bryce to sit down together and talk things out."

"You set this up without asking me?"

"Obviously. Otherwise it wouldn't come as a surprise."

Zach said in a steely tone, "Why didn't you check with me first?"

"I don't know. I just didn't think of it."

"Bullshit!"

"Okay, I didn't tell you because I knew you wouldn't want to do it."

Zach was seated on the sofa, his spine rigid, his hands on his thighs. "You thought that presenting me with a done deal would make me more cooperative?"

"No, of course not. It was stupid. I should have told you."

"So maybe you ought to call the meeting off."

"You have to do this. You can't just continue this pattern of responding to your son the same way you respond to your mother. If Bryce doesn't work things out with you, he may never be able to form healthy relationships with anyone."

"Have I told you lately how much I hate it when you throw psychobabble at me?"

"All right, don't do it for Bryce, do it for me. Please, Zach, it's really important to me that you at least listen to what he has to say."

"Listening to Bryce seldom makes me feel warm and fuzzy."

"He's not going to be on the attack this time. Please, Zach, don't let me down."

A deep frown carved itself into his face. "Isn't it against the rules to inflict therapy on your own family?"

"I just want you to listen."

"Shit," he grumbled. "I don't know why I give in to you all the time."

She could see his body begin to relax.

"All right, I'll go. But don't expect me to keep my mouth shut if he starts throwing zingers." Zach went upstairs to the computer room.

Trailing after him, Cassidy sat at her desk and started shuffling papers. A few minutes later, he came into the bedroom. "Where's that consent form? I need to fax it to Victor."

She dug it out of her purse and handed it to him.

"I almost forgot to tell you," Zach added. "The defense attorney got the locks back from the lab and it turns out we were right. We now have proof that the back door lock was picked."

"So the killer came in the back door, shot Kit, then closed the door behind him when he left."

"Seems a little odd, doesn't it?"

† † †

Cassidy had put on her nightshirt and was hanging her jeans in the closet when the phone rang.

"This is Angie. There's something I'd like to tell you. I probably shouldn't even be bothering you with this … It's pretty trivial except it isn't trivial to me and I really wanted to tell somebody, and you're the only one who knows … well, you know, about Bryce and me."

Cassidy smiled. "Don't make me wait. I'm dying to hear."

"Bryce called. After all this time. I thought I'd never hear from him again, but he called tonight and asked me to play pool with him. Well, I didn't even know how. Nobody's ever asked me before. But he said he'd teach me, so we went. I was kinda scared. I was afraid he'd be mad because, you know, I encouraged him. I mean, I almost feel like I took advantage of him. I suppose that sounds weird because it's usually the other way around—I mean, guys usually take advantage of girls. But Bryce didn't say a word about what happened. He just acted like everything was normal. At first it was awkward, but after a while it did seem pretty normal. So I guess everything's gonna be all right between us after all."

CHAPTER 35

"You want something to drink?" Bryce inquired of Cassidy and Zach, who were standing in his entryway. The boy flicked a guilty look at Cassidy, who kept her expression carefully neutral.

"I'll take a beer," Zach replied.

When they were settled in the red and black living room, the two men sipping from bottles, Zach said to Bryce, "So, how's school?"

"I'm a little behind. It's hard to concentrate."

"I don't know how you manage to study at all. If I were you, I'd probably drop out."

"Being in school helps keep my mind off the other shit. I have this political science class that's pretty interesting."

Both appeared riveted by the discussion of Bryce's schoolwork. Cassidy allowed them five minutes of small talk before she intervened.

She said to Bryce, "I believe you have some things to discuss with your father."

Drawing in a breath, Bryce said in a mild voice, "It bothers me that you make me do things. I'm an adult now. I shouldn't have to do what you say."

After a short hesitation, Zach replied, "I wouldn't push you around if you weren't such an obstructionist. Cass and I are doing our best to keep you out of prison, but anytime I ask for something simple, like a consent form, you refuse to cooperate."

"Yeah, but you don't really ask. You start off by telling me what to do and that makes me not want to do it."

Zach frowned. Cassidy was afraid he might shoot off an angry response, but instead he shifted in his chair, then took a long pull at his beer. "Okay, I can understand that. I don't do well when I'm ordered around either. If I stop coming on so strong, do you think you could be a little less hostile?"

"I don't know. Maybe."

The room fell silent.

Catching Bryce's eyes, Cassidy said, "You have to tell him the other part."

"Um … what other part?"

She didn't answer.

Bryce glanced at Zach, then away. Clearing his throat, he said, "I feel like I'm not important to you. Like I don't matter."

Zach ran a hand over his face. "That's not true. You are important. It's just that I'm not very good at showing it." He rubbed his forehead. "I've never even said 'I love you' to anybody but Cass."

"Well, I certainly wouldn't expect anything that extreme."

"You just did it again. I was trying to be honest and you took a dig at me."

"The reason I take digs is because of all the things you don't do. Take the night of the murder. It would've made all the difference if you could've said you believed me. Or put your arm around me. Or done *anything* to show you were on my side."

Zach stared at the floor, then ran a hand over his face again. "Yeah, I should've done those things. It's just ... I don't know why ... it doesn't come naturally."

"So I guess nothing's going to change," Bryce said bitterly.

Oh shit! What if your meddling makes things worse? Some people do better if they don't *talk.*

"Don't give up on me so fast," Zach said. "Just because it doesn't come naturally doesn't mean I can't do it. I do care about you. I'd like for us to be closer. If it means I have to be a little more expressive, I'll do it."

The anger cleared from Bryce's face. Tipping up his bottle, he took a long swig of beer. "If you're willing to work at this, I guess I could do the same."

† † †

They were less than a mile from home when Cassidy saw a cat cross the street half a block ahead of them. The cat walked with a slightly uneven gait.

"Slow down," she said. "That could be Milton."

"Why are we looking for Milton?"

"I haven't seen him for a couple of nights now. I think he might've stopped coming to the house."

Wandering across a nearby yard, the cat disappeared into a hedge.

"Stop the car," Cassidy said as they came abreast of the house. Zach braked and she jumped out. She inspected the hedge but it was too dark to see inside it.

Talking through the car window, she asked, "Would you mind waiting till he comes out?"

"Not if it's quick. If he takes too long, you can have the car and I'll walk home."

A short time later the cat emerged from the end of the hedge and began a leisurely stroll back across the street, with Cassidy following. She called "kitty, kitty," and the cat turned to look at her. One of his ears was missing.

She climbed back into the car. "It *is* Milton. I don't understand why he'd leave our block when I was providing regular meals."

"Don't ask me about cats."

"I guess he's moved on." *No good-bye, nothing. Just like so many of his two-legged male counterparts.*

"So now you don't have to be the neighborhood cat lady."

She let out a sigh.

"That should be a good thing."

† † †

Cassidy met Forest at O'Hare Airport at six Friday morning. As he approached, a slender teen with a knapsack on his back, she could see that his carriage was stiff and tense.

"So far so good," he said, the corners of his mouth lifting in a shy smile.

"I assume you don't have any checked luggage."

"Nah. I figured if I needed anything besides a toothbrush and a change of clothes, I'd buy it here."

"Once your dad finds out what we're up to, he's likely to cut off your credit."

"I borrowed a few bills on my card, so I'll be all right."

"You're pretty good at this stuff."

"I'm thinking I've got a future in the CIA."

They retrieved the Toyota from the parking garage and drove to Charity's apartment. Cassidy had told the young woman to expect them at seven, but they were held up by rush hour traffic and arrived twenty minutes late.

Cassidy rang the bell. After a while, the door was opened by a mocha-colored woman in a plush red robe.

"I'm LeToya. Chare told me what was going down. Come on upstairs." Their hostess scrambled upward, with Cassidy and Forest coming after her. Once they were inside the attic apartment, LeToya said, "How 'bout some coffee while you wait for Chare to get her skinny white ass out of bed?"

Cassidy said, "She isn't up yet?"

"She always has a hard time rolling out. She was gonna set the alarm but I guess she forgot."

Didn't want to set the alarm. Doesn't want to get out of bed. Most of all doesn't want to face what's coming next.

LeToya handed mugs to Cassidy and Forest. "You want anything in it?"

Cassidy indicated that she did, and the other woman set a sugar canister and a milk carton on the counter.

"You're on your own now, 'cause I gotta get ready for work." LeToya disappeared into the bathroom.

Leaning against the wall, Forest hooked his thumbs into the pockets of his khaki pants. Cassidy located a spoon in the sink, dried it off, and ladled sugar into her brew. Adding a large glug of milk, she propped her back against the counter and cradled her mug in her hands.

Several minutes later a pajama-clad Charity, cigarette in hand, shuffled into the kitchen and poured coffee for herself.

"Hey," Forest said, "I've been up all night. Least you could do is be dressed by now."

"Stuff it, treehead." She took a long drag. "There's no reason to hurry. Nothing we can do till Dad leaves the house anyway."

"He'll be gone by ten."

"That's more than two hours from now."

Charity took her time getting ready. She showered, blew her hair dry, donned Calvin Klein jeans and a clingy Liz Claiborne sweater, then spent twenty minutes on her makeup.

Wants to look good on the momentous occasion of her return to the family domicile. Even if her return is more of a home invasion than a homecoming.

✝ ✝ ✝

After they left LeToya's apartment, Cassidy found a nondescript café and pulled into its parking lot. "Charity's right. We do have a lot of time to kill." Inside they slid into a round booth with a cracked vinyl backrest.

Cassidy said to Forest, "So, you think we can count on your dad being out of the house by ten?"

"Yeah, chances are he will be."

"Chances are?" Charity squeaked. "I thought this was a sure thing."

Forest scowled at his sister. "He does leave most days. But I can't give you any guarantee."

"I know this is scary," Cassidy said to the young woman. "And it's going to be hard. But we've all done hard, scary things before. You went into treatment and stayed clean afterward. That was a very hard thing to do." She turned to Forest. "And you called me a second time, even though you got caught the first. That was hard too." She clasped Charity's left hand and Forest's right. "This mission is going to be difficult, but not impossible."

A young waitress with heavy makeup and thickly moussed black bangs that nearly covered her eyes asked for their orders. *So who's she trying to impress with the hair-in-the-eyes look? Maybe set her sights on a male sheepdog.*

"I don't want anything," Forest said.

"Me either," Charity echoed.

"Could you give us a few minutes?" Cassidy asked the waitress. When the woman was gone, she said, "You have to eat. We all need to be as alert and high-energy as possible, and that won't happen if we're running on empty. Order something with protein in it and force it down. That way you won't fade out a couple of hours from now."

And you're going to do the same, because these kids need to believe their leader is more fearless than she feels.

CHAPTER 36

CRUISING ONE OF MANY TREE-LINED STREETS IN an upscale section of Winnetka, Cassidy approached the Hopewell mansion. She tapped on the brake as she came abreast of it to give Charity more time to take in the Victorian in all its colonnaded, fish-scaled glory.

"There it is," Forest said from the backseat. "Home sweet home—not."

"Jesus!" Charity replied. "It's not a house, it's a freaking mausoleum."

Cassidy parked about ten yards beyond the detached garage. With trees and shrubbery blocking the view from the windows, she was confident the car wouldn't be seen.

Twisting around to address Forest, she said, "You ready?"

He stared at her for a moment, then jumped out of the Toyota, ran toward the garage, and peered in a window. His face beaming with vindication, he gave them a thumbs-up.

Cassidy and Charity were out of the car by the time he returned.

"Told you Dad'd be gone," Forest said to his sister.

"So now we have to go inside?"

"Just follow me. Everything's gonna be fine."

"What if we run into Peg?"

Cassidy said, "As long as we stick together and keep moving, I don't see how she can stop us." *Short of attacking us with a pistol or an Uzi.*

They circled around the back of the house, jogging to get past the area where they were most exposed, then gathered on the rear porch. Forest shoved his key in the lock. The door made a high-pitched squeak as it opened, Cassidy's scalp tingling at the sound. They traversed a cluttered utility porch, then followed a diagonal path across one corner of the state-of-the-art kitchen.

Passing through a doorway, they climbed a narrow back staircase. At the top, Forest leaned toward them and whispered, "You wait here." He went inside a room, then returned and shook his head. "She must be in the sunroom."

They followed Forest along a hall that went from the back of the house to the front, the corridor ending at the head of the grand staircase. Forest veered to the right, creeping along the balcony that ran in front of a row of closed doors. Cassidy's gaze swept the living room below. Much to her relief, it was uninhabited.

The boy turned into the room adjacent to the far wall, with Cassidy coming after him and Charity lagging behind. Sunlight poured through windows and greenery cascaded from pots on all sides. Adele lay on a velvet sofa, her face on a pillow, her eyes closed, an afghan wrapped around her.

"Omigod!" Charity said in a hushed voice as she came into the room. "She's so small. And so white. Like she never goes outside."

Forest began shaking the pale woman. "Mom, you have to wake up. Charity's here."

Adele opened her eyes and struggled to sit up. As the afghan fell away, Cassidy could see that she was wearing only a thin nightgown.

Crouching beside her mother, Charity reached for her hand. "It's me, Mom, it's me. I've come back to get you."

"We need to get her on her feet," Cassidy said. "Pull her arms over your shoulders and lift her up."

Forest made an attempt, but Charity stayed where she was, holding her mother's hand.

Noticing that Adele's feet were bare, Cassidy got down on her hands and knees and looked under the sofa for her slippers, which were nowhere to be seen.

The door burst open. Jumping to her feet, Cassidy saw Peg standing in the doorway with Heidi behind her.

Peg said to Forest, "What are you doing here? And who are these people?" She looked at Cassidy. "I remember you. You're that reporter's wife. I want you and that other girl out of here immediately."

"No wait," the boy protested, "this is my house and these are my friends and they can stay if I want them to."

Pushing past the housekeeper, Heidi ran to her brother and wrapped her arms around his waist. "Don't leave. I don't want you to go away anymore."

"Omigod!" Charity repeated, clapping a hand over her mouth. "That's Heidi!"

"I called Ben," Peg said. "He'll be home any minute."

"Maybe you should take your friends and go," Adele said to her son. "I don't want any trouble."

Turning her back on Peg, Cassidy spoke to Forest and Charity. "We still have some time before your dad gets here. We need to get your mother up and moving." Cassidy hunkered down beside Adele and drew her right arm over her shoulder. "You get her other side," she told Forest.

He didn't move.

"You can't do that," Peg said.

Cassidy kept her eyes on Forest's face. "This is your mother. It's now or never."

"You should just go," Adele said. "I'll be fine."

Peg started yelling but Cassidy tuned her out.

Forest draped Adele's left arm over his shoulder and helped Cassidy lift her off the sofa. As they walked Adele around the room, Cassidy whispered into the woman's ear. "Are you aware that the girl who came in with us is Charity? Do you recognize your daughter now that she's all grown up? She wants to take you away from Ben so he can't feed you drugs anymore. She still needs you. She needs to have her mother back."

Charity tried to pull Heidi into her arms but the little girl pushed her away.

Cassidy said, "If we move fast, we've got a chance of getting your mother out of here before your dad arrives. What we have to do is push our way past Peg." *Oh yeah? And where do you think you're going to find a battering ram?* "Charity, I need you to throw the afghan over your mother, then walk in front of her as we go through the doorway."

"Heidi's coming with us," Charity announced.

Cassidy said, "It's too much to handle all at once."

"I'm not leaving without her."

"For Christ's sake, Chare, stop acting like a dweeb."

Her face twisting in pain, Charity wrapped the afghan around her mother's shoulders.

Cassidy maneuvered Forest and Adele so that they faced the doorway, where Peg had planted herself, shoulders squared, hands gripping the frame. The housekeeper was taller and more solidly built than anyone else in the room.

A gloating look swept over Peg's face. "Now where is it you think you're going?"

Kept saying Peg couldn't stop all three of us, but there she is, doing it.

"Oh shit!" Forest exclaimed.

"You better watch your mouth, bub. Your father hears you talking like that, he'll put you on drugs too. And as for your poor sick mommy, you're disturbing her nap. Let her go back to lala land where she belongs." Peg's gaze settled on Adele. "Nothing bothers our little sleeping beauty, now does it?"

"You slut!" Charity said from behind them. She moved around to stand in front of Adele. "You goddamn fucking slut. Who do you think you are, talking to my mother like that? You're not fit to wash her feet."

Clenching her fists, Charity charged straight at Peg. The housekeeper raised an arm in front of her face but was unable to deflect Charity's blows. The younger woman punched Peg's left cheek, then hit her again in the ear.

Peg and Heidi screamed in unison. Charity grabbed a handful of Peg's hair and gave it a sharp yank. The housekeeper twisted out of Charity's grasp, stumbled backward across the balcony, grabbed hold of the railing and righted herself. She wiped a hand across her brow, then went barreling into Charity.

"You bitch!" Peg slapped the younger woman several times across the face.

Heidi crouched behind her brother. Adele moaned softly.

Charity stomped on Peg's instep, causing the housekeeper to gasp in pain. She tried to back away, but before she could put any distance between them, Charity lunged again. As the two women moved farther down the balcony, they receded from Cassidy's view.

"I have to go after them," she said to Forest. "Can you handle your mother alone?"

"Sure." He embraced Adele with both arms, almost as if they were dancing.

Cassidy rushed through the doorway to find Peg on the floor with Charity on top of her banging her head against the hardwood. Forcing herself not to scream, Cassidy came up behind the younger woman and grabbed one of her arms. "You have to stop."

"Get away from me! Leave me alone! I'm gonna kill her!"

"You can't do that. You'd go to jail. Then what would happen to Heidi and your mother?"

Gradually Charity's arms slackened. She let go of Peg, got to her feet, and stepped away. Peg lay still for a moment, then rolled over and dragged herself into a semi-upright position. "You just wait till Ben gets hold of you," she rasped.

Thank God she's coherent enough you don't have to call the paramedics.

"Let's get your mother out of here," Cassidy said.

The two women ran back to the sunroom. Cassidy said to Adele, "Peg is taken care of and if we move quickly there's a chance we can be gone before Ben gets home. But you have to let us take you away because we're not leaving without you."

Adele's pale lashes fluttered and a frightened look came into her light blue eyes.

"Okay, here we go." Forest removed his right arm from his mother's body and Cassidy hitched Adele's left arm over her shoulders. She said to Charity, "Can you tie up the ends of the afghan so it doesn't drag on the ground?"

"Her feet are bare," Charity noted as she adjusted the lightweight blanket.

"Nothing we can do about it."

She kissed her mother on the cheek. "Once we get you off the Thorazine, I'm gonna paint your toenails fire engine red. It'll be like the old days when you danced all night."

"Will you stop screwing around?" Forest said.

Charity went first and Cassidy, Adele, and Forest came after, with Heidi clinging to her brother's hand. "Why did that lady beat Peg up?" the child asked. "I never saw ladies fight before. Where are you taking Mom? I can come too, can't I? It's a good thing I had a cold and Peg kept me home today or I wouldn't be able to go with you."

They were halfway down the grand staircase when Ben charged through the front door and came to a stop at the bottom of the stairs. He scowled at Charity. "Didn't I tell you never to come near this family again? I won't have you corrupting your brother and sister with your evil ways."

Shrinking into herself, Charity muttered, "Heidi's my child, not yours."

"I advise you to leave now," Ben continued, "before I have time to think of an appropriate punishment." His gaze moved to Cassidy. "I should have you arrested, but Adele has been put through enough for one day. If you take this demon child and leave quietly, I won't press charges."

Cassidy felt a hot surge of anger pulse through her. She said to Adele, "Tell him you want to come with us."

Adele's whole body began to tremble.

"You have to. For Charity's sake. She's been without her mother long enough."

Removing her arms from her rescuers' shoulders, Adele bunched her hands together beneath her chin. "I can't."

Charity backed up a step, squeezing in between Forest and Adele. "Mom, please, don't do this to me again. When he sent me away the first time, I was sure you'd stand up for me, but you didn't. I can't believe you'd stay with him after all the things he's done to this family."

"Will you shut up and get out of here?" Hopewell thundered.

Adele blinked several times. "I used to be a good mother ... then Ben started giving me pills ... I don't want to let you down again." She started breathing rapidly through her mouth. "All right, I'll come with you."

"You have to tell Ben," Cassidy said.

Adele gazed downward for a long moment, then slowly raised her eyes and looked at her husband. "I'm going with my daughter."

"The only place you're going is back to your room. Forest, take your mother upstairs." He pinned his son with an intense stare. "And don't think there won't be repercussions for the part you played in this absurd scheme."

Forest stayed where he was.

Cassidy removed her cell phone from her pocket. "Are you saying you won't let your wife leave? Isn't that the same as holding her hostage? Maybe we ought to get the police over here to sort things out. And while they're at it, I believe I'll ask them to take Adele to the hospital for a tox screen."

His eyes blazing, Ben said to his wife, "You don't know what you're doing. You've been sick lately. Your mind isn't clear."

"I'm leaving with Charity."

Marching up the stairs, Hopewell pushed his son and daughter aside, grasped Adele by the arm, and tried to force her to go with him.

"Okay, that's it. I'm dialing 911," Cassidy said.

Hopewell made a grab for her phone but she slipped away and raced to the bottom of the stairs. As much as she would have preferred to keep the police out of it, she began punching in the emergency number.

"All right, you win!" Hopewell shouted. "Just don't forget to watch your back!"

"Let's get going," Cassidy said.

Forest and Heidi ran down the stairs and out the door, the boy dragging the child behind him. Adele, moving as if she were still half asleep, floated to the foot of the stairs. Cassidy and Charity each took one of her arms and guided her out to the street, where they all piled into the Toyota.

Cassidy drove to the treatment facility, an anonymous residence tucked away on a tree-studded lot in Lake Bluff. The Hopewell siblings and Heidi waited in straight-backed chairs in a room that used to be a front parlor while Cassidy shepherded Adele through the admission process. As they left the building, Cassidy reminded herself that her problems weren't over. *Three young people in your keeping and you haven't given a single thought as to where they go from here.*

CHAPTER 37

CASSIDY DROVE TO EVANSTON AND PARKED IN front of an old-fashioned ice cream parlor. With cones in hand, her rescue team assembled around a table and tried to figure it out.

"What am I gonna do?" Forest asked. "I can't go home. I don't think Heidi should go home either. We can't leave her in Herr Peg's clutches."

Cassidy said, "The two of you can stay with me … although getting you and Heidi back and forth to school might be tricky."

"Heidi's coming home with me," Charity asserted. Then, speaking to Forest, "You can come too. You've got money. You and Heidi can cab it to school. After Mom gets out of rehab, she can get an apartment and we can live with her."

Forest scowled. "I don't want to be stuck in that tiny attic place with a bunch of girls. At least not *sister* kind of girls." A moment passed, and then he sighed. "Oh well, after all the stuff I did today, I guess I can handle anything."

"You were a hero," Cassidy said, her chest swelling with pride at what her team had accomplished. "Both of you."

"What about me?" Heidi demanded. "Aren't I a hero too?"

"We're all heroes."

†††

After she dropped off the Hopewell progeny, Cassidy drove home, made coffee, and collapsed onto the bed. Now that her adrenaline had drained away, she felt empty and exhausted.

Climbing onto Cassidy's chest, Starshine purred rhapsodically and brushed her mouth against her human's lips. As Cassidy scratched beneath the cat's chin, her eyes squinted and a blissful look descended upon her triangular face.

Half an hour later, the phone rang and Cassidy twisted around to pick up the cordless from her nightstand. Annoyed at the interruption, Starshine abandoned Cassidy's lap, went to the end of the bed, and turned her back on her human.

Zach's voice said, "Since you're not in jail, can I assume your mission was a success?"

Cassidy had told her husband that she was going on a mission from God and that he should be prepared to round up another attorney in case the mission went south.

"Even though we were under heavy fire from the enemy, my stalwart team succeeded in pulling off a hostage rescue. I was planning to get permission from Forest to tell you about it, but I forgot, so I still can't provide any details."

"You can tell me later. I should be home by seven and I want to go out to dinner. A downtown restaurant. Two steps up from the kind of place we usually eat."

"Sounds perfect. I'm absolutely not in the mood to cook."

"I wrapped up my investigation today and by six o'clock tonight the story'll be ready to file."

"No wonder you'd like something a little fancier than Hamburger Helper."

"Aren't you going to ask how I did it so I can exert my bragging rights?"

"Yes, definitely. Brag away."

"You remember I told you I was interviewing patients at the nursing homes the docs worked out of? Well, the first dozen or so were too far gone to tell me anything, but yesterday I hit pay dirt. I found two women treated by two separate docs who sounded as if they have more marbles rolling around in their cortexes than I do."

"They probably drank less." *That wasn't nice. This is Zach's big moment and you shouldn't snipe at him.*

"These two women were transferred to the hospital in the last year and neither of them could get a straight answer as to why they were there. One was put through a CAT scan and a pretty miserable upper GI with no explanation as to why she was being tested. The other spent a week in the hospital without receiving any tests, even though Medicare was billed for three procedures supposedly administered to her."

"Why didn't the doctors stick to patients with dementia? It seems pretty stupid to transport people who could report them."

"Greed and carelessness. When people get away with something over a long period of time, they start to feel invincible."

"But these women can give evidence against only two of the docs. Didn't you say there was a whole ring?"

"Right. A ring of doctors plus the hospital owner who organized the scheme. I got signed statements from the women, then I grilled their doctors. The first one stonewalled me, but I was able to flip the second, who, it turns out, was suffering from a guilty conscience. He told me who the other docs were and that the owner—who'd recruited these bottom feeders—was taking a cut."

"Wow! That's fantastic! You broke the investigation wide open," she said, gushing a little to redeem herself for having sniped at him earlier.

"When I hear flattery, I always wonder what you're up to."

"Nothing. I'm just really impressed. So, we're going out tonight to celebrate the fact that you've finished your investigation."

"Not exactly. I'll tell you the real reason later."

"The real reason? What's that?"

"I just said I'll tell you later."

† † †

"I hope you're hungry," Zach said as he came into the bedroom.

"You bet I am." Cassidy rose from the bed and performed a small pirouette to show off the scoop-necked full-skirted wine-colored dress she had donned. Since her husband seldom saw her in anything but pants, she wanted to make sure he noticed.

"Hey, you look great!" His smoky eyes softened as he took her in.

She smiled in return.

"I better put on a jacket or the maître d' might not let me sit at the same table as you."

While Zach was changing, she took her low-heeled, pointy-toed pumps out of the closet. Putting the shoes on the floor in front of her, she sat in her desk chair. "I assume you won't mind dropping me off at the door."

"No, of course not." He frowned at her shoes. "Those don't look very comfortable."

"That's why I asked. I want to wear them but I don't want to walk in them." She slid her feet into the pumps.

"Why wear shoes that hurt?"

"Because they're stylish. And they look so spiffy. When I bought them, I thought I'd just wear them to do therapy."

"I didn't think you cared about fashion."

"I don't. Except for occasional lapses."

† † †

"That's an excellent choice," the earnest-looking waiter said in regard to the wine Zach had ordered.

As the young man turned away, Cassidy leaned in toward her husband. "So what's the real reason?"

"You have to wait till the wine's poured."

"Is this what I think it is?"

"It might be."

Excitement buzzed in her chest, images of the happy baby she'd seen at Iris's house flooding her mind. Removing her napkin from her wineglass, she spread it across her lap, then sat back to wait, too full of anticipation to attempt small talk.

The restaurant Zach had chosen hailed from a tradition of elegance that preceded the spare noisy bistros that were the current rage. A four-tier glass droplet chandelier hung from the ceiling, and looped red velvet drapes adorned the windows. The tables were widely spaced and Victorian paintings in carved wooden frames graced the floral walls.

After the wine was served, Zach raised his glass. "Here's to us making a baby together."

"Oh, Zach, this is a dream come true!" Clinking her glass against his, she gazed at her husband with a slap-happy grin on her face.

"Nobody's more surprised at my change of mind than me."

If his mind can change so quickly, maybe he doesn't mean it. Maybe he's just saying it because he's in a good mood tonight and tomorrow his mood will switch and he'll change his mind again.

For once in your life, just accept that something wonderful has happened and don't worry it to death.

She tried to keep her mouth shut but the words came out anyway. "Is this what you really want? Or are you just doing it for me?"

"No, I want it too. Or at least most of me does."

The waiter brought their dinners. Looking down at her plate, Cassidy realized that her appetite was gone. Too many questions were clamoring in her mind. *You have to give Zach a chance to eat. Can't go digging around in his psyche until his stomach is full.* She took small bites and waited until his plate was clean before she spoke again.

"What made you change your mind?"

"It was the talk with Bryce." Zach rubbed his fingers across the bottom of his chin. "I felt better after we hashed things out. More hopeful. I used to think family relationships were just too damn difficult. Too many expectations, too many compromises. Like there was no way I could be my own person and stay connected to my family."

"Well, but you're going to have to compromise if anything is going to improve with Bryce."

"Yeah, but he seems willing to meet me halfway. Maybe I'm wrong. Maybe we'll both slip back into our old bad habits. But being able to talk to Bryce without either of us getting pissed made me think I might like to have a kid after all."

"What's the connection between talking to Bryce and wanting a child?"

"I have no idea."

She waited.

"You always do that. If I say I don't know something, you just sit and act smug until I come up with an answer. Which is probably something I make up on the spot just to satisfy you."

No it's not. It's the truth bubbling up from his subconscious.

"I don't mean to be smug. It's just that it's so important for me to understand you."

"Me and everybody else. Sometimes I think you'd stop people on the street and ask personal questions if you thought you could get away with it."

"But you're the only one I really care about."

Creasing his brow, Zach stared into the middle distance. Several seconds passed, then he started talking. "I like it that I can do things to make you happy. Even small things, like bringing home those cans of diet cat food and telling you how great you look tonight. You get this big smile on your face and your eyes sparkle. Well, I was never able to get that reaction from Bryce. Even though we were getting along okay, nothing I did ever seemed to really please him. But things might be different now. He told me what he wants so maybe I'll finally be able to get a positive response out of him. You know, maybe he'll punch me on the shoulder or something."

"Yeah, I can see him doing that."

"So now the idea of having a baby doesn't seem so intimidating. If I could work things out with Bryce, where there's this whole history of misunderstanding, maybe I could figure out how to keep a kid happy. And maybe I'd enjoy getting a kid to smile the same way I enjoy getting you to smile."

"Getting a kid to smile at you. I think that might be one of the major joys of childrearing."

As a busboy cleared their plates, Zach emptied the remaining wine into their glasses.

"You said that most of you wants a baby. What about the part that doesn't?"

"Just because the scales have tipped doesn't mean I don't still have some reservations. How could anybody not have some ambivalence about a decision as life-changing as this?"

Cassidy's first reaction was to think that she was a hundred percent behind the idea, but then a small voice in the back of her head raised the questions she'd asked before. *What if it's like Melissa's baby? What if it comes between you and Zach? What if it turns into a druggie or joins a gang when it hits adolescence?*

Okay, so everything won't be perfect. But this is still the thing you've always wanted.

They finished their wine and got to their feet. Zach took her hand as they walked from the table to the door. "The parking gods smiled on me tonight. I found a spot just halfway down the block. But I can still pick you up at the door if you want."

She felt such a lightness of being that her pinched toes scarcely registered. "No, I'll walk."

CHAPTER 38

THEY STROLLED ALONG A BLOCK IN CHICAGO'S Gold Coast, one of the glitziest areas in the city. A peach-colored glow surrounded them, and the store windows were like little magic kingdoms, glittering with expensive objects Cassidy couldn't even imagine owning. They passed a man and woman so perfectly attired Cassidy experienced a brief twinge of feeling out of place.

Thought you always said appearances didn't matter.

As they approached the Subaru, Zach pressed the clicker to unlock the car. He opened Cassidy's door, then took his place behind the wheel. She buckled herself in. The engine turned over, the headlights went on, a stream of soft jazz issued from the radio. She watched a shorts and tee-shirt-clad cyclist zip through the slow-moving traffic.

A sound came from the back seat. Twisting her head, Cassidy glimpsed a man rising from the floor. Before she could make out his features, Zach gripped her chin and swiveled her face forward.

"Don't look!" he commanded.

Keeping his face forward as well, Zach said, "She didn't get a good enough look to identify you. You could let her go. She could leave her purse and cell in the car. We'd be long gone before she could get hold of the police."

Nobody'd fall for that. Well, but you shouldn't underestimate the stupidity of criminals.

"Don't waste my time," the man said. "Go south on Lake Shore Drive, then turn onto 55. You pull any stunts, I'll crack her head open."

Doesn't sound familiar. And he didn't use your name. Maybe a car-jacker instead of Kit's murderer. Maybe he'll dump us out on a country road and let us live.

"How on earth did you manage to break into a car on such a busy street?" Cassidy asked.

"Just can it, will ya?"

Guess you can forget about gaining rapport. Her hands clasped tightly in her lap, she tried to focus on taking deep breaths, but the picture in her mind of a shadowy figure holding a gun to Zach's head made it hard to concentrate.

Following their abductor's directions, Zach traveled on I-55 for a while, then turned south on Lamont Road, a lightly trafficked four-lane highway. Although Cassidy had never driven this route before, she knew they were headed toward the southwest suburbs.

"Hey Cass," the man said.

Oh shit! Knows your name. Not a car-jacker.

"Take off your underpants and toss 'em back here."

"Don't do it," Zach said. He stomped on the accelerator and the car leapt forward. Weaving through traffic, the Subaru hurtled past an ancient Cadillac, a minivan with a dog's head sticking out the window, and a shiny new bug.

"Whassamatter, Zach? You forget I got an automatic pointed at your skull?"

"You going to shoot me at ninety miles an hour?"

"I'll drill her." Cassidy felt the gun barrel bump up against her head. "My finger's starting to twitch, Zach."

"You shoot her, I'm running the car off the road. We've got front seat airbags, that's all."

Chicken like you never imagined.

"Okay, okay, I'll let her alone for now."

The car returned to normal speed. They drove through the town of Lamont, continuing south for another ten minutes or so, then turned onto a two-lane road, and from there onto an even narrower road that took them into a wooded area. The trees were short and sparse, the spaces between them crowded with underbrush. They passed a couple of tire-tracks leading off to the left, then the gunman instructed Zach to take the next turn-off. They drove through a narrow tunnel of trees, branches thumping the top and sides of the Subaru, then emerged onto a small limestone platform that ended in a drop-off. Zach stopped the car.

Cassidy felt a sudden chill. Beyond the U-shaped clearing lay a broad gray ribbon. *A river. We're on a cliff overlooking a river.* A jagged shoreline rose on the other side, and above the shoreline, a huge orange-colored moon.

Zach asked, "What are we waiting for?"

"Tell you one thing, it ain't your guardian angel." A snort of laughter.

Obviously plans to kill you. Since you're probably going to die anyway, might as well see what he looks like.

Swiveling backward, she gazed into a face with alert blue eyes and a bristly little mustache, topped by a baseball cap with the brim pulled down over the collar of his denim jacket. *Seen him before. Where?* She tried to dredge up a memory but nothing came.

"Whatcha lookin' at? Just turn around and keep your yap shut."

She did as she was told. Zach laid his hand on her knee and she put her hand on top of his. A wave of hopelessness came over her, but a small voice fought against despair. *You can't give up. You have to try something.*

Time dragged by as she envisioned one escape scenario after another, each more absurd than the last. Then an idea came to her that seemed to offer a slim chance of success. *Lame definitely. Probably even feeble. But not totally beyond the pale.*

Contorting her features, aiming for an expression of extreme discomfort, she turned to face the gunman again. "I need to pee."

"You just gotta hold it."

"I've been holding it ever since we left the restaurant. I can't hold it any longer."

"Guess you'll have to piss on yourself, then."

"That's so humiliating! Plus it'll stink up the car. Please, please, just let me step outside."

Zach said, "You've got your gun on her. She can't get away."

"Well, now that you mention it, it might be interesting to watch. You gimme your underpants if I let you go outside?"

"Anything. Just please, don't make me wet myself."

"You gotta squat right here next to the car. You can't go behind no trees."

"Oh yes, yes, I'll do exactly what you say."

Moving slowly, clamping her thighs together, she opened the door and placed one foot on the ground. Then, pushing off from the car and breaking into a run, she bolted for the woods. Bullets whizzed past her and she didn't know for sure whether she'd been hit.

Raising an arm in front of her face, she crashed into the underbrush. Sharp dry branches tore at her dress and skin and sent up a loud thrashing sound as she broke through them. She heard another burst of gunfire and tried to run faster but her shoes slowed her down. Dashing a few yards farther, she was brought to an abrupt halt when her skirt got tangled in the brush. She yanked it free, tearing a hole in the back of her dress.

After stumbling forward several steps, the toe of her shoe caught in the bushes and she plunged forward, her hands landing on the ground's spiky surface, the branches and rocks cutting her palms like thin knives. She gasped in pain, then clenched her teeth to keep from sobbing out loud.

Sitting up, she realized that one of her shoes was missing. *You'll never be able to walk barefoot through this underbrush.* Her only real option seemed to be to lie low and hope the gunman didn't find her. The thick cover of bushes prevented her from seeing any distance at all, so she put all her effort into listening. She heard the rustle of dry leaves, a whir of insects, but no voices. *Oh God—what if that thug shot Zach while you were making all that noise?*

Taking off her other shoe, she crawled behind a tree and stood up so she could see into the clearing. Shock pulsed through her when she realized she was only about twenty feet from the car. At first she didn't see the gunman, then she realized he was standing near the driver's door, aiming his flashlight into the woods on the opposite side of the clearing.

Looking for Zach. He must've gotten away while the gunman was shooting at you. She felt a glimmer of hope.

The gunman switched off his flashlight, lit a cigarette, and sat behind the wheel, leaving the car door open. A stretch of time went by, then another car pulled up behind the Subaru. The gunman and the other driver got out of their cars and strode toward each other.

"What took you so long?" the gunman demanded.

Victor's voice yelled back. "Hey, Al, what's going on? I don't see anybody in the car."

Victor! Zach wanted to see the trust, now Victor's trying to kill us!

"Yeah, well, they ain't there," Al replied.

"You moron! How'd they get out of the car?"

"They just did, that's all. If you'd been on time it wouldn't've happened."

"If you'd put a bullet in their heads like I told you to, it wouldn't've happened either."

"Didn't I tell you I wasn't gonna be your triggerman? There's no way I'm going down on a murder charge for you."

Cassidy suddenly realized where she'd seen Al before. *The guy who winked at you in Victor's office.*

"Hey, don't forget—you're the one who snatched them," Victor said. "You're already in almost as deep as I am."

"An accessory. Accessories don't end up on death row."

"We're dumping them in the quarry, for Chrissake. Nobody's going to be able to trace their bodies back to us."

"Spoken like a guy who never spent a night in jail. I got three arrests on my sheet. I never thought anybody'd be able to trace anything back to me, either."

"Look, we've got a job to do. Where are they?"

"The girl ran over there," Al pointed toward Cassidy's side of the clearing, "and Zach took off on the other side. You get her, I'll get him."

Victor removed a flashlight from his pocket, a gun from his waistband, and headed into the woods.

Oh God, what're you going to do? You can't run because you don't have shoes, and even if you could run, you'd make so much noise he'd find you right away.

The tree Cassidy was standing behind had a crook in it not far off the ground. She climbed into it to get a better look at what Victor was doing. He'd started at the edge of the quarry and was moving toward the road on a course parallel to the clearing, about five feet into the woods. He swept his flashlight beam in a broad arc ahead of him, stopping from time to time to aim it into the branches overhead.

He continued slowly until he reached the road, then moved a few feet deeper into the woods and started back toward the quarry. Cassidy studied his movements. He seemed to be covering every inch of ground with his light, but looking only sporadically into the trees.

Peering into the upper reaches of her tree, she saw two crooks above the one she was in, but since she'd never done any body-building, she wasn't sure she had the physical strength to climb to the highest one.

Probably not worth it. He's looking up as well as down.

Yeah, but there's a slim possibility he'd miss you in the tree and no possibility he'd miss you on the ground.

She boosted herself into the middle crook, then wrapped her arms and legs around the trunk and started hoisting herself upward, the bark tearing her dress and scraping her skin. Pain seared her bruised palms and she could feel her arms getting weaker as she pulled herself up inch by inch. By the time she hauled herself into the highest crook, she could barely move.

Victor can save his bullet. You'll be dead of exhaustion before he finds you.

After clinging to her branch for several seconds, she propped herself upright, leaned her back against the trunk, and locked her legs around the branch beneath her. The tree still held enough dry curling leaves to provide a small amount of cover.

Victor's light was now moving toward the road again. Reaching his destination, he moved deeper into the woods and headed back toward the quarry. He was still in the area between her tree and the clearing. As he approached, she could see that this time he would pass beneath her tree's outer limbs. But before he reached that point, he directed his light upward, bouncing the beam through all the nearby branches.

Cassidy closed her eyes and stopped breathing. She thought she could feel the light moving across her chest. Her skin prickly with fear, she waited for the bullet to hit her. She held her breath as long as she could, then opened her eyes and exhaled. Victor had moved past her tree.

He arrived at the quarry, moved deeper into the woods, and began a return path toward the road. This time he was on the opposite side of her tree, moving on a course that would take him about three feet from the trunk.

Leaning forward, Cassidy grasped her branch with both hands, pulled her legs up, and got into a crouch. Victor shone his light upward but aimed it at a tree beyond hers. He stepped beneath the branches of her tree, approached the trunk, moved past it.

She threw herself on his shoulders. Yelping, he fell to the ground with Cassidy on top of him. As he struggled to rise, her hand reached out for a rock, her fingers wrapping around a large chunk of limestone. Victor's body jerked. He fought against her effort to hold him down, unsteadily rising onto his hands and knees, nearly knocking her off her perch. She grabbed his collar with her left hand, brought her right arm back, and bashed the rock into his head. And bashed again and again.

He crumpled beneath her. She was preparing to swing one more time when she realized he wasn't moving. Her arm drew back of its own accord. Then her mind cleared and she was able to stop herself.

She couldn't believe she'd knocked him out. Adrenaline coursing through her system, she waited for him to move. She counted to ten, counted again, then expelled a breath.

Shifting her gaze to the flashlight, lodged in a bush a few feet ahead of her, she felt a rush of panic. *What if Al heard Victor yell? What if he sees the light and comes after you?* Tottering toward the bush, she turned the flashlight off and sat down. She could detect the distant sound of someone moving through the underbrush, but it was coming from the other side of the clearing.

Al's making so much noise, he couldn't have heard Victor yell. The person you need to be afraid for is Zach, not yourself.

Al said he wouldn't be Victor's triggerman.

Yes, but you can't count on it. After all, he did shoot at you.

She thought about what she had to do. Take Victor's gun. Find her shoes. Get over to the other side of the clearing and rescue her husband. *What if you can't stop Al? What if he kills Zach before you get there?* Thick black dread filled her chest. *You can't allow yourself to think these thoughts.* She pushed the horrible what-ifs out of her mind.

Returning to Victor's body, she turned on the flashlight and located his gun. An automatic. The same kind of gun she'd used before. She'd never been able to hit a target, but at least she knew enough to cock the firearm and release the safety.

Aiming her beam at the back of Victor's head, she sucked in her breath when she saw what a bloody mess it was.

No time to think about Victor. Have to save Zach.

But she needed to know whether or not she'd killed him. Following the example of cops she'd seen on TV, she moved her fingers around the base of his neck. *You want to find a pulse or not?* One small part of her wanted the kind of vengeance only his death would provide. But the largest part was relieved when she felt a pulse.

Okay, now you can go. She took a step away from the body. *But not without shoes. A snail would move faster than you without shoes.*

Finding the shoe she'd taken off was not difficult, but she couldn't remember where she'd been when she lost the first one. Her light probing the ground, she wandered back and forth, branches stabbing her feet, her fear for Zach creating pinpricks of anxiety in her stomach. Eventually she discovered the shoe in a clump of gnarly branches. With her feet ensconced in pointy-toed leather again, she crept toward the clearing.

CHAPTER 39

IRCLING AROUND TO ITS OPPOSITE SIDE, SHE stopped at a point parallel to the Subaru's rear bumper, about five feet from the edge of the woods. The driver's door still hung open. Gazing at the dome light, she felt an urge to close it.

If the battery runs down, you'll be trapped. Can't even call for help because you don't know where you are.

Don't be stupid. You can always drive Victor's car.

She turned away from the clearing and focused on the sound of Al crashing though the underbrush. She couldn't tell where he was but she was sure he wasn't moving in her direction.

Doesn't have Zach yet. They'd be headed toward the clearing if he did.

Just then she heard Al yell. *Now he's got him.* The crashing sound began moving toward her. She took it to mean that Al was bringing her husband in. From the direction of the sound, she could tell they were moving on a path not far from the edge of the quarry. With the gun in her right hand and the flashlight in her left, she ventured closer to the clearing. She could feel beads of sweat popping out on her forehead. A moment later Zach stepped into the open space, his hands clasped behind his neck. Al followed, his gun trained on the small of Zach's back.

Hoping to divert Al's attention, she directed the beam of her flashlight into his face. Whirling toward her, he fired off a couple of shots. At the same time, Zach swung around and slugged him in the shoulder. As Al stumbled backward, Zach went after him. Al teetered on the edge of the quarry, his arms swinging wildly, and then Zach lunged again and they both disappeared.

Cassidy ran to the precipice and aimed her light downward. The face of the wall looked like a multi-layered cake, the various layers jostled out of alignment. She saw two heads bobbing in the water six feet below. Al raised a hand with a pistol in it and clipped Zach on the side of the head. Zach's body went limp and he slowly sank beneath the surface.

Oh God! Oh God! Without quite realizing what she was doing, Cassidy dropped the flashlight, gripped her weapon in both hands, released the safety, cocked the gun, and pointed it at Al. *No wait— you might hit Zach. Have to stop Al. Too dangerous, can't shoot. No way out—you've got to!*

As she was firing, the crack blasting her eardrums, the recoil knocking her backward, she saw Al's head jerk to the side. His arms stopped paddling, and for a moment she thought he might be dead. Then he began making a feeble effort to swim to shore.

She caught a movement out of the corner of her eye. Zach had resurfaced, his arms flailing, his head bent backward so he was looking toward the sky. He was alive but clearly in trouble. Although he was now only a couple of yards from shore, he appeared so disoriented she doubted he would be able to make it out of the water on his own.

Looking for a place where she might be able to descend to the lake, she discovered that a few feet to her right, the offset layers were almost like a stairway created by a drunken stone mason. *You can go down there. But it won't be easy with a gun in your hand and these stupid shoes.* She briefly considered leaving the gun behind but was too fearful of Al to part with it.

She went to the spot that resembled a stairway and lowered herself over the side, gripping the wall with one hand and the gun with the other. Inching her way from step to step, she made it down to a large slab of rock at the water's edge.

Al's voice called for help. He was hanging onto a rock not far from where she stood, apparently too weak to pull himself out. Both hands clutched at the limestone's jagged edge. *No gun! It got away from him after he hit Zach.* She breathed a sigh of relief.

If Zach drowns, I'll personally stomp on Al's fingers. Without a second thought, she continued picking her way along the shoreline until she found a large flat rock near the spot where Zach was thrashing in the water.

She took off her shoes, got down on her hands and knees, and leaned out toward him. "Zach, I'm here," she shouted. "You have to swim over to me."

He gave no indication of hearing her.

Her heart was slamming into her rib cage. If she swam out to him, she knew there was a good chance he'd take her down with him.

"Zach, you have to listen. You have to do what I say."

Still no response.

She set the gun near her shoes and lowered herself into the water, its frigid temperature setting off a bout of violent shivering. At first she was unable to do anything more than hang on. Then, as her body adjusted to the cold, she felt around beneath the rock for a handhold. Digging her fingers into an indentation, she anchored herself with her left hand and stretched her right hand out toward Zach.

He slapped her hand aside, apparently unaware of her presence. She reached out again, and this time succeeded in grasping his wrist. He continued flailing but was too weak to break her hold, and she was able to drag him over to the rock. By the time she got him there, he'd stopped fighting. Letting go of his wrist, she grabbed his chin and forced him to look at her.

"Zach, can you hear me?"

His eyes began to focus. He made a noise she took to be an assent.

"Hold onto the rock."

He clutched at it with both hands.

She crawled out of the water, her torn skirt clinging to her legs. Goosebumps covered her skin and her teeth were chattering. She rubbed her arms, trying to reduce the chill, then knelt on the edge of the flat rock and looped her arm through Zach's armpit.

"You have to help. I can't do this by myself."

He hoisted and she pulled and before long he was lying face-down on the rock beside her. She was afraid he'd need CPR, which she'd never learned, but he drew himself upright and began coughing up water. When his coughing subsided, they lay down together, bodies intertwined, and warmed themselves.

Cassidy said, "I suppose I should do something about Al. The last time I saw him he was holding onto a rock and couldn't pull himself out."

"What's wrong with letting him drown?"

"I know there's an answer to that question but I can't think what it is."

Zach gave it some consideration. "You'd probably beat yourself up afterward."

"Yeah, that's it. That's the answer." Wearily she got to her feet.

"I'll do it," Zach said, but he couldn't get himself vertical.

Cassidy helped Al out of the water. When he collapsed on top of a boulder, she walked away, feeling no further responsibility. Returning to Zach's side, she collected her shoes and the gun and they waited until he'd regained enough strength to climb the quarry wall.

After they made it to the top, Cassidy sat in the Subaru and dug her cell phone out of her purse. "I can't give directions to the police. I don't know where we are."

"I do," Zach said.

CHAPTER 40

"THAT BLACK COP," BRYCE SAID TO ZACH. "What's his name? Jeffers? He leaked Victor's confession to you?"

Cassidy and the two men in her life were assembled in her living room, the hearty aroma of meatloaf permeating the air. It was Sunday afternoon, less than two days since their ordeal at the quarry.

Zach replied, "I did Jeffers a favor a few years ago. I came across some information that would have been damaging to his career and I didn't use it."

Cassidy said, "I didn't think you ever held anything back."

"I didn't need it for the story. Besides, I trade in favors. Anytime I get a chance to set it up so somebody owes me, I grab at it. Look how it paid off this time."

Bryce asked, "You gonna write up what he told you for the *Post?*"

"The story went to another reporter. I can't do it because I'm not objective. And even if I could, I wouldn't use Jeffers's information because it might get him in trouble."

"So tell me what happened. I can't wait to hear why my good buddy Victor would try to kill me or you or anybody else."

A grave look settled over Zach's face. Cassidy wrapped her hand around the base of her throat. She opened her mouth to speak but Zach pre-empted her.

"What I'm about to tell you is seriously bad news. It's going to affect the rest of your life." He glanced at Cassidy. "If you want a beer or something, I wouldn't object."

"What?" The boy's eyes narrowed. His shoulders stiffened as he braced himself. "Just tell me."

"Victor emptied out your trust fund. He stole all your money. There isn't anything left."

"No, that can't be true! He wouldn't do that!"

Zach didn't respond.

"Oh my God! I'll have to give up my townhouse and drop out of college."

"You may have to find cheaper digs," Zach said, "but I'm prepared to make sure you get through college."

"I thought you didn't have that kind of money."

"My grandparents set up a trust fund. My mother and uncle are first in line, but after they die, it comes down to me. Martin won't have any problem taking money out of my inheritance to pay for your education."

But Zach'll have a problem asking. However, he'll swallow his pride and do it for Bryce.

"If you pay for everything, I'll lose my independence. You'll feel entitled to order me around."

Zach laughed. "Yeah, right. I'll have you running errands all over town."

Cassidy said, "Your father may not put any strings on the money, but I intend to. I want you over here for dinner once a month."

Bryce stared at the window, then brought his eyes back to Zach's face. "I shouldn't have said that. Okay, tell me about Victor."

"You know he has a disabled kid?"

Bryce nodded.

"A while back Victor started stealing client funds so he could keep his kid in this gold-plated facility. But a couple of clients caught on and reported him to the ABA. After that, he was scared to death he'd get disbarred if he ever got reported again."

"But why try to kill *me*? I had no idea he was taking money out of my fund."

"I'm getting to that. After he got reported, Victor decided that outright stealing was too risky. But he knew a guy who had a gold thumb when it came to making money in the market, so he started borrowing money from various funds to do day trading based on tips from this guru. Initially he was successful enough to return the money he'd borrowed, but then he got cocky and tried trading on margin and lost his ass."

"My ass, you mean."

"Yeah. He did most of his borrowing from your fund because you never asked questions and didn't complain when he failed to send you an annual report. Meanwhile, you were demanding handfuls of cash to pay for tuition and the townhouse. The only way he could come up with the moola to give you was to steal from other clients, and he was terrified of getting caught again."

"But if I died, wouldn't somebody go over the records and discover that the money was missing?"

Cassidy looked at her watch. The meatloaf and scalloped potatoes had been in the oven for half an hour and a pot of chicken soup was simmering on the stove. "I have to check on dinner but I don't want either of you to say *one word* till I get back."

"Don't make me wait," Bryce complained. "I want to hear it now."

"Another minute or so won't kill you."

Walking gingerly, she went into the kitchen, her feet and palms still throbbing with pain. The soup was boiling too hard. She lowered the flame, then hurried back to the living room. "Okay," she said to Zach, "now you can explain why Victor's scheme would have worked if he hadn't killed the wrong person."

"Your mother made you the first beneficiary and Victor the second, but none of us knew Victor would inherit until Jeffers passed the word on to me. Victor was also the only one with a copy of the trust." He looked at Bryce. "He didn't even give you one, did he?"

"No."

"If you were killed, I wouldn't be able to get a copy without going to court. And if you'd been shot in a home invasion, which is what Victor intended it to look like, I wouldn't have had any reason to go to the trouble of obtaining a copy."

"You told me you were irritated with Victor and hadn't been talking to him lately," Cassidy said. "He didn't know you were living with anybody. He wouldn't have broken into your house if he had."

"It's my fault Kit died. It should've been me instead of her."

"If I were Pastor Hopewell, I'd probably say something trite like 'Everything happens for a reason.' But since I'm not, I think I'll smack you instead."

Bryce stared at her in confusion.

"You're too smart to be so martyrish. It isn't your fault Victor killed the wrong person. It's his."

Bryce sighed. "I miss her so much."

Cassidy felt a pang of guilt for her smart-ass remarks. "I'm sorry. I know this is hard on you."

After a short silence, Zach said, "So, you want to know how it all went down?"

"Yeah."

"After taking lessons from his jailbird buddy, Victor picked the back door lock and went into the living room to wait for you. He thought it would look more like a home invasion if you walked in on him, but he was prepared to kill you in your bed if you didn't come downstairs. Then Kit came flying into the room and he popped her. When he realized his mistake, he was so rattled he dropped the gun and went running out to the alley. But then he stopped to think about what he'd done, and he had this impulsive, completely unthought out idea that he could frame you by locking the back door."

"Yeah, and it worked perfectly."

"Not exactly. By the time he came back to the townhouse to act as your attorney, he realized he'd made a big mistake. It costs a ton of money to mount a defense. That thirty grand we gave the attorney was just a retainer. A trial would've run up a lot more, and then there might've been appeals. The more he thought about it, the more he became convinced he really would have to kill you, but he couldn't figure out how to do it. He didn't want it to look like a homicide because the murder of two people who were living together would cause the police to broaden their investigation, possibly leading to their subpoenaing his records. The other possibilities were to fake an accident or a suicide, but that's damned hard to pull off."

"What are you saying? That I didn't really try to kill myself?"

"When you said you weren't feeling suicidal, you were right."

"But how did he do it?"

"You left your cell phone behind when you walked out of Angie's apartment, and she was so freaked she called everybody on your speed dial and left a message saying you were depressed and had gone back to your townhouse. As soon as Victor heard that, he thought it might be the opportunity he'd been waiting for. He went straight to your place, and when you didn't answer the door, he picked the lock and found you passed out on the sofa. He would have gotten away with it too, if Cassidy hadn't arrived shortly after he left."

"I always thought he was a nice guy." Bryce looked at his father. "I thought he liked me more than you did."

"That was my fault. I should've done a better job of letting you know how I felt."

Cassidy said, "If Victor wanted to keep Bryce's death from looking like a homicide, why plant the car bomb?"

"Desperation. He kept obsessing about how much a trial would cost and finally decided he'd rather risk the possibility of being investigated than the certainty of having to steal so much money from his other clients."

The room fell silent. Since neither Bryce nor Zach seemed to know what to say next, Cassidy rescued them. "Dinner's almost ready but there's one more thing I'd like an answer to." She looked at Bryce. "That neighbor who heard you yelling at Kit? Why did you lie about it?"

"Do I have to tell you?"

"I doubt we'd resort to torture," Zach replied.

"Then I'm not going to."

After another beat of silence, Cassidy stood. "I better go get dinner on the table."

"No, wait. I guess I owe you something."

She sat back down.

Gazing at the floor, Bryce rubbed his hands against his knees. "Kit was in one of her moods. She wanted to talk about Raul, and when I said I was going to leave the house if she didn't stop, she did one of those flips of hers. She got all sexy and playful, and before I knew it, we were in bed together. But then I couldn't ... well, I couldn't ... you know."

"I can see how difficult it would be."

"Yeah, well, then I got pissed. I mean, really pissed. I started yelling at her. I said a bunch of things I didn't mean. I might even have said I wished she was dead. And then when the cops asked me about it, I absolutely didn't want to tell them. I figured nobody could prove that the neighbor really did hear me, so I lied."

"Yeah, I can understand that," Zach said.

"Me too."

Bryce didn't seem to have anything more to say, so Cassidy excused herself to go into the kitchen. She served the soup first, then meatloaf, scalloped potatoes, and green beans. She thought the meatloaf was dry and the beans overcooked.

Zach and Bryce heaped compliments upon her.

"Please don't say things you don't mean. I know the food isn't that great."

"When do I ever say things I don't mean?" Zach protested.

He didn't. *They probably really do like it and you're just being hypercritical.*

"Thank you," she said.

When she was done eating, she pushed her chair a couple of inches back from the table and said to Bryce, "There's one more part of the story I think you should know. Zach's already heard it but I'm sure he won't mind hearing it again." She licked a crumb from the corner of her mouth. "Do you remember my telling you that Forest Hopewell contacted me about setting up a meeting and then didn't show?"

"So did you find out what he wanted?"

"At first he insisted on keeping it confidential, then he gave me permission to tell you and Zach. But that's all, understand? You can't tell anybody, not even Angie."

Bryce nodded.

Cassidy recounted everything she knew about the Hopewells.

"That asshole actually kept his wife drugged for seven years?"

"From what Adele tells me, Ben still believes his mission as a pastor justifies everything he did."

"You talked to Adele?" Zach asked.

"This morning. She's still in the rehab center. Getting her off Thorazine was easy, but after being drugged and bullied for so long, she's developed a serious problem with anxiety and is panicked at the thought of going out on her own. Her counselor thinks she'll regain her spirit once she realizes Ben can't get at her anymore. The one thing she has managed to do is hire an attorney, who assures her he can get a court order requiring Ben to pay for everything. Charity's already shopping for an apartment where they can all live."

Bryce and Zach cleaned up the kitchen, then the boy announced that he was ready to take off. As they were standing in the entryway, he said, "It really sucks that you two nearly got killed because of me." He pulled Cassidy into a bear hug, then threw his arms around his father. Zach stiffened momentarily, then hugged the boy back.

After Bryce left, Zach said to Cassidy, "That should make you happy."

"It does," she replied, not sounding happy at all. She rearranged the cushions on the sofa, wiped at a smudge on the coffee table. Straightening, she wrapped her arms around her midsection.

"There's something I need to talk to you about," she said.

"You want to sit here?"

"I suppose it's too cold on the porch."

"I'll get the comforter off the bed."

They sat close together on the wicker couch, the comforter encasing them like a giant sleeping bag. A dusky twilight rendered the houses across the street soft and hazy. Cassidy stared through the porch windows at trees with tops that were still green and gold, despite the crumbly orange leaves littering the ground beneath them.

"What is it?" Zach asked, laying his arm across her shoulders.

"We came so close to dying at the quarry."

"Yeah, it was pretty hairy there for a while."

"I can't stop thinking about it. I haven't been able to get the pictures out of my mind since it happened."

Zach drew her closer.

"If we had a child, it might've lost both its parents."

"But we survived."

"Just barely. And it's not the first time. We do stupid things. Take too many risks. Get involved when we shouldn't."

"So what are you saying?"

"I want a child so badly." Her eyes filled and she covered her mouth with her hand. "But I think we shouldn't have one."

"You don't really mean that, do you?"

"Yes. No. I don't know." Pulling away from Zach, she dashed into the house for a box of tissues. She blew her nose, then said, "Aren't you going to try to change my mind?"

"We'll have to modify our lifestyle, that's all. In fact, having you stay home and take care of a baby instead of running around trying to catch criminals would suit me just fine."

"You'd have to change too."

"I can take care of myself."

He's already forgotten who fished who out of the lake.

Zach said, "You'd just have to settle down and stop getting involved in these risky propositions."

You could do that, couldn't you?

Who are you trying to kid?

A long silence. Then she said, "I don't think either of us could change. We both get such a rush out of throwing ourselves into dicey situations. It's who we are."

"It took me so long to reach the point where I wanted a baby, now I don't want to let go." He let out a sigh. "But I have to admit you're right."

Tears began running down Cassidy's face. "This is so hard."

She leaned her forehead against Zach's chest and sobbed. He rubbed her back and whispered soothing phrases. When her nose was so clogged she couldn't breathe, she pulled away and sucked in great shuddering gasps of air through her mouth. Grabbing a handful of tissues, she mopped her face, and after a while the tears began to come more slowly.

When she'd cried herself out, Zach said, "I know we both feel bad about this, but we need to keep in mind we still have a good life. We've got each other, we've got Starshine, and now we seem to have Bryce. It even looks like he's going to show up for Sunday dinner and teach me how to be a father."